THE
CONTINENTAL
OP

THE CONTINENTAL OP

DASHIELL HAMMETT

Edited and with an Introduction by
STEVEN MARCUS

VINTAGE BOOKS
A Division of Random House
New York

FIRST VINTAGE BOOKS EDITION, November 1975
Introduction Copyright © 1974 by Steven Marcus
Copyright © 1974 by Lillian Hellman, Executrix of
the Estate of Dashiell Hammett
Copyright 1923, 1924, 1930 by
Pro-distributors Publishing Co., Inc.
Copyright renewed 1951, 1952, 1958
by Arthur W. A. Cowan and
Lillian Hellman.

Library of Congress Cataloging in Publication Data

Hammett, Dashiell, 1894-1961.
  The Continental Op.

  CONTENTS: The tenth clew.—The golden horse-
shoe.—The house in Turk Street. [etc.]
  1. Detective and mystery stories, American.
I. Title.
[PZ3.H1884Cq7] [PS3515.A4347]   813'.5'2
ISBN 0-394-72013-X   75-11735

Manufactured in the United States of America

INTRODUCTION

1

Dashiell Hammett—creator of such figures in the mythology of American culture as the Continental Op, Sam Spade, and the Thin Man—was born Samuel Dashiell Hammett, in St. Mary's County, Maryland, in May 1894. The family was of Scottish and French extraction, and they were Catholic. Hammett's early years were spent in Philadelphia and Baltimore, and his formal education was brought to an end at the age of fourteen, when he left high school after less than a year of attendance. His father's relative lack of success in the world seems, at least in part, to be reflected in this decision.

For the next several years Hammett worked with indifferent success and even less interest at a number of odd jobs—on the Baltimore and Ohio Railroad, in factories, at stockbrokers', and as a casual laborer. When he was about twenty he answered an advertisement in a

Baltimore newspaper, and as a result, found himself employed by Pinkerton's, the most famous of American private-detective agencies. The young man had found a vocation that engaged his liveliest interests. The work was challenging, exciting, adventurous, dangerous, and humorous. It took him around the country and into and out of a large variety of walks of life, classes of society, and social and dramatic situations. These experiences were formative; their influence in his education as a writer can hardly be overestimated.

In 1918 he enlisted in the Ambulance Corps of the United States Army and was stationed near Baltimore. During his year of military service he came down with influenza, which led to the activation in him of tuberculosis. It was his first encounter with the series of lung diseases from which he was eventually to die. In 1919 he returned to his work at Pinkerton's and his travels and adventures in the service of the Agency. The active and arduous work of a private-detective agent in the field brought on another attack of tuberculosis, and he was hospitalized in 1920 and 1921 in government hospitals on the West Coast. While he was in the hospital he became involved with one of the nurses who worked there, and they were married toward the end of 1920.

Hammett was discharged from the hospital in May 1921, and he and his wife made their way along the West Coast to San Francisco. The town awakened Hammett's interest, and he went back to work there for the local branch of the Pinkerton Agency. He was to live in San Francisco for the next eight years, and the city provided him with the locale and material for a large part of his writing. Yet even as he was returning to work as a detective, other interests began to make themselves felt in him. He had conceived of the idea of becoming a writer, and was beginning to write bits of verse, small sketches from his experiences as a detective, and other pieces of apprentice work. Finally, the successful solution of a case led to his leaving the Agency. Some $200,000 in gold was missing on an Australian ship that had put into San Francisco. The Pinkerton Agency was employed by the insurance company involved to find the gold—which they believed was stashed away on the ship. Hammett and another operative were sent to search the ship, and found nothing. It was decided to send Hammett back to Australia on the ship in the belief that he might still find the missing loot. Hammett looked forward to the adventure. Just before the ship was to leave San Francisco, he made one last routine search and found the gold—it was hidden in a smokestack. He had solved the case and lost the trip to Australia. Frustrated and outdone by his own success, he handed in his resignation.

Soon after this, while working at odd jobs, Hammett began to hemorrhage again. Feeling that he had little time left to live, and that the one thing he wanted to do before he died was to write, he moved away from his family, took a cheap single room, and started to write. Sometime around here he also began to work for a local jewelry store as a writer of advertising copy. It was an odd and uncertain Bohemian existence; sometimes he lived on soup; frequently he drank too much. By the end of 1922, however, he began to break into print, with a number of small pieces in *Smart Set* and *Black Mask*. This latter, a popular pulp-fiction magazine, soon became Hammett's regular place of appearance in print, and his career and the career of the magazine traversed almost identical arcs. In October 1923 the first story in which the Continental Op appears—in his never-to-bevaried figure as anonymous narrator—was published. From then until 1930, as Hammett's writing underwent rapid and continuous development, this was the essential (though not the exclusive) form into which his fiction was cast. It was certainly the most successful, both in itself and in its appeal to a rapidly growing audience of readers. By the middle years of the 1920's Hammett was becoming known as an original talent, an innovator in a popular form of fiction, and as the central figure in a new school of writing about crime—the "hard-boiled school," as it came quickly to be called. And it was also beginning to be recognized as being within its own context the structural equivalent of what Hemingway and the writers who clustered naturally about Hemingway were doing in their kind of writing during the same period.

By 1927 Hammett was ready to work on a larger scale. He began to publish serially, in *Black Mask,* large units of fiction that were in fact quasi-independent sections of novels. After they had been published in the magazine he would revise them, and they would appear as volumes. *Red Harvest* was published as a volume in 1929, as was *The Dain Curse.* These two novels bring the Op's career to a climax (although three more short stories featuring the Op were later to appear), and Hammett was rapidly becoming both well known and affluent. In 1929 he invented Sam Spade and *The Maltese Falcon,* and became immediately famous. This was followed at once in 1930 by *The Glass Key. The Thin Man,* Hammett's last published novel, and another large success, came out in 1934.

Sometime during the late 1920's Hammett's marriage —two daughters were born of it—broke up for good. His life as a writer, as he continued to prosper, remained as intense, demanding, anarchic, and casually self-destructive as it had been in the years of his apprenticeship. On the one hand, there was a great deal of heavy drinking, there was a great deal of womanizing, and an even greater deal of compulsive and wild squandering of money. On the other hand, there were rigorous bouts of self-discipline and periods of extremely intense, ascetic, and self-denying hard work. After 1930 these latter began to diminish in frequency. Hammett had left San Francisco in 1929 and moved to New York; from there, in 1930, with the Great Depression setting deeply in, Hammett moved out to Hollywood. Warner Brothers had bought the film rights for *The Maltese Falcon,* and Hammett was offered high-paying work on a variety of film projects. It was here, one night in November, as he was coming out of a monumental drunk that had lasted for days, that he met a young woman named Lillian Hellman. The two were immediately attracted to one another, and there then began what was for both of them the most important relation in their lives. It was impassioned and tempestuous; it was often cruel and harsh and harmful; and there were times when neither was faithful to the other and when they went their own ways and lived apart. But in the end it endured; it lasted for thirty years, until his death.

By 1934 Hammett's career as a creative writer was finished. He did not know this, of course, and in 1932 in an interview, said that he was planning to write a play. That play never got written, but another one did. It was called *The Children's Hour,* and Hammett's work as a careful reader, stern schoolmaster, and relentlessly honest critic was instrumental in its realization. His connection with Lillian Hellman's career as a playwright was to remain close, intimate, and instrumental as the years went on.

During the1930's Hammett continued to work at various kinds of writing and rewriting jobs in the movie industry. He also became involved, as did so many other writers and intellectuals of the period, in various left-wing and anti-fascist causes. He had become a Marxist; he had also committed himself to the cause of the Communist Party in America, and became a member of it probably sometime during 1937. Although he never surrendered his personal critical sense about the limitations and absurdities of many of his political associates and allies, both here and abroad, the commitment he had made was deep, and it was lasting, and he would pay for it in the end. It was characteristic of him—as both man and writer—that he was willing to pay the price.

Shortly after America entered World War II, Hammett—at the age of forty-eight—enlisted in the Army. Through some inexplicable sleight of hand and mouth he managed to persuade the Army doctors that the scars on his lungs that showed up on the X-rays were of no importance. He volunteered for overseas service and was sent to the Aleutians—where, among other things, he edited a daily newspaper for the troops. He apparently thoroughly enjoyed his tour of duty in the Army, and became a legendary character among his much younger fellow soldiers. When he was discharged from the Army in 1945, he was fifty-one, famous, and comparatively affluent. He had also developed emphysema. The adaptation of his novels and characters to movies and radio shows continued to bring in money, as did the steady sale of his novels. Times were changing, but his political loyalties were not. Neither were his drinking habits, which damaged and ravaged him until they brought him down in 1948 with the d.t.'s. From that time forward he never drank.

The Cold War was now on, the period identified with Senator Joseph McCarthy's name was taking shape, and many old scores were beginning to be paid off. In one of the numerous legal cases that characterized the period, Hammett was called to give evidence. He was asked to name the contributors to a fund (of which he was a trustee) that supplied bail for Communists and others who were brought to trial (in this particular case, a number of persons on trial had jumped bail and vanished). Hammett refused to testify, was found guilty of contempt of court, and was sentenced to six months in jail. He spent five months in various prisons and was then released. When he got out of prison he was an exhausted and very ill man.

His external troubles were by no means over. The money, which had once been so plentiful, was no longer there. He was blacklisted in Hollywood, and his radio shows had gone off the air. The government sued him for back taxes, won a judgment of $140,000 against him, and had his royalty, and all other, payments blocked. He took it all, as he had taken all that had come before, stoically and without complaint. He retired further into himself and lived a quiet and self-contained life until 1956, when his illness and weakness made it impossible to live alone. Thereafter he lived within the care and companionship of Lillian Hellman. In 1960 his lung condition worsened and became cancerous. He died on January 10, 1961. By his own wish, he was buried in Arlington National Cemetery. He had served the nation in two World Wars. He had also served it in other ways, which were his own.

2

I was first introduced to Dashiell Hammett by Humphrey Bogart. I was twelve years old at the time, and mention the occasion because I take it to be exemplary, that I share this experience with countless others. (Earlier than this, at the very dawn of consciousness, I can recall William Powell and Myrna Loy and a small dog on a leash and an audience full of adults laughing; but that had nothing to do with Hammett or anything else as far as I was concerned.) What was striking about the event was that it was one of the first encounters I can consciously recall with the experience of moral ambiguity. Here was this detective you were supposed to like— and did like—behaving and speaking in peculiar and unexpected ways. He acted up to the cops, partly for real, partly as a ruse. He connived with crooks, for his own ends and perhaps even for some of theirs. He slept with his partner's wife, fell in love with a lady crook, and then refused to save her from the police, even though he could have. Which side was he on? Was he on any side apart from his own? And which or what side was that? The experience was not only morally ambiguous; it was morally complex and enigmatic as well. The impression it made was a lasting one.

Years later, after having read *The Maltese Falcon* and seen the movie again and then reread the novel, I could begin to understand why the impact of the film had been so memorable, much more so than that of most other movies. The director, John Huston, had had the wit to recognize the power, sharpness, integrity, and bite of Hammett's prose—particularly the dialogue—and the film script consists almost entirely of speech taken directly and without modification from the written novel.

Moreover, this unusual situation is complicated still further. In selecting with notable intelligence the relevant scenes and passages from the novel, Huston had to make certain omissions. Paradoxically, however, one of the things that he chose to omit was the most important or central moment in the entire novel. It is also one of the central moments in all of Hammett's writing. I think we can make use of this oddly "lost" passage as a means of entry into Hammett's vision or imagination of the world.

It occurs as Spade is becoming involved with Brigid O'Shaughnessy in her struggle with the other thieves, and it is his way of communicating to her his sense of how the world and life go. His way is to tell her a story from his own experience. The form this story takes is that of a parable. It is a parable about a man named Flitcraft. Flitcraft was a successful, happily married, stable, and utterly respectable real-estate dealer in Tacoma. One day he went out to lunch and never returned. No reason could be found for his disappearance, and no account of it could be made. " 'He went like that,' Spade said, 'like a fist when you open your hand.' "

Five years later Mrs. Flitcraft came to the agency at which Spade was working and told them that " 'she had seen a man in Spokane who looked a lot like her husband.' " Spade went off to investigate and found that it was indeed Flitcraft. He had been living in Spokane for a couple of years under the name of Charles Pierce. He had a successful automobile business, a wife, a baby son, a suburban home, and usually played golf after four in the afternoon, just as he had in Tacoma. Spade and he sat down to talk the matter over. Flitcraft, Spade recounts, " 'had no feeling of guilt. He had left his family well provided for, and what he had done seemed to him perfectly reasonable. The only thing that bothered him was a doubt that he could make that reasonableness clear' " 'to his interlocutor. When Flitcraft went out to lunch that day five years before in Tacoma, " 'he passed an office-building that was being put up. . . . A beam or something fell eight or ten stories down and smacked the sidewalk alongside him.' " A chip of smashed sidewalk flew up and took a piece of skin off his cheek. He was otherwise unharmed. He stood there " 'scared stiff,' " he told Spade, " 'but he was more shocked than really frightened. He felt like somebody had taken the lid off his life and let him look at the works.' "

Until that very moment Flitcraft had been " 'a good citizen and a good husband and father, not by any outer compulsion, but simply because he was a man who was most comfortable in step with his surroundings. . . . The life he knew was a clean orderly sane responsible affair. Now a falling beam had shown him that life was fundamentally none of these things. . . . What disturbed him was the discovery that in sensibly ordering his affairs he had got out of step, and not into step, with life.' " By the time he had finished lunch, he had reached the decision " 'that he would change his life at random by simply going away.' " He went off that afternoon, wandered around for a couple of years, then drifted back to the Northwest, " 'settled in Spokane and got married. His second wife didn't look like the first, but they were more alike than they were different.' " And the same held true of his second life. Spade then moves on to his conclusion: " 'He wasn't sorry for what he had done. It seemed reasonable enough to him. I don't think he even knew he had settled back into the same groove that he had jumped out of in Tacoma. But that's the part of it I always liked. He adjusted himself to beams falling, and then no more of them fell, and he adjusted himself to

their not falling.' " End of parable. Brigid of course
understands nothing of this, as Spade doubtless knew
beforehand. Yet what he has been telling her has to do
with the forces and beliefs and contingencies that guide
his conduct and supply a structure to his apparently
enigmatic behavior.

To begin with, we may note that such a sustained
passage is not the kind of thing we ordinarily expect in
a detective story or novel about crime. That it is there,
and that comparable passages occur in all of Hammett's
best work, clearly suggests the kind of transformation
that Hammett was performing on this popular genre of
writing. The transformation was in the direction of literature. And what the passage in question is about among
other things is the ethical irrationality of existence, the
ethical unintelligibility of the world. For Flitcraft the
falling beam " 'had taken the lid off life and let him look
at the works.' " The works are that life is inscrutable,
opaque, irresponsible, and arbitrary—that human existence does not correspond in its actuality to the way we
live it. For most of us live as if existence itself were
ordered, ethical, and rational. As a direct result of his
realization in experience that it is not, Flitcraft leaves his
wife and children and goes off. He acts irrationally and
at random, in accordance with the nature of existence.
When after a couple of years of wandering aimlessly
about he decides to establish a new life, he simply repro-
duces the old one he had supposedly repudiated and
abandoned; that is to say, he behaves again as if life
were orderly, meaningful, and rational, and "adjusts" to
it. And this, with fine irony, is the part of it, Spade says,
that he " 'always liked,' " which means the part that he
liked best. For here we come upon the unfathomable
and most mysteriously irrational part of it all—how de-

spite everything we have learned and everything we know, men will persist in behaving and trying to behave sanely, rationally, sensibly, and responsibly. And we will continue to persist even when we know that there is no logical or metaphysical, no discoverable or demonstrable reason for doing so.* It is this sense of sustained contradiction that is close to the center—or to one of the centers—of Hammett's work. The contradiction is not ethical alone; it is metaphysical as well. And it is not merely sustained; it is sustained with pleasure. For Hammett and Spade and the Op, the sustainment in consciousness of such contradictions is an indispensable part of their existence and of their pleasure in that existence.

That this pleasure is itself complex, ambiguous, and problematic becomes apparent as one simply describes the conditions under which it exists. And the complexity, ambiguity, and sense of the problematical are not confined to such moments of "revelation"—or set pieces— as the parable of Flitcraft. They permeate Hammett's work and act as formative elements in its structure, including its deep structure. Hammett's work went through considerable and interesting development in the course of his career for twelve years as a writer. He also wrote in a considerable variety of forms and worked out a variety of narrative devices and strategies. At the same time, his work considered as a whole reveals a remarkable kind of coherence. In order to further the understanding of that coherence, we can propose for the purposes of the present analysis to construct a kind of "ideal type" of a Hammett or Op story. Which is not to say or

* It can hardly be an accident that the new name that Hammett gives to Flitcraft is that of an American philosopher—with two vowels reversed—who was deeply involved in just such speculations.

to imply in the least that he wrote according to a formula, but that an authentic imaginative vision lay beneath and informed the structure of his work.

Such an ideal-typical description runs as follows. The Op is called in or sent out on a case. Something has been stolen, someone is missing, some dire circumstance is impending, someone has been murdered—it doesn't matter. The Op interviews the person or persons most immediately accessible. They may be innocent or guilty—it doesn't matter; it is an indifferent circumstance. Guilty or innocent, they provide the Op with an account of what they know, of what they assert really happened. The Op begins to investigate; he compares these accounts with others that he gathers; he snoops about; he does research; he shadows people, arranges confrontations between those who want to avoid one another, and so on. What he soon discovers is that the "reality" that anyone involved will swear to is in fact itself a construction, a fabrication, a fiction, a faked and alternate reality—and that it has been gotten together before he ever arrived on the scene. And the Op's work therefore is to deconstruct, decompose, deplot and defictionalize that "reality" and to construct or reconstruct out of it a true fiction, i.e., an account of what "really" happened.

It should be quite evident that there is a reflexive and coordinate relation between the activities of the Op and the activities of Hammett, the writer. Yet the depth and problematic character of this self-reflexive process begin to be revealed when we observe that the reconstruction or true fiction created and arrived at by the Op at the end of the story is no more plausible—nor is it meant to be —than the stories that have been told to him by all parties, guilty or innocent, in the course of his work. The Op may catch the real thief or collar the actual crook—

that is not entirely to the point. What is to the point is that the story, account, or chain of events that the Op winds up with as "reality" is no more plausible and no less ambiguous than the stories that he meets with at the outset and later. What Hammet has done—unlike most writers of detective or crime stories before him or since —is to include as part of the contingent and dramatic consciousness of his narrative the circumstance that the work of the detective is itself a fiction-making activity, a discovery or creation by fabrication of something new in the world, or hidden, latent, potential, or as yet unde-veloped within it. The typical "classical" detective story —unlike Hammett's—can be described as a formal game with certain specified rules of transformation. What ordinarily happens is that the detective is faced with a situation of inadequate, false, misleading, and ambiguous information. And the story as a whole is an exercise in disambiguation—with the final scenes being a ratiocina-tive demonstration that the butler did it (or not); these scenes achieve a conclusive, reassuring clarity of expla-nation, wherein everything is set straight, and the game we have been party to is brought to its appropriate end. But this, as we have already seen, is not what ordinarily happens in Hammett or with the Op.

What happens is that the Op almost invariably walks into a situation that has already been elaborately fabri-cated or framed. And his characteristic response to his sense that he is dealing with a series of deceptions or fic-tions is—to use the words that he uses himself repeat-edly—"to stir things up." This corresponds integrally, both as metaphor and in logical structure, to what hap-pened in the parable of Flitcraft. When the falling beam just misses Flitcraft, "he felt like somebody had taken the lid off life." The Op lives with the uninterrupted awareness that for him the lid has been taken off life. When the lid has been lifted, the logical thing to do is to "stir things up"—which is what he does.* He actively undertakes to deconstruct, decompose, and thus demystify the fictional—and therefore false—reality created by the characters, crooks or not, with whom he is involved. More often than not he tries to substitute his own fictional-hypothetical representation for theirs—and this representation may also be "true" or mistaken, or both at once. In any event, his major effort is to make the fictions of others visible as fictions, inventions, concealments, falsehoods, and mystifications. When a fiction becomes visible as such, it begins to dissolve and disappear, and presumably should reveal behind it the "real" reality that was there all the time and that it was masking. Yet what happens in Hammett is that what is revealed as "reality" is a still further fiction-making activity—in the first place the Op's, and behind that yet another, the consciousness present in many of the Op stories and all the novels that Dashiell Hammett, the writer, is continually doing the same thing as the Op and all the other characters in the fiction he is creating. That is to say, he is making a fiction (in writing) in the real world; and this fiction, like the real world itself, is coherent but not necessarily rational. What one both begins and ends with, then, is a story, a narrative, a coherent yet questionable account of the world. This problematic penetrates to the bottom of Hammett's narrative imagination and shapes a number of its deeper

* These homely metaphors go deep into Hammett's life. One of the few things that he could recall from his childhood past was his mother's repeated advice that a woman who wasn't good in the kitchen wasn't likely to be much good in any other room in the house.

processes—in *The Dain Curse,* for example, it is the chief topic of explicit debate that runs throughout the entire novel.

Yet Hammett's writing is still more complex and integral than this. For the unresolvable paradoxes and dilemmas that we have just been describing in terms of narrative structure and consciousness are reproduced once again in Hammett's vision and representation of society, of the social world in which the Op lives. At this point we must recall that Hammett is a writer of the 1920's and that this was the era of Prohibition. American society had in effect committed itself to a vast collective fiction. Even more, this fiction was false not merely in the sense that it was made up or did not in fact correspond to reality; it was false in the sense that it was corrupt and corrupting as well. During this period every time an American took a drink he was helping to undermine the law, and American society had covertly committed itself to what was in practice collaborative illegality.* There is a kind of epiphany of these circumstances in "The Golden Horseshoe." The Op is on a case that takes him to Tijuana. In a bar there, he reads a sign:

---

* Matters were even murkier than this. The Eighteenth Amendment to the Constitution was in effect from January 1920 to December 1933, nearly fourteen years. During this period Americans were forbidden under penalty of law to manufacture, sell, or transport any intoxicating liquor. At the same time no one was forbidden to buy or drink such liquor. In other words, Americans were virtually being solicited by their own laws to support an illegal trade in liquor, even while Congress was passing the Volstead Act, which was intended to prevent such a trade.

ONLY GENUINE PRE-WAR AMERICAN AND
BRITISH WHISKEYS SERVED HERE

He responds by remarking that "I was trying to count how many lies could be found in those nine words, and had reached four, with promise of more," when he is interrupted by some call to action. That sign and the Op's response to it describe part of the existential character of the social world represented by Hammett.

Another part of that representation is expressed in another kind of story or idea that Hammett returned to repeatedly. The twenties were also the great period of organized crime and organized criminal gangs in America, and one of Hammett's obsessive imaginations was the notion of organized crime or gangs taking over an entire society and running it as if it were an ordinary society doing business as usual. In other words, society itself would become a fiction, concealing and belying the actuality of what was controlling it and perverting it from within. One can thus make out quite early in this native American writer a proto-Marxist critical representation of how a certain kind of society works. Actually, the point of view is pre- rather than proto-Marxist, and the social world as it is dramatized in many of these stories is Hobbesian rather than Marxist.* It is a world of universal warfare, the war of each against all, and of all against all. The only thing that prevents the criminal ascendancy from turning into permanent tyranny is that the crooks who take over society cannot cooperate with

* Again it can hardly be regarded as an accident that the name Hammett gives to the town taken over by the criminals in *Red Harvest* is "Personville"—pronounced "Poisonville." And what else is Personville except Leviathan, the "artificial man" represented by Hobbes as the image of society itself.

one another, repeatedly fall out with each other, and return to the Hobbesian anarchy out of which they have momentarily arisen. The social world as imagined by Hammett runs on a principle that is the direct opposite of that postulated by Erik Erikson as the fundamental and enabling condition for human existence. In Hammett, society and social relations are dominated by the principle of basic mistrust. As one of his detectives remarks, speaking for himself and for virtually every other character in Hammett's writing, "I trust no one."

When Hammett turns to the respectable world, the world of respectable society, of affluence and influence, of open personal and political power, he finds only more of the same. The respectability of respectable American society is as much a fiction and a fraud as the phony respectable society fabricated by the criminals. Indeed, he unwaveringly represents the world of crime as a reproduction in both structure and detail of the modern capitalist society that it depends on, preys off, and is part of. But Hammett does something even more radical than this. He not only continually juxtaposes and connects the ambiguously fictional worlds of art and of writing with the fraudulently fictional worlds of society; he connects them, juxtaposes them, and sees them in dizzying and baffling interaction. He does this in many ways and on many occasions. One of them, for example, is the Maltese Falcon itself, which turns out to be and contains within itself the history of capitalism. It is originally a piece of plunder, part of what Marx called the "primitive accumulation"; when its gold encrusted with gems is painted over, it becomes a mystified object, a commodity itself; it is a piece of property that belongs to no one —whoever possesses it does not really own it. At the same time it is another fiction, a representation or work of art—which turns out itself to be a fake, since it is made of lead. It is a *rara avis* indeed. As is the fiction in which it is created and contained, the novel by Hammett.

It is into this bottomlessly equivocal, endlessly fraudulent, and brutally acquisitive world that Hammett precipitates the Op. There is nothing glamorous about him. Short, thick-set, balding, between thirty-five and forty, he has no name, no home, no personal existence apart from his work. He is, and he regards himself as, "the hired man" of official and respectable society, who is paid so much per day to clean it up and rescue it from the crooks and thieves who are perpetually threatening to take it over. Yet what he—and the reader—just as perpetually learn is that the respectable society that employs him is itself inveterately vicious, deceitful, culpable, crooked, and degraded. How then is the Op to be preserved, to preserve himself, from being contaminated by both the world he works against and the world he is hired to work for?

To begin with, the Op lives by a code. This code consists in the first instance of the rules laid down by the Continental Agency, and they are "rather strict." The most important of them by far is that no operative in the employ of the Agency is ever allowed to take or collect part of a reward that may be attached to the solution of a case. Since he cannot directly enrich himself through his professional skills, he is saved from at least the characteristic corruption of modern society—the corruption that is connected with its fundamental acquisitive structure. At the same time, the Op is a special case of the Protestant ethic, for his entire existence is bound up in and expressed by his work, his vocation. He likes his work, and it is honest work, done as much for enjoyment and the exercise of his skills and abilities as it is for personal gain and self-sustainment. The work is something of an end in itself, and this circumstance also serves to protect him, as does his deliberate refusal to use high-class and fancy moral language about anything. The work is an end in itself and is therefore something more than work alone. As Spade says, in a passage that is the culmination of many such passages in Hammett:

> "I'm a detective and expecting me to run criminals down and then let them go free is like asking a dog to catch a rabbit and let it go. It can be done, all right, and sometimes it is done, but it's not the natural thing."

Being a detective, then, entails more than fulfilling a social function or performing a social role. Being a detective is the realization of an identity, for there are components in it which are beyond or beneath society—and cannot be touched by it—and beyond and beneath reason. There is something "natural" about it. Yet if we recall that the nature thus being expressed is that of a man-hunter, and Hammett's apt metaphor compels us to do so, and that the state of society as it is represented in Hammett's writing reminds us of the state of nature in Hobbes, we see that even here Hammett does not release his sense of the complex and the contradictory, and is making no simple-minded appeal to some benign idea of the "natural."

And indeed the Op is not finally or fully protected by his work, his job, his vocation. (We have all had to relearn with bitterness what multitudes of wickedness "doing one's job" can cover.) Max Weber has memorably remarked that "the decisive means for politics is violence." In Hammett's depiction of modern American society, violence is the decisive means indeed, along with fraud, deceit, treachery, betrayal, and general, endemic unscrupulousness. Such means are in no sense alien to Hammett's detective. As the Op says, " 'detecting is a hard business, and you use whatever tools come to hand.' " In other words, there is a paradoxical tension and unceasing interplay in Hammett's stories between means and ends; relations between the two are never secure or stable. And as Max Weber further remarked, in his great essay "Politics as a Vocation": "the world is governed by demons, and he who lets himself in for . . . power and force as means, contracts with diabolic powers, and for his action it is *not* true that good can follow only from good and evil only from evil, but that often the opposite is true. Anyone who fails to see this is, indeed, a political infant." Neither Hammett nor the Op is an infant; yet no one can be so grown up and inured to experience that he can escape the consequences that attach to the deliberate use of violent and dubious means.

These consequences are of various orders. "Good" ends themselves can be transformed and perverted by the use of vicious or indiscriminate means. (I am leaving to one side those even more perplexing instances in Hammett in which the ends pursued by the Op correspond with ends desired by a corrupted yet respectable official society.) The consequences are also visible inwardly, on the inner being of the agent of such means, the Op himself. The violence begins to get to him:

I began to throw my right fist into him.
I liked that. His belly was flabby, and it got softer every time I hit it. I hit it often.

Another side of this set of irresolvable moral predicaments is revealed when we see that the Op's toughness is not merely a carapace within which feelings of tenderness and humanity can be nourished and preserved. The toughness is toughness through and through, and as the Op continues his career, and continues to live by the means he does, he tends to become more callous and less and less able to feel. At the very end, awaiting him, he knows, is the prospect of becoming like his boss, the head of the Agency, the Old Man, "with his gentle eyes behind gold spectacles and his mild smile, hiding the fact that fifty years of sleuthing had left him without any feelings at all on any subject." This is the price exacted by the use of such means in such a world; these are the consequences of living fully in a society moved by the principle of basic mistrust. "Whoever fights monsters," writes Nietzsche, "should see to it that in the process he does not become a monster. And when you look long into an abyss, the abyss also looks into you." The abyss looks into Hammett, the Old Man, and the Op.

It is through such complex devices as I have merely sketched here that Hammett was able to raise the crime story into literature. He did it over a period of ten years. Yet the strain was finally too much to bear—that shifting, entangled, and equilibrated state of contradictions out of which his creativity arose and which it expressed could no longer be sustained. His creative career ends when he is no longer able to handle the literary, social, and moral opacities, instabilities, and contradictions that characterize all his best work. His life then splits apart and goes in the two opposite directions that were implicit in his earlier, creative phase, but that the creativity held suspended and in poised yet fluid tension. His politics go in one direction; the way he made his living went in another—he became a hack writer, and then finally no writer at all. That is another story. Yet for ten years he was able to do what almost no other writer in this genre has ever done so well—he was able to really write, to construct a vision of a world in words, to know that the writing was about the real world and referred to it and was part of it; and at the same time he was able to be self-consciously aware that the whole thing was problematical and about itself and "only" writing as well. For ten years, in other words, he was a true creator of fiction.

STEVEN MARCUS

THE
TENTH
CLEW.

"Mr. Leopold Gantvoort is not at home," the servant who opened the door said, "but his son, Mr. Charles, is —if you wish to see him."

"No, I had an appointment with Mr. Leopold Gantvoort for nine or a little after. It's just nine now. No doubt he'll be back soon. I'll wait."

"Very well, sir."

He stepped aside for me to enter the house, took my overcoat and hat, guided me to a room on the second floor—Gantvoort's library—and left me. I picked up a magazine from the stack on the table, pulled an ash tray over beside me, and made myself comfortable.

An hour passed. I stopped reading and began to grow impatient. Another hour passed—and I was fidgeting.

A clock somewhere below had begun to strike eleven when a young man of twenty-five or -six, tall and slender, with remarkably white skin and very dark hair and eyes, came into the room.

3

"My father hasn't returned yet," he said. "It's too bad that you should have been kept waiting all this time. Isn't there anything I could do for you? I am Charles Gantvoort."

"No, thank you." I got up from my chair, accepting the courteous dismissal. "I'll get in touch with him to-morrow."

"I'm sorry," he murmured, and we moved toward the door together.

As we reached the hall an extension telephone in one corner of the room we were leaving buzzed softly, and I halted in the doorway while Charles Gantvoort went over to answer it.

His back was toward me as he spoke into the instrument.

"Yes. Yes, Yes!"—sharply—"*What? Yes*"—very weakly—"Yes."

He turned slowly around and faced me with a face that was gray and tortured, with wide shocked eyes and gaping mouth—the telephone still in his hand.

"Father," he gasped, "is dead—killed!"

"Where? How?"

"I don't know. That was the police. They want me to come down at once."

He straightened his shoulders with an effort, pulling himself together, put down the telephone, and his face fell into less strained lines.

"You will pardon my—"

"Mr. Gantvoort," I interrupted his apology, "I am connected with the Continental Detective Agency. Your father called up this afternoon and asked that a detective be sent to see him tonight. He said his life had been threatened. He hadn't definitely engaged us, however, so unless you—"

"Certainly! You are employed! If the police haven't already caught the murderer I want you to do everything possible to catch him."

"All right! Let's get down to headquarters."

Neither of us spoke during the ride to the Hall of Justice. Gantvoort bent over the wheel of his car, sending it through the streets at a terrific speed. There were several questions that needed answers, but all his attention was required for his driving if he was to maintain the pace at which he was driving without piling us into something. So I didn't disturb him, but hung on and kept quiet.

Half a dozen police detectives were waiting for us when we reached the detective bureau. O'Gar—a bullet-headed detective sergeant who dresses like the village constable in a movie, wide-brimmed black hat and all, but who isn't to be put out of the reckoning on that account—was in charge of the investigation. He and I had worked on two or three jobs together before, and hit it off excellently.

He led us into one of the small offices below the assembly room. Spread out on the flat top of a desk there were a dozen or more objects.

"I want you to look these things over carefully," the detective-sergeant told Gantvoort, "and pick out the ones that belonged to your father."

"But where is he?"

"Do this first," O'Gar insisted, "and then you can see him."

I looked at the things on the table while Charles Gantvoort made his selections. An empty jewel case; a memorandum book; three letters in slit envelopes that were addressed to the dead man; some other papers; a bunch of keys; a fountain pen; two white linen handkerchiefs;

two pistol cartridges; a gold watch, with a gold knife and a gold pencil attached to it by a gold-and-platinum chain; two black leather wallets, one of them very new and the other worn; some money, both paper and silver; and a small portable typewriter, bent and twisted, and matted with hair and blood. Some of the other things were smeared with blood and some were clean.

Gantvoort picked out the watch and its attachments, the keys, the fountain pen, the memoranda book, the handkerchiefs, the letters and other papers, and the older wallet.

"These were Father's," he told us. "I've never seen any of the others before. I don't know, of course, how much money he had with him tonight, so I can't say how much of this is his."

"You're sure none of the rest of this stuff was his?" O'Gar asked.

"I don't think so, but I'm not sure. Whipple could tell you." He turned to me. "He's the man who let you in tonight. He looked after Father, and he'd know positively whether any of these other things belonged to him or not."

One of the police detectives went to the telephone to tell Whipple to come down immediately.

I resumed the questioning.

"Is anything that your father usually carried with him missing? Anything of value?"

"Not that I know of. All the things that he might have been expected to have with him seem to be here."

"At what time tonight did he leave the house?"

"Before seven-thirty. Possibly as early as seven."

"Know where he was going?"

"He didn't tell me, but I supposed he was going to call on Miss Dexter."

The faces of the police detectives brightened, and their eyes grew sharp. I suppose mine did, too. There are many, many murders with never a woman in them anywhere; but seldom a very conspicuous killing.

"Who's this Miss Dexter?" O'Gar took up the inquiry.

"She's, well—" Charles Gantvoort hesitated. "Well, Father was on very friendly terms with her and her brother. He usually called on them—on her several evenings a week. In fact, I suspected that he intended marrying her."

"Who and what is she?"

"Father became acquainted with them six or seven months ago. I've met them several times, but don't know them very well. Miss Dexter—Creda is her given name —is about twenty-three years old, I should judge, and her brother Madden is four or five years older. He is in New York now, or on his way there, to transact some business for Father."

"Did your father tell you he was going to marry her?" O'Gar hammered away at the woman angle.

"No; but it was pretty obvious that he was very much —ah—infatuated. We had some words over it a few days ago—last week. Not a quarrel, you understand, but words. From the way he talked I feared that he meant to marry her."

"What do you mean 'feared'?" O'Gar snapped at that word.

Charles Gantvoort's pale face flushed a little, and he cleared his throat embarrassedly.

"I don't want to put the Dexters in a bad light to you. I don't think—I'm sure they had nothing to do with Father's—with this. But I didn't care especially for them —didn't like them. I thought they were—well—fortune hunters, perhaps. Father wasn't fabulously wealthy, but he had considerable means. And, while he wasn't feeble, still he was past fifty-seven, old enough for me to feel that Creda Dexter was more interested in his money than in him."

"How about your father's will?"

"The last one of which I have any knowledge—drawn up two or three years ago—left everything to my wife and me, jointly. Father's attorney, Mr. Murray Abernathy, could tell you if there was a later will, but I hardly think there was."

"Your father had retired from business, hadn't he?"

"Yes; he turned his import and export business over to me about a year ago. He had quite a few investments scattered around, but he wasn't actively engaged in the management of any concern."

O'Gar tilted his village constable hat back and scratched his bullet head reflectively for a moment. Then he looked at me.

"Anything else you want to ask?"

"Yes. Mr. Gantvoort, do you know or did you ever hear your father or anyone else speak of an Emil Bonfils?"

"No."

"Did your father ever tell you that he had received a threatening letter? Or that he had been shot at on the street?"

"No."

"Was your father in Paris in 1902?"

"Very likely. He used to go abroad every year up until the time of his retirement from business."

O'Gar and I took Gantvoort around to the morgue to see his father, then. The dead man wasn't pleasant to look at, even to O'Gar and me, who hadn't known him except by sight. I remembered him as a small wiry man, always smartly tailored, and with a brisk springiness that was far younger than his years.

He lay now with the top of his head beaten into a red and pulpy mess.

We left Gantvoort at the morgue and set out afoot for the Hall of Justice.

"What's this deep stuff you're pulling about Emil Bonfils and Paris in 1902?" the detective-sergeant asked as soon as we were out in the street.

"This: the dead man phoned the Agency this afternoon and said he had received a threatening letter from an Emil Bonfils with whom he had had trouble in Paris in 1902. He also said that Bonfils had shot at him the previous evening, in the street. He wanted somebody to come around and see him about it tonight. And he said that under no circumstances were the police to be let in on it—that he'd rather have Bonfils get him than have the trouble made public. That's all he would say over the phone; and that's how I happened to be on hand when Charles Gantvoort was notified of his father's death."

O'Gar stopped in the middle of the sidewalk and whistled softly.

"That's something!" he exclaimed. "Wait till we get back to headquarters—I'll show you something."

Whipple was waiting in the assembly room when we arrived at headquarters. His face at first glance was as smooth and mask-like as when he had admitted me to the house on Russian Hill earlier in the evening. But beneath his perfect servant's manner he was twitching and trembling.

We took him into the little office where we had questioned Charles Gantvoort.

Whipple verified all that the dead man's son had told us. He was positive that neither the typewriter, the jewel case, the two cartridges, or the newer wallet had belonged to Gantvoort.

We couldn't get him to put his opinion of the Dexters in words, but that he disapproved of them was easily seen. Miss Dexter, he said, had called up on the telephone three times this night at about eight o'clock, at nine, and at nine-thirty. She had asked for Mr. Leopold Gantvoort each time, but she had left no message. Whipple was of the opinion that she was expecting Gantvoort, and he had not arrived.

He knew nothing, he said, of Emil Bonfils or of any threatening letters. Gantvoort had been out the previous night from eight until midnight. Whipple had not seen him closely enough when he came home to say whether he seemed excited or not. Gantvoort usually carried about a hundred dollars in his pockets.

"Is there anything that you know of that Gantvoort had on his person tonight which isn't among these things on the desk?" O'Gar asked.

"No, sir. Everything seems to be here—watch and chain, money, memorandum book, wallet, keys, handkerchiefs, fountain pen—everything that I know of."

"Did Charles Gantvoort go out tonight?"

"No, sir. He and Mrs. Gantvoort were at home all evening."

"Positive?"

Whipple thought a moment.

"Yes, sir, I'm fairly certain. But I know Mrs. Gantvoort wasn't out. To tell the truth, I didn't see Mr. Charles from about eight o'clock until he came downstairs with this gentleman"—pointing to me—"at eleven.

But I'm fairly certain he was home all evening. I think Mrs. Gantvoort said he was."

Then O'Gar put another question—one that puzzled me at the time.

"What kind of collar buttons did Mr. Gantvoort wear?"

"You mean Mr. Leopold?"

"Yes."

"Plain gold ones, made all in one piece. They had a London jeweler's mark on them."

"Would you know them if you saw them?"

"Yes, sir."

We let Whipple go home then.

"Don't you think," I suggested when O'Gar and I were alone with this desk-load of evidence that didn't mean anything at all to me yet, "it's time you were loosening up and telling me what's what?"

"I guess so—listen! A man named Lagerquist, a grocer, was driving through Golden Gate Park tonight, and passed a machine standing on a dark road, with its lights out. He thought there was something funny about the way the man in it was sitting at the wheel, so he told the first patrolman he met about it.

"The patrolman investigated and found Gantvoort sitting at the wheel—dead—with his head smashed in and this dingus"—putting one hand on the bloody typewriter—"on the seat beside him. That was at a quarter of ten. The doc says Gantvoort was killed—his skull crushed—with this typewriter.

"The dead man's pockets, we found, had all been turned inside out; and all this stuff on the desk, except this new wallet, was scattered about in the car—some of it on the floor and some on the seats. This money was there too—nearly a hundred dollars of it. Among the papers was this."

He handed me a sheet of white paper upon which the following had been typewritten:

L. F. G.—

I want what is mine. 6,000 miles and 21 years are not enough to hide you from the victim of your treachery. I mean to have what you stole.

E. B.

"L. F. G. could be Leopold F. Gantvoort," I said. "And E. B. could be Emil Bonfils. Twenty-one years is the time from 1902 to 1923, and 6,000 miles is, roughly, the distance between Paris and San Francisco."

I laid the letter down and picked up the jewel case. It was a black imitation leather one, lined with white satin, and unmarked in any way.

Then I examined the cartridges. There were two of them, S. W. .45-caliber, and deep crosses had been cut in their soft noses—an old trick that makes the bullet spread out like a saucer when it hits.

"These in the car, too?"

"Yep—and this."

From a vest pocket O'Gar produced a short tuft of blond hair—hairs between an inch and two inches in length. They had been cut off, not pulled out by the roots.

"Any more?"

There seemed to be an endless stream of things.

He picked up the new wallet from the desk—the one that both Whipple and Charles Gantvoort had said did not belong to the dead man—and slid it over to me.

"That was found in the road, three or four feet from the car."

It was of a cheap quality, and had neither manufacturer's name nor owner's initials on it. In it were two ten-dollar bills, three small newspaper clippings, and a typewritten list of six names and addresses, headed by Gantvoort's.

The three clippings were apparently from the Personal columns of three different newspapers—the type wasn't the same—and they read:

GEORGE—Everything is fixed. Don't wait too long.
                                              D. D. D.
R. H. T.—They do not answer.   FLO
CAPPY—Twelve on the dot and look sharp. BINGO

The names and addresses on the typewritten list, under Gantvoort's, were:

Quincy Heathcote, 1223 S. Jason Street, Denver; B. D. Thornton, 96 Hughes Circle, Dallas; Luther G. Randall, 615 Columbia Street, Portsmouth; J. H. Boyd Willis, 5444 Harvard Street, Boston; Hannah Hindmarsh, 218 E. 79th Street, Cleveland.

"What else?" I asked when I had studied these.

The detective-sergeant's supply hadn't been exhausted yet.

"The dead man's collar buttons—both front and back —had been taken out, though his collar and tie were still in place. And his left shoe was gone. We hunted high and low all around, but didn't find either shoe or collar buttons."

"Is that all?"

I was prepared for anything now.

"What the hell do you want?" he growled. "Ain't that enough?"

"How about fingerprints?"

"Nothing stirring! All we found belonged to the dead man."

"How about the machine he was found in?"

"A coupe belonging to a Dr. Wallace Girargo. He phoned in at six this evening that it had been stolen from near the corner of McAllister and Polk streets. We're checking up on him—but I think he's all right."

The things that Whipple and Charles Gantvoort had identified as belonging to the dead man told us nothing. We went over them carefully, but to no advantage. The memorandum book contained many entries, but they all seemed totally foreign to the murder. The letters were quite as irrelevant.

The serial number of the typewriter with which the murder had been committed had been removed, we found—apparently filed out of the frame.

"Well, what do you think?" O'Gar asked when we had given up our examination of our clews and sat back burning tobacco.

"I think we want to find Monsieur Emil Bonfils."

"It wouldn't hurt to do that," he grunted. "I guess our best bet is to get in touch with these five people on the list with Gantvoort's name. Suppose that's a murder list? That this Bonfils is out to get all of them?"

"Maybe. We'll get hold of them anyway. Maybe we'll find that some of them have already been killed. But whether they have been killed or are to be killed or not, it's a cinch they have some connection with this affair. I'll get off a batch of telegrams to the Agency's branches, having the names on the list taken care of. I'll try to have the three clippings traced, too."

O'Gar looked at his watch and yawned.

"It's after four. What say we knock off and get some sleep? I'll leave word for the department's expert to compare the typewriter with that letter signed E. B. and with that list to see if they were written on it. I guess they were, but we'll make sure. I'll have the park searched all around where we found Gantvoort as soon as it gets light enough to see, and maybe the missing shoe and the collar buttons will be found. And I'll have a couple of the boys out calling on all the typewriter shops in the city to see if they can get a line on this one."

I stopped at the nearest telegraph office and got off a wad of messages. Then I went home to dream of nothing even remotely connected with crime or the detecting business.

At eleven o'clock that same morning, when, brisk and fresh with five hours' sleep under my belt, I arrived at the police detective bureau, I found O'Gar slumped down at his desk, staring dazedly at a black shoe, half a dozen collar buttons, a rusty flat key, and a rumpled newspaper—all lined up before him.

"What's all this? Souvenir of your wedding?"

"Might as well be." His voice was heavy with disgust. "Listen to this: one of the porters of the Seamen's National Bank found a package in the vestibule when he started cleaning up this morning. It was this shoe—Gantvoort's missing one—wrapped in this sheet of a five-day-old *Philadelphia Record,* and with these collar buttons and this old key in it. The heel of the shoe, you'll notice, has been pried off, and is still missing. Whipple identifies it all right, as well as two of the collar buttons, but he never saw the key before. These other four collar buttons are new, and common gold-rolled ones. The key don't look like it had had much use for a long time. What do you make of all that?"

I couldn't make anything out of it.

"How did the porter happen to turn the stuff in?"

"Oh, the whole story was in the morning papers—all about the missing shoe and collar buttons and all."

"What did you learn about the typewriter?" I asked.

"The letter and the list were written with it, right enough; but we haven't been able to find where it came from yet. We checked up the doc who owns the coupe, and he's in the clear. We accounted for all his time last night. Lagerquist, the grocer who found Gantvoort, seems to be all right, too. What did you do?"

"Haven't had any answers to the wires I sent last night. I dropped in at the Agency on my way down this morning, and got four operatives out covering the hotels and looking up all the people named Bonfils they can find—there are two or three families by that name listed in the directory. Also I sent our New York branch a wire to have the steamship records searched to see if an Emil Bonfils had arrived recently; and I put a cable through to our Paris correspondent to see what he could dig up over there."

"I guess we ought to see Gantvoort's lawyer—Abernathy—and that Dexter woman before we do anything else," the detective-sergeant said.

"I guess so," I agreed, "let's tackle the lawyer first. He's the most important one, the way things now stand."

Murray Abernathy, attorney-at-law, was a long, stringy, slow-spoken old gentleman who still clung to starched-bosom shirts. He was too full of what he thought were professional ethics to give us as much help as we had expected; but by letting him talk—letting him ramble along in his own way—we did get a little information from him. What we got amounted to this:

The dead man and Creda Dexter had intended being married the coming Wednesday. His son and her brother were both opposed to the marriage, it seemed, so Gantvoort and the woman had planned to be married secretly in Oakland, and catch a boat for the Orient that same afternoon; figuring that by the time their lengthy honeymoon was over they could return to a son and brother who had become resigned to the marriage.

A new will had been drawn up, leaving half of Gantvoort's estate to his new wife and half to his son and daughter-in-law. But the new will had not been signed yet, and Creda Dexter knew it had not been signed. She knew—and this was one of the few points upon which Abernathy would make a positive statement—that under the old will, still in force, everything went to Charles Gantvoort and his wife.

The Gantvoort estate, we estimated from Abernathy's roundabout statements and allusions, amounted to about a million and a half in cash value. The attorney had never heard of Emil Bonfils, he said, and had never heard of any threats or attempts at murder directed toward the dead man. He knew nothing—or would tell us nothing—that threw any light upon the nature of the thing that the threatening letter had accused the dead man of stealing.

From Abernathy's office we went to Creda Dexter's apartment, in a new and expensively elegant building only a few minutes' walk from the Gantvoort residence.

Creda Dexter was a small woman in her early twenties. The first thing you noticed about her were her eyes. They were large and deep and the color of amber, and their pupils were never at rest. Continuously they changed size, expanded and contracted—slowly at times, suddenly at others—ranging incessantly from the size of pinheads to an extent that threatened to blot out the amber irises.

With the eyes for a guide, you discovered that she was pronouncedly feline throughout. Her every movement was the slow, smooth, sure one of a cat; and the contours of her rather pretty face, the shape of her mouth, her small nose, the set of her eyes, the swelling of her brows, were all cat-like. And the effect was heightened by the way she wore her hair, which was thick and tawny.

"Mr. Gantvoort and I," she told us after the preliminary explanations had been disposed of, "were to have been married the day after tomorrow. His son and daughter-in-law were both opposed to the marriage, as was my brother Madden. They all seemed to think that the difference between our ages was too great. So to avoid any unpleasantness, we had planned to be married quietly and then go abroad for a year or more, feeling sure that they would all have forgotten their grievances by the time we returned.

"That was why Mr. Gantvoort persuaded Madden to go to New York. He had some business there—something to do with the disposal of his interest in a steel mill—so he used it as an excuse to get Madden out of the way until we were off on our wedding trip. Madden lived here with me, and it would have been nearly impossible for me to have made any preparations for the trip without him seeing them."

"Was Mr. Gantvoort here last night?" I asked her.

"No, I expected him—we were going out. He usually walked over—it's only a few blocks. When eight o'clock came and he hadn't arrived, I telephoned his house, and Whipple told me that he had left nearly an hour before. I called up again, twice, after that. Then, this morning, I called up again before I had seen the papers, and I was told that he—"

She broke off with a catch in her voice—the only sign of sorrow she displayed throughout the interview. The impression of her we had received from Charles Gantvoort and Whipple had prepared us for a more or less elaborate display of grief on her part. But she disappointed us. There was nothing crude about her work— she didn't even turn on the tears for us.

"Was Mr. Gantvoort here night before last?"

"Yes. He came over at a little after eight and stayed until nearly twelve. We didn't go out."

"Did he walk over and back?"

"Yes, so far as I know."

"Did he ever say anything to you about his life being threatened?"

"No."

She shook her head decisively.

"Do you know Emil Bonfils?"

"No."

"Ever hear Mr. Gantvoort speak of him?"

"No."

"At what hotel is your brother staying in New York?"

The restless black pupils spread out abruptly, as if they were about to overflow into the white areas of her eyes. That was the first clear indication of fear I had seen. But, outside of those tell-tale pupils, her composure was undisturbed.

"I don't know."

"When did he leave San Francisco?"

"Thursday—four days ago."

O'Gar and I walked six or seven blocks in thoughtful silence after we left Creda Dexter's apartment, and then he spoke.

"A sleek kitten—that dame! Rub her the right way, and she'll purr pretty. Rub her the wrong way—and look out for the claws!"

"What did that flash of her eyes when I asked about her brother tell you?" I asked.

"Something—but I don't know what! It wouldn't hurt to look him up and see if he's really in New York. If he is there today it's a cinch he wasn't here last night —even the mail planes take twenty-six or twenty-eight hours for the trip."

"We'll do that," I agreed. "It looks like this Creda Dexter wasn't any too sure that her brother wasn't in on the killing. And there's nothing to show that Bonfils didn't have help. I can't figure Creda being in on the murder, though. She knew the new will hadn't been signed. There'd be no sense in her working herself out of that three-quarters of a million berries."

We sent a lengthy telegram to the Continental's New York branch, and then dropped in at the Agency to see if any replies had come to the wires I had got off the night before.

They had.

None of the people whose names appeared on the typewritten list with Gantvoort's had been found; not the least trace had been found of any of them. Two of the addresses given were altogether wrong. There were no houses with those numbers on those streets—and there never had been.

. . .

What was left of the afternoon, O'Gar and I spent going over the street between Gantvoort's house on Russian Hill and the building in which the Dexters lived. We questioned everyone we could find—man, woman and child—who lived, worked, or played along any of the three routes the dead man could have taken.

We found nobody who had heard the shot that had been fired by Bonfils on the night before the murder. We found nobody who had seen anything suspicious on the night of the murder. Nobody who remembered having seen him picked up in a coupe.

Then we called at Gantvoort's house and questioned Charles Gantvoort again, his wife, and all the servants—and we learned nothing. So far as they knew, nothing belonging to the dead man was missing—nothing small enough to be concealed in the heel of a shoe.

The shoes he had worn the night he was killed were one of three pairs made in New York for him two months before. He could have removed the heel of the left one, hollowed it out sufficiently to hide a small object in it, and then nailed it on again; though Whipple insisted that he would have noticed the effects of any tampering with the shoe unless it had been done by an expert repairman.

This field exhausted, we returned to the Agency. A telegram had just come from the New York branch, saying that none of the steamship companies' records showed the arrival of an Emil Bonfils from either England, France, or Germany within the past six months.

The operatives who had been searching the city for Bonfils had all come in empty-handed. They had found and investigated eleven persons named Bonfils in San Francisco, Oakland, Berkeley, and Alameda. Their investigations had definitely cleared all eleven. None of these Bonfilses knew an Emil Bonfils. Combing the hotels had yielded nothing.

O'Gar and I went to dinner together—a quiet grouchy sort of meal during which we didn't speak six words apiece—and then came back to the Agency to find that another wire had come in from New York.

> *Madden Dexter arrived McAlpin Hotel this morning with Power of Attorney to sell Gantvoort interest in B. F. and F. Iron Corporation. Denies knowledge of Emil Bonfils or of murder. Expects to finish business and leave for San Francisco tomorrow.*

I let the sheet of paper upon which I had decoded the telegram slide out of my fingers, and we sat listlessly facing each other across my desk looking vacantly each at the other, listening to the clatter of charwomen's buckets in the corridor.

"It's a funny one," O'Gar said softly to himself at last. I nodded. It was.

"We got nine clews," he spoke again presently, "and none of them have got us a damned thing.

"Number one: the dead man called up you people and told you that he had been threatened and shot at by an Emil Bonfils that he'd had a run-in with in Paris a long time ago.

"Number two: the typewriter he was killed with and that the letter and list were written on. We're still trying to trace it, but with no breaks so far. What the hell kind of a weapon was that, anyway? It looks like this fellow Bonfils got hot and hit Gantvoort with the first thing he put his hand on. But what was the typewriter doing in a stolen car? And why were the numbers filed off it?"

I shook my head to signify that I couldn't guess the answer, and O'Gar went on enumerating our clews.

"Number three: the threatening letter, fitting in with what Gantvoort had said over the phone that afternoon.

"Number four: those two bullets with the crosses in their snoots.

"Number five: the jewel case.

"Number six: that bunch of yellow hair.

"Number seven: the fact that the dead man's shoe and collar buttons were carried away.

"Number eight: the wallet, with two ten-dollars bills, three clippings, and the list in it, found in the road.

"Number nine: finding the shoe next day, wrapped up in a five-day-old Philadelphia paper, and with the missing collar buttons, four more, and a rusty key in it.

"That's the list. If they mean anything at all, they mean that Emil Bonfils whoever he is—was flimflammed out of something by Gantvoort in Paris in 1902, and that Bonfils came to get it back. He picked Gantvoort up last night in a stolen car, bringing his typewriter with him—for God knows what reason! Gantvoort put up an argument, so Bonfils bashed in his noodle with the typewriter, and then went through his pockets, apparently not taking anything. He decided that what he was looking for was in Gantvoort's left shoe, so he took the shoe away with him. And then—but there's no sense to the collar button trick, or the phony list, or—"

"Yes there is!" I cut in, sitting up, wide awake now. "That's our tenth clew—the one we're going to follow from now on. That list was, except for Gantvoort's name and address, a fake. Our people would have found at least one of the five people whose names were on it if it

23

had been on the level. But they didn't find the least trace of any of them. And two of the addresses were of street numbers that didn't exist!

"That list was faked up, put in the wallet with the clippings and twenty dollars—to make the play stronger —and planted in the road near the car to throw us off-track. And if that's so, then it's a hundred to one that the rest of the things were cooked up too.

"From now on I'm considering all those nine lovely clews as nine bum steers. And I'm going just exactly contrary to them. I'm looking for a man whose name isn't Emil Bonfils, and whose initials aren't either E or B; who isn't French, and who wasn't in Paris in 1902. A man who hasn't light hair, doesn't carry a .45-caliber pistol, and has no interest in Personal advertisements in newspapers. A man who didn't kill Gantvoort to recover anything that could have been hidden in a shoe or on a collar button. That's the sort of a guy I'm hunting for now!"

The detective-sergeant screwed up his little green eyes reflectively and scratched his head.

"Maybe that ain't so foolish!" he said. "You might be right at that. Suppose you are—what then? That Dexter kitten didn't do it—it cost her three-quarters of a million. Her brother didn't do it—he's in New York. And, besides, you don't croak a guy just because you think he's too old to marry your sister. Charles Gantvoort? He and his wife are the only ones who make any money out of the old man dying before the new will was signed. We have only their word for it that Charles was home that night. The servants didn't see him between eight and eleven. You were there, and you didn't see him until eleven. But me and you both believe him when he says he *was* home all that evening. And neither of us think he bumped the old man off—though of course he might. Who then?"

"This Creda Dexter," I suggested, "was marrying Gantvoort for his money, wasn't she? You don't think she was in love with him, do you?"

"No. I figure, from what I saw of her, that she was in love with the million and a half."

"All right," I went on. "Now she isn't exactly homely —not by a long shot. Do you reckon Gantvoort was the only man who ever fell for her?"

"I got you! I got you!" O'Gar exclaimed. "You mean there might have been some young fellow in the running who didn't have any million and a half behind him, and who didn't take kindly to being nosed out by a man who did. Maybe—maybe."

"Well, suppose we bury all this stuff we've been working on and try out that angle."

"Suits me," he said. "Starting in the morning, then, we spend our time hunting for Gantvoort's rival for the paw of this Dexter kitten."

Right or wrong, that's what we did. We stowed all those lovely clews away in a drawer, locked the drawer, and forgot them. Then we set out to find Creda Dexter's masculine acquaintances and sift them for the murderer.

But it wasn't as simple as it sounded.

All our digging into her past failed to bring to light one man who could be considered a suitor. She and her brother had been in San Francisco three years. We traced them back the length of that period, from apartment to apartment. We questioned everyone we could find who even knew her by sight. And nobody could tell us of a single man who had shown an interest in her besides Gantvoort. Nobody, apparently, had ever seen her with any man except Gantvoort or her brother.

All of which, while not getting us ahead, at least convinced us that we were on the right trail. There must have been, we argued, at least one man in her life in those three years besides Gantvoort. She wasn't—unless we were very much mistaken—the sort of woman who would discourage masculine attention; and she was certainly endowed by nature to attract it. And if there was another man; then the very fact that he had been kept so thoroughly under cover strengthened the probability of him having been mixed up in Gantvoort's death.

We were unsuccessful in learning where the Dexters had lived before they came to San Francisco, but we weren't so very interested in their earlier life. Of course it was possible that some oldtime lover had come upon the scene again recently; but in that case it should have been easier to find the recent connection than the old one.

There was no doubt, our explorations showed, that Gantvoort's son had been correct in thinking the Dexters were fortune hunters. All their activities pointed to that, although there seemed to be nothing downright criminal in their pasts.

I went up against Creda Dexter again, spending an entire afternoon in her apartment, banging away with question after question, all directed toward her former love affairs. Who had she thrown over for Gantvoort and his million and a half? And the answer was always *nobody*—an answer that I didn't choose to believe.

We had Creda Dexter shadowed night and day—and it carried us ahead not an inch. Perhaps she suspected that she was being watched. Anyway, she seldom left her apartment, and then on only the most innocent of errands. We had her apartment watched whether she was in it or not. Nobody visited it. We tapped her telephone—and all our listening-in netted us nothing. We had her mail covered—and she didn't receive a single letter, not even an advertisement.

Meanwhile, we had learned where the three clippings found in the wallet had come from—from the Personal columns of a New York, a Chicago, and a Portland newspaper. The one in the Portland paper had appeared two days before the murder, the Chicago one four days before, and the New York one five days before. All three of those papers would have been on the San Francisco newsstands the day of the murder—ready to be purchased and cut out by anyone who was looking for material to confuse detectives with.

The Agency's Paris correspondent had found no less than six Emil Bonfilses—all bloomers so far as our job was concerned—and had a line on three more.

But O'Gar and I weren't worrying over Emil Bonfils any more—that angle was dead and buried. We were plugging away at our new task—the finding of Gantvoort's rival.

Thus the days passed, and thus the matter stood when Madden Dexter was due to arrive home from New York.

Our New York branch had kept an eye on him until he left that city, and had advised us of his departure, so I knew what train he was coming on. I wanted to put a few questions to him before his sister saw him. He could tell me what I wanted to know, and he might be willing to if I could get to him before his sister had an opportunity to shut him up.

If I had known him by sight I could have picked him up when he left his train at Oakland, but I didn't

know him; and I didn't want to carry Charles Gantvoort or anyone else along with me to pick him out for
me.

So I went up to Sacramento that morning, and
boarded his train there. I put my card in an envelope
and gave it to a messenger boy in the station. Then I
followed the boy through the train, while he called out:

"Mr. Dexter! Mr. Dexter!"

In the last car—the observation-club car—a slender,
dark-haired man in well-made tweeds turned from
watching the station platform through a window and
held out his hand to the boy.

I studied him while he nervously tore open the envelope and read my card. His chin trembled slightly
just now, emphasizing the weakness of a face that
couldn't have been strong at its best. Between twenty-
five and thirty, I placed him; with his hair parted in the
middle and slicked down; large, too-expressive brown
eyes; small well-shaped nose; neat brown mustache;
very red, soft lips—that type.

I dropped into the vacant chair beside him when he
looked up from the card.

"You are Mr. Dexter?"

"Yes," he said. "I suppose it's about Mr. Gantvoort's
death that you want to see me?"

"Uh-huh. I wanted to ask you a few questions, and
since I happened to be in Sacramento, I thought that
by riding back on the train with you I could ask them
without taking up too much of your time."

"If there's anything I can tell you," he assured me,
"I'll be only too glad to do it. But I told the New York
detectives all I knew, and they didn't seem to find it of
much value."

"Well, the situation has changed some since you left

New York." I watched his face closely as I spoke. "What we thought of no value then may be just what we want now."

I paused while he moistened his lips and avoided my eyes. He may not know anything, I thought, but he's certainly jumpy. I let him wait a few minutes while I pretended deep thoughtfulness. If I played him right, I was confident I could turn him inside out. He didn't seem to be made of very tough material.

We were sitting with our heads close together, so that the four or five other passengers in the car wouldn't overhear our talk; and that position was in my favor. One of the things that every detective knows is that it's often easy to get information—even a confession—out of a feeble nature simply by putting your face close to his and talking in a loud tone. I couldn't talk loud here, but the closeness of our faces was by itself an advantage.

"Of the men with whom your sister was acquainted," I came out with it at last, "who, outside of Mr. Gantvoort, was the most attentive?"

He swallowed audibly, looked out of the window, fleetingly at me, and then out of the window again.

"Really, I couldn't say."

"All right. Let's get at it this way. Suppose we check off one by one all the men who were interested in her and in whom she was interested."

He continued to stare out of the window.

"Who's first?" I pressed him.

His gaze flickered around to meet mine for a second, with a sort of timid desperation in his eyes.

"I know it sounds foolish, but I, her brother, couldn't give you the name of even one man in whom Creda was interested before she met Gantvoort. She never, so far as I know, had the slightest feeling for any man before she met him. Of course it is possible that there may have been someone that I didn't know anything about, but—"

It did sound foolish, right enough! The Creda Dexter I had talked to—a sleek kitten as O'Gar had put it—didn't impress me as being at all likely to go very long without having at least one man in tow. This pretty little guy in front of me was lying. There couldn't be any other explanation.

I went at him tooth and nail. But when we reached Oakland early that night he was still sticking to his original statement—that Gantvoort was the only one of his sister's suitors that he knew anything about. And I knew that I had blundered, had underrated Madden Dexter, had played my hand wrong in trying to shake him down too quickly—in driving too directly at the point I was interested in. He was either a lot stronger than I had figured him, or his interest in concealing Gantvoort's murderer was much greater than I had thought it would be.

But I had this much: if Dexter was lying—and there couldn't be much doubt of that—then Gantvoort *had* had a rival, and Madden Dexter believed or knew that this rival had killed Gantvoort.

When we left the train at Oakland I knew I was licked, that he wasn't going to tell me what I wanted to know—not this night, anyway. But I clung to him, stuck at his side when we boarded the ferry for San Francisco, in spite of the obviousness of his desire to get away from me. There's always a chance of something unexpected happening; so I continued to ply him with questions as our boat left the slip.

Presently a man came toward where we were sitting

—a big burly man in a light overcoat, carrying a black bag.

"Hello, Madden!" he greeted my companion, striding over to him with outstretched hand. "Just got in and was trying to remember your phone number," he said, setting down his bag, as they shook hands warmly.

Madden Dexter turned to me.

"I want you to meet Mr. Smith," he told me, and then gave my name to the big man, adding, "he's with the Continental Detective Agency here."

That tag—clearly a warning for Smith's benefit—brought me to my feet, all watchfulness. But the ferry was crowded—a hundred persons were within sight of us, all around us. I relaxed, smiled pleasantly, and shook hands with Smith. Whoever Smith was, and whatever connection he might have with the murder—and if he hadn't any, why should Dexter have been in such a hurry to tip him off to my identity?—he couldn't do anything here. The crowd around us was all to my advantage.

That was my second mistake of the day.

Smith's left hand had gone into his overcoat pocket —or rather, through one of those vertical slits that certain styles of overcoats have so that inside pockets may be reached without unbuttoning the overcoat. His hand had gone through that slit, and his coat had fallen away far enough for me to see a snub-nosed automatic in his hand—shielded from everyone's sight but mine— pointing at my waist-line.

"Shall we go on deck?" Smith asked—and it was an order.

I hesitated. I didn't like to leave all these people who were so blindly standing and sitting around us. But

Smith's face wasn't the face of a cautious man. He had the look of one who might easily disregard the presence of a hundred witnesses.

I turned around and walked through the crowd. His right hand lay familiarly on my shoulder as he walked behind me; his left hand held his gun, under the overcoat, against my spine.

The deck was deserted. A heavy fog, wet as rain—the fog of San Francisco Bay's winter nights—lay over boat and water, and had driven everyone else inside. It hung about us, thick and impenetrable; I couldn't see so far as the end of the boat, in spite of the lights glowing overhead.

I stopped.

Smith prodded me in the back.

"Farther away, where we can talk," he rumbled in my ear.

I went on until I reached the rail.

The entire back of my head burned with sudden fire . . . tiny points of light glittered in the blackness before me . . . grew larger . . . came rushing toward me. . . .

Semi-consciousness! I found myself mechanically keeping afloat somehow and trying to get out of my overcoat. The back of my head throbbed devilishly. My eyes burned. I felt heavy and logged, as if I had swallowed gallons of water.

The fog hung low and thick on the water—there was nothing else to be seen anywhere. By the time I had freed myself of the encumbering overcoat my head had cleared somewhat, but with returning consciousness came increased pain.

A light glimmered mistily off to my left, and then

vanished. From out of the misty blanket, from every direction, in a dozen different keys, from near and far, fog-horns sounded. I stopped swimming and floated on my back, trying to determine my whereabouts.

After a while I picked out the moaning, evenly spaced blasts of the Alcatraz siren. But they told me nothing. They came to me out of the fog without direction— seemed to beat down upon me from straight above.

I was somewhere in San Francisco Bay, and that was all I knew, though I suspected the current was sweeping me out toward the Golden Gate.

A little while passed, and I knew that I had left the path of the Oakland ferries—no boat had passed close to me for some time. I was glad to be out of that track. In this fog a boat was a lot more likely to run me down than to pick me up.

The water was chilling me, so I turned over and began swimming, just vigorously enough to keep my blood circulating while I saved my strength until I had a definite goal to try for.

A horn began to repeat its roaring note nearer and nearer, and presently the lights of the boat upon which it was fixed came into sight. One of the Sausalito ferries, I thought.

It came quite close to me, and I halloed until I was breathless and my throat was raw. But the boat's siren, crying its warning, drowned my shouts.

The boat went on and the fog closed in behind it.

The current was stronger now, and my attempts to attract the attention of the Sausalito ferry had left me weaker. I floated, letting the water sweep me where it would, resting.

Another light appeared ahead of me suddenly—hung there for an instant—disappeared.

I began to yell, and worked my arms and legs madly, trying to drive myself through the water to where it had been.

I never saw it again.

Weariness settled upon me, and a sense of futility. The water was no longer cold. I was warm with a comfortable, soothing numbness. My head stopped throbbing; there was no feeling at all in it now. No lights, now, but the sound of fog-horns . . . fog-horns . . . fog-horns ahead of me, behind me, to either side; annoying me, irritating me.

But for the moaning horns I would have ceased all effort. They had become the only disagreeable detail of my situation—the water was pleasant, fatigue was pleasant. But the horns tormented me. I cursed them petulantly and decided to swim until I could no longer hear them, and then, in the quiet of the friendly fog, go to sleep. . . .

Now and then I would doze, to be goaded into wakefulness by the wailing voice of a siren.

"Those damned horns! Those damned horns!" I complained aloud, again and again.

One of them, I found presently, was bearing down upon me from behind, growing louder and stronger. I turned and waited. Lights, dim and steaming, came into view.

With exaggerated caution to avoid making the least splash, I swam off to one side. When this nuisance was past I could go to sleep. I sniggered softly to myself as the lights drew abreast, feeling a foolish triumph in my cleverness in eluding the boat. Those damned horns. . . .

Life—the hunger for life—all at once surged back into my being.

I screamed at the passing boat, and with every iota of my being struggled toward it. Between strokes I tilted up my head and screamed. . . .

When I returned to consciousness for the second time that evening, I was lying on my back on a baggage truck, which was moving. Men and women were crowding around, walking beside the truck, staring at me with curious eyes. I sat up.

"Where are we?" I asked.

A little red-faced man in uniform answered my question.

"Just landing in Sausalito. Lay still. We'll take you over to the hospital."

I looked around.

"How long before this boat goes back to San Francisco?"

"Leaves right away."

I slid off the truck and started back aboard the boat.

"I'm going with it," I said.

Half an hour later, shivering and shaking in my wet clothes, keeping my mouth clamped tight so that my teeth wouldn't sound like a dice-game, I climbed into a taxi at the Ferry Building and went to my flat.

There, I swallowed half a pint of whisky, rubbed myself with a coarse towel until my skin was sore, and, except for an enormous weariness and a worse headache, I felt almost human again.

I reached O'Gar by phone, asked him to come up to my flat right away, and then called up Charles Gantvoort.

"Have you seen Madden Dexter yet?" I asked him.

"No, but I talked to him over the phone. He called me up as soon as he got in. I asked him to meet me in Mr. Abernathy's office in the morning, so we could go over that business he transacted for Father."

"Can you call him up now and tell him that you have been called out of town—will have to leave early in the morning—and that you'd like to run over to his apartment and see him tonight?"

"Why yes, if you wish."

"Good! Do that. I'll call for you in a little while and go over to see him with you."

"What is—"

"I'll tell you about it when I see you," I cut him off.

O'Gar arrived as I was finishing dressing.

"So he told you something?" he asked, knowing of my plan to meet Dexter on the train and question him.

"Yes," I said with sour sarcasm, "but I came near forgetting what it was. I grilled him all the way from Sacramento to Oakland, and couldn't get a whisper out of him. On the ferry coming over he introduces me to a man he calls Mr. Smith, and he tells Mr. Smith that I'm a gum-shoe. This, mind you, all happens in the middle of a crowded ferry! Mr. Smith puts a gun in my belly, marches me out on deck, raps me across the back of the head, and dumps me into the bay."

"You have a lot of fun, don't you?" O'Gar grinned, and then wrinkled his forehead. "Looks like Smith would be the man we want then—the buddy who turned the Gantvoort trick. But what the hell did he want to give himself away by chucking you overboard for?"

"Too hard for me," I confessed, while trying to find which of my hats and caps would sit least heavily upon my bruised head. "Dexter knew I was hunting for one of his sister's former lovers, of course. And he must have thought I knew a whole lot more than I do, or

36

he wouldn't have made that raw play—tipping my mitt to Smith right in front of me.

"It may be that after Dexter lost his head and made that break on the ferry, Smith figured that I'd be on to him soon, if not right away; and so he'd take a desperate chance on putting me out of the way. But we'll know all about it in a little while," I said, as we went down to the waiting taxi and set out for Gantvoort's.

"You ain't counting on Smith being in sight, are you?" the detective-sergeant asked.

"No. He'll be holed up somewhere until he sees how things are going. But Madden Dexter will have to be out in the open to protect himself. He has an alibi, so he's in the clear so far as the actual killing is concerned. And with me supposed to be dead, the more he stays in the open, the safer he is. But it's a cinch that he knows what this is all about, though he wasn't necessarily involved in it. As near as I could see, he didn't go out on deck with Smith and me tonight. Anyway he'll be home. And this time he's going to talk—he's going to tell his little story!"

Charles Gantvoort was standing on his front steps when we reached his house. He climbed into our taxi and we headed for the Dexters' apartment. We didn't have time to answer any of the questions that Gantvoort was firing at us with every turning of the wheels.

"He's home and expecting you?" I asked him.

"Yes."

Then we left the taxi and went into the apartment building.

"Mr. Gantvoort to see Mr. Dexter," he told the Philippine boy at the switchboard.

The boy spoke into the phone.

"Go right up," he told us.

At the Dexters' door I stepped past Gantvoort and pressed the button.

Creda Dexter opened the door. Her amber eyes widened and her smile faded as I stepped past her into the apartment.

I walked swiftly down the little hallway and turned into the first room through whose open door a light showed.

And came face to face with Smith!

We were both surprised, but his astonishment was a lot more profound than mine. Neither of us had expected to see the other; but I had known he was still alive, while he had every reason for thinking me at the bottom of the bay.

I took advantage of his greater bewilderment to the extent of two steps toward him before he went into action.

One of his hands swept down.

I threw my right fist at his face—threw it with every ounce of my 180 pounds behind it, re-enforced by the memory of every second I had spent in the water, and every throb of my battered head.

His hand, already darting down for his pistol, came back up too late to fend off my punch.

Something clicked in my hand as it smashed into his face, and my hand went numb.

But he went down—and lay where he fell.

I jumped across his body to a door on the opposite side of the room, pulling my gun loose with my left hand.

"Dexter's somewhere around!" I called over my shoulder to O'Gar, who with Gantvoort and Creda, was coming through the door by which I had entered. "Keep your eyes open!"

I dashed through the four other rooms of the apartment, pulling closet doors open, looking everywhere— and I found nobody.

Then I returned to where Creda Dexter was trying to revive Smith, with the assistance of O'Gar and Gantvoort.

The detective-sergeant looked over his shoulder at me.

"Who do you think this joker is?" he asked.

"My friend Mr. Smith."

"Gantvoort says he's Madden Dexter."

I looked at Charles Gantvoort, who nodded his head.

"This is Madden Dexter," he said.

We worked upon Dexter for nearly ten minutes before he opened his eyes.

As soon as he sat up we began to shoot questions and accusations at him, hoping to get a confession out of him before he recovered from his shakiness—but he wasn't that shaky.

All we could get out of him was:

"Take me in if you want to. If I've got anything to say I'll say it to my lawyer, and to nobody else."

Creda Dexter, who had stepped back after her brother came to, and was standing a little way off, watching us, suddenly came forward and caught me by the arm.

"What have you got on him?" she demanded, imperatively.

"I wouldn't want to say," I countered, "but I don't mind telling you this much. We're going to give him a chance in a nice modern court-room to prove that he didn't kill Leopold Gantvoort."

"He was in New York!"

"He was not! He had a friend who went to New York as Madden Dexter and looked after Gantvoort's business under that name. But if this is the real Madden Dexter then the closest he got to New York was when he met his friend on the ferry to get from him the papers connected with the B. F. & F. Iron Corporation transaction; and learned that I had stumbled upon the truth about his alibi—even if I didn't know it myself at the time."

She jerked around to face her brother.

"Is that on the level?" she asked him.

He sneered at her, and went on feeling with the fingers of one hand the spot on his jaw where my fist had landed.

"I'll say all I've got to say to my lawyer," he repeated.

"You will?" she shot back at him. "Well, I'll say what I've got to say right now!"

She flung around to face me again.

"Madden is not my brother at all! My name is Ives. Madden and I met in St. Louis about four years ago, drifted around together for a year or so, and then came to Frisco. He was a con man—still is. He made Mr. Gantvoort's acquaintance six or seven months ago, and was getting him all ribbed up to unload a fake invention on him. He brought him here a couple of times, and introduced me to him as his sister. We usually posed as brother and sister.

"Then, after Mr. Gantvoort had been here a couple times, Madden decided to change his game. He thought Mr. Gantvoort liked me, and that we could get more money out of him by working a fancy sort of badger-game on him. I was to lead the old man on until I had

40

him wrapped around my finger—until we had him tied up so tight he couldn't get away—had something on him—something good and strong. Then we were going to shake him down for plenty of money.

"Everything went along fine for a while. He fell for me—fell hard. And finally he asked me to marry him. We had never figured on that. Blackmail was our game. But when he asked me to marry him I tried to call Madden off. I admit the old man's money had something to do with it—it influenced me—but I had come to like him a little for himself. He was mighty fine in lots of ways—nicer than anybody I had ever known.

"So I told Madden all about it, and suggested that we drop the other plan, and that I marry Gantvoort. I promised to see that Madden was kept supplied with money—I knew I could get whatever I wanted from Mr. Gantvoort. And I was on the level with Madden. I liked Mr. Gantvoort, but Madden had found him and brought him around to me; and so I wasn't going to run out on Madden. I was willing to do all I could for him.

"But Madden wouldn't hear of it. He'd have got more money in the long run by doing as I suggested—but he wanted his little handful right away. And to make him more unreasonable he got one of his jealous streaks. He beat me one night!

"That settled it. I made up my mind to ditch him. I told Mr. Gantvoort that my brother was bitterly opposed to our marrying, and he could see that Madden was carrying a grouch. So he arranged to send Madden East on that steel business, to get him out of the way until we were off on our wedding trip. And we thought Madden was completely deceived—but I should have known that he would see through our scheme. We planned to be gone about a year, and by that time I thought Madden would have forgotten me—or I'd be fixed to handle him if he tried to make any trouble.

"As soon as I heard that Mr. Gantvoort had been killed I had a hunch that Madden had done it. But then it seemed like a certainty that he was in New York the next day, and I thought I had done him an injustice. And I was glad he was out of it. But now—"

She whirled around to her erstwhile confederate.

"Now I hope you swing, you big sap!"

She spun around to me aagin. No sleek kitten, this, but a furious, spitting cat, with claws and teeth bared.

"What kind of looking fellow was the one who went to New York for him?"

I described the man I had talked to on the train.

"Evan Felter," she said, after a moment of thought. "He used to work with Madden. You'll probably find him hiding in Los Angeles. Put the screws on him and he'll spill all he knows—he's a weak sister! The chances are he didn't know what Madden's game was until it was all over."

"How do you like that?" she spat at Madden Dexter. "How do you like that for a starter? You messed up my little party, did you? Well, I'm going to spend every minute of my time from now until they pop you off helping them pop you!"

And she did, too—with her assistance it was no trick at all to gather up the rest of the evidence we needed to hang him. And I don't believe her enjoyment of her three-quarters of a million dollars is spoiled a bit by any qualms over what she did to Madden. She's a very respectable woman *now,* and glad to be free of the con man.

THE
GOLDEN
HORSESHOE

"I haven't anything very exciting to offer you this time," Vance Richmond said as we shook hands. "I want you to find a man for me—a man who is not a criminal."

There was an apology in his voice. The last couple of jobs this lean, gray-faced attorney had thrown my way had run to gun-play and other forms of rioting, and I suppose he thought anything less than that would put me to sleep. Was a time when he might have been right—when I was a young sprout of twenty or so, newly attached to the Continental Detective Agency. But the fifteen years that had slid by since then had dulled my appetite for rough stuff.

"The man I want found," the lawyer went on, as we sat down, "is an English architect named Norman Ashcraft. He is a man of about thirty-seven, five feet ten inches tall, well built, and fair-skinned, with light hair and blue eyes. Four years ago he was a typical specimen of the clean-cut blond Britisher. He may not be like that now—those four years have been rather hard ones for him, I imagine.

"Here is the story. Four years ago the Ashcrafts were living together in England, in Bristol. It seems that Mrs. Ashcraft is of a very jealous disposition, and he was rather high-strung. Furthermore, he had only what money he earned at his profession, while she had inherited quite a bit from her parents. Ashcraft was rather foolishly sensitive about being the husband of a wealthy woman—was inclined to go out of his way to show that he was not dependent upon her money, that he wouldn't be influenced by it. Foolish, of course, but just the sort of attitude a man of his temperament would assume. One night she accused him of paying too much attention to another woman. They quarreled, and he packed up and left.

"She was repentant within a week—especially repentant since she had learned that her suspicion had had no foundation outside of her own jealousy—and she tried to find him. But he was gone. She succeeded in tracing him from Bristol to New York, and then to Detroit, where he had been arrested and fined for disturbing the peace in a drunken row of some sort. After that he dropped out of sight until he bobbed up in Seattle ten months later." The attorney hunted through the papers on his desk and found a memorandum.

"On May 23, 1923, he shot and killed a burglar in his room in a hotel there. The Seattle police seem to have suspected that there was something funny about the shooting, but had nothing to hold Ashcraft on. The man he killed was undoubtedly a burglar. Then Ashcraft disappeared again, and nothing was heard of him until just about a year ago. Mrs. Ashcraft had advertisements inserted in the Personal columns of papers in the principal American cities.

"One day she received a letter from him, from San Francisco. It was a very formal letter, and simply requested her to stop advertising. Although he was through with the name Norman Ashcraft, he wrote, he disliked seeing it published in every newspaper he read.

"She mailed a letter to him at the General Delivery window here, and used another advertisement to tell him about it. He answered it, rather caustically. She wrote him again, asking him to come home. He refused, though he seemed less bitter toward her. They exchanged several letters, and she learned that he had become a drug addict, and what was left of his pride would not let him return to her until he looked—and was at least somewhat like—his former self. She persuaded him to accept enough money from her to straighten himself out. She sent him this money each month, in care of General Delivery, here.

"Meanwhile she closed up her affairs in England— she had no close relatives to hold her there—and came to San Francisco, to be on hand when her husband was ready to return to her. A year has gone. She still sends him money each month. She still waits for him to come back to her. He has repeatedly refused to see her, and his letters are evasive—filled with accounts of the struggle he is having, making headway against the drug one month, slipping back the next.

"She suspects by now, of course, that he has no intention of ever coming back to her; that he does not intend giving up the drug; that he is simply using her as a source of income. I have urged her to discontinue the monthly allowance for a while. But she will not do that. You see, she blames herself for his present condition. She thinks her foolish flare of jealousy is responsible for his plight, and she is afraid to do anything that might either hurt him or induce him to hurt himself further. Her mind is unchangeably made up in that respect. She wants him back, wants him straightened out; but if he will not come, then she is content to continue the payments for the rest of his life. But she wants to know what she is to expect. She wants to end this devilish uncertainty in which she has been living.

"What we want, then, is for you to find Ashcraft. We want to know whether there is any likelihood of his ever becoming a man again, or whether he is gone beyond redemption. There is your job. Find him, learn whatever you can about him, and then, after we know something, we'll decide whether it's wiser to force an interview between them—in hopes that she will be able to influence him—or not."

"I'll try it," I said. "When does Mrs. Ashcraft send him his monthly allowance?"

"On the first of each month."

"Today is the twenty-eighth. That'll give me three days to wind up a job I have on hand. Got a photo of him?"

"Unfortunately, no. In her anger immediately after their row, Mrs. Ashcraft destroyed everything she had that would remind her of him."

I got up and reached for my hat.

"See you around the second of the month," I said, as I left the office.

On the afternoon of the first, I went down to the post office and got hold of Lusk, the inspector in charge of the division at the time.

"I've got a line on a scratcher from up north," I told Lusk, "who is supposed to be getting his mail at the window. Will you fix it up so I can get a spot on him?"

Post office inspectors are all tied up with rules and regulations that forbid their giving assistance to private detectives except on certain criminal matters. But a friendly inspector doesn't have to put you through the third degree. You lie to him—so that he will have an alibi in case there's a kick-back—and whether he thinks you're lying or not doesn't matter.

So presently I was downstairs again, loitering within sight of the A to D window, with the clerk at the window instructed to give me the office when Ashcraft's mail was called for. There was no mail for him there at the time. Mrs. Ashcraft's letter would hardly get to the clerks that afternoon, but I was taking no chances. I stayed on the job until the windows closed.

At a few minutes after ten the next morning I got my action. One of the clerks gave me the signal. A small man in a blue suit and a soft gray hat was walking away from the window with an envelope in his hand. A man of perhaps forty years, though he looked older. His face was pasty, his feet dragged, and his clothes needed brushing and pressing.

He came straight to the desk in front of which I stood fiddling with some papers. He took a large envelope from his pocket, and I got just enough of a glimpse of its front to see that it was already stamped and addressed. He kept the addressed side against his body, put the letter he had got from the window in it, and licked the flap backward, so that there was no possible way for anybody to see the front of the envelope. Then he rubbed the flap down carefully and turned toward the mailing slots. I went after him. There was nothing to do but to pull the always reliable stumble.

I overtook him, stepped close and faked a fall on the marble floor, bumping into him, grabbing him as if to regain my balance. It went rotten. In the middle of my stunt my foot really did slip, and we went down on the floor like a pair of wrestlers.

I scrambled up, yanked him to his feet, mumbled an apology and almost had to push him out of the way to beat him to the envelope that lay face down on the floor. I had to turn it over as I handed it to him in order to get the address:

Mr. Edward Bohannon,
Golden Horseshoe Café,
Tijuana, Baja California,
Mexico

I had the address, but I had tipped my mitt. There was no way in God's world for this little man in blue to miss knowing that I had been trying to get that address.

I dusted myself off while he put his envelope through a slot. He didn't come back past me, but went on down toward the Mission Street exit. I couldn't let him get away with what he knew. I didn't want Ashcraft tipped off before I got to him. I would have to try another trick as ancient as the one the slippery floor had bungled for me. I set out after the little man again.

Just as I reached his side he turned his head to see if he was being followed.

"Hello, Micky!" I hailed him. "How's everything in Chi?"

"You got me wrong." He spoke out of the side of his gray-lipped mouth, not stopping. "I don't know nothin' about Chi."

His eyes were pale blue, with needlepoint pupils—the eyes of a heroin or morphine user.

"Quit stalling," I said. "You fell off the rattler only this morning."

He stopped on the sidewalk and faced me.

"Me? Who do you think I am?"

"You're Micky Parker. The Dutchman gave us the rap that you were headed here."

"You're cuckoo," he sneered. "I don't know what the hell you're talkin' about!"

That was nothing—neither did I. I raised my right hand in my overcoat pocket.

"Now I'll tell one," I growled.

He flinched away from my bulging pocket.

"Hey, listen, brother!" he begged. "You got me wrong—on the level. My name ain't Micky Parker, an' I been here in Frisco for a solid year."

"You got to show me."

"I can do it," he exclaimed, all eagerness. "You come down the drag with me, an' I'll show you. My name's Ryan, an' I been livin' aroun' the corner here on Sixth Street."

"Ryan?" I asked.

"Yes—John Ryan."

I chalked that up against him. I don't suppose there are three old-time yeggs in the country who haven't used the name at least once; it's the John Smith of yeggdom.

This particular John Ryan led me around to a house on Sixth Street, where the landlady—a rough-hewn woman of fifty, with bare arms that were haired and

51

muscled like the village smithy's—assured me that her tenant had to her positive knowledge been in San Francisco for months, and that she remembered seeing him at least once a day for a couple of weeks back. If I had been really suspicious that this Ryan was my mythical Micky Parker from Chicago, I wouldn't have taken the woman's word for it, but as it was I pretended to be satisfied.

That seemed to be all right then. Mr. Ryan had been led astray, had been convinced that I had mistaken him for another crook, and that I was not interested in the Ashcraft letter. I would be safe—reasonably safe—in letting the situation go as it stood. But loose ends worry me. This bird was a hop-head, and he had given me a phony-sounding name, so . . .

"What do you do for a living?" I asked him.

"I ain't been doin' nothin' for a coupla months," he pattered, "but I expec' to open a lunch room with a fella nex' week."

"Let's go up to your room," I suggested. "I want to talk to you."

He wasn't enthusiastic, but he took me up. He had two rooms and a kitchen on the third floor. They were dirty, foul-smelling rooms.

"Where's Ashcraft?" I threw at him.

"I don't know what you're talkin' about," he mumbled.

"You'd better figure it out," I advised him, "or there's a nice cool cell down at the booby-hatch that will be wrapped around you."

"You ain't got nothin' on me."

"What of that? How'd you like to do a thirty or a sixty on a vag charge?"

"Vag, hell!" he snarled. "I got five hundred smacks in my kick."

I grinned at him.

"You know better than that, Ryan. A pocketful of money'll get you nothing in California. You've got no job. You can't show where your money comes from. You're made to order for the vag law."

I had this bird figured as a dope peddler. If he was —or was anything else off color that might come to light when he was vagged—the chances were that he would be willing to sell Ashcraft out to save himself; especially since, so far as I knew, Ashcraft wasn't on the wrong side of the criminal law.

"If I were you," I went on while he stared at the floor and thought, "I'd be a nice, obliging fellow and do my talking now. You're—"

He twisted sidewise in his chair and one of his hands went behind him.

I kicked him out of his chair.

The table slipped under me or I would have stretched him. As it was, that shot that I aimed at his jaw took him on the chest and carried him over backward, with the rocking-chair piled on top of him. I pulled the chair off and took his gun—a cheap nickleplated .32. Then I went back to my seat on the corner of the table.

He had only that one flash of fight in him. He got up sniveling.

"I'll tell you. I don't want no trouble. This Ashcraft told me he was jus' stringin' his wife along. He give me ten bucks a throw to get his letter ever' month an' send it to him in Tijuana. I knowed him here, an' when he went south six months ago—he's got a girl

down there—I promised I'd do it for him. I knowed
it was money—he said it was his 'alimony'—but I
didn't know there was somethin' wrong."

"What sort of a hombre is this Ashcraft? What's his
graft?"

"I don't know. He could be a con man—he's got a
good front. He's a Englishman, an' mostly goes by
the name of Ed Bohannon. He hits the hop. I don't use
it myself"—that was a good one—"but you know how
it is in a burg like this, a man runs into all kinds of
people. I don't know nothin' about what he's up to."

That was all I could get out of him. He couldn't—
or wouldn't—tell me where Ashcraft had lived in San
Francisco or who he had mobbed up with.

Ryan squawked his head off when he found that I
was going to vag him.

"You said you'd spring me if I talked," he wailed.

"I did not. But if I had—when a gent flashes a rod
on me I figure it cancels any agreement we might have
had. Come on."

I couldn't afford to let him run around loose until
I got in touch with Ashcraft.

He would have been sending a telegram before I was
three blocks away, and my quarry would be on his
merry way to points north, east, south and west.

It was a good hunch I played in nabbing Ryan.
When he was fingerprinted at the Hall of Justice he
turned out to be one Fred Rooney, alias "Jamocha,"
a pedlar and smuggler who had crushed out of the Federal Prison at Leavenworth, leaving eight years of a
tenner still unserved.

"Will you sew him up for a couple of days?" I asked
the captain of the city jail. "I've got work to do that

will go smoother if he can't get any word out for a while."

"Sure," the captain promised. "The federal people won't take him off our hands for two or three days. I'll keep him airtight till then."

From the jail I went up to Vance Richmond's office and turned my news over to him.

"Ashcraft is getting his mail in Tijuana. He's living down there under the name of Ed Bohannon, and maybe has a woman there. I've just thrown one of his friends—the one who handled the mail and an escaped con—in the cooler."

The attorney reached for the telephone.

He called a number. "Is Mrs. Ashcraft there? . . . This is Mr. Richmond. . . . No, we haven't exactly found him, but I think we know where he is. . . . Yes. . . . In about fifteen minutes."

He put down the telephone and stood up.

"We'll run up to Mrs. Ashcraft's house and see her."

Fifteen minutes later we were getting out of Richmond's car in Jackson Street near Gough. The house was a three-story white stone building, set behind a carefully sodded little lawn with an iron railing around it.

Mrs. Ashcraft received us in a drawing-room on the second floor. A tall woman of less than thirty, slimly beautiful in a gray dress. Clear was the word that best fit her; it described the blue of her eyes, the pink-white of her skin, and the light brown of her hair.

Richmond introduced me to her, and then I told her what I had learned, omitting the part about the woman in Tijuana. Nor did I tell her that the chances were her husband was a crook nowadays.

"Mr. Ashcraft is in Tijuana, I have been told. He

left San Francisco six months ago. His mail is being forwarded to him in care of a café there, under the name of Edward Bohannon."

Her eyes lighted up happily, but she didn't throw a fit. She wasn't that sort. She addressed the attorney:

"Shall I go down? Or will you?"

Richmond shook his head.

"Neither. You certainly shouldn't go, and I cannot—not at present." He turned to me. "You'll have to go. You can no doubt handle it better than I could. You will know what to do and how to do it. Mrs. Ashcraft doesn't wish to force herself on him, but neither does she wish to leave anything undone that might help him."

Mrs. Ashcraft held a strong, slender hand out to me.

"You will do whatever you think wisest."

It was partly a question, partly an expression of confidence.

"I will," I promised.

I liked this Mrs. Ashcraft.

Tijuana hadn't changed much in the two years I had been away. Still the same six or seven hundred feet of dusty and dingy street running between two almost solid rows of saloons, with dirtier side streets taking care of the dives that couldn't find room on the main street.

The automobile that had brought me down from San Diego dumped me into the center of the town early in the afternoon, and the day's business was just getting under way. That is, there were only two or three drunks wandering around among the dogs and loafing Mexicans in the street, although there was already a bustle of potential drunks moving from one saloon to the next.

In the middle of the next block I saw a big gilded horseshoe. I went down the street and into the saloon behind the sign. It was a fair sample of the local joint. A bar on your left as you came in, running half the length of the building, with three or four slot machines on one end. Across from the bar, against the right-hand wall, a dance floor that ran from the front wall to a raised platform, where a greasy orchestra was now preparing to go to work. Behind the orchestra was a row of low stalls or booths, with open fronts and a table and two benches apiece.

It was early in the day, and there were only a few buyers present. I caught a bartender's eye. He was a beefy, red-faced Irishman, with sorrel hair plastered down in two curls that hid what little forehead he had.

"I want to see Ed Bohannon," I told him confidentially.

He turned blank eyes on me.

"I don't know no Ed Bohannon."

Taking out a piece of paper and a pencil I scribbled, *Jamocha is copped,* and slid the paper over to him.

"If a man who says he's Ed Bohannon asks for that, will you give it to him?"

"I guess so."

"Good," I said. "I'll hang around a while."

I walked down the room and sat at a table in one of the stalls. A lanky girl who had done something to her hair that made it purple was camped beside me before I had settled in my seat.

"Buy me a little drink?" she asked.

The face she made at me was probably meant for a smile. Whatever it was, it beat me. I was afraid she'd do it again, so I surrendered.

"Yes," I said, and ordered a bottle of beer for myself from the waiter who was already hanging over my shoulder.

The purple-haired woman at my side downed her shot of whiskey, and was opening her mouth to suggest that we have another drink—hustlers down there don't waste any time at all—when a voice spoke from behind me.

"Cora, Frank wants you."

Cora scowled, looking over my shoulder.

Then she made that damned face at me again, said "All right, Kewpie. Will you take care of my friend here?" and left me.

Kewpie slid into the seat beside me. She was a little chunky girl of perhaps eighteen—not a day more than that. Just a kid. Her short hair was brown and curly over a round, boyish face with laughing, impudent eyes.

I bought her a drink and got another bottle of beer.

"What's on your mind?" I asked.

"Hooch." She grinned at me—a grin that was as boyish as the straight look of her brown eyes. "Gallons of it."

"And besides that?"

I knew this switching of girls on me hadn't been purposeless.

"I hear you're looking for a friend of mine," Kewpie said.

"That might be. What friends have you got?"

"Well, there's Ed Bohannon for one. You know Ed?"

"No—not yet."

"But you're looking for him?"

"Uh-huh."

"What's the racket? Maybe I could get word to Ed."

"Let it go," I bluffed. "This Ed of yours seem to be as

exclusive as all hell. Well, it's no skin off *my* face. I'll buy you another drink and trot along."

She jumped up.

"Wait a minute. I'll see if I can get him. What's your name?"

"Parker will do as well as any other," I said, the name I had used on Ryan popping first into my mind.

"You wait," she called back as she moved toward the back door. "I think I can find him."

"I think so too," I agreed.

Ten minutes went by, and a man came to my table from the front of the establishment. He was a blond Englishman of less than forty, with all the marks of the gentleman gone to pot on him. Not altogether on the rocks yet, but you could see evidence of the down-hill slide plainly in the dullness of his blue eyes, in the pouches under his eyes, in the blurred lines around his mouth and the mouth's looseness, and in the grayish tint of his skin. He was still fairly attractive in appearance— enough of his former wholesomeness remained for that.

He sat down facing me.

"You're looking for me?"

"You're Ed Bohannon?"

He nodded.

"Jamocha was picked up a couple of days ago," I told him, "and ought to be riding back to the Kansas big house by now. He got word out for me to give you the rap. He knew I was heading this way."

He frowned at the table. Then he looked sharply at me again.

"Did he tell you anything else?"

"*He* didn't tell me anything. He got word out to me by somebody's mouthpiece. I didn't see him."

"You're staying down here a while?"

"Yes, for two or three days," I said. "I've got something on the fire."

He smiled, and held out his hand.

"Thanks for the tip, Parker," he said. "If you'll take a walk with me I'll give you something real to drink."

I didn't have anything against that. He led me out of the Golden Horseshoe and down a side street to an adobe house set out where the town fringed off into the desert. In the front room he waved me to a chair and went into the next room.

"What do you fancy?" he called through the door. "Rye, gin, Scotch—"

"The last one wins," I interrupted his catalog.

He brought in a bottle of Black and White, a siphon and some glasses, and we settled down to drinking. We drank and talked, drank and talked, and each of us pretended to be drunker than he really was—though before long we were both as full as a pair of goats.

It was a drinking contest pure and simple. He was trying to drink me into a pulp—a pulp that would easily give up all of its secrets—and I was trying the same game on him. Neither of us made much progress.

"You know," he was saying somewhere along toward dark, "I've been a damn' ass. Got a wife—the nicesh woman in the worl'. Wantsh me t' come back to her, an' all tha' short of thing. Yet I hang around here, lappin' up this shtuff—hittin' the pipe—when I could be shomebody. Arc—architec', y'un'ershtand—good one, too. But I got in rut—got misxh up with theshe people. C-can't sheem to break 'way. Goin' to, though—no spoofin'. Goin' back to li'l wife, nicesh woman in the worl'. Breakin' 'way from p-pipe an' ever'-thing. Look at me. D' I look like a hop-head? Course not! Curin' m'self,

60

tha's why. I'll show you—take a smoke now—show you I can take it or leave it alone."

Pulling himself dizzily up out of his chair, he wandered into the next room, and came staggering back into the room again carrying an elaborate opium layout—all silver and ebony—on a silver tray. He put it on the table and flourished a pipe at me.

"Have a li'l rear on me, Parker."

I told him I'd stick to the Scotch.

"Give y' shot of C. 'f y'd rather have it," he invited me.

I declined the cocaine, so he sprawled himself comfortably on the floor beside the table, rolled and cooked a pill, and our party went on—with him smoking his hop and me punishing the liquor—each of us still talking for the other's benefit, and trying to get the other to talk for our own.

I was holding down a lovely package by the time Kewpie came in, at midnight.

"Looks like you folks are enjoying yourselves," she laughed, leaning down to kiss the Englishman's rumpled hair.

She perched herself on the table and reached for the Scotch.

"Everything's lovely," I assured her, though probably I didn't say it that clear.

"You ought to stay oiled all the time, Shorty; it improves you."

I don't know whether I made any answer to that or not. Shortly afterward, I know, I spread myself beside the Englishman on the floor and went to sleep.

The next two days were pretty much like the first one. Ashcraft and I were together twenty-four hours each of the days, and usually the girl was with us, and the only time we weren't drinking was when we were sleeping off what we had been drinking. We spent most of those three days in either the adobe house or the Golden Horseshoe, but we found time to take in most of the other joints in town now and then. I had only a hazy idea of some of the things that went on around me, though I don't think I missed anything entirely.

Ashcraft and I were as thick as thieves, on the surface, but neither of us ever lost his distrust of the other, no matter how drunk we got—and we got plenty drunk. He went up against his mud-pipe regularly. I don't think the girl used the stuff, but she had a pretty capacity for hard liquor.

Three days of this, and then, sobering up, I was riding back to San Francasco, making a list of what I knew and guessed about Norman Ashcraft, alias Ed Bohannon.

The list went something like this:

(1) He suspected, if he didn't know, that I had come down to see him on his wife's account: he had been too smooth and entertained me too well for me to doubt that; (2) he apparently had decided to return to his wife, though there was no guarantee that he would actually do so; (3) he was not incurably addicted to drugs; (4) he might pull himself together under his wife's influence, but it was doubtful: physically he hadn't gone to the dogs, but he had had his taste of the gutter and seemed to like it; (5) the girl Kewpie was crazily in love with him, while he liked her, but wasn't turning himself inside out over her.

A good night's sleep on the train between Los Angeles and San Francisco set me down in the Third and Townsend Street station with nearly normal head and stomach and not too many kinks in my nerves. I put away a breakfast of more food than I had eaten in three days, and went up to Vance Richmond's office.

"Mr. Richmond is in Eureka," his stenographer told me.

"Can you get him on the phone?"

She could, and did.

Without mentioning any names, I told the attorney what I knew and guessed.

"I see," he said. "Suppose you go out to Mrs. A's house and tell her I will write her tonight, and I probably shall be back in the city by the day after tomorrow. I think we can safely delay action until then."

I caught a street car, transferred at Van Ness Avenue, and went out to Mrs. Ashcraft's house. Nothing happened when I rang the bell. I rang it several times before I noticed that there were two morning newspapers in the vestibule. I looked at the dates—this morning's and yesterday morning's.

An old man in faded overalls was watering the lawn next door.

"Do you know if the people who live here have gone away?" I called.

"I don't guess so. The back door's open, I seen this mornin'."

He stopped to scratch his chin.

"They may of gone," he said slowly. "Come to think on it, I ain't seen any of 'em for—I don't remember seein' any of 'em yesterday."

I left the front steps and went around the house, climbed the low fence in back and went up the back steps. The kitchen door stood about a foot open. Nobody was visible in the kitchen, but there was a sound of running water.

I knocked on the door with my knuckles, loudly. There was no answering sound. I pushed the door open and went in. The sound of water came from the sink. I looked in the sink.

Under a thin stream of water running from one of the faucets lay a carving knife with nearly a foot of keen blade. The knife was clean, but the back of the porcelain sink—where water had splashed with only small, scattered drops—was freckled with red-brown spots. I scraped one of them with a fingernail—dried blood.

Except for the sink, I could see nothing out of order in the kitchen. I opened a pantry door. Everything seemed all right there. Across the room another door led to the front of the house. I opened the door and went into a passageway. Not enough light came from the kitchen to illuminate the passageway. I fumbled in the dusk for the light-button that I knew should be there. I stepped on something soft.

Pulling my foot back, I felt in my pocket for matches, and struck one. In front of me, his head and shoulders on the floor, his hips and legs on the lower steps of a flight of stairs, lay a Filipino boy in his underclothes.

He was dead. One eye was cut, and his throat was gashed straight across close up under his chin. I could see the killing without even shutting my eyes. At the top of the stairs—the killer's left hand dashing into the Filipino's face—thumb-nail gouging into eye—pushing the brown face back—tightening the brown throat for the knife's edge—the slash—and the shove down the steps.

The light from my second match showed me the button. I clicked on the lights, buttoned my coat, and went up the steps. Dried blood darkened them here and there, and at the second-floor landing the wall paper was stained with a big blot. At the head of the stairs I found another light-button, and pressed it.

I walked down the hall, poked my head into two rooms that seemed in order, and then turned a corner— and pulled up with a jerk, barely in time to miss stumbling over a woman who lay there.

She was bunched on the floor, face down, with knees drawn up under her and both hands clasped to her stomach. She wore a nightgown, and her hair was in a braid down her back.

I put a finger on the back of her neck. Stone-cold.

Kneeling on the floor—to avoid the necessity of turning her over—I looked at her face. She was the maid who had admitted Richmond and me four days ago.

I stood up again and looked around. The maid's head was almost touching a closed door. I stepped around her and pushed the door open. A bedroom, and not the maid's. It was an expensively dainty bedroom in cream and gray, with French prints on the walls. Nothing in the room was disarranged except the bed. The bed clothes were rumpled and tangled, and piled high in the center of the bed—in a pile that was too large . . .

Leaning over the bed, I began to draw the covers off. The second piece came away stained with blood. I yanked the rest off.

Mrs. Ashcraft was dead there.

Her body was drawn up in a little heap, from which her head hung crookedly, dangling from a neck that had been cut clean through to the bone. Her face was marked with four deep scratches from temple to chin. One sleeve had been torn from the jacket of her blue silk pajamas. Bedding and pajamas were soggy with the blood that the clothing piled over her had kept from drying.

I put the blanket over her again, edged past the dead woman in the hall, and went down the front stairs, switching on more lights, hunting for the telephone. Near the foot of the stairs I found it. I called the police detective bureau first, and then Vance Richmond's office.

"Get word to Mr. Richmond that Mrs. Ashcraft has been murdered," I told his stenographer. "I'm at her house, and he can get in touch with me here."

Then I went out of the front door and sat on the top step, smoking a cigarette while I waited for the police.

I felt rotten. I've seen dead people in larger quantities than three in my time, but this thing had fallen on me while my nerves were ragged from three days of boozing.

The police automobile swung around the corner and began disgorging men before I had finished my first cigarette. O'Gar, the detective-sergeant in charge of the Homicide Detail, was the first man up the steps.

"Hullo," he greeted me. "What have you got hold of this time?"

"I found three bodies in there before I quit looking," I told him as I led him indoors. "Maybe a regular detective like you can find more."

"You didn't do bad—for a lad," he said.

My wooziness had passed. I was eager to get to work.

I showed the Filipino to O'Gar first, and then the two women. We didn't find any more. Detail work occupied all of us—O'Gar, the eight men under him, and me—for the next few hours. The house had to be gone over from roof to cellar. The neighbors had to be grilled. The employment agencies through which the servants had been hired had to be examined. Relatives and friends of the Filipino and the maid had to be traced and questioned. Newsboys, mail carriers, grocers' delivery men, laundrymen, had to be found, questioned and investigated.

When the bulk of the reports were in, O'Gar and I sneaked away from the others and locked ourselves in the library.

"Night before last, huh? Wednesday night?" O'Gar grunted when we were comfortable in a couple of leather chairs, burning tobacco.

I nodded. The report of the doctor who had examined the bodies, the presence of the two newspapers in the vestibule, and the fact that neither neighbor, grocer nor butcher had seen any of them since Wednesday, combined to make Wednesday night—or early Thursday morning—the correct date.

"I'd say the killer cracked the back door," O'Gar went on, staring at the ceiling through smoke, "picked up the carving knife in the kitchen, and went upstairs. Maybe he went straight to Mrs. Ashcraft's room—maybe not. But after a bit he went in there. The torn sleeve and the scratches on her face mean that there was a tussle. The Filipino and the maid heard the noise—heard her scream maybe—and rushed to her room to find out what was the matter. The maid most likely got there just as the killer was coming out—and got hers. I guess the Filipino saw him then and ran. The killer caught him at the head of the back stairs—and finished him. Then he went down to the kitchen, washed his hands, dropped the knife, and blew."

"So far, so good," I agreed; "but I notice you skip over the question of who he was and why he killed."

"Don't crowd me," he rumbled: "I'll get around to that. There seem to be just three guesses to take your pick from. The killer was either a maniac who did the job for the fun of it, a burglar who was discovered and ran wild, or somebody who had a reason for bumping off Mrs. Ashcraft, and then had to kill the two servants when they discovered him. My personal guess is that the job was done by somebody who wanted to wipe out Mrs. Ashcraft."

"Not so bad," I applauded. "Now listen to this: Mrs. Ashcraft has a husband in Tijuana, a mild sort of hop-head who is mixed up with a bunch of thugs. She was trying to persuade him to come back to her. He has a girl down there who is young, goofy over him, and a bad actor—one tough youngster. He was planning to run out on the girl and come back home."

"So-o-o?" O'Gar said softly.

"But," I continued, "I was with both him and the girl, in Tijuana, night before last—when this killing was done."

"So-o?"

A knock on the door interrupted our talk. It was a policeman to tell me that I was wanted on the phone. I went down to the first floor, and Vance Richmond's voice came over the wire.

"What is it? Miss Henry delivered your message, but she couldn't give me any details."

I told him the whole thing.

"I'll leave for the city tonight," he said when I had finished. "You go ahead and do whatever you want. You're to have a free hand."

"Right," I replied. "I'll probably be out of town when you get back. You can reach me through the Agency. I'm going to wire Ashcraft to come up—in your name."

After Richmond had hung up, I called the city jail and asked the captain if John Ryan, alias Fred Rooney, alias Jamocha, was still there.

"No. Federal officers left for Leavenworth with him yesterday morning."

Up in the library again, I told O'Gar hurriedly:

"I'm catching the evening train south, betting my marbles that the job was made in Tijuana. I'm wiring Ashcraft to come up. I want to get him away from the Mexican town for a day or two, and if he's up here you can keep an eye on him. I'll give you a description of him, and you can pick him up at Vance Richmond's office."

Half an hour of the little time I had left I spent writing and sending three telegrams. The first was to Ashcraft.

EDWARD BOHANNON,
GOLDEN HORSESHOE CAFE,
TIJUANA, MEXICO.

MRS. ASHCRAFT IS DEAD. CAN YOU COME IMMEDIATELY?

VANCE RICHMOND

The other two were in code. One went to the Continental Detective Agency's Kansas City branch, asking that an operative be sent to Leavenworth to question Jamocha. The other requested the Los Angeles branch to have a man meet me in San Diego the next day.

Then I dashed out to my rooms for a bagful of clean clothes, and went to sleep riding south again.

San Diego was gay and packed when I got off the train early the next afternoon—filled with the crowd that the first Saturday of the racing season across the border had drawn. Movie folk from Los Angeles, farmers from the Imperial Valley, sailors from the Pacific Fleet, gamblers, tourists, grifters, and even regular people, from everywhere. I lunched, registered and left my bag at a hotel, and went up to the U. S. Grant Hotel to pick up the Los Angeles operative I had wired for.

I found him in the lobby—a freckle-faced youngster of twenty-two or so, whose bright gray eyes were busy just now with a racing program, which he held in a hand that had a finger bandaged with adhesive tape. I passed him and stopped at the cigar stand, where I bought a package of cigarettes and straightened out an imaginary dent in my hat. Then I went out to the street again. The bandaged finger and the business with the hat were our introductions. Somebody invented those tricks back before the Civil War, but they still worked smoothly, so their antiquity was no reason for discarding them.

I strolled up Fourth Street, getting away from Broadway—San Diego's main stem—and the operative caught up with me. His name was Gorman, and I gave him the lay.

"You're to go down to Tijuana and take a plant on the Golden Horseshoe Café. There's a little chunk of a girl hustling drinks in there—short, curly brown hair; brown eyes; round face; rather large red mouth; square shoulders. You can't miss her; she's a nice-looking kid of about eighteen, called Kewpie. She's the target for your eye. Keep away from her. Don't try to rope her. I'll give you an hour's start. Then I'm coming down to talk to her. I want to know what she does right after I leave, and what she does for the next few days. You can get in touch with me at the"—I gave him the name of my hotel and my room number—"each night. Don't give me a tumble anywhere else."

We parted, and I went down to the plaza and sat on a bench for an hour. Then I went up to the corner and fought for a seat on a Tijuana stage.

Fifteen or more miles of dusty riding—packed five in a seat meant for three—a momentary halt at the Immigration Station on the line, and I was climbing out of the stage at the entrance to the race track. The ponies had been running for some time, but the turnstiles were still spinning a steady stream of customers into the track. I turned my back on the gate and went over to the row of jitneys in front of the Monte Carlo—the big wooden casino—got into one, and was driven over to the Old Town.

The Old Town had a deserted look. Nearly everybody was over watching the dogs do their stuff. Gorman's freckled face showed over a drink of mescal when I entered the Golden Horseshoe. I hoped he had a good constitution. He needed one if he was going to do his sleuthing on a distilled cactus diet.

The welcome I got from the Horseshoers was just like a homecoming. Even the bartender with the plastered-down curls gave me a grin.

"Where's Kewpie?" I asked.

"Brother-in-lawing Ed?" a big Swede girl leered at me. "I'll see if I can find her for you."

Kewpie came through the back door just then and climbed all over me, hugging me, rubbing her face against mine, and the Lord knows what all. "Down for another souse?"

"No," I said, leading her back toward the stalls. "Business this time. Where's Ed?"

"Up north. His wife kicked off and he's gone to collect the remains."

"That makes you sorry?"

"You bet! It's tough on me that papa has come into a lot of sugar."

71

I looked at her out of the corner of my eyes—a glance that was supposed to be wise.

"And you think Ed's going to bring the jack back to you?"

Her eyes snapped darkly at me.

"What's eating you?" she demanded.

I smiled knowingly.

"One of two things is going to happen," I predicted. "Ed's going to ditch you—he was figuring on that, anyway—or he's going to need every brownie he can scrape up to keep his neck from being—"

"You God-damned liar!"

Her right shoulder was to me, touching my left. Her left hand flashed down under her short skirt. I pushed her shoulder forward, twisting her body sharply away from me. The knife her left hand had whipped up from her leg jabbed deep into the underside of the table. A thick-bladed knife, balanced for accurate throwing.

She kicked backward, driving one of her sharp heels into my ankle. I slid my left arm around behind her and pinned her elbow to her side just as she freed the knife from the table.

"What th' hell's all 'is?"

I looked up.

Across the table a man stood glaring at me—legs apart, fists on hips. A tall, raw-boned man with wide shoulders, out of which a long, skinny, yellow neck rose to support a little round head. His eyes were black shoe-buttons stuck close together at the top of a little mashed nose.

"Where d'yuh get 'at stuff?" this lovely person roared at me.

He was too tough to reason with.

"If you're a waiter," I told him, "bring me a bottle of

beer and something for the kid. If you're not a waiter—sneak."

"I'll bring yuh a—"

The girl wriggled out of my hands and shut him up.

"Mine's liquor," she said sharply.

He snarled, looked from one of us to the other, showed me his dirty teeth again, and wandered away.

"Who's your friend?"

"You'll do well to lay off him," she advised me, not answering my question.

Then she slid her knife back in its hiding place under her skirt and twisted around to face me.

"Now what's all this about Ed being in trouble?"

"You read about the killing in the papers?"

"Yes."

"You oughtn't need a map, then," I said. "Ed's only out is to put the job on you. But I doubt if he can get away with that. If he can't, he's nailed."

"You're crazy!" she exclaimed. "You weren't too drunk to know that both of us were here with you when the killing was done."

"I'm not crazy enough to think that proves anything," I corrected her. "But I am crazy enough to expect to go back to San Francisco wearing the killer on my wrist."

She laughed at me. I laughed back and stood up.

"See you some more," I said as I strolled toward the door.

I returned to San Diego and sent a wire to Los Angeles, asking for another operative. Then I got something to eat and spent the evening in my hotel room waiting for Gorman.

It was late when he arrived, and he smelled of mescal from San Diego to St. Louis and back, but his head seemed level enough.

"Looked like I was going to have to shoot you loose from the place for a moment," he grinned.

"You let me alone," I ordered. "Your job is to see what goes on, and that's all. What did you turn up?"

"After you blew, the girl and the big guy put their noodles together. They seemed kind of agitated—all agog, you might say. He slid out, so I dropped the girl and slid along behind him. He came to town and got a wire off. I couldn't crowd him close enough to see who it was to. Then he went back to the joint."

"Who is the big guy?"

"He's no sweet dream, from what I hear. 'Gooseneck' Flinn is the name on his calling cards. He's bouncer and general utility man for the joint."

So this Gooseneck party was the Golden Horseshoe's cleanup man, and he hadn't been in sight during my three-day spree? I couldn't possibly have been so drunk that I'd forget his ugliness. And it had been on one of those three days that Mrs. Ashcraft and her servants had been killed.

"I wired your office for another op," I told Gorman. "He's to connect with you. Turn the girl over to him, and you camp on Gooseneck's trail. I think we're going to hang three killings on him, so watch your step."

"Aye, aye, Cap," and he went off to get some sleep.

The next afternoon I spent at the race track, fooling around with the bangtails while I waited for night.

After the last race, I got something to eat at the Sunset Inn, and then drifted over to the big casino—the other end of the same building. A thousand or more people of all sorts were jostling one another there, fighting to go up against poker, craps, chuck-a-luck, wheels of fortune, roulette and twenty-one with whatever money the race track had left or given them. I didn't buck any of the games. My playtime was over. I walked around through the crowd looking for my men.

I spotted the first one—a sun-burned man who was plainly a farm hand in his Sunday clothes. He was pushing toward the door, and his face held that peculiar emptiness which belongs to the gambler who has gone broke before the end of the game. It's a look of regret that is not so much for the loss of the money as for the necessity of quitting.

I got between the farm hand and the door.

"Clean you?" I asked sympathetically when he reached me.

A sheepish sort of nod.

"How'd you like to pick up five bucks for a few minutes' work?" I tempted him.

He would like it, but what was the work?

"I want you to go over to the Old Town with me and look at a man. Then you get your pay. There are no strings to it."

That didn't exactly satisfy him, but five bucks are five bucks; and he could drop out any time he didn't like the looks of things. He decided to try it.

I put the farm hand over by a door, and went after another—a little, plump man with round, optimistic eyes and a weak mouth. He was willing to earn five dollars in the simple and easy manner I had outlined. The next man I braced was a little too timid to take a chance on a blind game. Then I got a Filipino—glorious in a fawn-colored suit, and a stocky young Greek who was probably either a waiter or a barber.

Four men were enough. My quartet pleased me immensely. They didn't look too intelligent for my purpose, and they didn't look like thugs or sharpers. I put them in a jitney and took them over to the Old Town.

"Now this is it," I coached them when we had arrived. "I'm going into the Golden Horseshoe Café, around the corner. Give me two or three minutes, and then come in and buy yourselves a drink." I gave the farm hand a five-dollar bill. "You pay for the drinks with that—it isn't part of your wages. There's a tall, broad-shouldered man with a long, yellow neck and a small ugly face in there. You can't miss him. I want you all to take a good look at him without letting him get wise. When you're sure you'd know him again anywhere, give me the nod, and come back here and you get your money. Be careful when you give me the nod. I don't want anybody in there to find out that you know me."

It sounded queer to them, but there was the promise of five dollars apiece, and there were the games back in the casino, where five dollars might buy a man into a streak of luck that—write the rest of it yourself. They asked questions, which I refused to answer, but they stuck.

Gooseneck was behind the bar, helping out the bartenders, when I entered the place. They needed help. The joint bulged with customers.

I couldn't find Gorman's freckled face in the crowd, but I picked out the hatchet-sharp white face of Hooper, another Los Angeles operative, who, I knew then, had been sent down in response to my second telegram. Kewpie was farther down the bar, drinking with a little man whose meek face had the devil-may-care expression of a model husband on a tear. She nodded at me, but didn't leave her client.

Gooseneck gave me a scowl and the bottle of beer I had ordered. Presently my four hired men came in. They did their parts beautifully!

First they peered through the smoke, looking from

face to face, and hastily avoiding eyes that met theirs. A little of this, and one of them, the Filipino, saw the man I had described, behind the bar. He jumped a foot in the excitement of his discovery, and then, finding Gooseneck glaring at him, turned his back and fidgeted. The three others spotted Gooseneck now, and sneaked looks at him that were as conspicuously furtive as a set of false whiskers. Gooseneck glowered at them.

The Filipino turned around, looked at me, ducking his head sharply, and bolted for the street. The three who were left shot their drinks down their gullets and tried to catch my eye. I was reading a sign high on the wall behind the bar:

ONLY GENUINE PRE-WAR AMERICAN AND
BRITISH WHISKEYS SERVED HERE

I was trying to count how many lies could be found in those nine words, and had reached four, with promise of more, when one of my confederates, the Greek, cleared his throat with the noise of a gasoline engine's backfire. Gooseneck was edging down the bar, a bung-starter in one hand, his face purple.

I looked at my assistants. Their nods wouldn't have been so terrible had they come one at a time; but they were taking no chances on my looking away again before they could get their reports in. The three heads bobbed together—a signal that nobody within twenty feet could, or, did, miss—and they scooted out of the door, away from the long-necked man and his bung-starter.

I emptied my glass of beer, sauntered out of the saloon and around the corner. They were clustered where I had told them to wait.

"We'd know him! We'd know him!" they chorused.

"That's fine," I praised them. "You did great. I think you're all natural-born gumshoes. Here's your pay. Now if I were you boys, I think I'd sort of avoid that place after this; because, in spite of the clever way you covered yourselves up—and you did nobly!—he might possibly suspect something. There's no use taking chances."

They grabbed their wages and were gone before I had finished my speech.

Hooper came into my room in the San Diego hotel at a little before two the next morning.

"Gooseneck disappeared, with Gorman tailing him, immediately after your first visit," he said. "Afterward the girl went around to a 'dobe house on the edge of town, and she was still there when I knocked off. The place was dark."

Gorman didn't show up.

A bell-hop with a telegram roused me at ten o'clock in the morning. The telegram was from Mexicali:

> DROVE HERE LAST NIGHT
> HOLED UP WITH FRIENDS
> SENT TWO WIRES.
>
> GORMAN

That was good news. The long-necked man had fallen for my play, had taken my four busted gamblers for four witnesses, had taken their nods for identifications. Gooseneck was the lad who had done the actual killing, and Gooseneck was in flight.

I had shed my pajamas and was reaching for my union suit when the boy came back with another wire. This one was from O'Gar, through the Agency:

ASHCRAFT DISAPPEARED YESTERDAY

I used the telephone to get Hooper out of bed.

"Get down to Tijuana," I told him. "Stick up the house where you left the girl last night, unless you run across her at the Golden Horseshoe. Stay there until she shows. Stay with her until she connects with a big blond Englishman, and then switch to him. He's a man of less than forty, tall, with blue eyes and yellow hair. Don't let him shake you—he's the big boy in this party just now. I'll be down. If the Englishman and I stay together and the girl leaves us, take her, but otherwise stick to him."

I dressed, put down some breakfast and caught a stage for the Mexican town. The boy driving the stage made fair time, but you would have thought we were standing still to see a maroon roadster pass us near Palm City. Ashcraft was driving the roadster.

The roadster was empty, standing in front of the adobe house, when I saw it again. Up in the next block, Hooper was doing an imitation of a drunk, talking to two Indians in the uniforms of the Mexican Army.

I knocked on the door of the adobe house.

Kewpie's voice: "Who is it?"

"Me—Parker. Just heard that Ed is back."

"Oh!" she exclaimed. A pause. "Come in."

I pushed the door open and went in. The Englishman sat tilted back in a chair, his right elbow on the table, his right hand in his coat pocket—if there was a gun in that pocket it was pointing at me.

"Hello," he said. "I hear you've been making guesses about me."

"Call 'em anything you like." I pushed a chair over to

79

within a couple of feet of him, and sat down. "But don't let's kid each other. You had Gooseneck knock your wife off so you could get what she had. The mistake you made was in picking a sap like Gooseneck to do the turn —a sap who went on a killing spree and then lost his nerve. Going to read and write just because three or four witnesses put the finger on him! And only going as far as Mexicali! That's a fine place to pick! I suppose he was so scared that the five- or six-hours ride over the hills seemed like a trip to the end of the world!"

I kept my chin going.

"You aren't a sap, Ed, and neither am I. I want to take you riding north with bracelets on, but I'm in no hurry. If I can't take you today, I'm willing to wait until tomorrow. I'll get you in the end, unless somebody beats me to you—and that won't break my heart. There's a rod between my vest and my belly. If you'll have Kewpie get it out, we'll be all set for the talk I want to make."

He nodded slowly, not taking his eyes from me. The girl came close to my back. One of her hands came over my shoulder, went under my vest, and my old black gun left me. Before she stepped away she laid the point of her knife against the nape of my neck for an instant—a gentle reminder.

"Good," I said when she gave my gun to the Englishman, who pocketed it with his left hand. "Now here's my proposition. You and Kewpie ride across the border with me—so we won't have to fool with extradition papers—and I'll have you locked up. We'll do our fighting in court. I'm not absolutely certain that I can tie the killings on either of you, and if I flop, you'll be free. If I make the grade—as I hope to—you'll swing, of course.

"What's the sense of scooting? Spending the rest of

your life dodging bulls? Only to be nabbed finally—or bumped off trying to get away? You'll maybe save your neck, but what of the money your wife left? That money is what you are in the game for—it's what you had your wife killed for. Stand trial and you've a chance to collect it. Run—and you kiss it good-bye."

My game just now was to persuade Ed and his girl to bolt. If they let me throw them in the can I might be able to convict one of them, but my chances weren't any too large. It depended on how things turned out later. It depended on whether I could prove that Gooseneck had been in San Francisco on the night of the killings, and I imagined that he would be well supplied with all sorts of proof to the contrary. We had not been able to find a single fingerprint of the killer's in Mrs. Ashcraft's house. And if I *could* convince a jury that he was in San Francisco at the time, then I would have to show that he had done the killing. And after that I would have the toughest part of the job still ahead of me—to prove that he had done the killing for one of these two, and not on his own account.

What I was working for was to make this pair dust out. I didn't care where they went or what they did, so long as they scooted. I'd trust to luck and my own head to get profit out of their scrambling—I was still trying to stir things up.

The Englishman was thinking hard. I knew I had him worried, chiefly through what I had said about Gooseneck Flinn. Then he chuckled.

"You're balmy, Painless," he said. "But you—"

I don't know what he was going to say—whether I was going to win or lose.

The front door slammed open, and Gooseneck Flinn came into the room.

His clothes were white with dust. His face was thrust forward to the full length of his long, yellow neck.

His shoe-button eyes focused on me. His hands turned over. That's all you could see. They simply turned over —and there was a heavy revolver in each.

"Your paws on the table, Ed," he snarled.

Ed's gun—if that is what he had in his pocket—was blocked from a shot at the man in the doorway by a corner of the table. He took his hand out of his pocket, empty, and laid both palms down on the table-top.

"Stay where y'r at!" Gooseneck barked at the girl.

Gooseneck glared at me for nearly a minute.

When he spoke it was to Ed and Kewpie.

"So this is what y' wired me to come back for, huh? A trap! Me the goat for yur! I'll be y'r goat! I'm goin' to speak my piece, an' then I'm goin' out o' here if I have to smoke my way through the whole damn' Mex army! I killed yur wife all right—an' her help, too. Killed 'em for the thousand bucks—"

The girl took a step toward him, screaming:

"Shut up, damn you!"

"Shut up, yourself!" Gooseneck roared back at her, and his thumb raised the hammer of the gun that threatened her. "I'm doin' the talkin'. I killed her for—"

Kewpie bent forward. Her left hand went under the hem of her skirt. The hand came up—empty. The flash from Gooseneck's gun lit on a flying steel blade.

The girl spun back across the room—hammered back by the bullets that tore through her chest. Her back hit the wall. She pitched forward to the floor.

Gooseneck stopped shooting and tried to speak. The brown haft of the girl's knife stuck out of his yellow throat. He couldn't get his words past the blade. He dropped one gun and tried to take hold of the protruding haft. Halfway up to it his hand came, and dropped. He went down slowly—to his knees—hands and knees—rolled over on his side—and lay still.

I jumped for the Englishman. The revolver Gooseneck had dropped turned under my foot, spilling me sidewise. My hand brushed the Englishman's coat, but he twisted away from me, and got his guns out.

His eyes were hard and cold and his mouth was shut until you could hardly see the slit of it. He backed slowly across the floor, while I lay still where I had tumbled. He didn't make a speech. A moment of hesitation in the doorway. The door jerked open and shut. He was gone.

I scooped up the gun that had thrown me, sprang to Gooseneck's side, tore the other gun out of his dead hand, and plunged into the street. The maroon roadster was trailing a cloud of dust into the desert behind it. Thirty feet from me stood a dirt-caked black touring car. That would be the one in which Gooseneck had driven back from Mexicali.

I jumped for it, climbed in, brought it to life, and pointed it at the dust-cloud ahead.

The car under me, I discovered, was surprisingly well engined for its battered looks—its motor was so good that I knew it was a border-runner's car. I nursed it along, not pushing it. For half an hour or more the dust-cloud ahead and I held our respective positions, and then I found that I was gaining.

The going was roughening. Any road that we might originally have been using had petered out. I opened up a little, though the jars it cost me were vicious.

I missed a boulder that would have smashed me up—

missed it by a hair—and looked ahead again to see that the maroon roadster was no longer stirring up the grit. It had stopped.

The roadster was empty. I kept on.

From behind the roadster a pistol snapped at me, three times. It would have taken good shooting to plug me at that instant. I was bouncing around in my seat like a pellet of quicksilver in a nervous man's palm.

He fired again from the shelter of his car, and then dashed for a narrow arroyo—a sharp-edged, ten-foot crack in the earth—off to the left. On the brink, he wheeled to snap another cap at me—and jumped down out of sight.

I twisted the wheel in my hands, jammed on the brakes and slid the black touring car to the spot where I had seen him last. The edge of the arroyo was crumbling under my front wheels. I released the brake. Tumbled out.

The car plunged down into the gully after him.

Sprawled on my belly, one of Gooseneck's guns in each hand, I wormed my head over the edge. On all fours, the Englishman was scrambling out of the way of the car. The car was mangled, but still sputtering. One of the man's fists was bunched around a gun—mine.

"Drop it and stand up, Ed!" I yelled.

Snake-quick, he flung himself around in a sitting position on the arroyo bottom, swung his gun up—and I smashed his forearm with my second shot.

He was holding the wounded arm with his left hand when I slid down beside him, picked up the gun he had dropped, and frisked him to see if he had any more. Then twisting a handkerchief into a tourniquet of a sort, I knotted it around his wounded arm.

"Let's go upstairs and talk," I suggested, and helped him up the steep side of the gully.

We climbed into his roadster.

"Go ahead, talk your head off," he invited, "but don't expect me to add much to the conversation. You've got nothing on me. You saw Kewpie bump Gooseneck off to keep him from peaching on her."

"So that's your play?" I inquired. "The girl hired Gooseneck to kill your wife—out of jealousy—when she learned that you were planning to shake her and return to your own world?"

"Exactly."

"Not bad, Ed, but there's one rough spot in it. You are not Ashcraft!"

He jumped, and then laughed.

"Now your enthusiasm is getting the better of your judgment," he kidded me. "Could I have deceived another man's wife? Don't you think her lawyer, Richmond, made me prove my identity?"

"Well, I'll tell you, Ed, I think I'm a smarter baby than either of them. Suppose you had a lot of stuff that belonged to Ashcraft—papers, letters, things in his handwriting? If you were even a fair hand with a pen, you could have fooled his wife. As for the lawyer—his making you identify yourself was only a matter of form. It never occurred to him you weren't Ashcraft.

"At first your game was to bleed Mrs. Ashcraft for an allowance—to take the cure. But after she closed out her affairs in England and came here, you decided to wipe her out and take everything. You knew she was an orphan and had no close relatives to come butting in. You knew it wasn't likely that there were many people in America who could say you were not Ashcraft."

"Where do you think Ashcraft would be while I was spending his money?"

"Dead," I said.

That got to him, though he didn't get excited. But his eyes became thoughtful behind his smile.

"You may be right, of course," he drawled. "But even at that, I don't see just how you expect to hang me. Can you prove that Kewpie didn't think I was Ashcraft? Can you prove that she knew why Mrs. Ashcraft was sending me money? Can you prove that she knew anything about my game? I rather think not."

"You may get away with it," I admitted. "Juries are funny, and I don't mind telling you that I'd be happier if I knew a few things about those murders that I don't know. Do you mind telling me about the ins and outs of your switch with Ashcraft?"

He puckered his lips and then shugged. "I'll tell you. It won't matter greatly. I'm due to go over for this impersonation, so a confession to a little additional larceny won't matter.

"The hotel-sneak used to be my lay," the Englishman said after a pause. "I came to the States after England and the Continent got uncomfortable. Then, one night in a Seattle hotel, I worked the tarrel and put myself into a room on the fourth floor. I had hardly closed the door behind me before another key was rattling in it. The room was night-dark. I risked a flash from my light, picked out a closet door, and got behind it.

"The clothes closet was empty; rather a stroke of luck, since there was nothing in it for the room's occupant to come for. He—it was a man—had switched on the lights by then.

"He began pacing the floor. He paced it for three solid hours—up and down, up and down, up and down

86

—while I stood behind the closet door with my gun in my hand, in case he should pull it open. For three solid hours he paced that damned floor. Then he sat down and I heard a pen scratching on paper. Ten minutes of that and he was back at his pacing; but he kept it up for only a few minutes this time. I heard the latches of a valise click. And a shot!

"I bounded out of my retreat. He was stretched on the floor, with a hole in the side of his head. A bad break for me, and no mistake! I could hear excited voices in the corridor. I stepped over the dead chap, found the letter he had been writing on the writing-desk. It was addressed to Mrs. Norman Ashcraft at a Wine Street number in Bristol, England. I tore it open. He had written that he was going to kill himself, and it was signed Norman. I felt better. A murder couldn't be made out of it.

"Nevertheless, I was here in this room with a flash-light, skeleton keys, and a gun—to say nothing of a handful of jewelry that I had picked up on the next floor. Somebody was knocking on the door.

"Get the police!" I called through the door, playing for time.

"Then I turned to the man who had let me in for all this. I would have pegged him for a fellow Britisher even if I hadn't seen the address on his letter. There are thousands of us on the same order—blond, fairly tall, well set up. I took the only chance there was. His hat and top-coat were on a chair where he had tossed them. I put them on and dropped my hat beside him. Kneeling, I emptied his pockets, and my own, gave him all my stuff, pouched all of his. Then I traded guns with him and opened the door.

"What I had in mind was that the first arrivals might

not know him by sight, or not well enough to recognize him immediately. That would give me several seconds to arrange my disappearance in. But when I opened the door I found that my idea wouldn't work out as I had planned. The house detective was there, and a policeman, and I knew I was licked. But I played my hand out. I told them I had come up to my room and found this chap on the floor going through my belongings. I had seized him, and in the struggle had shot him.

"Minutes went by like hours, and nobody denounced me. People were calling me Mr. Ashcraft. My impersonation was succeeding. It had me gasping then, but after I learned more about Ashcraft it wasn't so surprising. He had arrived at the hotel only that afternoon, and no one had seen him except in his hat and coat—the hat and coat I was wearing. We were of the same size and type—typical blond Englishmen.

"Then I got another surprise. When the detective examined the dead man's clothes he found that the maker's labels had been ripped out. When I got a look at his diary, later, I found the explanation of that. He had been tossing mental coins with himself, alternating between a determination to kill himself, and another to change his name and make a new place for himself in the world. It was while he was considering the second plan that he had removed the markers from all of his clothing. But I didn't know that while I stood there among those people. All I knew was that miracles were happening.

"I had to talk small just then, but after I went through the dead man's stuff I knew him inside and outside, backward and forward. He had nearly a bushel of papers, and a diary that had everything he had ever done or thought in it. I put in the first night studying those things—memorizing them—and practicing his signature.

Among the other things I had taken from his pockets were fifteen hundred dollars' worth of traveler's checks, and I wanted to cash them in the morning.

"I stayed in Seattle for three days—as Norman Ashcraft. I had tumbled on to something rich and I wasn't going to throw it away. The letter to his wife should keep me from being charged with murder if anything slipped, and I knew I was safer seeing the thing through than running. When the excitement had quieted down I packed up and came down to San Francisco, resuming my own name—Edward Bohannon. But I held onto all of Ashcraft's property, because I had learned from it that his wife had money, and I knew I could get some of it if I played my cards right. She saved me the trouble. I ran across one of her advertisements in the *Examiner,* answered it, and—here we are."

"But you didn't have Mrs. Ashcraft killed?"

He shook his head.

I took a package of cigarettes out of my pocket and put two of them on the seat between us.

"Suppose we play a game. This is just for my own satisfaction. It won't tie anybody to anything—won't prove anything. If you did a certain thing, pick up the cigarette that is nearer me. If you didn't, pick up the one nearer you. Will you play?"

"No, I won't," he said emphatically. "I don't like your game. But I do want a cigarette."

He reached out his uninjured arm and picked up the cigarette nearer *me.*

"Thanks, Ed," I said. "Now I hate to tell you this, but I'm going to swing you."

"You're balmy, my son."

"You're thinking of the San Francisco job, Ed," I explained. "I'm talking about Seattle. You, a hotel sneak-thief, were discovered in a room with a man who had just died with a bullet in his head. What do you think a jury will make out of that, Ed?"

He laughed at me. And then something went wrong with the laugh. It faded into a sickly grin.

"Of course you did," I said. "When you started to work out your plan to inherit all of Mrs. Ashcraft's wealth by having her killed, the first thing you did was to destroy that suicide letter of her husband's. No matter how carefully you guarded it, there was always a chance that somebody would stumble onto it and knock your game on the head. It had served its purpose—you wouldn't need it. It would be foolish to chance it turning up.

"I can't put you up for the murders you engineered in San Francisco; but I can sock you with the one you didn't do in Seattle—so justice won't be cheated. You're going to Seattle, Ed, to hang for Ashcraft's suicide."

And he did.

THE
HOUSE IN
TURK STREET

I had been told that the man for whom I was hunting lived in a certain Turk Street block, but my informant hadn't been able to give me his house number. Thus it came about that late one rainy afternoon I was canvassing this certain block, ringing each bell, and reciting a myth that went like this:

"I'm from the law office of Wellington and Berkeley. One of our clients—an elderly lady—was thrown from the rear platform of a street car last week and severely injured. Among those who witnessed the accident was a young man whose name we don't know. But we have been told that he lives in this neighborhood." Then I would describe the man I wanted, and wind up: "Do you know of anyone who looks like that?"

All down one side of the block the answers were: "No," "No," "No."

I crossed the street and started on the other side. The

first house: "No." The second: "No." The third. The fourth. The fifth—

No one came to the door in answer to my first ring. After a while, I rang again. I had just decided that no one was at home, when the knob turned slowly and a little old woman opened the door. She was a very fragile little old woman, with a piece of gray knitting in one hand, and faded eyes that twinkled pleasantly behind goldrimmed spectacles. She wore a stiffly starched apron over a black dress.

"Good evening," she said in a thin friendly voice. "I hope you didn't mind waiting. I always have to peep out to see who's there before I open the door—an old woman's timidity."

"Sorry to disturb you," I apologized. "But—"

"Won't you come in, please?"

"No; I just want a little information. I won't take much time."

"I wish you would come in," she said, and then added with mock severity, "I'm sure my tea is getting cold."

She took my damp hat and coat, and I followed her down a narrow hall to a dim room, where a man got up as we entered. He was old too, and stout, with a thin white beard that fell upon a white vest that was as stiffly starched as the woman's apron.

"Thomas," the little fragile woman told him; "this is Mr.—"

"Tracy," I said, because that was the name I had given the other residents of the block; but I came as near blushing when I said it as I have in fifteen years. These folks weren't made to be lied to.

Their name, I learned, was Quarre; and they were an affectionate old couple. She called him "Thomas" every time she spoke to him, rolling the name around in her mouth as if she liked the taste of it. He called her "my dear" just as frequently, and twice he got up to adjust a cushion more comfortably to her frail back.

I had to drink a cup of tea with them and eat some little spiced cookies before I could get them to listen to a question. Then Mrs. Quarre made little sympathetic clicking sounds with her tongue and teeth, while I told about the elderly lady who had fallen off a street car. The old man rumbled in his beard that it was "a damn shame," and gave me a fat cigar.

Finally I got away from the accident, and described the man I wanted.

"Thomas," Mrs. Quarre said, "isn't that the young man who lives in the house with the railing—the one who always looks so worried?"

The old man stroked his snowy beard and pondered for a moment.

"But, my dear," he rumbled at last, "hasn't he got dark hair?"

She beamed upon her husband. "Thomas is *so* observant," she said with pride. "I had forgotten; but the young man I spoke of does have dark hair, so he couldn't be the one."

The old man then suggested that one who lived in the block below might be my man. They discussed this one at some length before they decided that he was too tall and too old. Mrs. Quarre suggested another. They discussed that one, and voted against him. Thomas offered a candidate; he was weighed and discarded. They chattered on.

Darkness settled. The old man turned on a light in a tall lamp that threw a soft yellow circle upon us, and left the rest of the room dim. The room was a large one, and heavy with the thick hangings and bulky horsehair furniture of a generation ago. I didn't expect to get any information here; but I was comfortable, and the cigar was a good one. Time enough to go out into the drizzle when I had finished my smoke.

Something cold touched the nape of my neck.

"Stand up!"

I didn't stand up: I couldn't. I was paralyzed. I sat and blinked at the Quarres.

And looking at them, I knew that something cold *couldn't* be against the back of my neck; a harsh voice *couldn't* have ordered me to stand up. It wasn't possible!

Mrs. Quarre still sat primly upright against the cushions her husband had adjusted to her back; her eyes still twinkled with friendliness behind her glasses. The old man still stroked his white beard, and let cigar smoke drift unhurriedly from his nostrils.

They would go on talking about the young men in the neighborhood who might be the man I wanted. Nothing had happened. I had dozed.

"Get up!" The cold thing against my neck jabbed deep into the flesh.

I stood up. "Frisk him," the harsh voice came from behind.

The old man carefully laid his cigar down, came to me, and ran his hands over my body. Satisfied that I was unarmed, he emptied my pockets, dropping the contents upon the chair that I had just left.

"That's all," he told the man behind me, and returned to his chair.

"Turn around, you!" the harsh voice ordered.

I turned and faced a tall, gaunt, raw-boned man of about my own age, which is thirty-five. He had an ugly face—hollow-cheeked, bony, and spattered with big pale freckles. His eyes were of a watery blue, and his nose and chin stuck out abruptly. "Know me?" he asked.

"No."

"You're a liar!"

I didn't argue the point; he was holding a gun in one big freckled hand.

"You're going to know me pretty well before you're through with me," this big ugly man threatened. "You're going to—"

"Hook!" a voice came from a portièred doorway— the doorway through which the ugly man had no doubt crept up behind me. "Hook, come here!" The voice was feminine—young, clear, and musical.

"What do you want?" the ugly man called over his shoulder.

"*He's* here."

"All right!" He turned to Thomas Quarre. "Keep this joker safe."

From somewhere among his whiskers, his coat, and his stiff white vest, the old man brought out a big black revolver, which he handled with no signs of unfamiliarity.

The ugly man swept up the things that had been taken from my pockets, and carried them through the portières with him.

Mrs. Quarre smiled up at me. "Do sit down, Mr. Tracy," she said.

I sat.

Through the portières a new voice came from the next room; a drawling baritone voice whose accent was unmistakably British; cultured British. "What's up, Hook?" this voice was asking.

The harsh voice of the ugly man:

"Plenty's up, I'm telling you! They're on to us! I

started out a while ago; and as soon as I got to the street, I seen a man I knowed on the other side. He was pointed out to me in Philly five-six years ago. I don't know his name, but I remember his mug—he's a Continental Detective Agency man. I came back in right away, and me and Elvira watched him out of the window. He went to every house on the other side of the street, asking questions or something. Then he came over and started to give this side a whirl, and after a while he rings the bell. I tell the old woman and her husband to get him in, stall him along, and see what he says for himself. He's got a song and dance about looking for a guy what seen an old woman bumped by a street car—but that's the bunk! He's gunning for us. I went in and stuck him up just now. I meant to wait till you come, but I was scared he'd get nervous and beat it."

The British voice: "You shouldn't have shown yourself to him. The others could have taken care of him."

Hook: "What's the diff? Chances is he knows us all anyway. But supposing he didn't, what diff does it make?"

The drawling British voice: "It may make a deal of difference. It was stupid."

Hook, blustering: "Stupid, huh? You're always bellyaching about other people being stupid. To hell with you, I say! Who does all the work? Who's the guy that swings all the jobs? Huh? Where—"

The young feminine voice: "Now, Hook, for God's sake don't make that speech again. I've listened to it until I know it by heart!"

A rustle of papers, and the British voice: "I say, Hook, you're correct about his being a detective. Here is an identification card."

The feminine voice from the next room: "Well, what's to be done? What's our play?"

Hook: "That's easy to answer. We're going to knock this sleuth off!"

The feminine voice: "And put our necks in the noose?"

Hook, scornfully: "As if they ain't there if we don't! You don't think this guy ain't after us for the L.A. job, do you?"

The British voice: "You're an ass, Hook, and a quite hopeless one. Suppose this chap is interested in the Los Angeles affair, as is probable; what then? He is a Continental operative. Is it likely that his organization doesn't know where he is? Don't you think they know he was coming up here? And don't they know as much about us—chances are—as he does? There's no use killing him. That would only make matters worse. The thing to do is to tie him up and leave him here. His associates will hardly come looking for him until to-morrow."

My gratitude went out to the British voice! Somebody was in my favor, at least to the extent of letting me live. I hadn't been feeling very cheerful these last few minutes. Somehow, the fact that I couldn't see these people who were deciding whether I was to live or die, made my plight seem all the more desperate. I felt better now, though far from gay; I had confidence in the drawling British voice; it was the voice of a man who habitually carries his point.

Hook, bellowing: "Let me tell you something, brother: that guy's going to be knocked off! That's flat! I'm taking no chances. You can jaw all you want to about it, but I'm looking out for my own neck and it'll be a lot safer with that guy where he can't talk. That's flat."

The feminine voice, disgustedly: "Aw, Hook, be reasonable!"

The British voice, still drawling, but dead cold: "There's no use reasoning with you, Hook, you've the instincts and the intellect of a troglodyte. There is only one sort of language that you understand; and I'm going to talk that language to you, my son. If you are tempted to do anything silly between now and the time of our departure, just say this to yourself two or three times: 'If he dies, I die.' Say it as if it were out of the Bible —because it's that true."

There followed a long space of silence, with a tenseness that made my not particularly sensitive scalp tingle.

When, at last, a voice cut the silence, I jumped as if a gun had been fired; though the voice was low and smooth enough.

It was the British voice, confidently victorious, and I breathed again.

"We'll get the old people away first," the voice was saying. "You take charge of our guest, Hook. Tie him up while I get the bonds, and we'll be gone in less than half an hour."

The portières parted and Hook came into the room —a scowling Hook whose freckles had a greenish tinge against the sallowness of his face. He pointed a revolver at me, and spoke to the Quarres, short and harsh:

"He wants you." They got up and went into the next room.

Hook, meanwhile, had stepped back to the doorway,

still menacing me with his revolver; and pulled loose the plush ropes that were around the heavy curtains. Then he came around behind me, and tied me securely to the highbacked chair; my arms to the chair's arms, my legs to the chair's legs, my body to the chair's back and seat; and he wound up by gagging me with the corner of a cushion that was too well-stuffed.

As he finished lashing me into place, and stepped back to scowl at me, I heard the street door close softly, and then light footsteps ran back and forth overhead.

Hook looked in the direction of those footsteps, and his little watery blue eyes grew cunning. "Elvira!" he called softly.

The portières bulged as if someone had touched them, and the musical feminine voice came through. "What?"

"Come here."

"I'd better not. He wouldn't—"

"Damn him!" Hook flared up. "Come here!"

She came into the room and into the circle of light from the tall lamp; a girl in her early twenties, slender and lithe, and dressed for the street, except that she carried her hat in one hand. A white face beneath a bobbed mass of flame-colored hair. Smoke-gray eyes that were set too far apart for trustworthiness—though not for beauty—laughed at me; and her red mouth laughed at me, exposing the edges of little sharp animal-teeth. She was as beautiful as the devil, and twice as dangerous.

She laughed at me—a fat man, all trussed up with red plush rope, and with the corner of a green cushion in my mouth—and she turned to the ugly man. "What do you want?"

He spoke in an undertone, with a furtive glance at the ceiling, above which soft steps still padded back and forth.

"What say we shake him?"

Her smoke-gray eyes lost their merriment and became calculating.

"There's a hundred thousand he's holding—a third of it's mine. You don't think I'm going to take a Mickey Finn on that, do you?"

"Course not! Supposing we get the hundred-grand?"

"How?"

"Leave it to me, kid; leave it to me! If I swing it, will you go with me? You know I'll be good to you."

She smiled contemptuously, I thought—but he seemed to like it.

"You're whooping right you'll be good to me," she said. "But listen, Hook: we couldn't get away with it—not unless you *get him*. I know him! I'm not running away with anything that belongs to him unless he is fixed so that he can't come after it."

Hook moistened his lips and looked around the room at nothing. Apparently he didn't like the thought of tangling with the owner of the British drawl. But his desire for the girl was too strong for his fear.

"I'll do it!" he blurted. "I'll get him! Do you mean it, kid? If I get him, you'll go with me?"

She held out her hand. "It's a bet," she said and he believed her.

His ugly face grew warm and red and utterly happy, and he took a deep breath and straightened his shoulders. In his place, I might have believed her myself—all of us have fallen for that sort of thing at one time or another—but sitting tied up on the side-lines, I knew that he'd have been better off playing with a gallon of nitro than with this baby. She was dangerous! There was a rough time ahead for Hook!

"This is the lay—" Hook began, and stopped, tongue-tied.

A step had sounded in the next room.

Immediately the British voice came through the portières, and there was exasperation to the drawl now:

"This is really too much! I can't"—he said *reahly* and *cawnt*—"leave for a moment without having things done all wrong. Now just what got into you, Elvira, that you must go in and exhibit yourself to our detective?"

Fear flashed into her smoke-gray eyes, and out again, and she spoke airily. "Don't be altogether yellow," she said. "Your precious neck can get along all right without so much guarding."

The portières parted, and I twisted my head around as far as I could get it for my first look at this man who was responsible for my still being alive. I saw a short fat man, hatted and coated for the street, and carrying a tan traveling bag in one hand.

Then his face came into the yellow circle of light, and I saw that it was a Chinese face. A short fat Chinese, immaculately clothed in garments that were as British as his accent.

"It isn't a matter of color," he told the girl—and I understood now the full sting of her jibe; "it's simply a matter of ordinary wisdom."

His face was a round yellow mask, and his voice was the same emotionless drawl that I had heard before; but I knew that he was as surely under the girl's sway as the ugly man—or he wouldn't have let her taunt bring him into the room. But I doubted that she'd find this Anglicized Oriental as easily handled as Hook.

"There was no particular need," the Chinese was still talking, "for this chap to have seen any of us." He looked at me now for the first time, with little opaque eyes that were like two black seeds. "It's quite possible that he didn't know any of us, even by description. This showing ourselves to him is the most arrant sort of nonsense."

"Aw, hell, Tai!" Hook blustered. "Quit your belly-aching, will you? What's the diff? I'll knock him off, and that takes care of that!"

The Chinese set down his tan bag and shook his head.

"There will be no killing," he drawled, "or there will be quite a bit of killing. You don't mistake my meaning, do you, Hook?"

Hook didn't. His Adam's apple ran up and down with the effort of his swallowing and behind the cushion that was choking me, I thanked the yellow man again.

Then this red-haired she-devil put her spoon in the dish.

"Hook's always offering to do things that he has no intention of doing," she told the Chinese.

Hook's ugly face blazed red at this reminder of his promise to *get* the Chinese, and he swallowed again, and his eyes looked as if nothing would have suited him better than an opportunity to crawl under something. But the girl had him; her influence was stronger than his cowardice.

He suddenly stepped close to the Chinese, and from his advantage of a full head in height scowled down into the round yellow face.

"Tai," the ugly man snarled; "you're done. I'm sick and tired of all this dog you put on—acting like you was a king or something. I'm going to—"

He faltered, and his words faded away into silence. Tai looked up at him with eyes that were as hard and black and inhuman as two pieces of coal. Hook's lips twitched and he flinched away a little.

I stopped sweating. The yellow man had won again. But I had forgotten the red-haired she-devil. She laughed now—a mocking laugh that must have been like a knife to the ugly man.

A bellow came from deep in his chest, and he hurled one big fist into the round blank face of the yellow man.

The force of the punch carried Tai all the way across the room, and threw him on his side in one corner.

But he had twisted his body around to face the ugly man even as he went hurtling across the room—a gun was in his hand before he went down—and he was speaking before his legs had settled upon the floor— and his voice was a cultured British drawl.

"Later," he was saying; "we will settle this thing that is between us. Just now you will drop your pistol and stand very still while I get up."

Hook's revolver—only half out of his pocket when the Oriental had covered him—thudded to the rug. He stood rigidly still while Tai got to his feet, and Hook's breath came out noisily, and each freckle stood ghastlily out against the dirty scared white of his face.

I looked at the girl. There was contempt in the eyes with which she looked at Hook, but no disappointment.

Then I made a discovery: *something had changed in the room near her!*

I shut my eyes and tried to picture that part of the

room as it had been before the two men had clashed. Opening my eyes suddenly, I had the answer.

On the table beside the girl had been a book and some magazines. They were gone now. Not two feet from the girl was the tan bag that Tai had brought into the room. Suppose the bag had held the bonds from the Los Angeles job that they had mentioned. It probably had. What then? It probably now held the book and magazines that had been on the table. The girl had stirred up the trouble between the two men to distract their attention while she made a switch. Where would the loot be, then? I didn't know, but I suspected that it was too bulky to be on the girl's slender person.

Just beyond the table was a couch, with a wide red cover that went all the way down to the floor. I looked from the couch to the girl. She was watching me, and her eyes twinkled with a flash of mirth as they met mine coming from the couch. The couch it was!

By now the Chinese had pocketed Hook's revolver, and was talking to him: "If I hadn't a dislike for murder, and didn't think that you will perhaps be of some value to Elvira and me in effecting our departure, I should certainly relieve us of the handicap of your stupidity now. But I'll give you one more chance. I would suggest, however, that you think carefully before you give way to any more of your violent impulses." He turned to the girl. "Have you been putting foolish ideas in our Hook's head?"

She laughed. "Nobody could put any kind in it."

"Perhaps you're right," he said, and then came over to test the lashings about my arms and body.

Finding them satisfactory, he picked up the tan bag,

and held out the gun he had taken from the ugly man a few minutes before.

"Here's your revolver, Hook, now try to be sensible. We may as well go now. The old man and his wife will do as they were told. They are on their way to a city that we needn't mention by name in front of our friend here, to wait for us and their share of the bonds. Needless to say, they will wait a long while—they are out of it now. But between ourselves there must be no more treachery. If we're to get clear, we must help each other."

According to the best dramatic rules, these folks should have made sarcastic speeches to me before they left, but they didn't. They passed me without even a farewell look, and went out of sight into the darkness of the hall.

Suddenly the Chinese was in the room again, running tiptoe—an open knife in one hand, a gun in the other. This was the man I had been thanking for saving my life! He bent over me.

The knife moved on my right side, and the rope that held that arm slackened its grip. I breathed again, and my heart went back to beating.

"Hook will be back," Tai whispered, and was gone.

On the carpet, three feet in front of me, lay a revolver.

The street door closed, and I was alone in the house for a while.

You may believe that I spent that while struggling with the red plush ropes that bound me. Tai had cut one length, loosening my right arm somewhat and giving my body more play, but I was far from free. And his whispered "Hook will be back" was all the spur I needed to throw my strength against my bonds.

I understood now why the Chinese had insisted so strongly upon my life being spared. *I was the weapon with which Hook was to be removed!* The Chinese figured that Hook would make some excuse as soon as they reached the street, slip back into the house, knock me off, and rejoin his confederates. If he didn't do it on his own initiative, I suppose the Chinese would suggest it.

So he had put a gun within reach and had loosened my ropes as much as he could, not to have me free before he himself got away.

This thinking was a side-issue. I didn't let it slow up my efforts to get loose. The *why* wasn't important to me just now—the important thing was to have that revolver in my hand when the ugly man came back.

Just as the front door opened, I got my right arm completely free, and plucked the strangling cushion from my mouth. The rest of my body was still held by the ropes—held loosely—but held.

I threw myself, chair and all, forward, breaking the fall with my free arm. The carpet was thick. I went down on my face, with the heavy chair atop me, all doubled up, but my right arm was free of the tangle, and my right hand grasped the gun. The dim light hit upon a man hurrying into the room—a glint of metal in his hand.

I fired.

He caught both hands to his belly, bent double, and slid out across the carpet.

That was over. But that was far from being all. I wrenched at the plush ropes that held me, while my mind tried to sketch what lay ahead.

The girl had switched the bonds, hiding them under the couch—there was no question of that. She had

intended coming back for them before I had time to
get free. But Hook had come back first, and she would
have to change her plan. What more likely than that
she would now tell the Chinese that Hook had made
the switch? What then? There was only one answer:
Tai would come back for the bonds—both of them
would come. Tai knew that I was armed now, but
they had said that the bonds represented a hundred
thousand dollars. That would be enough to bring them
back!

I kicked the last rope loose and scrambled to the
couch. The bonds were beneath it: four thick bundles,
done up with heavy rubber bands. I tucked them under one arm, and went over to the man who was dying
near the door. His gun was under one of his legs. I
pulled it out, stepped over him, and went into the
dark hall. Then I stopped to consider.

The girl and the Chinese would split to tackle me.
One would come in the front door and the other in the
rear. That would be the safest way for them to handle
me. My play, obviously, was to wait just inside one of
those doors for them. It would be foolish for me to
leave the house. That's exactly what they would be expecting at first—and they would be lying in ambush.

Decidedly, my play was to lie low within sight of
this front door and wait until one of them came through
it—as one of them surely would, when they had tired
of waiting for me to come out.

Toward the street door, the hall was lighted with the
glow that filtered through the glass from the street
lights. The stairway leading to the second-story threw
a triangular shadow across part of the hall—a shadow
that was black enough for any purpose. I crouched low
in this three-cornered slice of night, and waited.

I had two guns: the one the Chinese had given me, and the one I had taken from Hook. I had fired one shot; that would leave me eleven still to use—unless one of the weapons had been used since it was loaded. I broke the gun Tai had given me, and in the dark ran my fingers across the back of the cylinder. My fingers touched *one* shell—under the hammer. Tai had taken no chances; he had given me one bullet—the bullet with which I had dropped Hook.

I put that gun down on the floor, and examined the one I had taken from Hook. It was *empty*. The Chinese had taken no chances at all! He had emptied Hook's gun before returning it to him after their quarrel.

I was in a hole! Alone, unarmed, in a strange house that would presently hold two who were hunting me—and that one of them was a woman didn't soothe me any—she was none the less deadly on that account.

For a moment I was tempted to make a dash for it; the thought of being out in the street again was pleasant; but I put the idea away. That would be foolishness, and plenty of it. Then I remembered the bonds under my arm. They would have to be my weapon; and if they were to serve me, they would have to be concealed.

I slipped out of my triangular shadow and went up the stairs. Thanks to the street lights, the upstairs rooms were not too dark for me to move around. Around and around I went through the rooms, hunting for a place to hide the bonds. But when suddenly a window rattled, as if from the draught created by the opening of an outside door somewhere, I still had the loot in my hands.

There was nothing to do now but to chuck them out

of a window and trust to luck. I grabbed a pillow from a bed, stripped off the white case, and dumped the bonds into it. Then I leaned out of an already open window and looked down into the night, searching for a desirable dumping place: I didn't want the bonds to land on anything that would make a racket.

And, looking out of the window, I found a better hiding place. The window opened into a narrow court, on the other side of which was a house of the same sort as the one I was in. That house was of the same height as this one, with a flat tin roof that sloped down the other way. The roof wasn't far from me—not too far to chuck the pillow case. I chucked it. It disappeared over the edge of the roof and crackled softly on the tin.

Then I turned on all the lights in the room, lighted a cigarette (we all like to pose a little now and then), and sat down on the bed to await my capture. I might have stalked my enemies through the dark house, and possibly have nabbed them; but most likely I would simply have succeeded in getting myself shot. And I don't like to be shot.

The girl found me.

She came creeping up the hall, an automatic in each hand, hesitated for an instant outside the door, and then came in on the jump. And when she saw me sitting peacefully on the side of the bed, her eyes snapped scornfully at me, as if I had done something mean. I suppose she thought I should have given her an opportunity to shoot.

"I got him, Tai," she called, and the Chinese joined us.

"What did Hook do with the bonds?" he asked point blank.

I grinned into his round yellow face and led my ace.

"Why don't you ask the girl?"

His face showed nothing, but I imagined that his fat body stiffened a little within its fashionable British clothing. That encouraged me, and I went on with my little lie that was meant to stir things up.

"Haven't you rapped to it," I asked, "that they were fixing up to ditch you?"

"You dirty liar!" the girl screamed, and took a step toward me.

Tai halted her with an imperative gesture. He stared through her with his opaque black eyes, and as he stared the blood slid out of his face. She had this fat yellow man on her string, right enough, but he wasn't exactly a harmless toy.

"So that's how it is?" he said slowly, to no one in particular. Then to me: "Where did they put the bonds?"

The girl went close to him and her words came tumbling over each other:

"Here's the truth of it, Tai, so help me God! I switched the stuff myself. Hook wasn't in it. I was going to run out on both of you. I stuck them under the couch downstairs, but they're not there now. That's the God's truth!"

He was eager to believe her, and her words had the ring of truth to them. And I knew that—in love with her as he was—he'd more readily forgive her treachery with the bonds than he would forgive her for planning to run off with Hook; so I made haste to stir things up again.

"Part of that is right enough," I said. "She did stick the bonds under the couch—but Hook was in on it. They fixed it up between them while you were upstairs.

He was to pick a fight with you, and during the argument she was to make the switch, and that is exactly what they did."

I had him! As she wheeled savagely toward me, he stuck the muzzle of an automatic in her side—a smart jab that checked the angry words she was hurling at me.

"I'll take your guns, Elvira," he said, and took them.

"Where are the bonds now?" he asked me.

I grinned. "I'm not with you, Tai. I'm against you."

"I don't like violence," he said slowly, "and I believe you are a sensible person. Let us traffic, my friend."

"You name it," I suggested.

"Gladly! As a basis for our bargaining, we will stipulate that you have hidden the bonds where they cannot be found by anyone else; and that I have you completely in my power, as the shilling shockers used to have it."

"Reasonable enough," I said; "go on."

"The situation, then, is what gamblers call a standoff. Neither of us has the advantage. As a detective, you want us; but we have you. As thieves, we want the bonds; but you have them. I offer you the girl in exchange for the bonds, and that seems to me an equitable offer. It will give me the bonds and a chance to get away. It will give you no small degree of success in your task as a detective. Hook is dead. You will have the girl. All that will remain is to find me and the bonds again—by no means a hopeless task. You will have turned a defeat into half a victory, with an excellent chance to make it a complete one."

"How do I know that you'll give me the girl?"

He shrugged. "Naturally, there can be no guarantee.

But, knowing that she planned to desert me for the swine who lies dead below, you can't imagine that my feelings for her are the most friendly. Too, if I take her with me, she will want a share in the loot."

I turned the lay-out over in my mind.

"This is the way it looks to me," I told him at last. "You aren't a killer. I'll come through alive no matter what happens. All right, why should I swap? You and the girl will be easier to find again than the bonds, and they are the most important part of the job anyway. I'll hold on to them, and take my chances on finding you folks again. Yes, I'm playing it safe."

"No, I'm not a killer," he said, very softly; and he smiled the first smile I had seen on his face. It wasn't a pleasant smile: and there was something in it that made you want to shudder. "But I am other things, perhaps, of which you haven't thought. But this talking is to no purpose. Elvira!"

The girl came obediently forward.

"You will find sheets in one of the bureau drawers," he told her. "Tear one or two of them into strips strong enough to tie up our friend securely."

The girl went to the buerau. I wrinkled my head, trying to find a not too disagreeable answer to the question in my mind. The answer that came first wasn't nice: *torture*.

Then a faint sound brought us all into tense motionlessness.

The room we were in had two doors: one leading into the hall, the other into another bedroom. It was through the hall door that the faint sound had come—the sound of creeping feet.

Swiftly, silently, Tai moved backward to a position from which he could watch the hall door without losing sight of the girl and me—and the gun poised like a live thing in his fat hand was all the warning we needed to make no noise.

The faint sound again, just outside the door.

The gun in Tai's hand seemed to quiver with eagerness.

Through the other door—the door that gave to the next room—popped Mrs. Quarre, an enormous cocked revolver in her thin hand.

"Let go it, you nasty heathen," she screeched.

Tai dropped his pistol before he turned to face her, and he held his hands up high—all of which was very wise.

Thomas Quarre came through the hall door then; he also held a cocked revolver—the mate of his wife's— though, in front of his bulk, his didn't look so enormously large.

I looked at the old woman again, and found little of the friendly fragile one who had poured tea and chatted about the neighbors. This was a witch if there ever was one—a witch of the blackest, most malignant sort. Her little faded eyes were sharp with ferocity, her withered lips were taut in a wolfish snarl, and her thin body fairly quivered with hate.

"I knew it," she was shrilling. "I told Tom as soon as we got far enough away to think things over. I knew it was a frame-up! I knew this supposed detective was a pal of yours! I knew it was just a scheme to beat Thomas and me out of our shares! Well, I'll show you, you yellow monkey! Where are them bonds? Where are they?"

The Chinese had recovered his poise, if he had ever lost it.

"Our stout friend can tell you perhaps," he said. "I

was about to extract the information from him when you so—ah—dramatically arrived."

"Thomas, for goodness sakes don't stand there dreaming," she snapped at her husband, who to all appearances was still the same mild old man who had given me an excellent cigar. "Tie up this Chinaman! I don't trust him an inch, and I won't feel easy until he's tied up."

I got up from my seat on the side of the bed, and moved cautiously to a spot that I thought would be out of the line of fire if the thing I expected happened.

Tai had dropped the gun that had been in his hand, but he hadn't been searched. The Chinese are a thorough people; if one of them carries a gun at all, he usually carries two or three or more. One gun had been taken from Tai, and if they tried to truss him up without frisking him, there was likely to be fireworks. So I moved to one side.

Fat Thomas Quarre went phlegmatically up to the Chinese to carry out his wife's orders—and bungled the job perfectly.

He put his bulk between Tai and the old woman's gun.

Tai's hands moved. An automatic was in each.

Once more Tai ran true to racial form. When a Chinese shoots he keeps on until his gun is empty.

When I yanked Tai over backward by his fat throat, and slammed him to the floor, his guns were still barking metal; and they clicked empty as I got a knee on one of his arms. I didn't take any chances. I worked on his throat until his eyes and tongue told me that he was out of things for a while. Then I looked around.

Thomas Quarre was against the bed, plainly dead, with three round holes in his starched white vest.

Across the room, Mrs. Quarre lay on her back. Her

clothes had somehow settled in place around her fragile body, and death had given her once more the gentle friendly look she had worn when I first saw her.

The red-haired girl Elvira was gone.

Presently Tai stirred, and after taking another gun from his clothes, I helped him sit up. He stroked his bruised throat with one fat hand and looked coolly around the room.

"Where's Elvira?" he asked.

"Got away—for the time being."

He shrugged. "Well, you can call it a decidedly successful operation. The Quarres and Hook dead; the bonds and I in your hands."

"Not so bad," I admitted, "but will you do me a favor?"

"If I may."

"Tell me what the hell this is all about!"

"All about?" he asked.

"Exactly! From what you people have let me overhear, I gather that you pulled some sort of job in Los Angeles that netted you a hundred-thousand-dollars' worth of bonds; but I can't remember any recent job of that size down there."

"Why, that's preposterous!" he said with what, for him, was almost wild-eyed amazement. "Preposterous! Of course you know all about it!"

"I do not! I was trying to find a young fellow named Fisher who left his Tacoma home in anger a week or two ago. His father wants him found on the quiet, so that he can come down and try to talk him into going home again. I was told that I might find Fisher in this block of Turk Street, and that's what brought me here."

He didn't believe me. He never believed me. He went to the gallows thinking me a liar.

When I got out into the street again (and Turk Street was a lovely place when I came free into it after my evening in that house!) I bought a newspaper that told me most of what I wanted to know.

A boy of twenty—a messenger in the employ of a Los Angeles stock and bond house—had disappeared two days before, while on his way to a bank with a wad of bonds. That same night this boy and a slender girl with bobbed red hair had registered at a hotel in Fresno as *J. M. Riordan and wife*. The next morning the boy had been found in his room—murdered. The girl was gone. The bonds were gone.

That much the paper told me. During the next few days, digging up a little here and a little there, I succeeded in piecing together most of the story.

The Chinese—whose full name was Tai Choon Tau —had been the brains of the mob. Their game had been a variation of the always-reliable badger game. Tai would pick out some youth who was messenger or runner for a banker or broker—one who carried either cash or negotiable securities in large quantities.

The girl Elvira would then *make* this lad, get him all fussed up over her—which shouldn't have been very hard for her—and then lead him gently around to running away with her and whatever he could grab in the way of his employer's bonds or currency.

Wherever they spent the first night of their flight, there Hook would appear—foaming at the mouth and loaded for bear. The girl would plead and tear her hair and so forth, trying to keep Hook—in his rôle of irate husband—from butchering the youth. Finally she would succeed, and in the end the youth would find himself without either girl or the fruits of his thievery.

Sometimes he had surrendered to the police. Two

we found had committed suicide. The Los Angeles lad had been built of tougher stuff than the others. He had put up a fight, and Hook had had to kill him. You can measure the girl's skill in her end of the game by the fact that not one of the half dozen youths who had been trimmed had said the least thing to implicate her; and some of them had gone to great trouble to keep her out of it.

The house in Turk Street had been the mob's retreat, and, that it might be always a safe one, they had not worked their game in San Francisco. Hook and the girl were supposed by the neighbors to be the Quarres' son and daughter—and Tai was the Chinese cook. The Quarres' benign and respectable appearances had also come in handy when the mob had securities to be disposed of.

The Chinese went to the gallows. We threw out the widest and finest-meshed of dragnets for the red-haired girl; and we turned up girls with bobbed red hair by the scores. But the girl Elvira was not among them.

I promised myself that some day . . .

THE GIRL
WITH THE
SILVER EYES

A bell jangled me into wakefulness. I rolled to the edge of my bed and reached for the telephone. The neat voice of the Old Man—the Continental Detective Agency's San Francisco manager—came to my ears:

"Sorry to disturb you, but you'll have to go up to the Glenton Apartments on Leavenworth Street. A man named Burke Pangburn, who lives there, phoned me a few minutes ago asking to have someone sent up to see him at once. He seemed rather excited. Will you take care of it? See what he wants." I said I would and, yawning, stretching and cursing Pangburn—whoever he was—got my fat body out of pajamas and into street clothes.

The man who had disturbed my Sunday morning sleep—I found when I reached the Glenton—was a slim, white-faced person of about twenty-five, with big brown eyes that were red-rimmed just now from either sleeplessness or crying, or both. His long brown hair was rumpled when he opened the door to admit me; and he wore a mauve dressing-robe spotted with big jade parrots over wine-colored silk pajamas.

The room into which he led me resembled an auctioneer's establishment just before the sale—or maybe one of these alley tea rooms. Fat blue vases, crooked red vases, lanky yellow vases, vases of various shapes and colors; marble statuettes, ebony statuettes, statuettes of any material; lanterns, lamps and candlesticks; draperies, hangings and rugs of all sorts; odds and ends of furniture that were all somehow queerly designed; peculiar pictures hung here and there in unexpected places. A hard room to feel comfortable in.

"My fiancée," he began immediately in a high-pitched voice that was within a notch of hysteria, "has disappeared! Something has happened to her! Foul play of some horrible sort! I want you to find her—to save her from this terrible thing that . . ."

I followed him this far and then gave it up. A jumble of words came out of his mouth—"spirited away . . . mysterious something . . . lured into a trap"—but they were too disconnected for me to make anything out of them. So I stopped trying to understand him, and waited for him to babble himself empty of words.

I have heard ordinarily reasonable men, under stress of excitement, run on even more crazily than this wild-eyed youth; but his dress—the parroted robe and gay pajamas—and his surroundings—this deliriously furnished room—gave him too theatrical a setting; made his words sound utterly unreal.

He himself, when normal, should have been a rather nice-looking lad: his features were well spaced and, though his mouth and chin were a little uncertain, his broad forehead was good. But standing there listening to the occasional melodramatic phrase that I could pick out of the jumbled noises he was throwing at me, I thought that instead of parrots on his robe he should have had cuckoos.

Presently he ran out of language and was holding his long, thin hands out to me in an appealing gesture, saying:

"Will you?" over and over. "Will you? Will you?"

I nodded soothingly, and noticed that tears were on his thin cheeks.

"Suppose we begin at the beginning," I suggested, sitting down carefully on a carved bench affair that didn't look any too strong.

"Yes! Yes!" He was standing legs apart in front of me, running his fingers through his hair. "The beginning. I had a letter from her every day until—"

"That's not the beginning," I objected. "Who is she? What is she?"

"She's Jeanne Delano!" he exclaimed in surprise at my ignorance. "And she is my fiancée. And now she is gone, and I know that—"

The phrases *"victim of foul play," "into a trap"* and so on began to flow hysterically out again.

Finally I got him quieted down and, sandwiched in between occasional emotional outbursts, got a story out of him that amounted to this:

This Burke Pangburn was a poet. About two months before, he had received a note from a Jeanne Delano— forwarded from his publishers—praising his latest book of rhymes. Jeanne Delano happened to live in San Francisco, too, though she hadn't known that he did. He had answered her note, and had received another. After a little of this they met. If she really was as beautiful as he claimed, then he wasn't to be blamed for falling in love with her. But whether or not she was really beautiful, he thought she was, and he had fallen hard.

This Delano girl had been living in San Francisco for only a little while, and when the poet met her she was living alone in an Ashbury Avenue apartment. He did not know where she came from or anything about her former life. He suspected—from certain indefinite suggestions and peculiarities of conduct which he couldn't put in words—that there was a cloud of some sort hanging over the girl; that neither her past nor her present were free from difficulties. But he hadn't the least idea what those difficulties might be. He hadn't cared. He knew absolutely nothing about her, except that she was beautiful, and he loved her, and she had promised to marry him. Then, on the third of the month —exactly twenty-one days before this Sunday morning —the girl had suddenly left San Francisco. He had received a note from her, by messenger.

This note, which he showed me after I had insisted point blank on seeing it, read:

Burkelove:

Have just received a wire, and must go East on next train. Tried to get you on the phone, but couldn't. Will write you as soon as I know what my address will be. If anything. [These two words were erased and could be read only with great difficulty.] *Love me until I'm back with you forever.*

Your JEANNE

Nine days later he had received another letter from her, from Baltimore, Maryland. This one, which I had a still harder time getting a look at, read:

Dearest Poet:

It seems like two years since I have seen you, and I have a fear that it's going to be between one and two months before I see you again.

I can't tell you now, beloved, about what brought me here. There are things that can't be written. But as soon as I'm back with you, I shall tell you the whole wretched story.

If anything should happen—I mean to me— you'll go on loving me forever, won't you, beloved? But that's foolish. Nothing is going to happen. I'm just off the train, and tired from traveling.

Tomorrow I shall write you a long, long letter to make up for this.

My address here is 215 N. Stricker St. Please, Mister, at least one letter a day!

Your own JEANNE

For nine days he had had a letter from her each day —with two on Monday to make up for the none on Sunday. And then her letters had stopped. And the daily letters he had sent to the address she gave—215 N. Stricker Street—had begun to come back to him, marked "Not known." He had sent a telegram, and the telegraph company had informed him that its Baltimore office had been unable to find a Jeanne Delano at the North Stricker Street address.

For three days he had waited, expecting hourly to hear from the girl, and no word had come. Then he had bought a ticket for Baltimore.

"But," he wound up, "I was afraid to go. I know she's in some sort of trouble—I can feel that—but I'm a silly poet. I can't deal with mysteries. Either I would find nothing at all or, if by luck I did stumble on the right track, the probabilities are that I would only muddle things; add fresh complications, perhaps endanger her life still further. I can't go blundering at it in that fashion, without knowing whether I am helping or harming her. It's a task for an expert in that sort of thing. So I thought of your agency. You'll be careful, won't you? It may be—I don't know—that she won't want assistance. It may be that you can help her without her knowing anything about it. You are accustomed to that sort of thing; you can do it, can't you?"

I turned the job over and over in my mind before answering him. The two great bugaboos of a reputable detective agency are the persons who bring in a crooked plan or a piece of divorce work all dressed up in the garb of a legitimate operation, and the irresponsible person who is laboring under wild and fanciful delusions—who wants a dream run out.

This poet—sitting opposite me now twining his long, white fingers nervously—was, I thought, sincere; but I wasn't so sure of his sanity.

"Mr. Pangburn," I said after a while, "I'd like to handle this thing for you, but I'm not sure that I can. The Continental is rather strict, and, while I believe this thing is on the level, still I am only a hired man and have to go by the rules. Now if you could give us the endorsement of some firm or person of standing—a reputable lawyer, for instance, or any legally responsible party—we'd be glad to go ahead with the work. Otherwise, I am afraid—"

"But I know she's in danger!" he broke out. "I know that—And I can't be advertising her plight—airing her affairs—to everyone."

"I'm sorry, but I can't touch it unless you can give me some such endorsement." I stood up. "But you can find plenty of detective agencies that aren't so particular."

His mouth worked like a small boy's, and he caught his lower lip between his teeth. For a moment I thought he was going to burst into tears. But instead he said slowly: "I dare say you are right. Suppose I refer you to my brother-in-law, Roy Axford. Will his word be sufficient?"

"Yes."

Roy Axford—R. F. Axford—was a mining man who had a finger in at least half of the big business enterprises of the Pacific Coast; and his word on anything was commonly considered good enough for anybody.

"If you can get in touch with him now," I said, "and arrange for me to see him today, I can get started without much delay."

Pangburn crossed the room and dug a telephone out from among a heap of his ornaments. Within a minute or two he was talking to someone whom he called "Rita."

"Is Roy home? . . . Will he be home this afternoon? . . . No, you can give him a message for me, though. . . . Tell him I'm sending a gentleman up to see him this afternoon on a personal matter—personal from me—and that I'll be very grateful if he'll do what I want. . . . Yes. . . . You'll find out, Rita. . . . It isn't a thing to talk about over the phone. . . . Yes, thanks!"

He pushed the telephone back into its hiding place and turned to me.

"He'll be at home until two o'clock. Tell him what

I told you and if he seems doubtful, have him call me up. You'll have to tell him the whole thing; he doesn't know anything at all about Miss Delano."

"All right. Before I go, I want a description of her."

"She's beautiful! The most beautiful woman in the world!"

That would look nice on a reward circular.

"That isn't exactly what I want," I told him. "How old is she?"

"Twenty-two."

"Height?"

"About five feet eight inches, or possibly nine."

"Slender, medium or plump?"

"She's inclined toward slenderness, but she—"

There was a note of enthusiasm in his voice that made me fear he was about to make a speech, so I cut him off with another question.

"What color hair?"

"Brown—so dark it's almost black—and it's soft and thick and—"

"Yes, yes. Long or bobbed?"

"Long and thick and—"

"What color eyes?"

"You've seen shadows on polished silver when—"

I wrote down *gray eyes* and hurried on with the interrogation.

"Complexion?"

"Perfect!"

"Uh-huh. But is it light, or dark, or florid, or sallow, or what?"

"Fair."

"Face oval, or square, or long and thin, or what shape?"

"Oval."

"What shaped nose? Large, small, turned-up—"

"Small and regular!" There was a touch of indignation in his voice.

"How did she dress? Fashionably? Did she favor bright or quiet colors?"

"Beaut—" And then as I opened my mouth to head him off he came down to earth with: "Very quietly—usually dark blues and browns."

"What jewelry did she wear?"

"I've never seen her wear any."

"Any scars, or moles?" The horrified look on his white face urged me on to give him a full shot. "Or warts, or deformities that you know?"

He was speechless, but he managed to shake his head.

"Have you a photograph of her?"

"Yes, I'll show you."

He bounded to his feet, wound his way through the room's excessive furnishings and out through a curtained doorway. Immediately he was back with a large photograph in a carved ivory frame. It was one of these artistic photographs—a thing of shadows and hazy outlines—not much good for identification purposes. She was beautiful—right enough—but that meant nothing; that's the purpose of an artistic photograph.

"This the only one you have?"

"Yes."

"I'll have to borrow it, but I'll get it back to you as soon as I have my copies made."

"No! No!" he protested against having his lady love's face given to a lot of gumshoes. "That would be terrible!"

I finally got it, but it cost me more words than I like to waste on an incidental.

"I want to borrow a couple of her letters, or something in her writing, too," I said.

"For what?"

"To have photostatic copies made. Handwriting specimens come in handy—give you something to go over hotel registers with. Then, even if going under fictitious names, people now and then write notes and make memorandums."

We had another battle, out of which I came with three envelopes and two meaningless sheets of paper, all bearing the girl's angular writing.

"She have much money?" I asked, when the disputed photograph and handwriting specimens were safely tucked away in my pocket.

"I don't know. It's not the sort of thing that one would pry into. She wasn't poor; that is, she didn't have to practice any petty economies; but I haven't the faintest idea either as to the amount of her income or its source. She had an account at the Golden Gate Trust Company, but naturally I don't know anything about its size."

"Many friends here?"

"That's another thing I don't know. I think she knew a few people here, but I don't know who they were. You see, when we were together we never talked about anything but ourselves. There was nothing we were interested in but each other. We were simply—"

"Can't you even make a guess at where she came from, who she was?"

"No. Those things didn't matter to me. She was Jeanne Delano, and that was enough for me."

"Did you and she ever have any financial interests in common? I mean, was there ever any transaction in money or other valuables in which both of you were interested?"

What I meant, of course, was had she got into him for a loan, or had she sold him something, or got money out of him in any other way.

He jumped to his feet, and his face went fog-gray. Then he sat down—slumped down—and blushed scarlet.

"Pardon me," he said thickly. "You didn't know her, and of course you must look at the thing from all angles. No, there was nothing like that. I'm afraid you are going to waste time if you are going to work on the theory that she was an adventuress. There was nothing like that! She was a girl with something terrible hanging over her; something that called her to Baltimore suddenly; something that has taken her away from me. Money? What could money have to do with it? I love her!"

R. F. Axford received me in an office-like room in his Russian Hill residence: a big blond man, whose forty-eight or -nine years had not blurred the outlines of an athlete's body. A big, full-blooded man with the manner of one whose self-confidence is complete and not altogether unjustified. "What's our Burke been up to now?" he asked amusedly when I told him who I was. His voice was a pleasant vibrant bass.

I didn't give him all the details.

"He was engaged to marry a Jeanne Delano, who went East about three weeks ago and then suddenly disappeared. He knows very little about her; thinks something has happened to her; and wants her found."

"Again?" His shrewd blue eyes twinkled. "And to a

Jeanne this time! She's the fifth within a year, to my knowledge, and no doubt I missed one or two while I was in Hawaii. But where do I come in?"

"I asked him for responsible endorsement. I think he's all right, but he isn't, in the strictest sense, a responsible person. He referred me to you."

"You're right about his not being, in the strictest sense, a responsible person." The big man screwed up his eyes and mouth in thought for a moment. Then: "Do you think that something has really happened to the girl? Or is Burke imagining things?"

"I don't know. I thought it was a dream at first. But in a couple of her letters there are hints that something was wrong."

"You might go ahead and find her then," Axford said. "I don't suppose any harm will come from letting him have his Jeanne back. It will at least give him something to think about for a while."

"I have your word for it then, Mr. Axford, that there will be no scandal or anything of the sort connected with the affair?"

"Assuredly! Burke is all right, you know. It's simply that he is spoiled. He has been in rather delicate health all his life; and then he has an income that suffices to keep him modestly, with a little over to bring out books of verse and buy doo-daws for his rooms. He takes himself a little too solemnly—is too much the poet—but he's sound at bottom."

"I'll go ahead with it, then," I said, getting up. "By the way, the girl has an account at the Golden Gate Trust Company, and I'd like to find out as much about it as possible, especially where her money came from. Clement, the cashier, is a model of caution when it comes to giving out information about depositors. If you could put in a word for me it would make my way smoother."

"Be glad to."

He wrote a couple of lines across the back of a card and gave it to me; and, promising to call on him if I needed further assistance, I left.

I telephoned Pangburn that his brother-in-law had given the job his approval. I sent a wire to the agency's Baltimore branch, giving what information I had. Then I went up to Ashbury Avenue, to the apartment house in which the girl had lived.

The manager—an immense Mrs. Clute in rustling black—knew little, if any, more about the girl than Pangburn. The girl had lived there for two and a half months; she had had occasional callers, but Pangburn was the only one that the manager could describe to me. The girl had given up the apartment on the third of the month, saying that she had been called East, and she had asked the manager to hold her mail until she sent her new address. Ten days later Mrs. Clute had received a card from the girl instructing her to forward her mail to 215 N. Stricker Street, Baltimore, Maryland. There had been no mail to forward.

The single thing of importance that I learned at the apartment house was that the girl's two trunks had been taken away by a green transfer truck. Green was the color used by one of the city's largest transfer companies.

I went then to the office of this transfer company, and found a friendly clerk on duty. (A detective, if he is wise, takes pains to make and keep as many friends as possible among transfer company, express company and railroad employees.) I left the office with a memorandum of the transfer company's check numbers and the Ferry baggageroom to which the two trunks had been taken.

At the Ferry Building, with this information, it didn't take me many minutes to learn that the trunks had been checked to Baltimore. I sent another wire to the Baltimore branch, giving the railroad check numbers.

Sunday was well into night by now, so I knocked off and went home.

Half an hour before the Golden Gate Trust Company opened for business the next morning I was inside, talking to Clement, the cashier. All the traditional caution and conservatism of bankers rolled together would but be one-two-three to the amount usually displayed by this plump, white-haired old man. But one look at Axford's card, with *"Please give the bearer all possible assistance"* inked across the back of it, made Clement even eager to help me.

"You have, or have had, an account here in the name of Jeanne Delano," I said. "I'd like to know as much as possible about it: to whom she drew checks, and to what amounts; but especially all you can tell me about where her money came from."

He stabbed one of the pearl buttons on his desk with a pink finger, and a lad with polished yellow hair oozed silently into the room. The cashier scribbled with a pencil on a piece of paper and gave it to the noiseless youth, who disappeared. Presently he was back, laying a handful of papers on the cashier's desk.

Clement looked through the papers and then up at me.

"Miss Delano was introduced here by Mr. Burke Pangburn on the sixth of last month, and opened an account with eight hundred and fifty dollars in cash. She made the following deposits after that: four hundred dollars on the tenth; two hundred and fifty on the twenty-first; three hundred on the twenty-sixth; two hundred on the thirtieth; and twenty thousand dollars on the second of this month. All of these deposits except the last were made with cash. The last one was a check."

He handed it to me: a Golden Gate Trust Company check.

Pay to the order of Jeanne Delano, twenty thousand dollars.

(Signed) BURKE PANGBURN

It was dated the second of the month.

"Burke Pangburn!" I exclaimed, a little stupidly. "Was it usual for him to draw checks to that amount?"

"I think not. But we shall see."

He stabbed the pearl button again, ran his pencil across another slip of paper, and the youth with the polished yellow hair made a noiseless entrance, exit, entrance, and exit. The cashier looked through the fresh batch of papers that had been brought to him.

"On the first of the month, Mr. Pangburn deposited twenty thousand dollars—a check against Mr. Axford's account here."

"Now how about Miss Delano's withdrawals?" I asked.

He picked up the papers that had to do with her account again.

"Her statement and canceled checks for last month haven't been delivered to her yet. Everything is here. A check for eighty-five dollars to the order of H. K. Clute on the fifteenth of last month; one 'to cash' for three hundred dollars on the twentieth, and another of the same kind for one hundred dollars on the twenty-fifth. Both of these checks were apparently cashed here by her. On the third of this month she closed out her account, with a check to her own order for twenty-one thousand, five hundred and fifteen dollars."

"And that check?"

"Was cashed here by her."

I lighted a cigarette, and let these figures drift around in my head. None of them—except those that were fixed to Pangburn's and Axford's signatures—seemed to be of any value to me. The Clute check—the only one the girl had drawn in anyone else's favor—had almost certainly been for rent.

"This is the way of it," I summed up aloud. "On the first of the month, Pangburn deposited Axford's check for twenty thousand dollars. The next day he gave a check to that amount to Miss Delano, which she deposited. On the following day she closed her account, taking between twenty-one and twenty-two thousand dollars in currency."

"Exactly," the cashier said.

Before going up to the Glenton Apartments to find out why Pangburn hadn't come clean with me about the twenty thousand dollars, I dropped in at the agency, to see if any word had come from Baltimore. One of the clerks had just finished decoding a telegram. It read:

> *Baggage arrived Mt. Royal Station on eighth. Taken away same day. Unable to trace. 215 North Stricker Street is Baltimore Orphan Asylum. Girl not known there. Continuing our efforts to find her.*

The Old Man came in from luncheon as I was leaving. I went back into his office with him for a couple of minutes.

"Did you see Pangburn?" he asked.

"Yes. I'm working on his job now—but I think it's a bust."

"What is it?"

"Pangburn is R. F. Axford's brother-in-law. He met a girl a couple of months ago, and fell for her. She sizes up as a worker. He doesn't know anything about her. The first of the month he got twenty thousand dollars from his brother-in-law and passed it over to the girl. She blew, telling him she had been called to Baltimore, and giving him a phony address that turns out to be an orphan asylum. She sent her trunks to Baltimore, and sent him some letters from there—but a friend could have taken care of the baggage and could have remailed her letters for her. Of course, she would have needed a ticket to check the trunks on, but in a twenty-thousand-dollar game that would be a small expense. Pangburn held out on me; he didn't tell me a word about the money. Ashamed of being easy pickings, I reckon. I'm going to the bat with him on it now."

The Old Man smiled his mild smile that might mean anything, and I left.

Ten minutes of ringing Pangburn's bell brought no answer. The elevator boy told me he thought Pangburn hadn't been in all night. I put a note in his box and went down to the railroad company's offices, where I arranged to be notified if an unused Baltimore-San Francisco ticket was turned in for redemption.

That done, I went up to the *Chronicle* office and searched the files for weather conditions during the past month, making a memorandum of four dates upon which it had rained steadily day and night. I carried my memorandum to the offices of the three largest taxicab companies.

That was a trick that had worked well for me before. The girl's apartment was some distance from the street car line, and I was counting upon her having gone out—or having had a caller—on one of those rainy dates. In either case, it was very likely that she —or her caller—had left in a taxi in preference to walking through the rain to the car line. The taxicab companies' daily records would show any calls from her address, and the fares' destinations.

The ideal trick, of course, would have been to have the records searched for the full extent of the girl's occupancy of the apartment; but no taxicab company would stand for having that amount of work thrust upon them, unless it was a matter of life and death. It was difficult enough for me to persuade them to turn clerks loose on the four days I had selected.

I called up Pangburn again after I left that last taxicab office, but he was not at home. I called up Axford's residence, thinking that the poet might have spent the night there, but was told that he had not.

Late that afternoon I got my copies of the girl's photograph and handwriting, and put one of each in the mail for Baltimore. Then I went around to the three taxicab companies' offices and got my reports. Two of them had nothing for me. The third's records showed two calls from the girl's apartment.

On one rainy afternoon a taxi had been called, and one passenger had been taken to the Glenton Apartments. That passenger, obviously, was either the girl or Pangburn. At half-past twelve one night another call had come in, and this passenger had been taken to the Marquis Hotel.

The driver who had answered this second call remembered it indistinctly when I questioned him, but he thought that his fare had been a man. I let the matter rest there for the time; the Marquis isn't a large hotel as San Francisco hotels go, but it is too large to make canvassing its guests for the one I wanted practicable.

I spent the evening trying to reach Pangburn, with no success. At eleven o'clock I called up Axford, and asked him if he had any idea where I might find his brother-in-law.

"Haven't seen him for several days," the millionaire said. "He was supposed to come up for dinner last night, but didn't. My wife tried to reach him by phone a couple times today, but couldn't."

The next morning I called Pangburn's apartment before I got out of bed, and got no answer.

Then I telephoned Axford and made an appointment for ten o'clock at his office.

"I don't know what he's up to now," Axford said good-naturedly when I told him that Pangburn had apparently been away from his apartment since Sunday, "and I suppose there's small chance of guessing. Our Burke is nothing if not erratic. How are you progressing with your search for the damsel in distress?"

"Far enough to convince me that she isn't in a whole lot of distress. She got twenty thousand dollars from your brother-in-law the day before she vanished."

"Twenty thousand dollars from Burke? She must be a wonderful girl! But wherever did he get that much money?"

"From you."

Axford's muscular body straightened in his chair. "From me?"

"Yes—your check."

"He did not."

There was nothing argumentative in his voice; it simply stated a fact.

"You didn't give him a check for twenty thousand dollars on the first of the month?"

"No."

"Then," I suggested, "perhaps we'd better take a run over to the Golden Gate Trust Company."

Ten minutes later we were in Clement's office.

"I'd like to see my canceled checks," Axford told the cashier.

The youth with the polished yellow hair brought them in presently—a thick wad of them—and Axford ran rapidly through them until he found the one he wanted. He studied that one for a long while, and when he looked up at me he shook his head slowly but with finality.

"I've never seen it before."

Clement mopped his head with a white handkerchief, and tried to pretend that he wasn't burning up with curiosity and fears that his bank had been gypped.

The millionaire turned the check over and looked at the endorsement.

"Deposited by Burke," he said in the voice of one who talks while he thinks of something entirely different, "on the first."

"Could we talk to the teller who took in the twenty-thousand-dollar check that Miss Delano deposited?" I asked Clément.

He pressed one of his desk's pearl buttons with a fumbling pink finger, and in a minute or two a little sallow man with a hairless head came in.

"Do you remember taking a check for twenty thousand from Miss Jeanne Delano a few weeks ago?" I asked him.

"Yes, sir! Yes, sir! Perfectly."

"Just what do you remember about it?"

"Well, sir, Miss Delano came to my window with Mr. Burke Pangburn. It was his check. I thought it was a large check for him to be drawing, but the book-keepers said he had enough money in his account to cover it. They stood there—Miss Delano and Mr. Pangburn—talking and laughing while I entered the deposit in her book, and then they left, and that was all."

"This check," Axford said slowly, after the teller had gone back to his cage, "is a forgery. But I shall make it good, of course. That ends the matter, Mr. Clement, and there must be no more to-do about it."

"Certainly, Mr. Axford. Certainly."

Clement was all enormously relieved smiles and head-noddings, with this twenty-thousand-dollar load lifted from his bank's shoulders.

Axford and I left the bank then and got into his coupé, in which we had come from his office. But he did not immediately start the engine. He sat for a while staring at the traffic of Montgomery Street with unsee-ing eyes.

"I want you to find Burke," he said presently, and there was no emotion of any sort in his bass voice. "I want you to find him without risking the least whisper of scandal. If my wife knew of all this— She mustn't know. She thinks her brother is a choice morsel. I want you to find him for me. The girl doesn't matter any more, but I suppose that where you find one you will find the other. I'm not interested in the money, and I don't want you to make any special attempt to recover

143

that; it could hardly be done, I'm afraid, without publicity. I want you to find Burke before he does something else."

"If you want to avoid the wrong kind of publicity," I said, "your best bet is to spread the right kind first. Let's advertise him as missing, fill the papers up with his pictures and so forth. They'll play him up strong. He's your brother-in-law and he's a poet. We can say that he has been ill—you told me that he had been in delicate health all his life—and that we fear he has dropped dead somewhere or is suffering under some mental derangement. There will be no necessity of mentioning the girl or the money, and our explanation may keep people—especially your wife—from guessing the truth when the fact that he is missing leaks out. It's bound to leak out somehow."

He didn't like my idea at first, but I finally won him over.

We went up to Pangburn's apartment then, easily securing admittance on Axford's explanation that we had an engagement with him and would wait there for him. I went through the rooms inch by inch, prying into each hole and hollow and crack; reading everything that was written anywhere, even down to his manuscripts; and I found nothing that threw any light on his disappearance.

I helped myself to his photographs—pocketing five of the dozen or more that were there. Axford did not think that any of the poet's bags or trunks were missing from the pack-room. I did not find his Golden Gate Trust Company deposit book.

I spent the rest of the day loading the newspapers up with what we wished them to have; and they gave my ex-client one grand spread: first-page stuff with photographs and all possible trimmings. Anyone in San Francisco who didn't know that Burke Pangburn—brother-in-law of R. F. Axford and author of *Sandpatches and Other Verse*—was missing, either couldn't read or wouldn't.

This advertising brought results. By the following morning, reports were rolling in from all directions, from dozens of people who had seen the missing poet in dozens of places. A few of these reports looked promising—or at least possible—but the majority were ridiculous on their faces.

I came back to the agency from running out one that had—until run out—looked good, to find a note asking me to call up Axford.

"Can you come down to my office now?" he asked when I got him on the wire.

There was a lad of twenty-one or -two with Axford when I was ushered into his office: a narrow-chested, dandified lad of the sporting clerk type.

"This is Mr. Fall, one of my employees," Axford told me. "He says he saw Burke Sunday night."

"Where?" I asked Fall.

"Going into a roadhouse near Halfmoon Bay."

"Sure it was him?"

"Absolutely! I've seen him come in here to Mr. Axford's office often enough to know him. It was him all right."

"How'd you come to see him?"

"I was coming up from further down the shore with some friends, and we stopped in at the roadhouse to get something to eat. As we were leaving, a car drove up and Mr. Pangburn and a girl or woman—I didn't notice her particularly—got out and went inside. I didn't think anything of it until I saw in the paper last night that he hadn't been seen since Sunday. So then I thought to myself that—"

"What roadhouse was this?" I cut in.

"The White Shack."

"About what time?"

"Somewhere between eleven-thirty and midnight, I guess."

"He see you?"

"No. I was already in our car when he drove up."

"What did the woman look like?"

"I don't know. I didn't see her face, and I can't remember how she was dressed or even if she was short or tall."

That was all Fall could tell me. We shooed him out of the office, and I used Axford's telephone to call up "Wop" Healey's dive in North Beach and leave word that when "Porky" Grout came in he was to call up "Jack." That was a standing arrangement by which I got word to Porky whenever I wanted to see him, without giving anybody a chance to tumble to the connection between us.

"Know the White Shack?" I asked Axford, when I was through.

"I know where it is, but I don't know anything about it."

"Well, it's a tough hole. Run by 'Tin-Star' Joplin, an ex-yegg who invested his winnings in the place when Prohibition made the roadhouse game good. He makes more money now than he ever heard of in his piking safe-ripping days. Retailing liquor is a side-line with him; his real profit comes from acting as a relay station for the booze that comes through Halfmoon Bay for points beyond; and the dope is that half the booze put ashore by the Pacific rum fleet is put ashore in Halfmoon Bay.

"The White Shack is a tough hole, and it's no place for your brother-in-law to be hanging around. I can't go down there myself without stirring things up; Joplin and I are old friends. But I've got a man I can put in there for a few nights. Pangburn may be a regular visitor, or he may even be staying there. He wouldn't be the first one Joplin had ever let hide out there. I'll put this man of mine in the place for a week, anyway, and see what he can find."

"It's all in your hands," Axford said.

From Axford's office I went straight to my rooms, left the outer door unlocked, and sat down to wait for Porky Grout. I had waited an hour and a half when he pushed the door open and came in. "'Lo! How's tricks?" He swaggered to a chair, leaned back in it, put his feet on the table and reached for a pack of cigarettes that lay there.

That was Porky Grout. A pasty-faced man in his thirties, neither large nor small, always dressed flashily —even if sometimes dirtily—and trying to hide an enormous cowardice behind a swaggering carriage, a blustering habit of speech, and an exaggerated pretense of self-assurance.

But I had known him for three years; so now I crossed the room and pushed his feet roughly off the table, almost sending him over backward.

"What's the idea?" He came to his feet, crouching and snarling. "Where do you get that stuff? Do you want a smack in the——"

I took a step toward him. He sprang away, across the room.

"Aw, I didn't mean nothin'. I was only kiddin'!"

"Shut up and sit down," I advised him.

I had known this Porky Grout for three years, and had been using him for nearly that long, and I didn't know a single thing that could be said in his favor. He was a coward. He was a liar. He was a thief, and a hop-head. He was a traitor to his kind and, if not watched, to his employers. A nice bird to deal with! But detecting is a hard business, and you use whatever tools come to hand. This Porky was an effective tool if handled right, which meant keeping your hand on his throat all the time and checking up every piece of information he brought in.

His cowardice was—for my purpose—his greatest asset. It was notorious throughout the criminal Coast; and though nobody—crook or not—could possibly think him a man to be trusted, nevertheless he was not actually distrusted. Most of his fellows thought him too much the coward to be dangerous; they thought he would be afraid to betray them; afraid of the summary vengeance that crookdom visits upon the squealer. But they didn't take into account Porky's gift for convincing himself that he was a lion-hearted fellow, when no danger was near. So he went freely where he desired and where I sent him, and brought me otherwise unobtainable bits of information.

For nearly three years I had used him with considerable success, paying him well, and keeping him under my heel. *Informant* was the polite word that designated him in my reports; the underworld has even less lovely names than the common *stool-pigeon* to denote his kind.

"I have a job for you," I told him, now that he was seated again, with his feet on the floor. His loose mouth twitched up at the left corner, pushing that eye into a knowing squint. "I thought so." He always says something like that.

"I want you to go down to Halfmoon Bay and stick around Tin-Star Joplin's joint for a few nights. Here are two photos"—sliding one of Pangburn and one of the girl across the table. "Their names and descriptions are written on the backs. I want to know if either of them shows up down there, what they're doing, and where they're hanging out. It may be that Tin-Star is covering them up."

Porky was looking knowingly from one picture to the other. "I think I know this guy," he said out of the corner of his mouth that twitches. That's another thing about Porky. You can't mention a name or give a description that won't bring that same remark, even though you make them up.

"Here's some money." I slid some bills across the table. "If you're down there more than a couple of nights, I'll get some more to you. Keep in touch with me, either over this phone or the under-cover one at the office. And—remember this—lay off the stuff! If I come down there and find you all snowed up, I promise that I'll tip Joplin off to you."

He had finished counting the money by now—there wasn't a whole lot to count—and he threw it contemptuously back on the table.

"Save that for newspapers," he sneered. "How am I goin' to get anywheres if I can't spend no money in the joint?"

"That's plenty for a couple of days' expenses; you'll probably knock back half of it. If you stay longer than a couple of days, I'll get more to you. And you get your pay when the job is done, and not before."

He shook his head and got up. "I'm tired of pikin' along with you. You can turn your own jobs. I'm through!"

"If you don't get down to Halfmoon Bay tonight, you *are* through," I assured him, letting him get out of the threat whatever he liked.

After a little while, of course, he took the money and left. The dispute over expense money was simply a preliminary that went with every job I sent him out on.

After Porky had cleared out, I leaned back in my chair and burned half a dozen Fatimas over the job. The girl had gone first with the twenty thousand dollars, and then the poet had gone; and both had gone, whether permanently or not, to the White Shack. On its face, the job was an obvious affair. The girl had given Pangburn the *work* to the extent of having him forge a check against his brother-in-law's account; and then, after various moves whose value I couldn't determine at the time, they had gone into hiding together.

There were two loose ends to be taken care of. One of them—the finding of the confederate who had mailed the letters to Pangburn and who had taken care of the girl's baggage—was in the Baltimore branch's hands. The other was: Who had ridden in the taxicab that I had traced from the girl's apartment to the Marquis Hotel?

That might not have any bearing upon the job, or it might. Suppose I could find a connection between the Marquis Hotel and the White Shack. That would make a completed chain of some sort. I searched the back of the telephone directory and found the roadhouse number. Then I went up to the Marquis Hotel. The girl on duty at the hotel switchboard, when I got there, was one with whom I had done business before. "Who's been calling Halfmoon Bay numbers?" I asked her.

"My God!" She leaned back in her chair and ran a pink hand gently over the front of her rigidly waved red hair. "I got enough to do without remembering every call that goes through. This ain't a boarding-house. We have more'n one call a week."

"You don't have many Halfmoon Bay calls," I insisted, leaning an elbow on the counter and letting a folded five-spot peep out between the fingers of one hand. "You ought to remember any you've had lately."

"I'll see," she sighed, as if willing to do her best on a hopeless task.

She ran through her tickets.

"Here's one—from room 522, a couple weeks ago."

"What number was called?"

"Halfmoon Bay 51."

That was the roadhouse number. I passed over the five-spot.

"Is 522 a permanent guest?"

"Yes. Mr. Kilcourse. He's been here three or four months."

"What is he?"

"I don't know. A perfect gentleman, if you ask me."

"That's nice. What does he look like?"

"He's a young man, but his hair is turning gray. He's dark and handsome. Looks like a movie actor."

"Bull Montana?" I asked, as I moved off toward the desk.

The key to 522 was in its place in the rack. I sat down where I could keep an eye on it. Perhaps an hour later a clerk took it out and gave it to a man who did look somewhat like an actor. He was a man of thirty or so, with dark skin, and dark hair that showed gray around the ears. He stood a good six feet of fashionably dressed slenderness.

Carrying the key, he disappeared into an elevator.

I called up the agency then and asked the Old Man to send Dick Foley over. Ten minutes later Dick arrived. He's a little shrimp of a Canadian—there isn't a hundred and ten pounds of him—who is the smoothest shadow I've ever seen, and I've seen most of them.

"I have a bird in here I want tailed," I told Dick. "His name is Kilcourse and he's in room 522. Stick around outside, and I'll give you the spot on him. I went back to the lobby and waited some more.

At eight o'clock Kilcourse came down and left the hotel. I went after him for half a block—far enough to turn him over to Dick—and then went home, so that I would be within reach of a telephone if Porky Grout tried to get in touch with me. No call came from him that night.

When I arrived at the agency the next morning, Dick was waiting for me. "What luck?" I asked.

"Damnedest!" The little Canadian talks like a telegram when his peace of mind is disturbed, and just now he was decidedly peevish. "Took me two blocks. Shook me. Only taxi in sight."

"Think he made you?"

"No. Wise head. Playing safe."

"Try him again, then. Better have a car handy, in case he tries the same trick again."

My telephone jingled as Dick was going out. It was Porky Grout, talking over the agency's unlisted line. "Turn up anything?" I asked.

"Plenty," he bragged.

"Good! Are you in town?"

"Yes."

"I'll meet you in my rooms in twenty minutes," I said.

The pasty-faced informant was fairly bloated with pride in himself when he came through the door I had left unlocked for him. His swagger was almost a cake-walk; and the side of his mouth that twitches was twisted into a knowing leer that would have fit a Solomon.

"I knocked it over for you, kid," he boasted. "Nothin' to it—for me! I went down there and talked to ever'body that knowed anything, seen ever'thing there was to see, and put the X-rays on the whole dump. I made a—"

"Uh-huh," I interrupted. "Congratulations and so forth. But just what did you turn up?"

"Now le'me tell you." He raised a dirty hand in a traffic-cop sort of gesture. "Don't crowd me. I'll give you all the dope."

"Sure," I said. "I know. You're great, and I'm lucky to have you to knock off my jobs for me, and all that! But is Pangburn down there?"

"I'm gettin' around to that. I went down there and—"

"Did you see Pangburn?"

"As I was sayin', I went down there and—"

"Porky," I said, "I don't give a damn what you did! Did you see Pangburn?"

"Yes. I seen him."

"Fine! Now what did you see?"

"He's camping down there with Tin-Star. Him and the broad that you give me a picture of are both there. She's been there a month. I didn't see her, but one of the waiters told me about her. I seen Pangburn myself. They don't show themselves much—stick back in Tin-Star's part of the joint—where he lives—most of the time. Pangburn's been there since Sunday. I went down there and—"

"Learn who the girl is? Or anything about what they're up to?"

"No. I went down there and—"

"All right! *Went down there* again tonight. Call me up as soon as you know positively Pangburn is there—that he hasn't gone out. Don't make any mistakes. I don't want to come down there and scare them up on a false alarm. Use the agency's under-cover line, and just tell whoever answers that you won't be in town until late. That'll mean that Pangburn is there; and it'll let you call up from Joplin's without giving the play away."

"I got to have more dough," he said, as he got up. "It costs—"

"I'll file your application," I promised. "Now beat it, and let me hear from you tonight, the minute you're sure Pangburn is there."

Then I went up to Axford's office. "I think I have a line on him," I told the millionaire. "I hope to have him where you can talk to him tonight. My man says he was at the White Shack last night, and is probably living there. If he's there tonight, I'll take you down, if you want."

"Why can't we go now?"

"No. The place is too dead in the daytime for my man to hang around without making himself conspicuous, and I don't want to take any chances on either you or me showing ourselves there until we're sure we're coming face to face with Pangburn."

"What do you want me to do then?"

"Have a fast car ready tonight, and be ready to start as soon as I get word to you."

"Righto. I'll be at home after five-thirty. Phone me as soon as you're ready to go, and I'll pick you up."

At nine-thirty that evening I was sitting beside Axford

on the front seat of a powerfully engined foreign car, and we were roaring down a road that led to Halfmoon Bay. Porky's telephone call had come.

Neither of us talked much during that ride, and the imported monster under us made it a short ride. Axford sat comfortable and relaxed at the wheel, but I noticed for the first time that he had a rather heavy jaw.

The White Shack is a large building, square-built of imitation stone. It is set away back from the road, and is approached by two curving driveways, which, together, make a semi-circle whose diameter is the public road. The center of this semi-circle is occupied by sheds under which Joplin's patrons stow their cars, and here and there around the sheds are flower-beds and clumps of shrubbery. We were still going at a fair clip when we turned into one end of this semi-circular driveway, and—

Axford slammed on his brakes, and the big machine threw us into the windsheld as it jolted into an abrupt stop—barely in time to avoid smashing into a cluster of people who had suddenly loomed up.

In the glow from our headlights faces stood sharply out; white, horrified faces, furtive faces, faces that were callously curious. Below the faces, white arms and shoulders showed, and bright gowns and jewelry, against the duller background of masculine clothing.

This was the first impression I got, and then, by the time I had removed my face from the windshield, I realized that this cluster of people had a core, a thing about which it centered. I stood up, trying to look over the crowd's heads, but I could see nothing.

Jumping down to the driveway, I pushed through the crowd.

Face down on the white gravel a man sprawled—a

thin man in dark clothes—and just above his collar, where the head and neck join, was a hole. I knelt to peer into his face. Then I pushed through the crowd again, back to where Axford was just getting out of the car, the engine of which was still running, "Pangburn is dead—shot!"

Methodically, Axford took off his gloves, folded them and put them in a pocket. Then he nodded his understanding of what I had told him, and walked toward where the crowd stood around the dead poet. I looked after him until he had vanished in the throng. Then I went winding through the outskirts of the crowd, hunting for Porky Grout.

I found him standing on the porch, leaning against a pillar. I passed where he could see me, and went on around to the side of the roadhouse that afforded most shadow.

In the shadows Porky joined me. The night wasn't cool, but his teeth were chattering. "Who got him?" I demanded.

"I don't know," he whined, and that was the first thing of which I had ever known him to confess complete ignorance. "I was inside, keepin' an eye on the others."

"What others?"

"Tin-Star, and some guy I never seen before, and the broad. I didn't think the kid was going out. He didn't have no hat."

"What *do* you know about it?"

"A little while after I phoned you, the girl and Pangburn came out from Joplin's part of the joint and sat down at a table around on the other side of the porch, where it's fairly dark. They eat for a while and then this other guy comes over and sits down with 'em. I don't know his name, but I think I've saw him around town. He's a tall guy, in fancy rags."

That would be Kilcourse.

"They talk for a while and then Joplin joins 'em. They sit around the table laughin' and talkin' for maybe a quarter of a hour. Then Pangburn gets up and goes indoors. I got a table that I can watch 'em from, and the place is crowded, and I'm afraid I'll lose my table if I leave it, so I don't follow the kid. He ain't got no hat; I figure he ain't goin' nowhere. But he must of gone through the house and out front, because pretty soon there's a noise that I thought was a auto backfire, and then the sound of a car gettin' away quick. And then some guy squawks that there's a dead man outside. Ever'body runs out here, and it's Pangburn."

"You dead sure that Joplin, Kilcourse and the girl were all at the table when Pangburn was killed?"

"Absolutely," Porky said, "if this dark guy's name is Kilcourse."

"Where are they now?"

"Back in Joplin's hang-out. They went up there as soon as they seen Pangburn had been croaked."

I had no illusions about Porky. I knew he was capable of selling me out and furnishing the poet's murderer with an alibi. But there was this about it: if Joplin, Kilcourse or the girl had fixed him, and had fixed my informant, then it was hopeless for me to try to prove that they weren't on the rear porch when the shot was fired. Joplin had a crowd of hangers-on who would swear to anything he told them without batting an eye. There would be a dozen supposed witnesses to their presence on the rear porch.

Thus the only thing for me to do was to take it for

granted that Porky was coming clean with me. "Have you see Dick Foley?" I asked, since Dick had been shadowing Kilcourse.

"No."

"Hunt around and see if you can find him. Tell him I've gone up to talk to Joplin, and tell him to come on up. Then you can stick around where I can get hold of you if I want you."

I went in through a French window, crossed an empty dance-floor and went up the stairs that led to Tin-Star Joplin's living quarters in the rear second story. I knew the way, having been up there before. Joplin and I were old friends.

I was going up now to give him and his friends a shake-down on the off-chance that some good might come of it, though I knew that I had nothing on any of them. I could have tied something on the girl, of course, but not without advertising the fact that the dead poet had forged his brother-in-law's signature to a check. And that was no go.

"Come in," a heavy, familiar voice called when I rapped on Joplin's living-room door. I pushed the door open and went in.

Tin-Star Joplin was standing in the middle of the floor: a big-bodied ex-yegg with inordinately thick shoulders and an expressionless horse face. Beyond him Kilcourse sat dangling one leg from the corner of a table, alertness hiding behind an amused half-smile on his handsome dark face. On the other side of the room a girl whom I knew for Jeanne Delano sat on the arm of a big leather chair. And the poet hadn't exaggerated when he told me she was beautiful.

"You!" Joplin grunted disgustedly as soon as he recognized me. "What the hell do *you* want?"

"What've you got?"

My mind wasn't on this sort of repartee, however; I was studying the girl. There was something vaguely familiar about her—but I couldn't place her. Perhaps I hadn't seen her before; perhaps much looking at the picture Pangburn had given me was responsible for my feeling of recognition. Pictures will do that.

Meanwhile, Joplin had said: "Time to waste is one thing I ain't got."

And I had said: "If you'd saved up all the time different judges have given you, you'd have plenty."

I had seen the girl somewhere before. She was a slender girl in a glistening blue gown that exhibited a generous spread of front, back and arms that were worth showing. She had a mass of dark brown hair above an oval face of the color that pink ought to be. Her eyes were wide-set and a gray shade that wasn't altogether unlike the shadows on polished silver that the poet had compared them to. I studied the girl, and she looked back at me with level eyes, and still I couldn't place her. Kilcourse still sat dangling a leg from the table corner.

Joplin grew impatient. "Will you stop gandering at the girl, and tell me what you want of me?" he growled.

The girl smiled then, a mocking smile that bared the edges of razor-sharp little animal-teeth. And with the smile I knew her!

Her hair and skin had fooled me. The last time I had seen her—the only time I had seen her before—her face had been marble-white, and her hair had been short and the color of fire. She and an older woman and three men and I had played hide-and-seek one evening in a house in Turk Street over a matter of the murder of a bank messenger and the theft of a hundred thousand dollars' worth of Liberty Bonds. Through her intriguing three of her accomplices had died that evening, and the fourth—the Chinese—had eventually gone to the gallows at Folsom Prison. Her name had been Elvira then, and since her escape from the house that night we had been fruitlessly hunting her from border to border, and beyond.

Recognition must have shown in my eyes in spite of the effort I made to keep them blank, for, swift as a snake, she had left the arm of the chair and was coming forward, her eyes more steel than silver.

I put my gun in sight.

Joplin took a half-step toward me. "What's the idea?" he barked.

Kilcourse slid off the table, and one of his thin dark hands hovered over his necktie.

"This is the idea," I told them. "I want the girl for a murder a couple months back, and maybe—I'm not sure —for tonight's. Anyway, I'm—"

The snapping of a light-switch behind me, and the room went black.

I moved, not caring where I went so long as I got away from where I had been when the lights went out.

My back touched a wall and I stopped, crouching low.

"Quick, kid!" A hoarse whisper that came from where I thought the door should be.

But both of the room's doors, I thought, were closed, and could hardly be opened without showing gray rectangles. People moved in the blackness, but none got between me and the lighter square of windows.

Something clicked softly in front of me—too thin a click for the cocking of a gun—but it could have been the opening of a spring-knife, and I remembered that Tin-Star Joplin had a fondness for that weapon.

"Let's go!" A harsh whisper that cut through the dark like a blow.

Sounds of motion, muffled, indistinguishable . . . one sound not far away . . .

Abruptly a strong hand clamped one of my shoulders, a hard-muscled body strained against me. I stabbed out with my gun, and heard a grunt.

The hand moved up my shoulder toward my throat.

I snapped up a knee, and heard another grunt.

A burning point ran down my side.

I stabbed again with my gun—pulled it back until the muzzle was free of the soft obstacle that had stopped it, and squeezed the trigger. The crash of the shot. Joplin's voice in my ear, a curiously matter-of-fact voice: "God damn! That got me."

I spun away from him then, toward where I saw the dim yellow of an open door. I had heard no sounds of departure. I had been too busy. But I knew that Joplin had tied into me while the others made their get-away.

Nobody was in sight as I jumped, slid, tumbled down the steps—any number at a time. A waiter got in my path as I plunged toward the dance-floor. I don't know whether his interference was intentional or not. I didn't ask. I slammed the flat of my gun in his face and went on. Once I jumped a leg that came out to trip me; and at the outer door I had to smear another face.

Then I was out in the semi-circular driveway, from one end of which a red tail-light was turning east into the country road.

While I sprinted for Axford's car I noticed that Pangburn's body had been removed. A few people still stood around the spot where he had lain, and they gaped at me now with open mouths.

The car was as Axford had left it, with idling engine. I swung it through a flower-bed and pointed it east on the public road. Five minutes later I picked up the red point of a tail-light again.

The car under me had more power than I would ever need, more than I would have known how to handle. I don't know how fast the one ahead was going, but I closed in as if it had been standing still.

A mile and a half, or perhaps two—

Suddenly a man was in the road ahead—a little beyond the reach of my lights. The lights caught him, and I saw that it was Porky Grout!

Porky Grout standing facing me in the middle of the road, the dull metal of an automatic in each hand.

The guns in his hands seemed to glow dimly red and then go dark in the glare of my headlights—glow and then go dark, like two bulbs in an automatic electric sign.

The windshield fell apart around me.

Porky Grout—the informant whose name was a synonym for cowardice the full length of the Pacific Coast— stood in the center of the road shooting at a metal comet that rushed down upon him. . . .

I didn't see the end.

I confess frankly that I shut my eyes when his set white face showed close over my radiator. The metal monster under me trembled—not very much—and the road ahead was empty except for the fleeing red light. My windshield was gone. The wind tore at my uncovered hair and brought tears to my squinted-up eyes.

Presently I found that I was talking to myself, saying, "That was Porky. That was Porky." It was an amazing fact. It was no surprise that he had double-crossed me. That was to be expected. And for him to have crept up the stairs behind me and turned off the lights wasn't astonishing. But for him to have stood straight up and died—

An orange streak from the car ahead cut off my wonderment. The bullet didn't come near me—it isn't easy to shoot accurately from one moving car into another— but at the pace I was going it wouldn't be long before I was close enough for good shooting.

I turned on the searchlight above the dashboard. It didn't quite reach the car ahead, but it enabled me to see that the girl was driving. While Kilcourse sat screwed around beside her, facing me. The car was a yellow roadster.

I eased up a little. In a duel with Kilcourse here I would have been at a disadvantage, since I would have had to drive as well as shoot. My best play seemed to be to hold my distance until we reached a town, as we inevitably must. It wasn't midnight yet. There would be people on the streets of any town, and policemen. Then I could close in with a better chance of coming off on top.

A few miles of this and my prey tumbled to my plan. The yellow roadster slowed down, wavered, and came to rest with its length across the road. Kilcourse and the girl were out immediately and crouching in the road on the far side of their barricade.

I was tempted to dive pell-mell into them, but it was a weak temptation, and when its short life had passed I put on the brakes and stopped. Then I fiddled with my searchlight until it bore full upon the roadster.

A flash came from somewhere near the roadster's wheels, and the searchlight shook violently, but the glass wasn't touched. It would be their first target, of course, and . . .

Crouching in my car, waiting for the bullet that would smash the lens, I took off my shoes and overcoat.

The third bullet ruined the light.

I switched off the other lights, jumped to the road, and when I stopped running I was squatting down against the near side of the yellow roadster. As easy and safe a trick as can be imagined.

The girl and Kilcourse had been looking into the glare of a powerful light. When that light suddenly died, and the weaker ones around it went, too, they were left in pitch unseeing blackness, which must last for the minute or longer that their eyes would need to readjust themselves to the gray-black of the night. My stockinged feet had made no sound on the macadam road, and now there was only a roadster between us; and I knew it and they didn't.

From near the radiator Kilcourse spoke softly:

"I'm going to try to knock him off from the ditch. Take a shot at him now and then to keep him busy."

"I can't see him," the girl protested.

"Your eyes'll be all right in a second. Take a shot at the car anyway."

I moved toward the radiator as the girl's pistol barked at the empty touring car.

Kilcourse, on hands and knees, was working his way toward the ditch that ran along the south side of the road. I gathered my legs under me, intent upon a spring and a blow with my gun upon the back of his head. I didn't want to kill him, but I wanted to put him out of the way quick. I'd have the girl to take care of, and she was at least as dangerous as he.

As I tensed for the spring, Kilcourse, guided perhaps by some instinct of the hunted, turned his head and saw me—saw a threatening shadow.

Instead of jumping I fired.

I didn't look to see whether I had hit him or not. At that range there was little likelihood of missing. I bent double and slipped back to the rear of the roadster, keeping on my side of it. Then I waited.

The girl did what I would perhaps have done in her place. She didn't shoot or move toward the place the shot had come from. She thought I had forestalled Kilcourse in using the ditch and that my next play would be to circle around behind her. To offset this, she moved around the rear of the roadster, so that she could ambush me from the side nearest Axford's car.

Thus it was that she came creeping around the corner and poked her delicately chiseled nose plunk into the muzzle of the gun that I held ready for her.

She gave a little scream.

Women aren't always reasonable: they are prone to disregard trifles like guns held upon them. So I grabbed her gun hand, which was fortunate for me. As my hand closed around the weapon, she pulled the trigger, catching a chunk of my forefinger between hammer and frame. I twisted the gun out of her hand; released my finger.

But she wasn't done yet. With me standing there holding a gun not four inches from her body, she turned and bolted off toward where a clump of trees made a jet-black blot to the north.

When I recovered from my surprise at this amateurish procedure, I stuck both her gun and mine in my pockets, and set out after her, tearing the soles of my feet at every step.

She was trying to get over a wire fence when I caught her.

"Stop playing, will you?" I said crossly, as I set the

fingers of my left hand around her wrist and started to lead her back to the roadster. "This is a serious business. Don't be so childish!"

"You are hurting my arm."

I knew I wasn't hurting her arm, and I knew this girl for the direct cause of four, or perhaps five, deaths; yet I loosened my grip on her wrist until it wasn't much more than a friendly clasp. She went back willingly enough to the roadster, where, still holding her wrist, I switched on the lights. Kilcourse lay just beneath the headlight's glare, huddled on his face, with one knee drawn up under him.

I put the girl squarely in the line of light.

"Now stand there," I said, "and behave. The first break you make, I'm going to shoot a leg out from under you," and I meant it.

I found Kilcourse's gun, pocketed it, and knelt beside him.

He was dead, with a bullet-hole above his collar-bone.

"Is he—" her mouth trembled.

"Yes."

She looked down at him, and shivered a little.

"Poor Fag," she whispered.

I've gone on record as saying that this girl was beautiful, and, standing there in the dazzling white of the headlights, she was more than that. She was a thing to start crazy thoughts even in the head of an unimaginative middle-aged thief-catcher. She was—

Anyhow, I suppose that is why I scowled at her and said:

"Yes, poor Fag, and poor Hook, and poor Tai, and poor kind of a Los Angeles bank messenger, and poor Burke," calling the roll, so far as I knew it, of men who had died loving her.

She didn't flare up. Her big gray eyes lifted, and she looked at me with a gaze that I couldn't fathom, and her lovely oval face under the mass of brown hair—which I knew was phony—was sad.

"I suppose you do think—" she began.

But I had had enough of this; I was uncomfortable along the spine.

"Come on," I said. "We'll leave Kilcourse and the roadster here for now."

She said nothing, but went with me to Axford's big machine, and sat in silence while I laced my shoes. I found a robe on the back seat for her.

"Better wrap this around your shoulders. The windshield is gone. It'll be cool."

She followed my suggestion without a word, but when I had edged our vehicle around the rear of the roadster, and had straightened out in the road again, going east, she laid a hand on my arm.

"Aren't we going back to the White Shack?"

"No. Redwood City—the county jail."

A mile perhaps, during which, without looking at her, I knew she was studying my rather lumpy profile. Then her hand was on my forearm again and she was leaning toward me so that her breath was warm against my cheek. "Will you stop for a minute? There's something —some things I want to tell you."

I brought the car to a halt in a cleared space of hard soil off to one side of the road, and screwed myself a little around in the seat to face her more directly.

"Before you start," I told her, "I want you to understand that we stay here for just so long as you talk about the Pangburn affair. When you get off on any other line —then we finish our trip to Redwood City."

"Aren't you even interested in the Los Angeles affair?"

"No. That's closed. You and Hook Riordan and Tai Choon Tau and the Quarres were equally responsible for the messenger's death, even if Hook did the actual killing. Hook and the Quarres passed out the night we had our party in Turk Street. Tai was hanged last month. Now I've got you. We had enough evidence to swing the Chinese, and we've even more against you. That is done —finished—completed. If you want to tell me anything about Pangburn's death, I'll listen. Otherwise—"

I reached for the self-starter.

A pressure of her fingers on my arm stopped me.

"I do want to tell you about it," she said earnestly. "I want you to know the truth about it. You'll take me to Redwood City, I know. Don't think that I expect— that I have any foolish hopes. But I'd like you to know the truth about this thing. I don't know why I should care especially what you think, but—"

Her voice dwindled off to nothing.

Then she began to talk very rapidly—as people talk when they fear interruptions before their stories are told —and she sat leaning slightly forward, so that her beautiful oval face was very close to mine.

"After I ran out of the Turk Street house that night— while you were struggling with Tai—my intention was to get away from San Francisco. I had a couple of thousand dollars, enough to carry me any place. Then I thought that going away would be what you people would expect me to do, and that the safest thing for me to do would be to stay right here. It isn't hard for a woman to change her appearance. I had bobbed red hair, white skin, and wore gay clothes. I simply dyed my hair, bought these transformations to make it look long, put color on my face, and bought some dark clothes. Then I took an apartment on Ashbury Avenue under the name of Jeanne Delano, and I was an altogether different person.

"But, while I knew I was perfectly safe from recognition anywhere, I felt more comfortable staying indoors for a while, and, to pass the time, I read a good deal. That's how I happened to run across Burke's book. Do you read poetry?"

I shook my head. An automobile going toward Halfmoon Bay came into sight just then—the first one we'd seen since we left the White Shack. She waited until it had passed before she went on, still talking rapidly.

"Burke wasn't a genius, of course, but there was something about some of his things that—something that got inside me. I wrote him a little note, telling him how much I had enjoyed these things, and sent it to his publishers. A few days later I had a note from Burke, and I learned that he lived in San Francisco. I hadn't known that.

"We exchanged several notes, and then he asked if he could call, and we met. I don't know whether I was in love with him or not, even at first. I did like him, and, between the ardor of his love for me and the flattery of having a fairly well-known poet for a suitor, I really thought that I loved him. I promised to marry him.

"I hadn't told him anything about myself, though now I know that it wouldn't have made any difference to him. But I was afraid to tell him the truth, and I wouldn't lie to him, so I told him nothing.

"Then Fag Kilcourse saw me one day on the street, and knew me in spite of my new hair, complexion and clothes. Fag hadn't much brains, but he had eyes that could see through anything. I don't blame Fag. He acted according to his code. He came up to my apartment, having followed me home; and I told him that I was going to marry Burke and be a respectable housewife. That was dumb of me. Fag was square. If I had told him that I was ribbing Burke up for a trimming, Fag would have let me alone, would have kept his hands off. But when I told him that I was through with the graft, had 'gone queer,' that made me his meat. You know how crooks are: everyone in the world is either a fellow crook or a prospective victim. So if I was no longer a crook, then Fag considered me fair game.

"He learned about Burke's family connections, and then he put it up to me—twenty thousand dollars, or he'd turn me up. He knew about the Los Angeles job, and he knew how badly I was wanted. I was up against it then. I knew I couldn't hide from Fag or run away from him. I told Burke I had to have twenty thousand dollars. I didn't think he had that much, but I thought he could get it. Three days later he gave me a check for it. I didn't know at the time how he had raised it, but it wouldn't have mattered if I had known. I had to have it.

"But that night he told me where he got the money; that he had forged his brother-in-law's signature. He told me because, after thinking it over, he was afraid that when the forgery was discovered I would be caught with him and considered equally guilty. I'm rotten in spots, but I wasn't rotten enough to let him put himself in the pen for me, without knowing what it was all about. I told him the whole story. He didn't bat an eye. He insisted that the money be paid Kilcourse, so that I would be safe, and began to plan for my further safety.

"Burke was confident that his brother-in-law wouldn't send him over for forgery, but, to be on the safe side, he insisted that I move and change my name again and lay low until we knew how Axford was going to take it. But that night, after he had gone, I made some plans of my own. I did like Burke—I liked him too much to let him be the goat without trying to save him, and I didn't have a great deal of faith in Axford's kindness. This was the second of the month. Barring accidents, Axford wouldn't discover the forgery until he got his canceled checks early the following month. That gave me practically a month to work in.

"The next day I drew all my money out of the bank, and sent Burke a letter, saying that I had been called to Baltimore, and I laid a clear trail to Baltimore, with baggage and letters and all, which a pal there took care of for me. Then I went down to Joplin's and got him to put me up. I let Fag know I was there, and when he came down I told him I expected to have the money for him in a day or two.

"He came down nearly every day after that, and I stalled him from day to day, and each time it got easier. But my time was getting short. Pretty soon Burke's letters would be coming back from the phony address I had given him, and I wanted to be on hand to keep him from doing anything foolish. And I didn't want to get in touch with him until I could give him the twenty thousand, so he could square the forgery before Axford learned of it from his canceled checks.

"Fag was getting easier and easier to handle, but I still didn't have him where I wanted him. He wasn't willing to give up the twenty thousand dollars—which I was, of course, holding all this time—unless I'd promise to stick with him for good. And I still thought I was in love with Burke, and I didn't want to tie myself up with Fag, even for a little while.

"Then Burke saw me on the street one Sunday night. I was careless, and drove into the city in Joplin's roadster

—the one back there. And, as luck would have it, Burke saw me. I told him the truth, the whole truth. And he told me that he had just hired a private detective to find me. He was like a child in some ways: it hadn't occurred to him that the sleuth would dig up anything about the money. But I knew the forged check would be found in a day or two at the most. I knew it!

"When I told Burke that he went to pieces. All his faith in his brother-in-law's forgiveness went. I couldn't leave him the way he was. He'd have babbled the whole thing to the first person he met. So I brought him back to Joplin's with me. My idea was to hold him there for a few days, until we could see how things were going. If nothing appeared in the papers about the check, then we could take it for granted that Axford had hushed the matter up, and Burke could go home and try to square himself. On the other hand, if the papers got the whole story, then Burke would have to look for a permanent hiding-place, and so would I.

"Tuesday evening's and Wednesday morning's papers were full of the news of his disappearance, but nothing was said about the check. That looked good, but we waited another day for good measure. Fag Kilcourse was in on the game by this time, of course, and I had had to pass over the twenty thousand dollars, but I still had hopes of getting it—or most of it—back, so I continued to string him along. I had a hard time keeping off Burke, though, because he had begun to think he had some sort of right to me, and jealousy made him wicked. But I got Tin-Star to throw a scare into him, and I thought Burke was safe.

"Tonight one of Tin-Star's men came up and told us that a man named Porky Grout, who had been hanging around the place for a couple of nights, had made a couple of cracks that might mean he was interested in us. Grout was pointed out to me, and I took a chance on showing myself in the public part of the place, and sat at a table close to his. He was plain rat—as I guess you know—and in less than five minutes I had him at my table, and half an hour later I knew that he had tipped you off that Burke and I were in the White Shack. He didn't tell me all this right out, but he told me more than enough for me to guess the rest.

"I went up and told the others. Fag was for killing both Grout and Burke right away. But I talked him out of it. That wouldn't help us any, and I had Grout where he would jump in the ocean for me. I thought I had Fag convinced, but— We finally decided that Burke and I would take the roadster and leave, and that when you got here Porky Grout was to pretend he was hopped up, and point out a man and a woman—any who happened to be handy—as the ones he had taken for us. I stopped to get a cloak and gloves, and Burke went on out to the car alone—and Fag shot him. I didn't know he was going to! I wouldn't have let him! Please believe that! I wasn't as much in love with Burke as I had thought, but please believe that after all he had done for me I wouldn't have let them hurt him!

"After that it was a case of stick with the others whether I liked it or not, and I stuck. We ribbed Grout to tell you that all three of us were on the back porch when Burke was killed, and we had any number of others primed with the same story. Then you came up and recognized me. Just my luck that it had to be you— the only detective in San Francisco who knew me!

"You know the rest: how Porky Grout came up behind you and turned off the lights, and Joplin held you while we ran for the car; and then, when you closed in on us, Grout offered to stand you off while we got clear, and now. . . ."

Her voice died, and she shivered a little. The robe I had given her had fallen away from her white shoulders. Whether or not it was because she was so close against my shoulder, I shivered, too. And my fingers, fumbling in my pocket for a cigarette, brought it out twisted and mashed.

"That's all there is to the part you promised to listen to," she said softly, her face turned half away. "I wanted you to know. You're a hard man, but somehow I——"

I cleared my throat, and the hand that held the mangled cigarette was suddenly steady.

"Now don't be crude, sister," I said. "Your work has been too smooth so far to be spoiled by rough stuff now."

She laughed—a brief laugh that was bitter and reckless and just a little weary, and she thrust her face still closer to mine, and the gray eyes were soft and placid.

"Little fat detective whose name I don't know"—her voice had a tired huskiness in it, and a tired mockery—"you think I am playing a part, don't you? You think I am playing for liberty. Perhaps I am. I certainly would take it if it were offered me. But—— Men have thought me beautiful, and I have played with them. Women are like that. Men have loved me and, doing what I liked with them, I have found men contemptible. And then comes this little fat detective whose name I don't know, and he acts as if I were a hag—an old squaw. Can I help then being piqued into some sort of feeling for him? Women are like that. Am I so homely that any man has a right to look at me without even interest? Am I ugly?"

I shook my head. "You're quite pretty," I said, struggling to keep my voice as casual as the words.

"You beast!" she spat, and then her smile grew gentle again. "And yet it is because of that attitude that I sit here and turn myself inside out for you. If you were to take me in your arms and hold me close to the chest that I am already leaning against, and if you were to tell me that there is no jail ahead for me just now, I would be glad, of course. But, though for a while you might hold me, you would then be only one of the men with which I am familiar: men who love and are used and are succeeded by other men. But because you do none of these things, because you are a wooden block of a man, I find myself wanting you. Would I tell you this, little fat detective, if I were playing a game?"

I grunted non committally, and forcibly restrained my tongue from running out to moisten my dry lips.

"I'm going to this jail tonight if you are the same hard man who has goaded me into whining love into his un-caring ears, but before that, can't I have one whole-hearted assurance that you think me a little more than 'quite pretty'? Or at least a hint that if I were not a prisoner your pulse might beat a little faster when I touch you? I'm going to this jail for a long while—perhaps to the gallows. Can't I take my vanity there not quite in tatters to keep me company? Can't you do some slight thing to keep me from the afterthought of having bleated all this out to a man who was simply bored?"

Her lids had come down half over the silver-gray eyes, her head had tilted back so far that a little pulse showed throbbing in her white throat; her lips were motionless over slightly parted teeth, as the last word had left them. My fingers went deep into the soft white flesh of her shoulders. Her head went further back, her eyes closed, one hand came up to my shoulder.

"You're beautiful as all hell!" I shouted crazily into her face, and flung her against the door.

It seemed an hour that I fumbled with starter and gears before I had the car back in the road and thundering toward the San Mateo County jail. The girl had straightened herself up in the seat again, and sat huddled within the robe I had given her. I squinted straight ahead into the wind that tore at my hair and face, and the absence of the windshield took my thoughts back to Porky Grout.

Porky Grout, whose yellowness was notorious from Seattle to San Diego, standing rigidly in the path of a charging metal monster, with an inadequate pistol in each hand. She had done that to Porky Grout—this woman beside me! She had done that to Porky Grout, and he hadn't even been human! A slimy reptile whose highest thought had been a skinful of dope had gone grimly to death that she might get away—she—this woman whose shoulders I had gripped, whose mouth had been close under mine!

I let the car out another notch, holding the road somehow.

We went through a town: a scurrying of pedestrians for safety, surprised faces staring at us, street lights glistening on the moisture the wind had whipped from my eyes. I passed blindly by the road I wanted, circled back to it, and we were out in the country again.

At the foot of a long, shallow hill I applied the brakes and we snapped to motionless.

I thrust my face close to the girl's.

"Furthermore, you are a liar!" I knew I was shouting foolishly, but I was powerless to lower my voice. "Pangburn never put Axford's name on that check. He never

176

knew anything about it. You got in with him because you knew his brother-in-law was a millionaire. You pumped him, finding out everything he knew about his brother-in-law's account at the Golden Gate Trust. You stole Pangburn's bank book—it wasn't in his room when I searched it—and deposited the forged Axford check to his credit, knowing that under those circumstances the check wouldn't be questioned. The next day you took Pangburn into the bank, saying you were going to make a deposit. You took him in because with him standing beside you the check to which *his* signature had been forged wouldn't be questioned. You knew that, being a gentleman, he'd take pains not to see what you were depositing.

"Then you framed the Baltimore trip. He told the truth to me—the truth so far as he knew it. Then you met him Sunday night—maybe accidentally, maybe not. Anyway, you took him down to Joplin's, giving him some wild yarn that he would swallow and that would persuade him to stay there for a few days. That wasn't hard, since he didn't know anything about either of the twenty-thousand-dollar checks. You and your pal Kilcourse knew that if Pangburn disappeared nobody would ever know that he hadn't forged the Axford check, and nobody would ever suspect that the second check was phony. You'd have killed him quietly, but when Porky tipped you off that I was on my way down you had to move quick—so you shot him down. That's the truth of it!" I yelled.

All this while she watched me with wide gray eyes that were calm and tender, but now they clouded a little and a pucker of pain drew her brows together.

I yanked my head away and got the car in motion.

Just before we swept into Redwood City one of her hands came up to my forearm, rested there for a second, patted the arm twice, and withdrew.

I didn't look at her, nor, I think, did she look at me, while she was being booked. She gave her name as Jeanne Delano, and refused to make any statement until she had seen an attorney. It all took a very few minutes.

As she was being led away, she stopped and asked if she might speak privately with me.

We went together to a far corner of the room.

She put her mouth close to my ear so that her breath was warm again on my cheek, as it had been in the car, and whispered the vilest epithet of which the English language is capable.

Then she walked out to her cell.

THE
WHOSIS
KID

It started in Boston, back in 1917. I ran into Lew Maher on the Tremont Street sidewalk of the Touraine Hotel one afternoon, and we stopped to swap a few minutes' gossip in the snow.

I was telling him something or other when he cut in with:

"Sneak a look at this kid coming up the street. The one with the dark cap."

Looking, I saw a gangling youth of eighteen or so; pasty and pimply face, sullen mouth, dull hazel eyes, thick, shapeless nose. He passed the city sleuth and me without attention, and I noticed his ears. They weren't the battered ears of a pug, and they weren't conspicuously deformed, but their rims curved in and out in a peculiar crinkled fashion.

At the corner he went out of sight, turning down Boylston Street toward Washington.

"There's a lad that will make a name for hisself if he ain't nabbed or rocked off too soon," Lew predicted. "Better put him on your list. The Whosis Kid. You'll be looking for him some one of these days."

"What's his racket?"

"Stick-up, gunman. He's got the makings of a good one. He can shoot, and he's plain crazy. He ain't hampered by nothing like imagination or fear of consequences. I wish he was. It's these careful, sensible birds that are easiest caught. I'd swear the Kid was in on a coupla jobs that were turned in Brookline last month. But I can't fit him to 'em. I'm going to clamp him some day, though—and that's a promise."

Lew never kept his promise. A prowler killed him in an Audubon Road residence a month later.

A week or two after this conversation I left the Boston branch of the Continental Detective Agency to try army life. When the war was over I returned to the Agency payroll in Chicago, stayed there for a couple of years, and got transferred to San Francisco.

So, all in all, it was nearly eight years later that I found myself sitting behind the Whosis Kid's crinkled ears at the Dreamland Rink.

Friday nights is fight night at the Steiner Street house. This particular one was my first idle evening in several weeks. I had gone up to the rink, fitted myself to a hard wooden chair not too far from the ring, and settled down to watch the boys throw gloves at one another. The show was about a quarter done when I picked out this pair of odd and somehow familiar ears two rows ahead of me.

I didn't place them right away. I couldn't see their owner's face. He was watching Kid Cipriani and Bunny Keogh assault each other. I missed most of that fight.

But during the brief wait before the next pair of boys went on, the Whosis Kid turned his head to say something to the man beside him. I saw his face and knew him.

He hadn't changed much, and he hadn't improved any. His eyes were duller and his mouth more wickedly sullen than I had remembered them. His face was as pasty as ever, if not so pimply.

He was directly between me and the ring. Now that I knew him, I didn't have to pass up the rest of the card. I could watch the boys over his head without being afraid he would get out on me.

So far as I knew, the Whosis Kid wasn't wanted anywhere—not by the Continental, anyway—and if he had been a pickpocket, or a con man, or a member of any of the criminal trades in which we are only occasionally interested, I would have let him alone. But stick-ups are always in demand. The Continental's most important clients are insurance companies of one sort or another, and robbery policies make up a good percentage of the insurance business these days.

When the Whosis Kid left in the middle of the main event—along with nearly half of the spectators, not caring what happened to either of the musclebound heavies who were putting on a room-mate act in the ring—I went with him.

He was alone. It was the simplest sort of shadowing. The streets were filled with departing fight fans. The Kid walked down to Fillmore Street, took on a stack of wheats, bacon and coffee at a lunch room, and caught a No. 22 car.

He—and likewise I—transferred to a No. 5 car at McAllister Street, dropped off at Polk, walked north one block, turned back west for a block and a fraction, and went up the front stairs of a dingy light-house-keeping room establishment that occupied the second and third floors over a repair shop on the south side of Golden Gate Avenue, between Van Ness and Franklin.

That put a wrinkle in my forehead. If he had left the street car at either Van Ness or Franklin, he would have saved himself a block of walking. He had ridden down to Polk and walked back. For the exercise, maybe.

I loafed across the street for a short while, to see what—if anything—happened to the front windows. None that had been dark before the Kid went in lighted up now. Apparently he didn't have a front room—unless he was a very cautious young man. I knew he hadn't tumbled to my shadowing. There wasn't a chance of that. Conditions had been too favorable to me.

The front of the building giving me no information, I strolled down Van Ness Avenue to look at the rear. The building ran through to Redwood Street, a narrow back street that split the block in half. Four back windows were lighted, but they told me nothing. There was a back door. It seemed to belong to the repair shop. I doubted that the occupants of the upstairs rooms could use it.

On my way home to my bed and alarm clock, I dropped in at the office, to leave a note for the Old Man:

Tailing the Whosis Kid, stick-up, 25-27, 135, 5 foot 11 inches, sallow, br. hair, hzl. eyes, thick nose, crooked ears. Origin Boston. Anything on him? Will be vicinity Golden Gate and Van Ness.

Eight o'clock the next morning found me a block below the house in which the Kid had gone, waiting for him to appear. A steady, soaking rain was falling, but

I didn't mind that. I was closed up inside a black coupé, a type of car whose tamely respectable appearance makes it the ideal one for city work. This part of Golden Gate Avenue is lined with automobile repair shops, second-hand automobile dealers, and the like. There are always dozens of cars standing idle to the block. Although I stayed there all day, I didn't have to worry over my being too noticeable.

That was just as well. For nine solid, end-to-end hours I sat there and listened to the rain on the roof, and waited for the Whosis Kid, with not a glimpse of him, and nothing to eat except Fatimas. I wasn't any too sure he hadn't slipped me. I didn't know that he lived in this place I was watching. He could have gone to his home after I had gone to mine. However, in this detective business pessimistic guesses of that sort are always bothering you, if you let them. I stayed parked, with my eye on the dingy door into which my meat had gone the night before.

At a little after five that evening, Tommy Howd, our pug-nosed office boy, found me and gave me a memorandum from the Old Man:

Whosis Kid known to Boston branch as robbery-suspect, but have nothing definite on him. Real name believed to be Arthur Cory or Carey. May have been implicated in Tunnicliffe jewelry robbery in Boston last month. Employee killed, $60,-000 unset stones taken. No description of two bandits. Boston branch thinks this angle worth running out. They authorize surveillance.

After I had read this memorandum, I gave it back to the boy—there's no wisdom in carrying around a pocketful of stuff relating to your job—and asked him:

"Will you call up the Old Man and ask him to send somebody up to relieve me while I get a bite of food? I haven't chewed since breakfast."

"Swell chance!" Tommy said. "Everybody's busy. Hasn't been an op in all day. I don't see why you fellas don't carry a hunk or two of chocolate in your pockets to—"

"You've been reading about Arctic explorers," I accused him. "If a man's starving he'll eat anything, but when he's just ordinarily hungry he doesn't want to clutter up his stomach with a lot of candy. Scout around and see if you can pick me up a couple of sandwiches and a bottle of milk."

He scowled at me, and then his fourteen-year-old face grew cunning.

"I tell you what," he suggested. "You tell me what this fella looks like, and which building he's in, and I'll watch while you go get a decent meal. Huh? Steak, and French fried potatoes, and pie, and coffee."

Tommy has dreams of being left on the job in some such circumstance, of having everything break for him while he's there, and of rounding up regiments of desperadoes all by himself. I don't think he'd muff a good chance at that, and I'd be willing to give him a whack at it. But the Old Man would scalp me if he knew I turned a child loose among a lot of thugs.

So I shook my head.

"This guy wears four guns and carries an ax, Tommy. He'd eat you up."

"Aw, applesauce! You ops are all the time trying to make out nobody else could do your work. These crooks can't be such tough mugs—or they wouldn't let you catch 'em!"

There was some truth in that, so I put Tommy out of the coupé into the rain.

"One tongue sandwich, one ham, one bottle of milk. And make it sudden."

But I wasn't there when he came back with the food. He had barely gone out of sight when the Whosis Kid, his overcoat collar turned up against the rain that was driving down in close-packed earnest just now, came out of the rooming-house doorway.

He turned south on Van Ness.

When the coupé got me to the corner he was not in sight. He couldn't have reached McAllister Street. Unless he had gone into a building, Redwood Street— the narrow one that split the block—was my best bet. I drove up Golden Gate Avenue another block, turned south, and reached the corner of Franklin and Redwood just in time to see my man ducking into the back door of an apartment building that fronted on McAllister Street.

I drove on slowly, thinking.

The building in which the Kid had spent the night and this building into which he had just gone had their rears on the same back street, on opposite sides, a little more than half a block apart. If the Kid's room was in the rear of his building, and he had a pair of strong glasses, he could keep a pretty sharp eye on all the windows—and probably much of the interiors—of the rooms on that side of the McAllister Street building.

Last night he had ridden a block out of his way. Having seen him sneak into the back door just now, my guess was that he had not wished to leave the street car where he could be seen from his building. Either of his more convenient points of departure from the car would have been in sight of this building. This would add up to the fact that the Kid was watching someone in this building, and did not want them to be watching him.

He had now gone calling through the back door. That wasn't difficult to explain. The front door was locked, but the back door—as in most large buildings —probably was open all day. Unless the Kid ran into a janitor or someone of the sort, he could get in with no trouble. The Kid's call was furtive, whether his host was at home or not.

I didn't know what it was all about, but that didn't bother me especially. My immediate problem was to get to the best place from which to pick up the Kid when he came out.

If he left by the back door, the next block of Redwood Street—between Franklin and Gough—was the place for me and my coupé. But he hadn't promised me he would leave that way. It was more likely that he would use the front door. He would attract less attention walking boldly out the front of the building than sneaking out the back. My best bet was the corner of McAllister and Van Ness. From there I could watch the front door as well as one end of Redwood Street.

I slid the coupé down to that corner and waited.

Half an hour passed. Three quarters.

The Whosis Kid came down the front steps and walked toward me, buttoning his overcoat and turning up the collar as he walked, his head bent against the slant of the rain.

A curtained black Cadillac touring car came from behind me, a car I thought had been parked down near the City Hall when I took my plant there.

It curved around my coupé, slid with chainless recklessness in to the curb, skidded out again, picking up speed somehow on the wet paving.

A curtain whipped loose in the rain.

Out of the opening came pale fire-streaks. The bitter voice of a small-caliber pistol. Seven times.

The Whosis Kid's wet hat floated off his head—a slow balloon-like rising.

There was nothing slow about the Kid's moving.

Plunging, in a twisting swirl of coat-skirts, he flung into a shop vestibule.

The Cadillac reached the next corner, made a dizzy sliding turn, and was gone up Franklin Street. I pointed the coupé at it.

Passing the vestibule into which the Kid had plunged, I got a one-eyed view of him, on his knees, still trying to get a dark gun untangled from his overcoat. Excited faces were in the doorway behind him. There was no excitement in the street. People are too accustomed to automobile noises nowadays to pay much attention to the racket of anything less than a six-inch gun.

By the time I reached Franklin Street, the Cadillac had gained another block on me. It was spinning to the left, up Eddy Street.

I paralleled it on Turk Street, and saw it again when I reached the two open blocks of Jefferson Square. Its speed was decreasing. Five or six blocks further, and it crossed ahead of me—on Steiner Street—close enough for me to read the license plate. Its pace was moderate now. Confident that they had made a clean get-away, its occupants didn't want to get in trouble through speeding. I slid into their wake, three blocks behind.

Not having been in sight during the early blocks of

the fight, I wasn't afraid that they would suspect my interest in them now.

Out on Haight Street near the park panhandle, the Cadillac stopped to discharge a passenger. A small man —short and slender—with cream-white face around dark eyes and a tiny black mustache. There was something foreign in the cut of his dark coat and the shape of his gray hat. He carried a walking stick.

The Cadillac went on out Haight Street without giving me a look at the other occupants. Tossing a mental nickel, I stuck to the man afoot. The chances always are against you being able to trace a suspicious car by its license number, but there is a slim chance.

My man went into a drug store on the corner and used the telephone. I don't know what else he did in there, if anything. Presently a taxicab arrived. He got in and was driven to the Marquis Hotel. A clerk gave him the key to room 761. I dropped him when he stepped into an elevator.

At the Marquis I am among friends.

I found Duran, the house copper, on the mezzanine floor, and asked him:

"Who is 761?"

Duran is a white-haired old-timer who looks, talks, and acts like the president of an exceptionally strong bank. He used to be captain of detectives in one of the larger Middle Western cities. Once he tried too hard to get a confession out of a safe-ripper, and killed him. The newspapers didn't like Duran. They used that accident to howl him out of his job.

"761?" he repeated in his grandfatherly manner. "That is Mr. Maurois, I believe. Are you especially interested in him?"

"I have hopes," I admitted. "What do you know about him?"

"Not a great deal. He has been here perhaps two weeks. We shall go down and see what we can learn."

We went to the desk, the switchboard, the captain of bellhops, and upstairs to question a couple of chambermaids. The occupant of 761 had arrived two weeks ago, had registered as *Edouard Maurois, Dijon, France,* had frequent telephone calls, no mail, no visitors, kept irregular hours and tipped freely. Whatever business he was in or had was not known to the hotel people.

"What is the occasion of your interest in him, if I may ask?" Duran inquired after we had accumulated these facts. He talks like that.

"I don't exactly know yet," I replied truthfully. "He just connected with a bird who is wrong, but this Maurois may be all right himself. I'll give you a rap the minute I get anything solid on him."

I couldn't afford to tell Duran I had seen his guest snapping caps at a gunman under the eyes of the City Hall in daylight. The Marquis Hotel goes in for respectability. They would have shoved the Frenchman out in the streets. It wouldn't help me to have him scared up.

"Please do," Duran said. "You owe us something for our help, you know, so please don't withhold any information that might save us unpleasant notoriety."

"I won't," I promised. "Now will you do me another favor? I haven't had my teeth in anything except my mouth since seven-thirty this morning. Will you keep an eye on the elevators, and let me know if Maurois goes out? I'll be in the grill, near the door."

"Certainly."

On my way to the grillroom I stopped at the telephone booths and called up the office. I gave the night office man the Cadillac's license number.

"Look it up on the list and see who it belongs to."

The answer was: "H. J. Paterson, San Pablo, issued for a Buick roadster."

That about wound up that angle. We could look up Paterson, but it was safe betting it wouldn't get us anything. License plates, once they get started in crooked ways, are about as easy to trace as Liberty Bonds.

All day I had been building up hunger. I took it into the grillroom and turned it loose. Between bites I turned the day's events over in my mind. I didn't think hard enough to spoil my appetite. There wasn't that much to think about.

The Whosis Kid lived in a joint from which some of the McAllister Street apartments could be watched. He visited the apartment building furtively. Leaving, he was shot at from a car that must have been waiting somewhere in the vicinity. Had the Frenchman's companion in the Cadillac—or his companions, if more than one—been the occupant of the apartment the Kid had visited? Had they expected him to visit it? Had they tricked him into visiting it, planning to shoot him down as he was leaving? Or were they watching the front while the Kid watched the rear? If so, had either known that the other was watching? And who lived there?

I couldn't answer any of these riddles. All I knew was that the Frenchman and his companions didn't seem to like the Whosis Kid.

Even the sort of meal I put away doesn't take forever to eat. When I finished it, I went out to the lobby again.

Passing the switchboard, one of the girls—the one

whose red hair looks as if it had been poured into its waves and hardened—gave me a nod.

I stopped to see what she wanted.

"Your friend just had a call," she told me.

"You get it?"

"Yes. A man is waiting for him at Kearny and Broadway. Told him to hurry."

"How long ago?"

"None. They're just through talking."

"Any names?"

"No."

"Thanks."

I went on to where Duran was stalling with an eye on the elevators.

"Shown yet?" I asked.

"No."

"Good. The red-head on the switchboard just told me he had a phone call to meet a man at Kearny and Broadway. I think I'll beat him to it."

Around the corner from the hotel, I climbed into my coupé and drove down to the Frenchman's corner.

The Cadillac he had used that afternoon was already there, with a new license plate. I passed it and took a look at its one occupant—a thick-set man of forty-something with a cap pulled low over his eyes. All I could see of his features was a wide mouth slanting over a heavy chin.

I put the coupé in a vacant space down the street a way. I didn't have to wait long for the Frenchman. He came around the corner afoot and got into the Cadillac. The man with the big chin drove. They went slowly up Broadway. I followed.

*　　*　　*

We didn't go far, and when we came to rest again, the Cadillac was placed conveniently for its occupants to watch the Venetian Café, one of the gaudiest of the Italian restaurants that fill this part of town.

Two hours went by.

I had an idea that the Whosis Kid was eating at the Venetian. When he left, the fireworks would break out, continuing the celebration from where it had broken off that afternoon on McAllister Street. I hoped the Kid's gun wouldn't get caught in his coat this time. But don't think I meant to give him a helping hand in his two-against-one fight.

This party had the shape of a war between gunmen. It would be a private one as far as I was concerned. My hope was that by hovering on the fringes until somebody won, I could pick up a little profit for the Continental, in the form of a wanted crook or two among the survivors.

My guess at the Frenchman's quarry was wrong. It wasn't the Whosis Kid. It was a man and a woman. I didn't see their faces. The light was behind them. They didn't waste any time between the Venetian's door and their taxicab.

The man was big—tall, wide, and thick. The woman looked small at his side. I couldn't go by that. Anything weighing less than a ton would have seemed tiny beside him.

As the taxicab pulled away from the café, the Cadillac went after it. I ran in the Cadillac's wake.

It was a short chase.

The taxicab turned into a dark block on the edge of Chinatown. The Cadillac jumped to its side, bearing it over to the curb.

A noise of brakes, shouting voices, broken glass. A

woman's scream. Figures moving in the scant space between touring car and taxicab. Both cars rocking. Grunts. Thuds. Oaths.

A man's voice: "Hey! You can't do that! Nix! Nix!"

It was a stupid voice.

I had slowed down until the coupé was barely moving toward this tussle ahead. Peering through the rain and darkness, I tried to pick out a detail or so as I approached, but I could see little.

I was within twenty feet when the curbward door of the taxicab banged open. A woman bouncd out. She landed on her knees on the sidewalk, jumped to her feet, and darted up the street.

Putting the coupé closer to the curb, I let the door swing open. My side windows were spattered with rain. I wanted to get a look at the woman when she passed. If she should take the open door for an invitation, I didn't mind talking to her.

She accepted the invitation, hurrying as directly to the car as if she had expected me to be waiting for her. Her face was a small oval above a fur collar.

"Help me!" she gasped. "Take me from here— quickly."

There was a suggestion of foreignness too slight to be called an accent.

"How about—?"

I shut my mouth. The thing she was jabbing me in the body with was a snub-nosed automatic.

"Sure! Get in," I urged her.

She bent her head to enter. I looped an arm over her neck, throwing her down across my lap. She squirmed and twisted—a small-boned, hard-fleshed body with strength in it.

I wrenched the gun out of her hand and pushed her back on the seat beside me.

Her fingers dug into my arms.

"Quick! Quick! Ah, please, quickly! Take me—"

"What about your friend?" I asked.

"Not him! He is of the others! Please, quickly!"

A man filled the open coupé door—the big-chinned man who had driven the Cadillac.

His hand seized the fur at the woman's throat.

She tried to scream—made the gurgling sound of a man with a slit throat. I smacked his chin with the gun I had taken from her.

He tried to fall into the coupé. I pushed him out.

Before his head had hit the sidewalk, I had the door closed, and was twisting the coupé around in the street.

We rode away. Two shots sounded just as we turned the first corner. I don't know whether they were fired at us or not. I turned other corners. The Cadillac did not appear again.

So far, so good. I had started with the Whosis Kid, dropped him to take Maurois, and now let him go to see who this woman was. I didn't know what this confusion was all about, but I seemed to be learning *who* it was all about.

"Where to?" I asked presently.

"To home," she said, and gave me an address.

I pointed the coupé at it with no reluctance at all. It was the McAllister Street apartments the Whosis Kid had visited earlier in the evening.

We didn't waste any time getting there. My companion might know it or might not, but I knew that all the other players in this game knew that address. I wanted to get there before the Frenchman and Big Chin.

Neither of us said anything during the ride. She

crouched close to me, shivering. I was looking ahead, planning how I was to land an invitation into her apartment. I was sorry I hadn't held on to her gun. I had let it fall when I pushed Big Chin out of the car. It would have been an excuse for a later call if she didn't invite me in.

I needn't have worried. She didn't invite me. She insisted that I go in with her. She was scared stiff.

"You will not leave me?" she pleaded as we drove up McAllister Street. "I am in complete terror. You cannot go from me! If you will not come in, I will stay with you."

I was willing enough to go in, but I didn't want to leave the coupé where it would advertise me.

"We'll ride around the corner and park the car," I told her, "and then I'll go in with you."

I drove around the block, with an eye in each direction for the Cadillac. Neither eye found it. I left the coupé on Franklin Street and we returned to the McAllister Street building.

She had me almost running through the rain that had lightened now to a drizzle.

The hand with which she tried to fit a key to the front door was a shaky, inaccurate hand. I took the key and opened the door. We rode to the third floor in an automatic elevator, seeing no one. I unlocked the door to which she led me, near the rear of the building.

Holding my arm with one hand, she reached inside and snapped on the lights in the passageway.

I didn't know what she was waiting for, until she cried:

"Frana! Frana! Ah, Frana!"

The muffled yapping of a small dog replied. The dog did not appear.

She grabbed me with both arms, trying to crawl up my damp coat-front.

"They are here!" she cried in the thin dry voice of utter terror. "They are here!"

"Is anybody supposed to be here?" I asked, putting her around to one side, where she wouldn't be between me and the two doors across the passageway.

"No! Just my little dog Frana, but—"

I slid my gun half out of my pocket and back again, to make sure it wouldn't catch if I needed it, and used my other hand to get rid of the woman's arms.

"You stay here. I'll see if you've got company."

Moving to the nearest door, I heard a seven-year-old voice—Lew Maher's—saying: *"He can shoot and he's plain crazy. He ain't hampered by nothing like imagination or fear of consequences."*

With my left hand I turned the first door's knob. With my left foot I kicked it open.

Nothing happened.

I put a hand around the frame, found the button, switched on the lights.

A sitting-room, all orderly.

Through an open door on the far side of the room came the muffled yapping of Frana. It was louder now and more excited. I moved to the doorway. What I could see of the next room, in the light from this, seemed peaceful and unoccupied enough. I went into it and switched on the lights.

The dog's voice came through a closed door. I crossed to it, pulled it open. A dark fluffy dog jumped snapping at my leg. I grabbed it where its fur was thickest and lifted it squirming and snarling. The light hit it. It was purple—purple as a grape! Dyed purple!

Carrying this yapping, yelping artificial hound a little away from my body with my left hand, I moved on to the next room—a bedroom. It was vacant. Its closet hid nobody. I found the kitchen and bathroom. Empty. No one was in the apartment. The purple pup had been imprisoned by the Whosis Kid earlier in the day.

Passing through the second room on my way back to the woman with her dog and my report, I saw a slitted envelope lying face-down on a table. I turned it over. The stationery of a fashionable store, it was addressed to Mrs. Inés Almad, here.

The party seemed to be getting international. Maurois was French; the Whosis Kid was Boston American; the dog had a Bohemian name (at least I remember nabbing a Czech forger a few months before whose first name was Frana); and Inés, I imagine, was either Spanish or Portuguese. I didn't know what Almad was, but she was undoubtedly foreign, and not, I thought, French.

I returned to her. She hadn't moved an inch.

"Everything seems to be all right," I told her. "The dog got himself caught in a closet."

"There is no one here?"

"No one."

She took the dog in both hands, kissing its fluffy stained head, crooning affectionate words to it in a language that made no sense to me.

"Do your friends—the people you had your row with tonight—know where you live?" I asked.

I knew they did. I wanted to see what she knew.

She dropped the dog as if she had forgotten it, and her brows puckered.

"I do not know that," she said slowly. "Yet it may be. If they do—"

She shuddered, spun on her heel, and pushed the hall door violently shut.

"They may have been here this afternoon," she went on. "Frana has made himself prisoner in closets before, but I fear everything. I am coward-like. But there is none here now?"

"No one," I assured her again.

We went into the sitting-room. I got my first good look at her when she shed her hat and dark cape.

She was a trifle under medium height, a dark-skinned woman of thirty in a vivid orange gown. She was dark as an Indian, with bare brown shoulders round and sloping, tiny feet and hands, her fingers heavy with rings. Her nose was thin and curved, her mouth full-lipped and red, her eyes—long and thickly lashed—were of an extraordinary narrowness. They were dark eyes, but nothing of their color could be seen through the thin slits that separated the lids. Two dark gleams through veiling lashes. Her black hair was disarranged just now in fluffy silk puffs. A rope of pearls hung down on her dark chest. Earrings of black iron—in a peculiar club-like design—swung beside her cheeks.

Altogether, she was an odd trick. But I wouldn't want to be quoted as saying that she wasn't beautiful—in a wild way.

She was shaking and shivering as she got rid of her hat and cloak. White teeth held her lower lip as she crossed the room to turn on an electric heater. I took advantage of this opportunity to shift my gun from my overcoat pocket to my pants. Then I took off the coat.

Leaving the room for a second, she returned with a brown-filled quart bottle and two tumblers on a bronze tray, which she put on a little table near the heater.

The first tumbler she filled to within half an inch of its rim. I stopped her when she had the other nearly half full.

"That'll do fine for me," I said.

It was brandy, and not at all hard to get down. She shot her tumblerful into her throat as if she needed it, shook her bare shoulders, and sighed in a satisfied way.

"You will think, certainly, I am lunatic," she smiled at me. "Flinging myself on you, a stranger in the street, demanding of you time and troubles."

"No," I lied seriously. "I think you're pretty level-headed for a woman who, no doubt, isn't used to this sort of stuff."

She was pulling a little upholstered bench closer to the electric heater, within reach of the table that held the brandy. She sat down now, with an inviting nod at the bench's empty half.

The purple dog jumped into her lap. She pushed it out. It started to return. She kicked it sharply in the side with the pointed toe of her slipper. It yelped and crawled under a chair across the room.

I avoided the window by going the long way around the room. The window was curtained, but not thickly enough to hide all of the room from the Whosis Kid —if he happened to be sitting at his window just now with a pair of field glasses to his eyes.

"But I am not level-headed, really," the woman was saying as I dropped beside her. "I am coward-like, terribly. And even becoming accustomed— It is my husband, or he who was my husband. I should tell you. Your gallantry deserves the explanation, and I do not wish you should think a thing that is not so."

I tried to look trusting and credulous. I expected to disbelieve everything she said.

"He is most crazily jealous," she went on in her low-pitched, soft voice, with a peculiar way of saying words that just missed being marked enough to be called a foreign accent. "He is an old man, and incredibly wicked. These men he has sent to me! A woman there was once—tonight's men are not first. I don't know what —what they mean. To kill me, perhaps—to maim, to disfigure—I do not know."

"And the man in the taxi with you was one of them?" I asked. "I was driving down the street behind you when you were attacked, and I could see there was a man with you. He was one of them?"

"Yes! I did not know it, but it must have been that he was. He does not defend me. A pretense, that is all."

"Ever try sicking the cops on this hubby of yours?"

"It is what?"

"Ever notify the police?"

"Yes, but"—she shrugged her brown shoulders—"I would as well have kept quiet, or better. In Buffalo it was, and they—they bound my husband to keep the peace, I think you call it. A thousand dollars! Poof! What is that to him in his jealousy? And I—I cannot stand the things the newspapers say—the jesting of them. I must leave Buffalo. Yes, once I do try sicking the cops on him. But not more."

"Buffalo?" I explored a little. "I lived there for a while—on Crescent Avenue."

"Oh, yes. That is out by the Delaware Park."

That was right enough. But her knowing something about Buffalo didn't prove anything about the rest of her story.

She poured more brandy. By speaking quick I held

my drink down to a size suitable for a man who has work to do. Hers was as large as before. We drank, and she offered me cigarettes in a lacquered box—slender cigarettes, hand-rolled in black paper.

I didn't stay with mine long. It tasted, smelled and scorched like gunpowder.

"You don't like my cigarettes?"

"I'm an old-fashioned man," I apologized, rubbing its fire out in a bronze dish, fishing in my pocket for my own deck. "Tobacco's as far as I've got. What's in these fireworks?"

She laughed. She had a pleasant laugh, with a sort of coo in it.

"I am so very sorry. So many people do not like them. I have a Hindu incense mixed with the tobacco."

I didn't say anything to that. It was what you would expect of a woman who would dye her dog purple.

The dog moved under its chair just then, scratching the floor with its nails.

The brown woman was in my arms, in my lap, her arms wrapped around my neck. Close-up, opened by terror, her eyes weren't dark at all. They were gray-green. The blackness was in the shadow from her heavy lashes.

"It's only the dog," I assured her, sliding her back on her own part of the bench. "It's only the dog wriggling around under the chair."

"Ah!" she blew her breath out with enormous relief.

Then we had to have another shot of brandy.

"You see, I am most awfully the coward," she said when the third dose of liquor was in her. "But, ah, I have had so much trouble. It is a wonder that I am not insane."

I could have told her she wasn't far enough from it

to do much bragging, but I nodded with what was meant for sympathy.

She lit another cigarette to replace the one she had dropped in her excitement. Her eyes became normal black slits again.

"I do not think it is nice"—there was a suggestion of a dimple in her brown cheek when she smiled like that—"that I throw myself into the arms of a man even whose name I do not know, or anything of him."

"That's easy to fix. My name is Young," I lied; "and I can let you have a case of Scotch at a price that will astonish you. I think maybe I could stand it if you call me Jerry. Most of the ladies I let sit in my lap do."

"Jerry Young," she repeated, as if to herself. "That's is a nice name. And you are the bootlegger?"

"Not *the*," I corrected her; "just *a*. This is San Francisco."

The going got tough after that.

Everything else about this brown woman was all wrong, but her fright was real. She was scared stiff. And she didn't intend being left alone this night. She meant to keep me there—to massage any more chins that stuck themselves at her. Her idea—she being that sort—was that I would be most surely held with affection. So she must turn herself loose on me. She wasn't hampered by any pruderies or puritanisms at all.

I also have an idea. Mine is that when the last gong rings I'm going to be leading this baby and some of her playmates to the city prison. That is an excellent reason —among a dozen others I could think of—why I shouldn't get mushy with her.

I was willing enough to camp there with her until something happened. That apartment looked like the scene of the next action. But I had to cover up my own game. I couldn't let her know she was only a minor figure in it. I had to pretend there was nothing behind my willingness to stay but a desire to protect her. Another man might have got by with a chivalrous, knight-errant, protector-of-womanhood-without-personal-interest attitude. But I don't look, and can't easily act, like that kind of person. I had to hold her off without letting her guess that my interest wasn't personal. It was no cinch. She was too damned direct, and she had too much brandy in her.

I didn't kid myself that my beauty and personality were responsible for any of her warmth. I was a thick-armed male with big fists. She was in a jam. She spelled my name P-r-o-t-e-c-t-i-o-n. I was something to be put between her and trouble.

Another complication: I am neither young enough nor old enough to get feverish over every woman who doesn't make me think being blind isn't so bad. I'm at that middle point around forty where a man puts other feminine qualities—amiability, for one—above beauty on his list. This brown woman annoyed me. She was too sure of herself. Her work was rough. She was trying to handle me as if I were a farmer boy. But in spite of all this, I'm constructed mostly of human ingredients. This woman got more than a stand-off when faces and bodies were dealt. I didn't like her. I hoped to throw her in the can before I was through. But I'd be a liar if I didn't admit that she had me stirred up inside—between her cuddling against me, giving me the come-on, and the brandy I had drunk.

The going was tough—no fooling.

A couple of times I was tempted to bolt. Once I

looked at my watch—2:06. She put a ring-heavy brown hand on the timepiece and pushed it down to my pocket.

"Please, Jerry!" the earnestness in her voice was real. "You cannot go. You cannot leave me here. I will not have it so. I will go also, through the streets following. You cannot leave me to be murdered here!"

I settled down again.

A few minutes later a bell rang sharply.

She went to pieces immediately. She piled over on me, strangling me with her bare arms. I pried them loose enough to let me talk.

"What bell is that?"

"The street door. Do not heed it."

I patted her shoulder.

"Be a good girl and answer it. Let's see who it is."

Her arms tightened.

"No! No! No! They have come!"

The bell rang again.

"Answer it," I insisted.

Her face was flat against my coat, her nose digging into my chest.

"No! No!"

"All right," I said. "I'll answer it myself."

I untangled myself from her, got up and went into the passageway. She followed me. I tried again to persuade her to do the talking. She would not, although she didn't object to my talking. I would have liked it better if whoever was downstairs didn't learn that the woman wasn't alone. But she was too stubborn in her refusal for me to do anything with her.

"Well?" I said into the speaking-tube.

"Who the hell are you?" a harsh, deep-chested voice asked.

"What do you want?"

"I want to talk to Inés."

"Speak your piece to me," I suggested, "and I'll tell her about it."

The woman, holding one of my arms, had an ear close to the tube.

"Billie, it is," she whispered. "Tell him that he goes away."

"You're to go away," I passed the message on.

"Yeah?" the voice grew harsher and deeper. "Will you open the door, or will I bust it in?"

There wasn't a bit of playfulness in the question. Without consulting the woman, I put a finger on the button that unlocks the street door.

"Welcome," I said into the tube.

"He's coming up," I explained to the woman. "Shall I stand behind the door and tap him on the skull when he comes in? Or do you want to talk to him first?"

"Do not strike him!" she exclaimed. "It is Billie."

That suited me. I hadn't intended putting the slug to him—not until I knew who and what he was, anyway. I had wanted to see what she would say.

Billie wasn't long getting up to us. I opened the door when he rang, the woman standing beside me. He didn't wait for an invitation. He was through the doorway before I had the door half opened. He glared at me. There was plenty of him!

A big, red-faced, red-haired bale of a man—big in any direction you measured him—and none of him was fat. The skin was off his nose, one cheek was clawed, the other swollen. His hatless head was a tangled mass of red hair.

One pocket had been ripped out of his coat, and a

button dangled on the end of a six-inch ribbon of torn cloth.

This was the big heaver who had been in the taxicab with the woman.

"Who's this mutt?" he demanded, moving his big paws toward me.

I knew the woman was a goof. It wouldn't have surprised me if she had tried to feed me to the battered giant. But she didn't. She put a hand on one of his and soothed him.

"Do not be nasty, Billie. He is a friend. Without him I would not this night have escaped."

He scowled. Then his face straightened out and he caught her hand in both of his.

"So you got away it's all right," he said huskily. "I'd a done better if we'd been outside. There wasn't no room in that taxi for me to turn around. And one of them guys crowned me."

That was funny. This big clown was apologizing for getting mangled up protecting a woman who had scooted, leaving him to get out as well as he could.

The woman led him into the sitting-room, I tagging along behind. They sat on the bench. I picked out a chair that wasn't in line with the window the Whosis Kid ought to be watching.

"What did happen, Billie?" She touched his grooved cheek and skinned nose with her fingertips. "You are hurt."

He grinned with a sort of shamefaced delight. I saw that what I had taken for a swelling in one cheek was only a big hunk of chewing tobacco.

"I don't know all that happened," he said. "One of 'em crowned me, and I didn't wake up till a coupla hours afterwards. The taxi driver didn't give me no help in the fight, but he was a right guy and knowed where his money would come from. He didn't holler or nothing. He took me around to a doc that wouldn't squawk, and the doc straightened me out, and then I come up here."

"Did you see each one of those men?" she asked.

"Sure! I seen 'em, and felt 'em, and maybe tasted 'em."

"They were how many?"

"Just two of 'em. A little fella with a trick tickler, and a husky with a big chin on him."

"There was no other? There was not a younger man, tall and thin?"

That could be the Whosis Kid. She thought he and the Frenchman were working together?

Billie shook his shaggy, banged-up head.

"Nope. They was only two of 'em."

She frowned and chewed her lip.

Billie looked sidewise at me—a look that said "Beat it."

The woman caught the glance. She twisted around on the bench to put a hand on his head.

"Poor Billie," she cooed; "his head most cruelly hurt saving me, and now, when he should be at his home giving it rest, I keep him here talking. You go, Billie, and when it is morning and your poor head is better, you will telephone to me?"

His red face got dark. He glowered at me.

Laughing, she slapped him lightly on the cheek that bulged around his cud of tobacco.

"Do not become jealous of Jerry. Jerry is enamored of one yellow and white lady somewhere, and to her he is most faithful. Not even the smallest liking has he for dark women." She smiled a challenge at me. "Is it not so, Jerry?"

"No," I denied. "And, besides, all women are dark."

Billie shifted his chew to the scratched cheek and bunched his shoulders.

"What the hell kind of a crack is that to be making?" he rumbled.

"That means nothing it should not, Billie," she laughed at him. "It is only an epigram."

"Yeah?" Billie was sour and truculent. I was beginning to think he didn't like me. "Well, tell your little fat friend to keep his smart wheezes to himself. I don't like 'em."

That was plain enough. Billie wanted an argument. The woman, who held him securely enough to have steered him off, simply laughed again. There was no profit in trying to find the reason behind any of her actions. She was a nut. Maybe she thought that since we weren't sociable enough for her to keep both on hand, she'd let us tangle, and hold on to the one who rubbed the other out of the picture.

Anyway, a row was coming. Ordinarily I am inclined to peace. The day is past when I'll fight for the fun of it. But I've been in too many rumpuses to mind them much. Usually nothing very bad happens to you, even if you lose. I wasn't going to back down just because this big stiff was meatier than I. I've always been lucky against the large sizes. He had been banged up earlier in the evening. That would cut down his steam some. I wanted to hang around this apartment a little longer, if it could be managed. If Billie wanted to tussle—and it looked as if he did—he could.

It was easy to meet him half-way: anything I said would be used against me.

I grinned at his red face, and suggested to the woman, solemnly:

"I think if you'd dip him in blueing he'd come out the same color as the other pup."

As silly as that was, it served. Billie reared up on his feet and curled his paws into fists.

"Me and you'll take a walk," he decided; "out where there's space enough."

I got up, pushed my chair back with a foot, and quoted "Red" Burns to him: "If you're close enough, there's room enough."

He wasn't a man you had to talk to much. We went around and around.

It was fists at first. He started it by throwing his right at my head. I went in under it and gave him all I had in a right and left to the belly. He swallowed his chew of tobacco. But he didn't bend. Few big men are as strong as they look. Billie was.

He didn't know anything at all. His idea of a fight was to stand up and throw fists at your head—right, left, right, left. His fists were as large as wastebaskets. They wheezed through the air. But always at the head—the easiest part to get out of the way.

There was room enough for me to go in and out. I did that. I hammered his belly. I thumped his heart. I mauled his belly again. Every time I hit him he grew an inch, gained a pound and picked up another horsepower. I don't fool when I hit, but nothing I did to this human mountain—not even making him swallow his hunk of tobacco—had any visible effect on him.

I've always had a reasonable amount of pride in my ability to sock. It was disappointing to have this big heaver take the best I could give him without a grunt. But I wasn't discouraged. He couldn't stand it forever. I settled down to make a steady job of it.

Twice he clipped me. Once on the shoulder. A big fist

spun me half around. He didn't know what to do next. He came in on the wrong side. I made him miss, and got clear. The other time he caught me on the forehead. A chair kept me from going down. The smack hurt me. It must have hurt him more. A skull is tougher than a knuckle. I got out of his way when he closed in, and let him have something to remember on the back of his neck.

The woman's dusky face showed over Billie's shoulder as he straightened up. Her eyes were shiny behind their heavy lashes, and her mouth was open to let white teeth gleam through.

Billie got tired of the boxing after that, and turned the set-to into a wrestling match, with trimmings. I would rather have kept on with the fists. But I couldn't help myself. It was his party. He grabbed one of my wrists, yanked, and we thudded chest to chest.

He didn't know any more about this than he had about that. He didn't have to. He was big enough and strong enough to play with me.

I was underneath when we tumbled down on the floor and began rolling around. I did my best. It wasn't anything. Three times I put a scissors on him. His body was too big for my short legs to clamp around. He chucked me off as if he were amusing the baby. There was no use at all in trying to do things to his legs. No hold known to man could have held them. His arms were almost as strong. I quit trying.

Nothing I knew was any good against this monster. He was out of my range. I was satisfied to spend all that was left of my strength trying to keep him from crippling me—and waiting for a chance to out-smart him.

He threw me around a lot. Then my chance came.

I was flat on my back, with everything but one or two

of my most centrally located intestines squeezed out. Kneeling astride me, he brought his big hands up to my throat and fastened them there.

That's how much he didn't know!

You can't choke a man that way—not if his hands are loose and he knows a hand is stronger than a finger.

I laughed in his purple face and brought my own hands up. Each of them picked one of his little fingers out of my flesh. It wasn't a dream at that. I was all in, and he wasn't. But no man's little finger is stronger than another's hand. I twisted them back. They broke together.

He yelped. I grabbed the next—the ring fingers.

One of them snapped. The other was ready to pop when he let go.

Jerking up, I butted him in the face. I twisted from between his knees. We came on our feet together.

The doorbell rang.

Fight interest went out of the woman's face. Fear came in. Her fingers picked at her mouth.

"Ask who's there," I told her.

"Who—who is there?"

Her voice was flat and dry.

"Mrs. Keil," came from the corridor, the words sharp with indignation. "You will have to stop this noise immediately! The tenants are complaining—and no wonder! A pretty hour to be entertaining company and carrying on so!"

"The landlady," the dark woman whispered. Aloud: "I am sorry, Mrs. Keil. There will not be more noises."

Something like a sniff came through the door, and the sound of dimming footsteps.

Inés Almad frowned reproachfully at Billie.

"You should not have done this," she blamed him.

213

He looked humble, and at the floor, and at me. Looking at me, the purple began to flow back into his face.

"I'm sorry," he mumbled. "I told this fella we ought to take a walk. We'll do it now, and there won't be no more noise here."

"Billie!" her voice was sharp. She was reading the Law to him. "You will go out and have attention for your hurts. If you have not won these fights, because of that am I to be left here alone to be murdered?"

The big man shuffled his feet, avoided her gaze and looked utterly miserable. But he shook his head stubbornly.

"I can't do it, Inés," he said. "Me and this guy has got to finish it. He busted my fingers, and I got to bust his jaw."

"Billie!"

She stamped one small foot and looked imperiously at him. He looked as if he'd like to roll over on his back and hold his paws in the air. But he stood his ground.

"I got to," he repeated. "There ain't no way out of it."

Anger left her face. She smiled very tenderly at him.

"Dear old Billie," she murmured, and crossed the room to a secretary in a corner.

When she turned, an automatic pistol was in her hand. Its one eye looked at Billie.

"Now, *lechón*," she purred, "go out!"

The red man wasn't a quick thinker. It took a full minute for him to realize that this woman he loved was driving him away with a gun. The big dummy might have known that his three broken fingers had disqualified him. It took another minute for him to get his legs in motion. He went toward the door in slow bewilderment, still only half believing this thing was really happening.

The woman followed him step by step. I went ahead to open the door.

I turned the knob. The door came in, pushing me back against the opposite wall.

In the doorway stood Edouard Maurois and the man I had swatted on the chin. Each had a gun.

I looked at Inés Almad, wondering what turn her craziness would take in the face of this situation. She wasn't so crazy as I had thought. Her scream and the thud of her gun on the floor sounded together.

"Ah!" the Frenchman was saying. "The gentlemen were leaving? May we detain them?"

The man with the big chin—it was larger than ever now with the marks of my tap—was less polite.

"Back up, you birds!" he ordered, stooping for the gun the woman had dropped.

I still was holding the doorknob. I rattled it a little as I took my hand away—enough to cover up the click of the lock as I pushed the button that left it unlatched. If I needed help, and it came, I wanted as few locks as possible between me and it.

Then—Billie, the woman and I walking backward —we all paraded into the sitting-room. Maurois and his companion both wore souvenirs of the row in the taxicab. One of the Frenchman's eyes was bruised and closed—a beautiful shiner. His clothes were rumpled and dirty. He wore them jauntily in spite of that, and he still had his walking stick, crooked under the arm that didn't hold his gun.

Big Chin held us with his own gun and the woman's while Maurois ran his hand over Billie's and my clothes, to see if we were armed. He found my gun and pocketed it. Billie had no weapons.

"Can I trouble you to step back against the wall?" Maurois asked when he was through.

We stepped back as if it was no trouble at all. I found my shoulder against one of the window curtains. I pressed it against the frame, and turned far enough to drag the curtain clear of a foot or more of pane.

If the Whosis Kid was watching, he should have had a clear view of the Frenchman—the man who had shot at him earlier in the evening. I was putting it up to the Kid. The corridor door was unlocked. If the Kid could get into the building—no great trick—he had a clear path. I didn't know where he fit in, but I wanted him to join us, and I hoped he wouldn't disappoint me. If everybody got together here, maybe whatever was going on would come out where I could see it and understand it.

Meanwhile, I kept as much of myself as possible out of the window. The Kid might decide to throw lead from across the alley.

Maurois was facing Inés. Big Chin's guns were on Billie and me.

"I do not *comprends ze anglais* ver' good," the Frenchman was mocking the woman. "So it is when you say you meet wit' me, I t'ink you say in New Orleans. I do not know you say San Francisc'. I am ver' sorry to make ze mistake. I am mos' sorry zat I keep you wait. But now I am here. You have ze share for me?"

"I have not." She held her hands out in an empty gesture. "The Kid took those—everything from me."

"What? Maurois dropped his taunting smile and his vaudeville accent. His one open eye flashed angrily. "How could he, unless—?"

"He suspected us, Edouard." Her mouth trembled with earnestness. Her eyes pleaded for belief. She was lying. "He had me followed. The day after I am there he comes. He takes all. I am afraid to wait for you. I fear your unbelief. You would not——"

"*C'est incroyable!*" Maurois was very excited over it. "I was on the first train south after our—our theatricals. Could the Kid have been on that train without my knowing it? *Non!* And how else could he have reached you before I? You are playing with me, *ma petite* Inés. That you did join the Kid, I do not doubt. But not in New Orleans. You did not go there. You came here to San Francisco."

"Edouard!" she protested, fingering his sleeve with one brown hand, the other holding her throat as if she were having trouble getting the words out. "You cannot think that thing! Do not those weeks in Boston say it is not possible? For one like the Kid—or like any other —am I to betray you? You know me not more than to think I am like that?"

She was an actress. She was appealing, and pathetic, and anything else you like—including dangerous.

The Frenchman took his sleeve away from her and stepped back a step. White lines ringed his mouth below his tiny mustache, and his jaw muscles bulged. His one good eye was worried. She had got to him, though not quite enough to upset him altogether. But the game was young yet.

"I do not know what to think," he said slowly. "If I have been wrong—I must find the Kid first. Then I will learn the truth."

"You don't have to look no further, brother. I'm right among you!"

The Whosis Kid stood in the passageway door. A black revolver was in each of his hands. Their hammers were up.

* * *

It was a pretty tableau.

There is the Whosis Kid in the door—a lean lad in his twenties, all the more wicked-looking because his face is weak and slack-jawed and dull-eyed. The cocked guns in his hands are pointing at everybody or at nobody, depending on how you look at them.

There is the brown woman, her cheeks pinched in her two fists, her eyes open until their green-grayishness shows. The fright I had seen in her face before was nothing to the fright that is there now.

There is the Frenchman—whirled doorward at the Kid's first word—his gun on the Kid, his cane still under his arm, his face a tense white blot.

There is Big Chin, his body twisted half around, his face over one shoulder to look at the door, with one of his guns following his face around.

There is Billie—a big, battered statue of a man who hasn't said a word since Inés Almad started to gun him out of the apartment.

And, last, here I am—not feeling so comfortable as I would home in bed, but not actually hysterical either. I wasn't altogether dissatisfied with the shape things were taking. Something was going to happen in these rooms. But I wasn't friendly enough to any present to care especially what happened to whom. For myself, I counted on coming through all in one piece. Few men *get* killed. Most of those who meet sudden ends *get themselves* killed. I've had twenty years of experience at dodging that. I can count on being one of the survivors of whatever blow-up there is. And I hope to take most of the other survivors for a ride.

But right now the situation belonged to the men with guns—the Whosis Kid, Maurois and Big Chin.

The Kid spoke first. He had a whining voice that came disagreeably through his thick nose.

"This don't look nothing like Chi to me, but, anyways, we're all here."

"Chicago!" Maurois exclaimed. "You did not go to Chicago!"

The Kid sneered at him.

"Did you? Did she? What would I be going there for? You think me and her run out on you, don't you? Well, we would of if she hadn't put the two X's to me the same as she done to you, and the same as the three of us done to the boob."

"That may be," the Frenchman replied; "but you do not expect me to believe that you and Inés are not friends? Didn't I see you leaving here this afternoon?"

"You see me, all right," the Kid agreed; "but if my rod hadn't of got snagged in my flogger you wouldn't have seen nothing else. But I ain't got nothing against you now. I thought you and her had ditched me, just as you think me and her done you. I know different now, from what I heard while I was getting in here. She twisted the pair of us, Frenchy, just like we twisted the boob. Ain't you got it yet?"

Maurois shook his head slowly.

What put an edge to this conversation was that both men were talking over their guns.

"Listen," the Kid asked impatiently. "We was to meet up in Chi for a three-way split, wasn't we?"

The Frenchman nodded.

"But she tells me," the Kid went on, "she'll connect with me in St. Louis, counting you out; and she ribs you up to meet her in New Orleans, ducking me. And then she gyps the pair of us by running out here to Frisco with the stuff.

"We're a couple of suckers, Frenchy, and there ain't no use of us getting hot at each other. There's enough of it for a fat two-way cut. What I say is let's forget what's done, and me and you make it fifty-fifty. Understand, I ain't begging you. I'm making a proposition. If you don't like it, to hell with you! You know me. You never seen the day I wouldn't shoot it out with you or anybody else. Take your pick!"

The Frenchman didn't say anything for a while. He was converted, but he didn't want to weaken his hand by coming in too soon. I don't know whether he believed the Kid's words or not, but he believed the Kid's guns. You can get a bullet out of a cocked revolver a lot quicker than out of a hammerless automatic. The Kid had the bulge there. And the Kid had him licked because the Kid had the look of one who doesn't give a damn what happens next.

Finally Maurois looked a question at Big Chin. Big Chin moistened his lips, but said nothing.

Maurois looked at the Kid again, and nodded his head.

"You are right," he said. "We will do that."

"Good!" The Kid did not move from his door. "Now who are these plugs?"

"These two"—Maurois nodded at Billie and me—"are friends of our Inés. This"—indicating Big Chin—"is a confrere of mine."

"You mean he's in with you? That's all right with me." The Kid spoke crisply. "But, you understand, his cut comes out of yours. I get half, and no trimming."

The Frenchman frowned, but he nodded in agreement.

"Half is yours, if we find it."

"Don't get no headache over that," the Kid advised him. "It's here and we'll get it."

He put one of his guns away and came into the room, the other gun hanging loosely at his side. When he walked across the room to face the woman, he managed it so that Big Chin and Maurois were never behind him.

"Where's the stuff?" he demanded.

Inés Almad wet her red mouth with her tongue and let her mouth droop a little and looked softly at the Kid, and made her play.

"One of us is as bad as are the others, Kid. We all— each of us tried to get for ourselves everything. You and Edouard have put aside what is past. Am I more wrong than you? I have them, true, but I have not them here. Until tomorrow will you wait? I will get them. We will divide them among us three, as it was to have been. Shall we not do that?"

"Not any!" The Kid's voice had finality in it.

"Is that just?" she pleaded, letting her chin quiver a bit. "Is there a treachery of which I am guilty that also you and Edouard are not? Do you—?"

"That ain't the idea at all," the Kid told her. "Me and Frenchy are in a fix where we got to work together to get anywhere. So we're together. With you it's different. We don't need you. We can take the stuff away from you. You're out! Where's the stuff?"

"Not here! Am I foolish sufficient to leave them here where so easily you could find them? You *do* need my help to find them. Without me you cannot—"

"You're silly! I might flop for that if I didn't know you. But I know you're too damned greedy to let 'em get far away from you. And you're yellower than you're greedy. If you're smacked a couple of times, you'll kick

in. And don't think I got any objections to smacking you
over!"

She cowered back from his upraised hand.

The Frenchman spoke quickly.

"We should search the rooms first, Kid. If we don't
find them there, then we can decide what to do next."

The Whosis Kid laughed sneeringly at Maurois.

"All right. But, get this, I'm not going out of here
without that stuff—not if I have to take this rat apart.
My way's quicker, but we'll hunt first if you want to.
Your con-whatever-you-call-him can keep these plugs
tucked in while me and you upset the joint."

They went to work. The Kid put away his gun and
brought out a long-bladed spring-knife. The Frenchman
unscrewed the lower two-thirds of his cane, baring a
foot and a half of sword-blade.

No cursory search, theirs. They took the room we
were in first. They gutted it thoroughly, carved it to the
bone. Furniture and pictures were taken apart. Uphol-
stering gave up its stuffing. Floor coverings were cut. Suspicious lengths of wallpaper were scraped loose. They
worked slowly. Neither would let the other get behind
him. The Kid would not turn his back on Big Chin.

The sitting-room wrecked, they went into the next
room, leaving the woman, Billie and me standing among
the litter. Big Chin and his two guns watched over us.

As soon as the Frenchman and the Kid were out of
sight, the woman tried her stuff out on our guardian. She
had a lot of confidence in her power with men, I'll say
that for her.

For a while she worked her eyes on Big Chin, and
then, very softly:

"Can I—?"

"You can't!" Big Chin was loud and gruff. "Shut up!" The Whosis Kid appeared at the door.

"If nobody don't say nothing maybe nobody won't get hurt," he snarled, and went back to his work.

The woman valued herself too highly to be easily discouraged. She didn't put anything in words again, but she looked things at Big Chin—things that had him sweating and blushing. He was a simple man. I didn't think she'd get anywhere. If there had been no one present but the two of them, she might have put Big Chin over the jumps; but he wouldn't be likely to let her get to him with a couple of birds standing there watching the show.

Once a sharp yelp told us that the purple Frana—who had fled rearward when Maurois and Big Chin arrived— had got in trouble with the searchers. There was only that one yelp, and it stopped with a suddenness that suggested trouble for the dog.

The two men spent nearly an hour in the other rooms. They didn't find anything. Their hands, when they joined us again, held nothing but the cutlery.

"I said to you it was not here," Inés told them triumphantly. "Now will you—?"

"You can't tell me nothing I'll believe." The Kid snapped his knife shut and dropped it in his pocket. "I still think it's here."

He caught her wrist, and held his other hand, palm up, under her nose.

"You can put 'em in my hand, or I'll take 'em."

"They are not here! I swear it!"

His mouth lifted at the corner in a savage grimace. "Liar!"

He twisted her arm roughly, forcing her to her knees. His free hand went to the shoulder-strap of her orange gown.

"I'll damn soon find out," he promised.

Billie came to life.

"Hey!" he protested, his chest heaving in and out. "You can't do that!"

"Wait, Kid!" Maurois—putting his sword-cane together again—called. "Let us see if there is not another way."

The Whosis Kid let go of the woman and took three slow steps back from her. His eyes were dead circles without any color you could name—the dull eyes of the man whose nerves quit functioning in the face of excitement. His bony hands pushed his coat aside a little and rested where his vest bulged over the sharp corners of his hip-bones.

"Let's me and you get this right, Frenchy," he said in his whining voice. "Are you with me or her?"

"You, most certainly, but—"

"All right. Then *be* with me! Don't be trying to gum every play I make. I'm going to frisk this dolly, and don't think I ain't. What are you going to do about it?"

The Frenchman pursed his mouth until his little black mustache snuggled against the tip of his nose. He puckered his eyebrows and looked thoughtfully out of his one good eye. But he wasn't going to do anything at all about it, and he knew he wasn't. Finally he shrugged.

"You are right," he surrendered. "She should be searched."

The Kid grunted contemptuous disgust at him and went toward the woman again.

She sprang away from him, to me. Her arms clamped around my neck in the habit they seemed to have.

"Jerry!" she screamed in my face. "You will not allow him! Jerry, please not!"

I didn't say anything.

I didn't think it was exactly genteel of the Kid to frisk her, but there were several reasons why I didn't try to stop him. First, I didn't want to do anything to delay the unearthing of this "stuff" there had been so much talk about. Second, I'm no Galahad. This woman had picked her playmates, and was largely responsible for this angle of their game. If they played rough, she'd have to make the best of it. And, a good strong third, Big Chin was prodding me in the side with a gun-muzzle to remind me that I couldn't do anything if I wanted to—except get myself slaughtered.

The Kid dragged Inés away. I let her go.

He pulled her over to what was left of the bench by the electric heater, and called the Frenchman there with a jerk of his head.

"You hold her while I go through her," he said.

She filled her lungs with air. Before she could turn it loose in a shriek, the Kid's long fingers had fit themselves to her throat.

"One chirp out of you and I'll tie a knot in your neck," he threatened.

She let the air wheeze out of her nose.

Billie shuffled his feet. I turned my head to look at him. He was puffing through his mouth. Sweat polished his forehead under his matted red hair. I hoped he wasn't going to turn his wolf loose until the "stuff" came to the surface. If he would wait a while I might join him.

He wouldn't wait. He went into action when— Maurois holding her—the Kid started to undress the woman.

He took a step toward them. Big Chin tried to wave him back with a gun. Billie didn't even see it. His eyes were red on the three by the bench.

"Hey, you can't do that!" he rumbled. "You can't do that!"

"No?" The Kid looked up from his work. "Watch me."

"Billie!" the woman urged the big man on in his foolishness.

Billie charged.

Big Chin let him go, playing safe by swinging both guns on me. The Whosis Kid slid out of the plunging giant's path. Maurois hurled the girl straight at Billie—and got his gun out.

Billie and Inés thumped together in a swaying tangle.

The Kid spun behind the big man. One of the Kid's hands came out of his pocket with the spring-knife. The knife clicked open as Billie regained his balance.

The Kid jumped close.

He knew knives. None of your clumsy downward strokes with the blade sticking out the bottom of his fist.

Thumb and crooked forefinger guided blade. He struck upward. Under Billie's shoulder. Once. Deep.

Billie pitched forward, smashing the woman to the floor under him. He rolled off her and was dead on his back among the furniture-stuffing. Dead, he seemed larger than ever, seemed to fill the room.

The Whosis Kid wiped his knife clean on a piece of carpet, snapped it shut, and dropped it back in his pocket. He did this with his left hand. His right was close to his hip. He did not look at the knife. His eyes were on Maurois.

But if he expected the Frenchman to squawk, he was disappointed. Maurois' little mustache twitched, and his face was white and strained, but:

"We'd better hurry with what we have to do, and get out of here," he suggested.

The woman sat up beside the dead man, whimpering. Her face was ashy under her dark skin. She was licked. A shaking hand fumbled beneath her clothes. It brought out a little flat silk bag.

Maurois—nearer than the Kid—took it. It was sewed too securely for his fingers to open. He held it while the Kid ripped it with his knife. The Frenchman poured part of the contents out in one cupped hand.

Diamonds. Pearls. A few colored stones among them.

Big Chin blew his breath out in a faint whistle. His eyes were bright on the sparkling stones. So were the eyes of Maurois, the woman, and the Kid.

Big Chin's inattention was a temptation. I could reach his jaw. I could knock him over. The strength Billie had mauled out of me had nearly all come back by now. I could knock Big Chin over and have at least one of his guns by the time the Kid and Maurois got set. It was time for me to do something. I had let these comedians run the show long enough. The stuff had come to light. If I let the party break up there was no telling when, if ever, I could round up these folks again.

But I put the temptation away and made myself wait a bit longer. No use going off half-cocked. With a gun in my hand, facing the Kid and Maurois, I still would have less than an even break. That's not enough. The idea in this detective business is to catch crooks, not to put on heroics.

Maurois was pouring the stones back in the bag when I looked at him again. He started to put the bag in his pocket. The Whosis Kid stopped him with a hand on his arm.

"I'll pack 'em."

Maurois' eyebrows went up.

"There's two of you and one of me," the Kid explained. "I trust you, and all the like of that, but just the same I'm carrying my own share."

"But—"

The doorbell interrupted Maurois' protest.

The Kid spun to the girl.

"You do the talking—and no wise breaks!"

She got up from the floor and went to the passageway.

"Who is there?" she called.

The landlady's voice, stern and wrathful:

"Another sound, Mrs. Almad, and I shall call the police. This is disgraceful!"

I wondered what she would have thought if she had opened the unlocked door and taken a look at her apartment—furniture whittled and gutted; a dead man—the noise of whose dying had brought her up here this second time—lying in the middle of the litter.

I wondered—I took a chance.

"Aw, go jump down the sewer!" I told her.

A gasp, and we heard no more from her. I hoped she was speeding her injured feelings to the telephone. I might need the police she had mentioned.

The Kid's gun was out. For a while it was a toss-up. I would lie down beside Billie, or I wouldn't. If I could have been knifed quietly, I would have gone. But nobody was behind me. The Kid knew I wouldn't stand still and quiet while he carved me. He didn't want any more racket than necessary, now that the jewels were on hand.

"Keep your clam shut or I'll shut it for you!" was the worst I got out of it.

The Kid turned to the Frenchman again. The Frenchman had used the time spent in this side-play to pocket the gems.

"Either we divvy here and now, or I carry the stuff," the Kid announced. "There's two of you to see I don't take a Mickey Finn on you."

"But, Kid, we cannot stay here! Is not the landlady even now calling the police? We will go elsewhere to divide. Why cannot you trust me when you are with me?"

Two steps put the Kid between the door and both Maurois and Big Chin. One of the Kid's hands held the gun he had flashed on me. The other was conveniently placed to his other gun.

"Nothing stirring!" he said through his nose. "My cut of them stones don't go out of here in nobody else's kick. If you want to split 'em here, good enough. If you don't, I'll do the carrying. That's flat!"

"But the police!"

"You worry about them. I'm taking one thing at a time, and it's the stones right now."

A vein came out blue in the Frenchman's forehead. His small body was rigid. He was trying to collect enough courage to swap shots with the Kid. He knew, and the Kid knew, that one of them was going to have all the stuff when the curtain came down. They had started off by double-crossing each other. They weren't likely to change their habits. One would have the stones in the end. The other would have nothing—except maybe a burial.

Big Chin didn't count. He was too simple a thug to last long in his present company. If he had known anything, he would have used one of his guns on each of them right now. Instead, he continued to cover me, trying to watch them out of the tail of his eye.

The woman stood near the door, where she had gone to talk to the landlady. She was staring at the Frenchman and the Kid. I wasted precious minutes that seemed to run into hours trying to catch her eye. I finally got it.

I looked at the light-switch, only a foot from her. I looked at her. I looked at the switch again. At her. At the switch.

She got me. Her hand crept sidewise along the wall.

I looked at the two principal players in this button-button game.

The Kid's eyes were dead—and deadly—circles. Maurois' one open eye was watery. He couldn't make the grade. He put a hand in his pocket and brought out the silk bag.

The woman's brown finger topped the light-button. God knows she was nothing to gamble on, but I had no choice. I had to be in motion when the lights went. Big Chin would pump metal. I had to trust Inés not to balk. If she did, my name was Denis.

Her nail whitened.

I went for Maurois.

Darkness—streaked with orange and blue—filled with noise.

My arms had Maurois. We crashed down on dead Billie. I twisted around, kicking the Frenchman's face. Loosened one arm. Caught one of his. His other hand gouged at my face. That told me the bag was in the one I held. Clawing fingers tore my mouth. I put my teeth in them and kept them there. One of my knees was on his face. I put my weight on it. My teeth still held his hand. Both of my hands were free to get the bag.

Not nice, this work, but effective.

The room was the inside of a black drum on which a

giant was beating the long roll. Four guns worked together in a prolonged throbbing roar.

Maurois' fingernails dug into my thumb. I had to open my mouth—let his hand escape. One of my hands found the bag. He wouldn't let go. I screwed his thumb. He cried out. I had the bag.

I tried to leave him then. He grabbed my legs. I kicked at him—missed. He shuddered twice—and stopped moving. A flying bullet had hit him, I took it. Rolling over to the floor, snuggling close to him, I ran a hand over him. A hard bulge came under my hand. I put my hand in his pocket and took back my gun.

On hands and knees—one fist around my gun, the other clutching the silk sack of jewels—I turned to where the door to the next room should have been. A foot wrong, I corrected my course. As I went through the door, the racket in the room behind me stopped.

Huddled close to the wall inside the door, I stowed the silk bag away, and regretted that I hadn't stayed plastered to the floor behind the Frenchman. This room was dark. It hadn't been dark when the woman switched off the sitting-room lights. Every room in the apartment had been lighted then. All were dark now. Not knowing who had darkened them, I didn't like it.

No sounds came from the room I had quit.

The rustle of gently falling rain came from an open window that I couldn't see, off to one side.

Another sound came from behind me. The muffled tattoo of teeth on teeth.

That cheered me. Inés the scary, of course. She had left the sitting-room in the dark and put out the rest of the lights. Maybe nobody else was behind me.

231

Breathing quietly through wide-open mouth, I waited. I couldn't hunt for the woman in the dark without making noises. Maurois and the Kid had strewn furniture and parts of furniture everywhere. I wished I knew if she was holding a gun. I didn't want to have her spraying me.

Not knowing, I waited where I was.

Her teeth clicked on for minutes.

Something moved in the sitting-room. A gun thundered.

"Inés!" I hissed toward the chattering teeth.

No answer. Furniture scraped in the sitting-room. Two guns went off together. A groaning broke out.

"I've got the stuff," I whispered under cover of the groaning.

That brought an answer.

"Jerry! Ah, come here to me!"

The groans went on, but fainter, in the other room. I crawled toward the woman's voice. I went on hands and knees, bumping as carefully as possible against things. I couldn't see anything. Midway, I put a hand down on a soggy bundle of fur—the late purple Frana. I went on.

Inés touched my shoulder with an eager hand.

"Give them to me," were her first words.

I grinned at her in the dark, patted her hand, found her head, and put my mouth to her ear.

"Let's get back in the bedroom," I breathed, paying no attention to her request for the loot. "The Kid will be coming." I didn't doubt that he had bested Big Chin. "We can handle him better in the bedroom."

I wanted to receive him in a room with only one door.

She led me—both of us on hands and knees—to the bedroom. I did what thinking seemed necessary as we crawled. The Kid couldn't know yet how the Frenchman and I had come out. If he guessed, he would guess that the Frenchman had survived. He would be likely to put me in the chump class with Billie, and think the Frenchman could handle me. The chances were that he had got Big Chin, and knew it by now. It was black as black in the sitting-room, but he must know by now that he was the only living thing there.

He blocked the only exit from the apartment. He would think, then, that Inés and Maurois were still alive in it, with the spoils. What would he do about it? There was no pretense of partnership now. That had gone with the lights. The Kid was after the stones. The Kid was after them alone.

I'm no wizard at guessing the other guy's next move. But my idea was that the Kid would be on his way after us, soon. He knew—he must know—that the police were coming; but I had him doped as crazy enough to disregard the police until they appeared. He'd figure that there would be only a couple of them—prepared for nothing more violent than a drinking-party. He could handle them—or he would think he could. Meanwhile, he would come after the stones.

The woman and I reached the bedroom, the room farthest back in the apartment, a room with only one door. I heard her fumbling with the door, trying to close it. I couldn't see, but I got my foot in the way.

"Leave it open," I whispered.

I didn't want to shut the Kid out. I wanted to take him in.

On my belly, I crawled back to the door, felt for my watch, and propped it on the sill, in the angle between door and frame. I wriggled back from it until I was six or eight feet away, looking diagonally across the open doorway at the watch's luminous dial.

The phosphorescent numbers could not be seen from the other side of the door. They faced me. Anybody who came through the door—unless he jumped—must, if only for a split-second, put some part of himself between me and the watch.

On my belly, my gun cocked, its butt steady on the floor, I waited for the faint light to be blotted out.

I waited a time. Pessimism: perhaps he wasn't coming; perhaps I would have to go after him; perhaps he would run out, and I would lose him after all my trouble.

Inés, beside me, breathed quaveringly in my ear, and shivered.

"Don't touch me," I growled at her as she tried to cuddle against me.

She was shaking my arm.

Glass broke in the next room.

Silence.

The luminous patches on the watch burnt my eyes. I couldn't afford to blink. A foot could pass the dial while I was blinking. I couldn't afford to blink, but I had to blink. I blinked. I couldn't tell whether something had passed the watch or not. I had to blink again. Tried to hold my eyes stiffly opened. Failed. I almost shot at the third blink. I could have sworn something had gone between me and the watch.

The Kid, whatever he was up to, made no sound.

The dark woman began to sob beside me. Throat noises that could guide bullets.

I lumped her with my eyes and cursed the lot—not aloud, but from the heart.

My eyes smarted. Moisture filmed them. I blinked it away, losing sight of the watch for precious instants. The butt of my gun was slimy with my hand's sweat. I was thoroughly uncomfortable, inside and out.

Gunpowder burned at my face.

A screaming maniac of a woman was crawling all over me.

My bullet hit nothing lower than the ceiling.

I flung, maybe kicked, the woman off, and snaked backward. She moaned somewhere to one side. I couldn't see the Kid—couldn't hear him. The watch was visible again, farther away. A rustling.

The watch vanished.

I fired at it.

Two points of light near the floor gave out fire and thunder.

My gun-barrel as close to the floor as I could hold it, I fired between those points. Twice.

Twin flames struck at me again.

My right hand went numb. My left took the gun. I sped two more bullets on their way. That left one in my gun.

I don't know what I did with it. My head filled up with funny notions. There wasn't any room. There wasn't any darkness. There wasn't anything. . . .

I opened my eyes in dim light. I was on my back. Beside me the dark woman knelt, shivering and sniffling. Her hands were busy—in my clothes.

One of them came out of my vest with the jewel-bag.

Coming to life, I grabbed her arm. She squealed as if I were a stirring corpse. I got the bag again.

"Give them back, Jerry," she wailed, trying frantically to pull my fingers loose. "They are my things. Give them!"

Sitting up, I looked around.

Beside me lay a shattered bedside lamp, whose fall—caused by carelessness with my feet, or one of the Kid's bullets—had KO'd me. Across the room, face down, arms spread in a crucified posture, the Whosis Kid sprawled. He was dead.

From the front of the apartment—almost indistinguishable from the throbbing in my head—came the pounding of heavy blows. The police were kicking down the unlocked door.

The woman went quiet. I whipped my head around. The knife stung my cheek—put a slit in the lapel of my coat. I took it away from her.

There was no sense to this. The police were already here. I humored her, pretending a sudden coming to full consciousness.

"Oh, it's you!" I said. "Here they are."

I handed her the silk bag of jewels just as the first policeman come into the room.

I didn't see Inés again before she was taken back East to be hit with a life-sentence in the Massachusetts big house. Neither of the policemen who crashed into her apartment that night knew me. The woman and I were separated before I ran into anyone who did know me, which gave me an opportunity to arrange that she would not be tipped off to my identity. The most difficult part of the performance was to keep myself out of the newspapers, since I had to tell the coroner's jury about the deaths of Billie, Big Chin, Maurois and the Whosis Kid. But I managed it. So far as I know, the dark woman still thinks I am Jerry Young, the bootlegger.

The Old Man talked to her before she left San Francisco. Fitting together what he got from her and what the Boston branch got, the history runs like this:

A Boston jeweler named Tunnicliffe had a trusted employee named Binder. Binder fell in with a dark woman named Inés Almad. The dark woman, in turn, had a couple of shifty friends—a Frenchman named Maurois, and a native of Boston whose name was either Carey or Cory, but who was better known as the Whosis Kid. Out of that sort of combination almost anything was more than likely to come.

What came was a scheme. The faithful Binder—part of whose duties it was to open the shop in the morning and close it at night—was to pick out the richest of the unset stones bought for the holiday trade, carry them off with him one evening, and turn them over to Inés. She was to turn them into money.

To cover up Binder's theft, the Whosis Kid and the Frenchman were to rob the jeweler's shop immediately after the door was opened the following morning. Binder and the porter—who would not notice the absence of the most valuable pieces from the stock—would be the only ones in the shop. The robbers would take whatever they could get. In addition to their pickings, they were to be paid two hundred and fifty dollars apiece, and in case either was caught later, Binder could be counted on not to identify them.

That was the scheme as Binder knew it. There were angles he didn't suspect.

Between Inés, Maurois and the Kid there was another agreement. She was to leave for Chicago with the stones as soon as Binder gave them to her, and wait there for Maurois and the Kid. She and the Frenchman would have been satisfied to run off and let Binder hold the sack. The Whosis Kid insisted that the hold-up go through as planned, and that the foolish Binder be killed. Binder knew too much about them, the Kid said, and he would squawk his head off as soon as he learned he had been double-crossed.

The Kid had his way, and he had shot Binder.

Then had come the sweet mess of quadruple and sextuple crossing that had led all three into calamity: the woman's private agreements with the Kid and Maurois—to meet one in St. Louis and the other in New Orleans—and her flight alone with the loot to San Francisco.

Billie was an innocent bystander—or almost. A lumberhandler Inés had run into somewhere, and picked up as a sort of cushion against the rough spots along the rocky road she traveled.

THE
MAIN
DEATH

The Captain told me Hacken and Begg were handling the job. I caught them leaving the detectives' assembly room. Begg was a freckled heavyweight, as friendly as a Saint Bernard puppy, but less intelligent. Lanky detective-sergeant Hacken, not so playful, carried the team's brains behind his worried hatchet face.

"In a hurry?" I inquired.

"Always in a hurry when we're quitting for the day," Begg said, his freckles climbing up his face to make room for his grin.

"What do you want?" Hacken asked.

"I want the low-down on the Main doings—if any."

"You going to work on it?"

"Yes," I said, "for Main's boss—Gungen."

"Then you can tell us something. Why'd he have the twenty thou in cash?"

"Tell you in the morning," I promised. "I haven't

seen Gungen yet. Got a date with him tonight."

While we talked we had gone into the assembly room, with its schoolroom arrangement of desks and benches. Half a dozen police detectives were scattered among them, doing reports. We three sat around Hacken's desk and the lanky detective-sergeant talked:

"Main got home from Los Angeles at eight, Sunday night, with twenty thousand in his wallet. He'd gone down there to sell something for Gungen. You find out why he had that much in cash. He told his wife he had driven up from L.A. with a friend—no name. She went to bed around ten-thirty, leaving him reading. He had the money—two hundred hundred-dollar bills—in a brown wallet.

"So far, so good. He's in the living-room reading. She's in the bedroom sleeping. Just the two of them in the apartment. A racket wakes her. She jumps out of bed, runs into the living-room. There's Main wrestling with a couple of men. One's tall and husky. The other's little—kind of girlish built. Both have got black handkerchiefs over their mugs and caps pulled down.

"When Mrs. Main shows, the little one breaks away from Main and sticks her up. Puts a gun in Mrs. Main's face and tells her to behave. Main and the other guy are still scuffling. Main has got his gun in his hand, but the thug has him by the wrist, trying to twist it. He makes it pretty soon—Main drops the rod. The thug flashes his own, holding Main off while he bends down to pick up the one that fell.

"When the man stoops, Main piles on him. He manages to knock the fellow's gun out of his hand, but by that time the fellow had got the one on the floor —the one Main had dropped. They're heaped up there for a couple of seconds. Mrs. Main can't see what's happening. Then bang! Main's falling away, his vest burning where the shot had set fire to it, a bullet in his heart, his gun smoking in the masked guy's fist. Mrs. Main passes out.

"When she comes to there's nobody in the apartment but herself and her dead husband. His wallet's gone, and so is his gun. She was unconscious for about half an hour. We know that, because other people heard the shot and could give us the time—even if they didn't know where it came from.

"The Mains' apartment is on the sixth floor. It's an eight-story building. Next door to it, on the corner of Eighteenth Avenue, is a two-story building—grocery downstairs, grocer's flat upstairs. Behind these buildings runs a narrow back street—an alley. All right.

"Kinney—the patrolman on that beat—was walking down Eighteenth Avenue. He heard the shot. It was clear to him, because the Mains' apartment is on that side of the building—the side overlooking the grocer's —but Kinney couldn't place it right away. He wasted time scouting around up the street. By the time he got down as far as the alley in his hunting, the birds had flown. Kinney found signs of 'em though—they had dropped a gun in the alley—the gun they'd taken from Main and shot him with. But Kinney didn't see 'em— didn't see anybody who might have been them.

"Now, from a hall window of the apartment house's third floor to the roof of the grocer's building is easy going. Anybody but a cripple could make it—in or out —and the window's never locked. From the grocer's roof to the back street is almost as easy. There's a cast iron pipe, a deep window, a door with heavy hinges sticking out—a regular ladder up and down that back wall. Begg and I did it without working up a sweat.

The pair could have gone in that way. We know they left that way. On the grocer's roof we found Main's wallet—empty, of course—and a handkerchief. The wallet had metal corners. The handkerchief had caught on one of 'em, and went with it when the crooks tossed it away."

"Main's handkerchief?"

"A woman's—with an E in one corner."

"Mrs. Main's?"

"Her name is Agnes," Hacken said. "We showed her the wallet, the gun, and the handkerchief. She identified the first two as her husband's, but the handkerchief was a new one on her. However, she could give us the name of the perfume on it—*Désir du Coeur*. And—with it for a guide—she said the smaller of the masked pair could have been a woman. She had already described him as kind of girlish built."

"Any fingerprints, or the like?" I asked.

"No. Phels went over the apartment, the window, the roof, the wallet and the gun. Not a smear."

"Mrs. Main identify 'em?"

"She says she'd know the little one. Maybe she would."

"Got anything on the who?"

"Not yet," the lanky detective-sergeant said as we moved to the door.

In the street I left the police sleuths and set out for Bruno Gungen's home in Westwood Park.

The dealer in rare and antique jewelry was a little bit of a man and a fancy one. His dinner jacket was corset-tight around his waist, padded high and sharp at the shoulders. Hair, mustache and spade-shaped goatee were dyed black and greased until they were as shiny as his pointed pink fingernails. I wouldn't bet a cent that the color in his fifty-year-old cheeks wasn't rouge. He came out of the depths of a leather library chair to give me a soft, warm hand that was no larger than a child's, bowing and smiling at me with his head tilted to one side.

Then he introduced me to his wife, who bowed without getting up from her seat at the table. Apparently she was a little more than a third of his age. She couldn't have been a day over nineteen, and she looked more like sixteen. She was as small as he, with a dimpled olive-skinned face, round brown eyes, a plump painted mouth and the general air of an expensive doll in a toy-store window.

Bruno Gungen explained to her at some length that I was connected with the Continental Detective Agency, and that he had employed me to help the police find Jeffrey Main's murderers and recover the stolen twenty thousand dollars.

She murmured, "Oh, yes!" in a tone that said she was not the least bit interested, and stood up, saying, "Then I'll leave you to—"

"No, no, my dear!" Her husband was waving his pink fingers at her. "I would have no secrets from you."

His ridiculous little face jerked around to me, cocked itself sidewise, and he asked, with a little giggle: "Is not that so? That between husband and wife there should be no secrets?"

I pretended I agreed with him.

"You, I know, my dear," he addressed his wife, who had sat down again, "are as much interested in this as I, for did we not have an equal affection for dear Jeffrey? Is it not so?"

She repeated, "Oh, yes!" with the same lack of interest.

Her husband turned to me and said, "Now?" encouragingly.

"I've seen the police," I told him. "Is there anything you can add to their story? Anything new? Anything you didn't tell them?"

He whisked his face around toward his wife. "Is there, Enid, dear?"

"I know of nothing," she replied.

He giggled and made a delighted face at me.

"That is it," he said. "We know of nothing."

"He came back to San Francisco at eight o'clock Sunday night—three hours before he was killed and robbed—with twenty thousand dollars in hundred-dollar bills. What was he doing with it?"

"It was the proceeds of a sale to a customer," Bruno Gungen explained. "Mr. Nathaniel Ogilvie, of Los Angeles."

"But why cash?"

The little man's painted face screwed itself up into a shrewd leer.

"A bit of hanky-panky," he confessed complacently, "a trick of the trade, as one says. You know the genus collector? Ah, there is a study for you! Observe. I obtain a golden tiara of early Grecian workmanship, or let me be correct—purporting to be of early Grecian workmanship, purporting also to have been found in Southern Russia, near Odessa. Whether there is any truth in either of these suppositions I do not know, but certainly the tiara is a thing of beauty."

He giggled.

"Now I have a client, a Mr. Nathaniel Ogilvie, of Los Angeles, who has an appetite for curios of the sort —a very devil of a *cacoethes carpendi*. The value of these items, you will comprehend, is exactly what one can get for them—no more, little less. This tiara—now ten thousand dollars is the least I could have expected for it, if sold as one sells an ordinary article of the sort. But can one call a golden cap made long ago for some forgotten Scythian king an ordinary article of any sort? No! No! So, swaddled in cotton, intricately packed, Jeffrey carries this tiara to Los Angeles to show our Mr. Ogilvie.

"In what manner the tiara came into our hands Jeffrey will not say. But he will hint at devious intrigues, smuggling, a little of violence and lawlessness here and there, the necessity for secrecy. For your true collector, there is the bait! Nothing is anything to him except as it is difficultly come by. Jeffrey will not lie. No! *Mon Dieu,* that would be dishonest, despicable! But he will suggest much, and he will refuse, oh, so emphatically! to take a check for the tiara. No check, my dear sir! Nothing which may be traced! Cash moneys!

"Hanky-panky, as you see. But where is the harm? Mr. Ogilvie is certainly going to buy the tiara, and our little deceit simply heightens his pleasure in his purchase. He will enjoy its possession so much the more. Besides, who is to say that this tiara is not authentic? If it is, then these things Jeffrey suggests are indubitably true. Mr. Ogilvie does buy it, for twenty thousand dollars, and that is why poor Jeffrey had in his possession so much cash money."

He flourished a pink hand at me, nodded his dyed head vigorously, and finished with, "*Voilà!* That is it!"

"Did you hear from Main after he got back?" I asked.

The dealer smiled as if my question tickled him, turning his head so that the smile was directed at his wife.

"Did we, Enid, darling?" he passed on the question.

She pouted and shrugged her shoulders indifferently.

"The first we knew he had returned," Gungen interpreted these gestures to me, "was Monday morning, when we heard of his death. Is it not so, my dove?"

His dove murmured, "Yes," and left her chair, saying, "You'll excuse me? I have a letter to write."

"Certainly, my dear," Gungen told her as he and I stood up.

She passed close to him on her way to the door. His small nose twitched over his dyed mustache and he rolled his eyes in a caricature of ecstasy.

"What a delightful scent, my precious!" he exclaimed. "What a heavenly odor! What a song to the nostrils! Has it a name, my love?"

"Yes," she said, pausing in the doorway, not looking back.

"And it is?"

"*Désir du Coeur*," she replied over her shoulder as she left us.

Bruno Gungen looked at me and giggled.

I sat down again and asked him what he knew about Jeffrey Main.

"Everything, no less," he assured me. "For a dozen years, since he was a boy of eighteen he has been my right eye, my right hand."

"Well, what sort of man was he?"

Bruno Gungen showed me his pink palms side by side.

"What sort is any man?" he asked over them.

That didn't mean anything to me, so I kept quiet, waiting.

"I shall tell you," the little man began presently. "Jeffrey had the eye and the taste for this traffic of mine. No man living save myself alone has a judgment in these matters which I would prefer to Jeffrey's. And, honest, mind you! Let nothing I say mislead you on that point. Never a lock have I to which Jeffrey had not also the key, and might have it forever, if he had lived so long.

"But there is a but. In his private life, rascal is a word that only does him justice. He drank, he gambled, he loved, he spent—dear God, how he spent! He was, in this drinking and gaming and loving and spending, a most promiscuous fellow, beyond doubt. With moderation he had nothing to do. Of the moneys he got by inheritance, of the fifty thousand dollars or more his wife had when they were married, there is no remainder. Fortunately, he was insured—else his wife would have been left penniless. Oh, he was a true Heliogabalus, that fellow!"

Bruno Gungen went down to the front door with me when I left. I said, "Good night," and walked down the gravel path to where I had left my car. The night was clear, dark, moonless. High hedges were black walls on both sides of the Gungen place. To the left there was a barely noticeable hole in the blackness—a dark-gray hole—oval—the size of a face.

I got into my car, stirred up the engine and drove away. Into the first cross-street I turned, parked the machine, and started back toward Gungen's afoot. I was curious about that face-size oval.

When I reached the corner, I saw a woman coming toward me from the direction of Gungen's. I was in the shadow of a wall. Cautiously, I backed away from the corner until I came to a gate with brick buttresses sticking out. I made myself flat between them.

The woman crossed the street, went on up the driveway, toward the car line. I couldn't make out anything about her, except that she was a woman. Maybe she was coming from Gungen's grounds, maybe not. Maybe it was her face I had seen against the hedge, maybe not. It was a heads or tails proposition. I guessed yes and tailed her up the drive.

Her destination was a drug store on the car line. Her business there was with the telephone. She spent ten minutes at it. I didn't go into the store to try for an earful, but stayed on the other side of the street, contenting myself with a good look at her.

She was a girl of about twenty-five, medium in height, chunky in build, with pale gray eyes that had little pouches under them, a thick nose and a prominent lower lip. She had no hat over her brown hair. Her body was wrapped in a long blue cape.

From the drug store I shadowed her back to the Gungen house. She went in the back door.

A servant, probably, but not the maid who had opened the door for me earlier in the evening.

I returned to my car, drove back to town, to the office.

"Is Dick Foley working on anything?" I asked Fiske, who sits on the Continental Detective Agency's affairs at night.

"No. Did you ever hear the story about the fellow who had his neck operated on?" With the slightest encouragement, Fiske is good for a dozen stories without a stop, so I said:

"Yes. Get hold of Dick and tell him I've got a shadow job out Westwood Park way for him to start on in the morning."

I gave Fiske—to be passed on to Dick—Gungen's address and a description of the girl who had done the phoning from the drug store. Then I assured the night man that I had also heard the story about the pickaninny named Opium, and likewise the one about what the old man said to his wife on their golden wedding anniversary. Before he could try me with another, I escaped to my own office, where I composed and coded a telegram to our Los Angeles branch, asking that Main's recent visit to that city be dug into.

The next morning Hacken and Begg dropped in to see me and I gave them Gungen's version of why the twenty thousand had been in cash. The police detectives told me a stool-pigeon had brought them word that Bunky Dahl—a local guerrilla who did a moderate business in hijacking—had been flashing a roll since about the time of Main's death.

"We haven't picked him up yet," Hacken said. "Haven't been able to place him, but we've got a line on his girl. Course, he might have got his dough somewhere else."

At ten o'clock that morning I had to go over to Oakland to testify against a couple of flimflammers who had sold bushels of stock in a sleight-of-hand rubber manufacturing business. When I got back to the Agency, at six that evening, I found a wire from Los Angeles on my desk.

Jeffrey Main, the wire told me, had finished his business with Ogilvie Saturday afternoon, had checked out of his hotel immediately, and had left on the Owl that evening, which would have put him in San Francisco early Sunday morning. The hundred-dollar bills with which Ogilvie had paid for the tiara had been new ones, consecutively numbered, and Ogilvie's bank had given the Los Angeles operative the numbers.

Before I quit for the day, I phoned Hacken, gave him these numbers as well as the other dope in the telegram.

"Haven't found Dahl yet," he told me.

Dick Foley's report came in the next morning. The girl had left the Gungen house at 9:15 the previous night, had gone to the corner of Miramar Avenue and Southwood Drive, where a man was waiting for her in a Buick coupé. Dick described him: Age about 30; height about five feet ten; slender, weight about 140; medium complexion; brown hair and eyes; long thin face with pointed chin; brown hat, suit and shoes and gray overcoat.

The girl got into the car with him and they drove out to the beach, along the Great Highway for a little while, and then back to Miramar and Southwood, where the girl got out. She seemed to be going back to the house, so Dick let her go and tailed the man in the Buick down to the Futurity Apartments in Mason Street.

The man stayed in there for half an hour or so and then came out with another man and two women. This second man was of about the same age as the first, about five feet eight inches tall, would weigh about a hundred and seventy pounds, had brown hair and eyes, a dark complexion, a flat, broad face with high cheekbones, and wore a blue suit, gray hat, tan overcoat, black shoes, and a pear-shaped pearl tie-pin.

One of the women was about twenty-two years old, small, slender and blond. The other was probably three or four years older, red-haired, medium in height and build, with a turned-up nose.

The quartet had got in the car and gone to the Algerian Café, where they had stayed until a little after one in the morning. Then they had returned to the Futurity Apartments. At half-past three the two men had left, driving the Buick to a garage in Post Street, and then walking to the Mars Hotel. When I had finished reading this I called Mickey Linehan in from the operatives' room, gave him the report and instructions:

"Find out who these folks are."

Mickey went out. My phone rang.

Bruno Gungen: "Good morning. May you have something to tell me today?"

"Maybe," I said. "You're downtown?"

"Yes, in my shop. I shall be here until four."

"Right. I'll be in to see you this afternoon."

At noon Mickey Linehan returned. "The first bloke," he reported, "the one Dick saw with the girl, is named Benjamin Weel. He owns the Buick and lives in the Mars—room 410. He's a salesman, though it's not known what of. The other man is a friend of his who has been staying with him for a couple of days. I couldn't get anything on him. He's not registered. The two women in the Futurity are a couple of hustlers. They live in apartment 303. The larger one goes by the name of Mrs. Effie Roberts. The little blonde is Violet Evarts."

"Wait," I told Mickey, and went back into the file room, to the index-card drawers.

I ran through the W's—*Weel, Benjamin, alias Coughing Ben, 36,312W.*

The contents of folder No. 36,312W told me that Coughing Ben Weel had been arrested in Amador County in 1916 on a highgrading charge and had been sent to San Quentin for three years. In 1922 he had been picked up again in Los Angeles and charged with trying to blackmail a movie actress, but the case had fallen through. His description fit the one Dick had given of the man in the Buick. His photograph—a copy of the one taken by the Los Angeles police in '22—showed a sharp-featured young man with a chin like a wedge.

I took the photo back to my office and showed it to Mickey.

"This is Weel five years ago. Follow him around a while."

When the operative had gone I called the police detective bureau. Neither Hacken nor Begg was in. I got hold of Lewis, in the identification department.

"What does Bunky Dahl look like?" I asked him.

"Wait a minute," Lewis said, and then: "32, 67½, 174, medium, brown, brown, broad flat face with prominent cheekbones, gold bridge work in lower left jaw, brown mole under right ear, deformed little toe on right foot."

"Have you a picture of him to spare?"

"Sure."

"Thanks, I'll send a boy down for it."

I told Tommy Howd to go down and get it, and then went out for some food. After luncheon I went up to Gungen's establishment in Post Street. The little dealer was gaudier than ever this afternoon in a black coat that was even more padded in the shoulders and tighter in the waist than his dinner coat had been the other night, striped gray pants, a vest that leaned toward magenta, and a billowy satin tie wonderfully embroidered with gold thread.

We went back through his store, up a narrow flight of stairs to a small cube of an office on the mezzanine floor.

"And now you have to tell me?" he asked when we were seated, with the door closed.

"I've got more to ask than tell. First, who is the girl with the thick nose, the thick lower lip, and the pouches under gray eyes, who lives in your house?"

"That is one Rose Rubury." His little painted face was wrinkled in a satisfied smile. "She is my dear wife's maid."

"She goes riding with an ex-convict."

"She does?" He stroked his dyed goatee with a pink hand, highly pleased. "Well, she is my dear wife's maid, that she is."

"Main didn't drive up from Los Angeles with a friend, as he told his wife. He came up on the train Saturday night—so he was in town twelve hours before he showed up at home."

Bruno Gungen giggled, cocking his delighted face to one side.

"Ah!" he tittered. "We progress! We progress! Is it not so?"

"Maybe. Do you remember if this Rose Rubury was in the house on Sunday night—say from eleven to twelve?"

"I do remember. She was. I know it certainly. My dear wife was not feeling well that night. My darling had gone out early that Sunday morning, saying she was going to drive out into the country with some friends—what friends I do not know. But she came home at eight o'clock that night complaining of a distressing headache. I was quite frightened by her appearance, so that I went often to see how she was, and thus it happens that I know her maid was in the house all of that night, until one o'clock, at least."

"Did the police show you the handkerchief they found with Main's wallet?"

"Yes." He squirmed on the edge of his chair, his face like the face of a kid looking at a Christmas tree.

"You're sure it's your wife's?"

His giggle interfered with his speech, so he said, "Yes," by shaking his head up and down until the goatee seemed to be a black whiskbroom brushing his tie.

"She could have left it at the Mains' some time when she was visiting Mrs. Main," I suggested.

"That is not possible," he corrected me eagerly. "My darling and Mrs. Main are not acquainted."

"But your wife and Main were acquainted?"

He giggled and brushed his tie with his whisker again.

"How well acquainted?"

He shrugged his padded shoulders up to his ears.

"I know not," he said merrily. "I employ a detective."

"Yeah?" I scowled at him. "You employ this one to find out who killed and robbed Main—and for nothing else. If you think you're employing him to dig up your family secrets, you're as wrong as Prohibition."

"But why? But why?" He was flustered. "Have I not the right to know? There will be no trouble over it, no scandal, no divorce suing, of that be assured. Even Jeffrey is dead, so it is what one calls ancient history. While he lived I knew nothing, was blind. After he died I saw certain things. For my own satisfaction— that is all, I beg you to believe—I should like to know with certainty."

"You won't get it out of me," I said bluntly. "I don't know anything about it except what you've told me, and you can't hire me to go further into it. Besides, if you're not going to do anything about it, why don't you keep your hands off—let it sleep?"

"No, no, my friend." He had recovered his bright-eyed cheerfulness. "I am not an old man, but I am fifty-two. My dear wife is eighteen, and a truly lovely person." He giggled. "This thing happened. May it not happen again? And would it not be the part of hus-bandly wisdom to have—shall I say—a hold on her? A rein? A check? Or if it never happens again, still might not one's dear wife be the more docile for cer-tain information which her husband possesses?"

"It's your business." I stood up. "But I don't want any part of it."

"Ah, do not let us quarrel!" He jumped up and took one of my hands in his. "If you will not, you will not. But there remains the criminal aspect of the situation —the aspect that has engaged you thus far. You will not forsake that? You will fulfill your engagement there? Surely?"

"Suppose—just suppose—it should turn out that your wife had a hand in Main's death. What then?"

"That"—he shrugged, holding his hands out, palms up—"would be a matter for the law."

"Good enough. I'll stick—if you understand that you're entitled to no information except what touches your 'criminal aspect.' "

"Excellent! And if it so happens you cannot separate my darling from that—"

I nodded. He grabbed my hand again, patting it. I took it away from him and returned to the Agency.

A memorandum on my desk asked me to phone de-tective-sergeant Hacken. I did.

"Bunky Dahl wasn't in on the Main job," the hatchet-faced man told me. "He and a pal named Coughing Ben Weel were putting on a party in a roadhouse near Vallejo that night. They were there from around ten until they were thrown out after two in the morning for starting a row. It's on the up-and-up. The guy that gave it to me is right—and I got a check-up on it from two others."

I thanked Hacken and phoned Gungen's residence, asking for Mrs. Gungen, asking her if she would see me if I came out there.

"Oh, yes," she said.

It seemed to be her favorite expression, though the way she said it didn't express anything.

Putting the photos of Dahl and Weel in my pocket, I got a taxi and set out for Westwood Park. Using Fatima-smoke on my brains while I rode, I concocted a wonderful series of lies to be told my client's wife—a series that I thought would get me the information I wanted.

A hundred and fifty yards or so up the drive from the house I saw Dick Foley's car standing.

A thin, pasty-faced maid opened the Gungens' door and took me into a sitting-room on the second floor, where Mrs. Gungen put down a copy of *The Sun Also Rises* and waved a cigarette at a nearby chair. She was very much the expensive doll this afternoon in a Persian orange dress, sitting with one foot tucked under her in a brocaded chair.

Looking at her while I lighted a cigarette, remembering my first interview with her and her husband, and my second one with him, I decided to chuck the tale-of-woe I had spent my ride building.

"You've a maid—Rose Rubury," I began. "I don't want her to hear what's said."

She said, "Very well," without the least sign of surprise, added, "Excuse me a moment," and left her chair and the room.

Presently she was back, sitting down with both feet tucked under her now.

"She will be away for at least half an hour."

"That will be long enough. This Rose is friendly with an ex-convict named Weel."

The doll face frowned, and the plump painted lips pressed themselves together. I waited, giving her time to say something. She didn't say it. I took Weel's and Dahl's pictures out and held them out to her.

"The thin-faced one is your Rose's friend. The other's a pal of his—also a crook."

She took the photographs with a tiny hand that was as steady as mine, and looked at them carefully. Her mouth became smaller and tighter, her brown eyes darker. Then, slowly, her face cleared, she murmured, "Oh, yes," and returned the pictures to me.

"When I told your husband about it"—I spoke deliberately—"he said, 'She's my wife's maid,' and laughed."

Enid Gungen said nothing.

"Well?" I asked. "What did he mean by that?"

"How should I know?" she sighed.

"You know your handkerchief was found with Main's empty wallet." I dropped this in a by-the-way tone, pretending to be chiefly occupied putting cigarette ash in a jasper tray that was carved in the form of a lidless coffin.

"Oh, yes," she said wearily, "I've been told that."

"How do you think it happened?"

"I can't imagine."

"I can," I said, "but I'd rather know positively.

Mrs. Gungen, it would save a lot of time if we could talk plain language."

"Why not?" she asked listlessly. "You are in my husband's confidence, have his permission to question me. If it happens to be humiliating to me—well, after all, I am only his wife. And it is hardly likely that any new indignities either of you can devise will be worse than those to which I have already been submitted."

I grunted at this theatrical speech and went ahead.

"Mrs. Gungen, I'm only interested in learning who robbed and killed Main. Anything that points in that direction is valuable to me, but only insofar as it points in that direction. Do you understand what I mean?"

"Certainly," she said. "I understand you are in my husband's employ."

That got us nowhere. I tried again:

"What impression do you suppose I got the other evening, when I was here?"

"I can't imagine."

"Please try."

"Doubtless"—she smiled faintly—"you got the impression that my husband thought I had been Jeffrey's mistress."

"Well?"

"Are you"—her dimples showed; she seemed amused —"asking me if I really was his mistress?"

"No—though of course I'd like to know."

"Naturally you would," she said pleasantly.

"What impression did you get that evening?" I asked.

"I?" She wrinkled her forehead. "Oh, that my husband had hired you to prove that I had been Jeffrey's mistress." She repeated the word mistress as if she liked the shape of it in her mouth.

"You were wrong."

"Knowing my husband, I find that hard to believe."

"Knowing myself, I'm sure of it," I insisted. "There's no uncertainty about it between your husband and me, Mrs. Gungen. It is understood that my job is to find who stole and killed—nothing else."

"Really?" It was a polite ending of an argument of which she had grown tired.

"You're tying my hands," I complained, standing up, pretending I wasn't watching her carefully. "I can't do anything now but grab this Rose Rubury and the two men and see what I can squeeze out of them. You said the girl would be back in half an hour?"

She looked at me steadily with her round brown eyes.

"She should be back in a few minutes. You're going to question her?"

"But not here," I informed her. "I'll take her down to the Hall of Justice and have the men picked up. Can I use your phone?"

"Certainly. It's in the next room." She crossed to open the door for me.

I called Davenport 20 and asked for the detective bureau.

Mrs. Gungen, standing in the sitting-room, said, so softly I could barely hear it:

"Wait."

Holding the phone, I turned to look through the door at her. She was pinching her red mouth between thumb and finger, frowning. I didn't put down the phone until she took the hand from her mouth and held it out toward me. Then I went back into the sitting-room.

261

I was on top. I kept my mouth shut. It was up to her to make the plunge. She studied my face for a minute or more before she began:

"I won't pretend I trust you." She spoke hesitantly, half as if to herself. "You're working for my husband, and even the money would not interest him so much as whatever I had done. It's a choice of evils—certain on the one hand, more than probable on the other."

She stopped talking and rubbed her hands together. Her round eyes were becoming indecisive. If she wasn't helped along she was going to balk.

"There's only the two of us," I urged her. "You can deny everything afterward. It's my word against yours. If you don't tell me—I know now I can get it from the others. Your calling me from the phone lets me know that. You think I'll tell your husband everything. Well, if I have to fry it out of the others, he'll probably read it all in the papers. Your one chance is to trust me. It's not as slim a chance as you think. Anyway, it's up to you."

A half-minute of silence.

"Suppose," she whispered, "I should pay you to—"

"What for? If I'm going to tell your husband, I could take your money and still tell him, couldn't I?"

Her red mouth curved, her dimples appeared and her eyes brightened.

"That is reassuring," she said. "I shall tell you. Jeffrey came back from Los Angeles early so we could have the day together in a little apartment we kept. In the afternoon two men came in—with a key. They had revolvers. They robbed Jeffrey of the money. That was what they had come for. They seemed to know all about it and about us. They called us by name, and taunted us with threats of the story they would tell if we had them arrested.

"We couldn't do anything after they had gone. It was a ridiculously hopeless plight they had put us in. There wasn't anything we could do—since we couldn't possibly replace the money. Jeffrey couldn't even pretend he had lost it or had been robbed of it while he was alone. His secret early return to San Francisco would have been sure to throw suspicion on him. Jeffrey lost his head. He wanted me to run away with him. Then he wanted to go to my husband and tell him the truth. I wouldn't permit either course—they were equally foolish.

"We left the apartment, separating, a little after seven. We weren't, the truth is, on the best of terms by then. He wasn't—now that we were in trouble—as —No, I shouldn't say that."

She stopped and stood looking at me with a placid doll's face that seemed to have got rid of all its troubles by simply passing them to me.

"The pictures I showed you are the two men?" I asked.

"Yes."

"This maid of yours knew about you and Main? Knew about the apartment? Knew about his trip to Los Angeles and his plan to return early with the cash?"

"I can't say she did. But she certainly could have learned most of it by spying and eavesdropping and looking through my—I had a note from Jeffrey telling me about the Los Angeles trip, making the appointment for Sunday morning. Perhaps she could have seen it. I'm careless."

"I'm going now," I said. "Sit tight till you hear from me. And don't scare up the maid."

"Remember, I've told you nothing," she reminded me as she followed me to the sitting-room door.

From the Gungen house I went direct to the Mars Hotel. Mickey Linehan was sitting behind a newspaper in a corner of the lobby.

"They in?" I asked him.

"Yep."

"Let's go up and see them."

Mickey rattled his knuckles on door number 410. A metallic voice asked: "Who's there?"

"Package," Mickey replied in what was meant for a boy's voice.

A slender man with a pointed chin opened the door. I gave him a card. He didn't invite us into the room, but he didn't try to keep us out when we walked in.

"You're Weel?" I addressed him while Mickey closed the door behind us, and then, not waiting for him to say yes, I turned to the broad-faced man sitting on the bed. "And you're Dahl?"

Weel spoke to Dahl, in a casual, metallic voice: "A couple of gumshoes."

The man on the bed looked at us and grinned.

I was in a hurry.

"I want the dough you took from Main," I announced.

They sneered together, as if they had been practicing.

I brought out my gun.

Weel laughed harshly. "Get your hat, Bunky," he chuckled. "We're being taken into custody."

"You've got the wrong idea," I explained. "This isn't a pinch. It's a stick-up. Up go the hands!"

Dahl's hands went up quick.

Weel hesitated until Mickey prodded him in the ribs with the nose of a .38-special.

"Frisk 'em," I ordered Mickey.

He went through Weel's clothes, taking a gun, some papers, some loose money, and a money-belt that was fat. Then he did the same for Dahl.

"Count it," I told him.

Mickey emptied the belts, spit on his fingers and went to work.

"Nineteen thousand, one hundred and twenty-six dollars and sixty-two cents," he reported when he was through.

With the hand that didn't hold my gun, I felt in my pocket for the slip on which I had written the numbers of the hundred-dollar bills Main had got from Ogilvie. I held the slip out to Mickey.

"See if the hundreds check against this."

He took the slip, looked, said, "They do."

"Good—pouch the money and the guns and see if you can turn up any more in the room."

Coughing Ben Weel had got his breath by now.

"Look here!" he protested. "You can't pull this, fellow! Where do you think you are? You can't get away with this!"

"I can try," I assured him. "I suppose you're going to yell, *Police!* Like hell you are! The only squawk you've got coming is at your own dumbness in thinking because your squeeze on the woman was tight enough to keep her from having you copped, you didn't have to worry about anything. I'm playing the same game you played with her and Main—only mine's better, because you can't get tough afterward without facing stir. Now shut up!"

"No more jack," Mickey said. "Nothing but four postage stamps."

"Take 'em along," I told him. "That's practically eight cents. Now we'll go."

"Hey, leave us a couple of bucks," Weel begged.

"Didn't I tell you to shut up?" I snarled at him, backing to the door, which Mickey was opening.

The hall was empty. Mickey stood in it, holding his gun on Weel and Dahl while I backed out of the room and switched the key from the inside to the outside. Then I slammed the door, twisted the key, pocketed it, and we went downstairs and out of the hotel.

Mickey's car was around the corner. In it, we transferred our spoils—except the guns—from his pockets to mine. Then he got out and went back to the Agency. I turned the car toward the building in which Jeffrey Main had been killed.

Mrs. Main was a tall girl of less than twenty-five, with curled brown hair, heavily-lashed gray-blue eyes, and a warm, full-featured face. Her ample body was dressed in black from throat to feet.

She read my card, nodded at my explanation that Gungen had employed me to look into her husband's death, and took me into a gray and white living-room.

"This is the room?" I asked.

"Yes." She had a pleasant, slightly husky voice.

I crossed to the window and looked down on the grocer's roof, and on the half of the back street that was visible. I was still in a hurry.

"Mrs. Main," I said as I turned, trying to soften the abruptness of my words by keeping my voice low, "after your husband was dead, you threw the gun out the window. Then you stuck the handkerchief to the corner of the wallet and threw that. Being lighter than the gun, it didn't go all the way to the alley, but fell on the roof. Why did you put the handkerchief—?"

Without a sound she fainted.

I caught her before she reached the floor, carried her to a sofa, found cologne and smelling salts, applied them.

"Do you know whose handkerchief it was?" I asked when she was awake and sitting up.

She shook her head from left to right.

"Then why did you take that trouble?"

"It was in his pocket. I didn't know what else to do with it. I thought the police would ask about it. I didn't want anything to start them asking questions."

"Why did you tell the robbery story?"

No answer.

"The insurance?" I suggested.

She jerked up her head, cried defiantly:

"Yes! He had gone through his own money and mine. And then he had to—to do a thing like that. He—"

I interrupted her complaint:

"He left a note, I hope—something that will be evidence." Evidence that she hadn't killed him, I meant.

"Yes." She fumbled in the bosom of her black dress.

"Good," I said, standing. "The first thing in the morning, take that note down to your lawyer and tell him the whole story."

I mumbled something sympathetic and made my escape.

Night was coming down when I rang the Gungens' bell for the second time that day. The pasty-faced maid who opened the door told me Mr. Gungen was at home. She led me upstairs.

Rose Rubury was coming down the stairs. She stopped on the landing to let us pass. I halted in front of her while my guide went on toward the library.

"You're done, Rose," I told the girl on the landing. "I'll give you ten minutes to clear out. No word to anybody. If you don't like that—you'll get a chance to see if you like the inside of the can."

"Well—the idea!"

"The racket's flopped." I put a hand into a pocket and showed her one wad of the money I had got at the Mars Hotel. "I've just come from visiting Coughing Ben and Bunky."

That impressed her. She turned and scurried up the stairs.

Bruno Gungen came to the library door, searching for me. He looked curiously from the girl—now running up the steps to the third story—to me. A question was twisting the little man's lips, but I headed it off with a statement:

"It's done."

"Bravo!" he exclaimed as we went into the library. "You hear that, my darling? It is done!"

His darling, sitting by the table, where she had sat the other night, smiled with no expression in her doll's face, and murmured, "Oh, yes," with no expression in her words.

I went to the table and emptied my pockets of money.

"Nineteen thousand, one hundred and twenty-six dollars and seventy cents, including the stamps," I announced. "The other eight hundred and seventy-three dollars and thirty cents is gone."

"Ah!" Bruno Gungen stroked his spade-shaped black beard with a trembling pink hand and pried into my face with hard bright eyes. "And where did you find it? By all means sit down and tell us the tale. We are famished with eagerness for it, eh, my love?"

His love yawned, "Oh, yes!"

"There isn't much story," I said. "To recover the money I had to make a bargain, promising silence. Main was robbed Sunday afternoon. But it happens that we couldn't convict the robbers if we had them. The only person who could identify them—won't."

"But who killed Jeffrey?" The little man was pawing my chest with both pink hands. "Who killed him that night?"

"Suicide. Despair at being robbed under circumstances he couldn't explain."

"Preposterous!" My client didn't like the suicide.

"Mrs. Main was awakened by the shot. Suicide would have canceled his insurance—would have left her penniless. She threw the gun and wallet out the window, hid the note he left, and framed the robber story."

"But the handkerchief!" Gungen screamed. He was all worked up.

"That doesn't mean anything," I assured him solemnly, "except that Main—you said he was promiscuous—had probably been fooling with your wife's maid, and that she—like a lot of maids—helped herself to your wife's belongings."

He puffed up his rouged cheeks, and stamped his feet, fairly dancing. His indignation was as funny as the statement that caused it.

"We shall see!" He spun on his heel and ran out of the room, repeating over and over, "We shall see!"

Enid Gungen held a hand out to me. Her doll face was all curves and dimples.

"I thank you," she whispered.

"I don't know what for," I growled, not taking the hand. "I've got it jumbled so anything like proof is out of the question. But he can't help knowing—didn't I practically tell him?"

"Oh, that!" She put it behind her with a toss of her small head. "I'm quite able to look out for myself so long as he has no definite proof."

I believed her.

Bruno Gungen came fluttering back into the library, frothing at the mouth, tearing his dyed goatee, raging that Rose Rubury was not to be found in the house.

The next morning Dick Foley told me the maid had joined Weel and Dahl and had left for Portland with them.

THE
FAREWELL
MURDER

1

I was the only one who left the train at Farewell.

A man came through the rain from the passenger shed. He was a small man. His face was dark and flat. He wore a gray waterproof cap and a gray coat cut in military style.

He didn't look at me. He looked at the valise and gladstone bag in my hands. He came forward quickly, walking with short, choppy steps.

He didn't say anything when he took the bags from me. I asked:

"Kavalov's?"

He had already turned his back to me and was carrying my bags towards a tan Stutz coach that stood in the roadway beside the gravel station platform. In answer to my question he bowed twice at the Stutz without looking around or checking his jerky half-trot.

I followed him to the car.

Three minutes of riding carried us through the village. We took a road that climbed westward into the hills. The road looked like a seal's back in the rain.

The flat-faced man was in a hurry. We purred over the road at a speed that soon carried us past the last of the cottages sprinkled up the hillside.

Presently we left the shiny black road for a paler one curving south to run along a hill's wooded crest. Now and then this road, for a hundred feet or more at a stretch, was turned into a tunnel by tall trees' heavily leafed boughs interlocking overhead.

Rain accumulated in fat drops on the boughs and came down to thump the Stutz's roof. The dullness of rainy early evening became almost the blackness of night inside these tunnels.

The flat-faced man switched on the lights, and increased our speed.

He sat rigidly erect at the wheel. I sat behind him. Above his military collar, among the hairs that were clipped short on the nape of his neck, globules of moisture made tiny shining points. The moisture could have been rain. It could have been sweat.

We were in the middle of one of the tunnels.

The flat-faced man's head jerked to the left, and he screamed:

"A-a-a-a-a-a!"

It was a long, quivering, high-pitched bleat, thin with terror.

I jumped up, bending forward to see what was the matter with him.

The car swerved and plunged ahead, throwing me back on the seat again.

Through the side window I caught a one-eyed glimpse of something dark lying in the road.

I twisted around to try the back window, less rain-bleared.

I saw a black man lying on his back in the road, near the left edge. His body was arched, as if its weight rested on his heels and the back of his head. A knife handle that couldn't have been less than six inches long stood straight up in the air from the left side of his chest.

By the time I had seen this much we had taken a curve and were out of the tunnel.

"Stop," I called to the flat-faced man.

He pretended he didn't hear me. The Stutz was a tan streak under us. I put a hand on the driver's shoulder.

His shoulder squirmed under my hand, and he screamed "A-a-a-a-a!" again as if the dead black man had him.

I reached past him and shut off the engine.

He took his hands from the wheel and clawed up at me. Noises came from his mouth, but they didn't make any words that I knew.

I got a hand on the wheel. I got my other forearm under his chin. I leaned over the back of his seat so that the weight of my upper body was on his head, mashing it down against the wheel.

Between this and that and the help of God, the Stutz hadn't left the road when it stopped moving.

I got up off the flat-faced man's head and asked:

"What the hell's the matter with you?"

He looked at me with white eyes, shivered, and didn't say anything.

"Turn it around," I said. "We'll go back there."

He shook his head from side to side, desperately, and

made some more of the mouth-noises that might have been words if I could have understood them.

"You know who that was?" I asked.

He shook his head.

"You do," I growled.

He shook his head.

By then I was beginning to suspect that no matter what I said to this fellow I'd get only headshakes out of him.

I said:

"Get away from the wheel, then. I'm going to drive back there."

He opened the door and scrambled out.

"Come back here," I called.

He backed away, shaking his head.

I cursed him, slid in behind the wheel, said, "All right, wait here for me," and slammed the door.

He retreated backwards slowly, watching me with scared, whitish eyes while I backed and turned the coach.

I had to drive back farther than I had expected, something like a mile.

I didn't find the black man. The tunnel was empty.

If I had known the exact spot in which he had been lying, I might have been able to find something to show how he had been removed. But I hadn't had time to pick out a landmark, and now any one of four or five places looked like the spot.

With the help of the coach's lamps I went over the left side of the road from one end of the tunnel to the other.

I didn't find any blood. I didn't find any footprints. I didn't find anything to show that anybody had been lying in the road. I didn't find anything.

It was too dark by now for me to try searching the woods.

I returned to where I had left the flat-faced man.

He was gone.

It looked, I thought, as if Mr. Kavalov might be right in thinking he needed a detective.

2

Half a mile beyond the place where the flat-faced man had deserted me, I stopped the Stutz in front of a grilled steel gate that blocked the road. The gate was padlocked on the inside. From either side of it tall hedging ran off into the woods. The upper part of a brown-roofed small house was visible over the hedge-top to the left.

I worked the Stutz's horn.

The racket brought a gawky boy of fifteen or sixteen to the other side of the gate. He had on bleached whip-cord pants and a wildly striped sweater. He didn't come out to the middle of the road, but stood at one side, with one arm out of sight as if holding something that was hidden from me by the hedge.

"This Kavalov's?" I asked.

"Yes, sir," he said uneasily.

I waited for him to unlock the gate. He didn't unlock it. He stood there looking uneasily at the car and at me.

"Please, mister," I said, "can I come in?"

"What—who are you?"

"I'm the guy that Kavalov sent for. If I'm not going to be let in, tell me, so I can catch the six-fifty back to San Francisco."

The boy chewed his lip, said, "Wait till I see if I can find the key," and went out of sight behind the hedge.

He was gone long enough to have had a talk with somebody.

When he came back he unlocked the gate, swung it open, and said:

"It's all right, sir. They're expecting you."

When I had driven through the gate I could see lights on a hilltop a mile or so ahead and to the left.

"Is that the house?" I asked.

"Yes, sir. They're expecting you."

Close to where the boy had stood while talking to me through the gate, a double-barrel shotgun was propped up against the hedge.

I thanked the boy and drove on. The road wound gently uphill through farmland. Tall, slim trees had been planted at regular intervals on both sides of the road.

The road brought me at last to the front of a building that looked like a cross between a fort and a factory in the dusk. It was built of concrete. Take a flock of squat cones of various sizes, round off the points bluntly, mash them together with the largest one somewhere near the center, the others grouped around it in not too strict accordance with their sizes, adjust the whole collection to agree with the slopes of a hilltop, and you would have a model of the Kavalov house. The windows were steel-sashed. There weren't very many of them. No two were in line either vertically or horizontally. Some were lighted.

As I got out of the car, the narrow front door of this house opened.

A short, red-faced woman of fifty or so, with faded blond hair wound around and around her head, came out. She wore a high-necked, tight-sleeved, gray woolen dress. When she smiled her mouth seemed wide as her lips.

She said:

"You're the gentleman from the city?"

"Yeah. I lost your chauffeur somewhere back on the road."

"Lord bless you," she said amiably, "that's all right."

A thin man with thin dark hair plastered down above a thin, worried face came past her to take my bags when I had lifted them out of the car. He carried them indoors.

The woman stood aside for me to enter, saying:

"Now I suppose you'll want to wash up a little bit before you go in to dinner, and they won't mind waiting for you the few minutes you'll take if you hurry."

I said, "Yeah, thanks," waited for her to get ahead of me again, and followed her up a curving flight of stairs that climbed along the inside of one of the cones that made up the building.

She took me to a second-story bedroom where the thin man was unpacking my bags.

"Martin will get you anything you need," she assured me from the doorway, "and when you're ready, just come on downstairs."

I said I would, and she went away. The thin man had finished unpacking by the time I had got out of coat, vest, collar and shirt. I told him there wasn't anything else I needed, washed up in the adjoining bathroom, put on a fresh shirt and collar, my vest and coat, went downstairs.

The wide hall was empty. Voices came through an open doorway to the left.

One voice was a nasal whine. It complained:

"I will not have it. I will not put up with it. I am not a child, and I will not have it."

This voice's t's were a little too thick for t's, but not thick enough to be d's.

Another voice was a lively, but slightly harsh, baritone. It said cheerfully:

"What's the good of saying we won't put up with it, when we are putting up with it?"

The third voice was feminine, a soft voice, but flat and spiritless. It said:

"But perhaps he did kill him."

The whining voice said: "I do not care. I will not have it."

The baritone voice said, cheerfully as before: "Oh, won't you?"

A doorknob turned farther down the hall. I didn't want to be caught standing there listening. I advanced to the open doorway.

3

I was in the doorway of a low-ceilinged oval room furnished and decorated in gray, white and silver. Two men and a woman were there.

The older man—he was somewhere in his fifties—got up from a deep gray chair and bowed ceremoniously at me. He was a plump man of medium height, completely bald, dark-skinned and pale-eyed. He wore a wax-pointed gray mustache and a straggly gray imperial.

"Mr. Kavalov?" I asked.

"Yes, sir." His was the whining voice.

I told him who I was. He shook my hand and then introduced me to the others.

The woman was his daughter. She was probably thirty. She had her father's narrow, full-lipped mouth, but her eyes were dark, her nose was short and straight, and her skin was almost colorless. Her face had Asia in it. It was pretty, passive, unintelligent.

The man with the baritone voice was her husband. His name was Ringgo. He was six or seven years older than his wife, neither tall nor heavy, but well set-up. His left arm was in splints and a sling. The knuckles of his right hand were darkly bruised. He had a lean, bony, quick-witted face, bright dark eyes with plenty of lines around them, and a good-natured hard mouth.

He gave me his bruised hand, wriggled his bandaged arm at me, grinned, and said:

"I'm sorry you missed this, but the future injuries are yours."

"How did it happen?" I asked.

Kavalov raised a plump hand.

"Time enough it is to go into that when we have eaten," he said. "Let us have our dinner first."

We went into a small green and brown dining-room where a small square table was set. I sat facing Ringgo across a silver basket of orchids that stood between tall silver candlesticks in the center of the table. Mrs. Ringgo sat to my right, Kavalov to my left. When Kavalov sat down I saw the shape of an automatic pistol in his hip pocket.

Two men servants waited on us. There was a lot of food and all of it was well turned out. We ate caviar, some sort of consommé, sand dabs, potatoes and cucumber jelly, roast lamb, corn and string beans, asparagus, wild duck and hominy cakes, artichoke-and-tomato salad, and orange ice. We drank white wine, claret, Burgundy, coffee and *crème de menthe*.

Kavalov ate and drank enormously. None of us skimped.

Kavalov was the first to disregard his own order that

nothing be said about his troubles until after we had eaten. When he had finished his soup he put down his spoon and said:

"I am not a child. I will not be frightened."

He blinked pale, worried eyes defiantly at me, his lips pouting between mustache and imperial.

Ringgo grinned pleasantly at him. Mrs. Ringgo's face was as serene and unattentive as if nothing had been said.

"What is there to be frightened of?" I asked.

"Nothing," Kavalov said. "Nothing excepting a lot of idiotic and very pointless trickery and play-acting."

"You can call it anything you want to call it," a voice grumbled over my shoulder, "but I seen what I seen."

The voice belonged to one of the men who was waiting on the table, a sallow, youngish man with a narrow, slack-lipped face. He spoke with a subdued sort of stubbornness, and without looking up from the dish he was putting before me.

Since nobody else paid any attention to the servant's clearly audible remark, I turned my face to Kavalov again. He was trimming the edge of a sand dab with the side of his fork.

"What kind of trickery and play-acting?" I asked.

Kavalov put down his fork and rested his wrists on the edge of the table. He rubbed his lips together and leaned over his plate towards me.

"Supposing"—he wrinkled his forehead so that his bald scalp twitched forward—"you have done injury to a man ten years ago." He turned his wrists quickly, laying his hands palm-up on the white cloth. "You have done this injury in the ordinary business manner—you understand?—for profit. There is not anything personal concerned. You do not hardly know him. And then supposing he came to you after all those ten years and said to you: 'I have come to watch you die.' " He turned his hands over, palms down. "Well, what would you think?"

"I wouldn't," I replied, "think I ought to hurry up my dying on his account."

The earnestness went out of his face, leaving it blank. He blinked at me for a moment and then began eating his fish. When he had chewed and swallowed the last piece of sand dab he looked up at me again. He shook his head slowly, drawing down the corners of his mouth.

"That was not a good answer," he said. He shrugged, and spread his fingers. "However, you will have to deal with this Captain Cat-and-mouse. It is for that I engaged you."

I nodded.

Ringgo smiled and patted his bandaged arm, saying:

"I wish you more luck with him than I had."

Mrs. Ringgo put out a hand and let the pointed fingertips touch her husband's wrist for a moment.

I asked Kavalov:

"This injury I was to suppose I had done: how serious was it?"

He pursed his lip, made little wavy motions with the fingers of his right hand, and said:

"Oh—ah—ruin."

"We can take it for granted, then, that your captain's really up to something?"

"Good God!" said Ringgo, dropping his fork, "I wouldn't like to think he'd broken my arm just in fun."

Behind me the sallow servant spoke to his mate:

"He wants to know if we think the captain's really up to something."

"I heard him," the other said gloomily. "A lot of help he's going to be to us."

Kavalov tapped his plate with a fork and made angry faces at the servants.

"Shut up," he said. "Where is the roast?" He pointed the fork at Mrs. Ringgo. "Her glass is empty." He looked at the fork. "See what care they take of my silver," he complained, holding it out to me. "It has not been cleaned decently in a month."

He put the fork down. He pushed back his plate to make room for his forearms on the table. He leaned over them, hunching his shoulders. He sighed. He frowned. He stared at me with pleading pale eyes.

"Listen," he whined. "Am I a fool? Would I send to San Francisco for a detective if I did not need a detective? Would I pay you what you are charging me, when I could get plenty of good enough detectives for half of that, if I did not require the best detective I could secure? Would I require so expensive a one if I did not know this captain for a completely dangerous fellow?"

I didn't say anything. I sat still and looked attentive.

"Listen," he whined. "This is not April-foolery. This captain means to murder me. He came here to murder me. He will certainly murder me if somebody does not stop him from it."

"Just what has he done so far?" I asked.

"That is not it." Kavalov shook his bald head impatiently. "I do not ask you to undo anything that he has done. I ask you to keep him from killing me. What has he done so far? Well, he has terrorized my people most completely. He has broken Dolph's arm. He has done these things so far, if you must know."

"How long has this been going on? How long has he been here?" I asked.

"A week and two days."

284

"Did your chauffeur tell you about the black man we saw in the road?"

Kavalov pushed his lips together and nodded slowly.

"He wasn't there when I went back," I said.

He blew out his lips with a little puff and cried excitedly:

"I do not care anything about your black men and your roads. I care about not being murdered."

"Have you said anything to the sheriff's office?" I asked, trying to pretend I wasn't getting peevish.

"That I have done. But to what good? Has he threatened me? Well, he has told me he has come to watch me die. From him, the way he said it, that is a threat. But to your sheriff it is not a threat. He has terrorized my people. Have I proof that he has done that? The sheriff says I have not. What absurdity! Do I need proof? Don't I know? Must he leave fingerprints on the fright he causes? So it comes to this: the sheriff will keep an eye on him. 'An eye,' he said, mind you. Here I have twenty people, servants and farm hands, with forty eyes. And he comes and goes as he likes. An eye!"

"How about Ringgo's arm?" I asked.

Kavalov shook his head impatiently and began to cut up his lamb with short, quick strokes.

Ringgo said:

"There's nothing we can do about that. I hit him first." He looked at his bruised knuckles. "I didn't think he was that tough. Maybe I'm not as good as I used to be. Anyway, a dozen people saw me punch his jaw before he touched me. We performed at high noon in front of the post office."

"Who is this captain?"

"It's not him," the sallow servant said. "It's that black devil."

Ringgo said:

"Sherry's his name, Hugh Sherry. He was a captain in the British army when we knew him before—quartermaster's department in Cairo. That was in 1917, all of twelve years ago. The commodore"—he nodded his head at his father-in-law—"was speculating in military supplies. Sherry should have been a line officer. He had no head for desk work. He wasn't timid enough. Somebody decided the commodore wouldn't have made so much money if Sherry hadn't been so careless. They knew Sherry hadn't made any money for himself. They cashiered Sherry at the same time they asked the commodore please to go away."

Kavalov looked up from his plate to explain.

"Business is like that in wartime. They wouldn't let me go away if I had done anything they could keep me there for."

"And now, twelve years after you had him kicked out of the army in disgrace," I said, "he comes here, threatens to kill you, so you believe, and sets out to spread panic among your people. Is that it?"

"That is not it," Kavalov whined. "That is not it at all. I did not have him kicked out of my armies. I am a man of business. I take my profits where I find them. If somebody let me take a profit that angers his employers, what is their anger to me? Second, I do not believe he means to kill me. I know that."

I said:

"I'm trying to get it straight in my mind."

"There is nothing to get straight. A man is going to murder me. I ask you not to let him do it. Is not that simple enough?"

"Simple enough," I agreed, and I stopped trying to talk to him.

Kavalov and Ringgo were smoking cigars, Mrs. Ringgo and I cigarettes over *crème de menthe* when the red-faced blond woman in gray wool came in.

She came in hurriedly. Her eyes were wide open and dark.

She said:

"Anthony says there's a fire in the upper field."

Kavalov crunched his cigar between his teeth and looked pointedly at me.

I stood up, asking:

"How do I get there?"

"I'll show you the way," Ringgo said, leaving his chair.

"Dolph," his wife protested, "your arm."

He smiled gently at her and said:

"I'm not going to interfere. I'm only going along to see how an expert handles these things."

4

I ran up to my room for hat, coat, flashlight and gun.

The Ringgos were standing at the front door when I started downstairs again.

He had put on a dark raincoat, buttoned tight over his injured arm, its left sleeve hanging empty. His right arm was around his wife. Both of her bare arms were around his neck. She was bent far back, he far forward over her. Their mouths were together.

Retreating a little, I made more noise with my feet when I came into sight again. They were standing apart at the door, waiting for me. Ringgo was breathing heavily, as if he had been running. He opened the door.

Mrs. Ringgo addressed me:

"Please don't let my foolish husband be too reckless."

I said I wouldn't, and asked him:

"Worth while taking any of the servants or farm hands along?"

He shook his head.

"Those that aren't hiding would be as useless as those that are," he said. "They've all had it taken out of them."

He and I went out, leaving Mrs. Ringgo looking after us from the doorway. The rain had stopped for the time, but a black muddle overhead promised more presently.

Ringgo led me around the side of the house, along a narrow path that went downhill, through shrubbery, past a group of small buildings in a shallow valley, and diagonally up another, lower, hill.

The path was soggy. At the top of the hill we left the path, going through a wire gate and across a stubby field that was both gummy and slimy under our feet. We moved along swiftly. The gumminess of the ground, the sultriness of the night air, and our coats, made the going warm work.

When we had crossed this field we could see the fire, a spot of flickering orange beyond intervening trees. We climbed a low wire fence and wound through the trees.

A violent rustling broke out among the leaves overhead, starting at the left, ending with a solid thud against a tree trunk just to our right. Then something *plopped* on the soft ground under the tree.

Off to the left a voice laughed, a savage, hooting laugh.

The laughing voice couldn't have been far away. I went after it.

The fire was too small and too far away to be of much use to me: blackness was nearly perfect among the trees.

I stumbled over roots, bumped into trees, and found nothing. The flashlight would have helped the laugher more than me, so I kept it idle in my hand.

When I got tired of playing peek-a-boo with myself, I cut through the woods to the field on the other side, and went down to the fire.

The fire had been built in one end of the field, a dozen feet or less from the nearest tree. It had been built of dead twigs and broken branches that the rain had missed, and had nearly burnt itself out by the time I reached it.

Two small forked branches were stuck in the ground on opposite sides of the fire. Their forks held the ends of a length of green sapling. Spitted on the sapling, hanging over the fire, was an eighteen-inch-long carcass, headless, tail-less, footless, skinless, and split down the front.

On the ground a few feet away lay an Airedale puppy's head, pelt, feet, tail, insides, and a lot of blood.

There were some dry sticks, broken in convenient lengths, beside the fire. I put them on as Ringgo came out of the woods to join me. He carried a stone the size of a grapefruit in his hand.

"Get a look at him?" he asked.

"No. He laughed and went."

He held out the stone to me, saying:

"This is what was chucked at us."

Drawn on the smooth gray stone, in red, were round blank eyes, a triangular nose, and a grinning, toothy mouth—a crude skull.

I scratched one of the red eyes with a fingernail, and said:

"Crayon."

Ringgo was staring at the carcass sizzling over the fire and at the trimmings on the ground.

"What do you make of that?" I asked.

He swallowed and said:

"Mickey was a damned good little dog."

"Yours?"

He nodded.

I went around with my flashlight on the ground. I found some footprints, such as they were.

"Anything?" Ringgo asked.

"Yeah." I showed him one of the prints. "Made with rags tied around his shoes. They're no good."

We turned to the fire again.

"This is another show," I said. "Whoever killed and cleaned the pup knew his stuff; knew it too well to think he could cook him decently like that. The outside will be burnt before the inside's even warm, and the way he's put on the spit he'd fall off if you tried to turn him."

Ringgo's scowl lightened a bit.

"That's a little better," he said. "Having him killed is rotten enough, but I'd hate to think of anybody eating Mickey, or even meaning to."

"They didn't," I assured him. "They were putting on a show. This the sort of thing that's been happening?"

"Yes."

"What's the sense of it?"

He glumly quoted Kavalov:

"Captain Cat-and-mouse."

I gave him a cigarette, took one myself, and lighted them with a stick from the fire.

He raised his face to the sky, said, "Raining again; let's go back to the house," but remained by the fire, staring at the cooking carcass. The stink of scorched meat hung thick around us.

"You don't take this very seriously yet, do you?" he asked presently, in a low, matter-of-fact voice.

"It's a funny layout."

"He's cracked," he said in the same low voice. "Try to see this. Honor meant something to him. That's why we had to trick him instead of bribing him, back in

Cairo. Less than ten years of dishonor can crack a man like that. He'd go off and hide and brood. It would be either shoot himself when the blow fell—or that. I was like you at first." He kicked at the fire. "This is silly. But I can't laugh at it now, except when I'm around Miriam and the commodore. When he first showed up I didn't have the slightest idea that I couldn't handle him. I had handled him all right in Cairo. When I discovered I couldn't handle him I lost my head a little. I went down and picked a row with him. Well, that was no good either. It's the silliness of this that makes it bad. In Cairo he was the kind of man who combs his hair before he shaves, so his mirror will show an orderly picture. Can you understand some of this?"

"I'll have to talk to him first," I said. "He's staying in the village?"

"He has a cottage on the hill above. It's the first one on the left after you turn into the main road." Ringgo dropped his cigarette into the fire and looked thoughtfully at me, biting his lower lip. "I don't know how you and the commodore are going to get along. You can't make jokes with him. He doesn't undersand them, and he'll distrust you on that account."

"I'll try to be careful," I promised. "No good offering this Sherry money?"

"Hell, no," he said softly. "He's too cracked for that."

We took down the dog's carcass, kicked the fire apart, and trod it out in the mud before we returned to the house.

5

The country was fresh and bright under clear sunlight the next morning. A warm breeze was drying the ground and chasing raw-cotton clouds across the sky.

At ten o'clock I set out afoot for Captain Sherry's. I didn't have any trouble finding his house, a pinkish stuccoed bungalow with a terra cotta roof—reached from the road by a cobbled walk.

A white-clothed table with two places set stood on the tiled veranda that stretched across the front of the bungalow.

Before I could knock, the door was opened by a slim black man, not much more than a boy, in a white jacket. His features were thinner than most American Negroes', aquiline, pleasantly intelligent.

"You're going to catch colds lying around in wet roads," I said, "if you don't get run over."

His mouth-ends ran towards his ears in a grin that showed me a lot of strong yellow teeth.

"Yes, sir," he said, buzzing his s's, rolling the r, bowing. "The *capitaine* have waited breakfast that you be with him. You do sit down, sir. I will call him."

"Not dog meat?"

His mouth-ends ran back and up again and he shook his head vigorously.

"No, sir." He held up his black hands and counted the fingers. "There is orange and kippers and kidneys grilled and eggs and marmalade and toast and tea or coffee. There is not dog meat."

"Fine," I said, and sat down in one of the wicker armchairs on the veranda.

I had time to light a cigarette before Captain Sherry came out.

He was a gaunt tall man of forty. Sandy hair, parted in the middle, was brushed flat to his small head, above a sunburned face. His eyes were gray, with lower lids as straight as ruler-edges. His mouth was another hard straight line under a close-clipped sandy mustache.

Grooves like gashes ran from his nostrils past his mouth-corners. Other grooves, just as deep, ran down his cheeks to the sharp ridge of his jaw. He wore a gaily striped flannel bathrobe over sand-colored pajamas.

"Good morning," he said pleasantly, and gave me a semi-salute. He didn't offer to shake hands. "Don't get up. It will be some minutes before Marcus has breakfast ready. I slept late. I had a most abominable dream." His voice was a deliberately languid drawl. "I dreamed that Theodore Kavalov's throat had been cut from here to here." He put bony fingers under his ears. "It was an atrociously gory business. He bled and screamed horribly, the swine."

I grinned up at him, asking:

"And you didn't like that?"

"Oh, getting his throat cut was all to the good, but he bled and screamed so filthily." He raised his nose and sniffed. "That's honeysuckle somewhere, isn't it?"

"Smells like it. Was it throat-cutting that you had in mind when you threatened him?"

"When I threatened him," he drawled. "My dear fellow, I did nothing of the sort. I was in Udja, a stinking Moroccan town close to the Algerian frontier, and one morning a voice spoke to me from an orange tree. It said: 'Go to Farewell, in California, in the States, and there you will see Theodore Kavalov die.' I thought that a capital idea. I thanked the voice, told Marcus to pack, and I came here. As soon as I arrived I told Kavalov about it, thinking perhaps he would die then and I wouldn't be hung up here waiting. He didn't, though, and too late, I regretted not having asked the voice for a definite date. I should hate having to waste months here."

"That's why you've been trying to hurry it up?" I asked.

"I beg your pardon?"

"Schrecklichkeit," I said, "rocky skulls, dog barbecues, vanishing corpses."

"I've been fifteen years in Africa," he said. "I've too much faith in voices that come from orange trees where no one is to try to give them a hand. You needn't fancy I've had anything to do with whatever has happened."

"Marcus?"

Sherry stroked his freshly shaven cheeks and replied:

"That's possible. He has an incorrigible bent for the ruder sort of African horseplay. I'll gladly cane him for any misbehavior of which you've reasonably definite proof."

"Let me catch him at it," I said, "and I'll do my own caning."

Sherry leaned forward and spoke in a cautious undertone:

"Be sure he suspects nothing till you've a firm grip on him. He's remarkably effective with either of his knives."

"I'll try to remember that. The voice didn't say anything about Ringgo?"

"There was no need. When the body dies, the hand is dead."

Black Marcus came out carrying food. We moved to the table and I started on my second breakfast.

Sherry wondered whether the voice that had spoken to him from the orange tree had also spoken to Kavalov. He had asked Kavalov, he said, but hadn't received a very satisfactory answer. He believed that voices which announced deaths to people's enemies usually also warned the one who was to die. "That is," he said, "the conventional way of doing it, I believe."

"I don't know," I said. "I'll try to find out for you. Maybe I ought to ask him what he dreamed last night, too."

"Did he look nightmarish this morning?"

"I don't know. I left before he was up."

Sherry's eyes became hot gray points.

"Do you mean," he asked, "that you've no idea what shape he's in this morning, whether he's alive or not, whether my dream was a true one or not?"

"Yeah."

The hard line of his mouth loosened into a slow delighted smile.

"By Jove," he said, "that's capital! I thought—you gave me the impression of knowing positively that there was nothing to my dream, that it was only a meaningless dream."

He clapped his hands sharply.

Black Marcus popped out of the door.

"Pack," Sherry ordered. "The bald one is finished. We're off."

Marcus bowed and backed grinning into the house.

"Hadn't you better wait to make sure?" I asked.

"But I am sure," he drawled, "as sure as when the voice spoke from the orange tree. There is nothing to wait for now: I have seen him die."

"In a dream."

"Was it a dream?" he asked carelessly.

When I left, ten or fifteen minutes later, Marcus was making noises indoors that sounded as if he actually was packing.

Sherry shook hands with me, saying:

"Awfully glad to have had you for breakfast. Perhaps we'll meet again if your work ever brings you to northern

Africa. Remember me to Miriam and Dolph. I can't sincerely send condolences."

Out of sight of the bungalow, I left the road for a path along the hillside above, and explored the country for a higher spot from which Sherry's place could be spied on. I found a pip, a vacant ramshackle house on a jutting ridge off to the northeast. The whole of the bungalow's front, part of one side, and a good stretch of the cobbled walk, including its juncture with the road, could be seen from the vacant house's front porch. It was a rather long shot for naked eyes, but with field glasses it would be just about perfect, even to a screen of overgrown bushes in front.

When I got back to the Kavalov house Ringgo was propped up on gay cushions in a reed chair under a tree, with a book in his hand.

"What do you think of him?" he asked. "Is he cracked?"

"Not very. He wanted to be remembered to you and Mrs. Ringgo. How's the arm this morning?"

"Rotten. I must have let it get too damp last night. It gave me hell all night."

"Did you see Captain Cat-and-mouse?" Kavalov's whining voice came from behind me. "And did you find any satisfaction in that?"

I turned around. He was coming down the walk from the house. His face was more gray than brown this morning, but what I could see of his throat, above the v of a wing collar, was uncut enough.

"He was packing when I left," I said. "Going back to Africa."

6

That day was Thursday. Nothing else happened that day.

Friday morning I was awakened by the noise of my bedroom door being opened violently.

Martin, the thin-faced valet, came dashing into my room and began shaking me by the shoulder, though I was sitting up by the time he reached my bedside.

His thin face was lemon-yellow and ugly with fear.

"It's happened," he babbled. "Oh, my God, it's happened!"

"What's happened?"

"It's happened. It's happened."

I pushed him aside and got out of bed. He turned suddenly and ran into my bathroom. I could hear him vomiting as I pushed my feet into slippers.

Kavalov's bedroom was three doors below mine, on the same side of the building.

The house was full of noises, excited voices, doors opening and shutting, though I couldn't see anybody.

I ran down to Kavalov's door. It was open.

Kavalov was in there, lying on a low Spanish bed. The bedclothes were thrown down across the foot.

Kavalov was lying on his back. His throat had been cut, a curving cut that paralleled the line of his jaw between points an inch under his ear lobes.

Where his blood had soaked into the blue pillow case and blue sheet it was purple as grape-juice. It was thick and sticky, already clotting.

Ringgo came in wearing a bathrobe like a cape.

"It's happened," I growled, using the valet's words.

Ringgo looked dully, miserably, at the bed and began cursing in a choked, muffled voice.

The red-faced blond woman—Louella Qually, the housekeeper—came in, screamed, pushed past us, and ran to the bed, still screaming. I caught her arm when she reached for the covers.

"Let things alone," I said.

"Cover him up. Cover him up, the poor man!" she cried.

I took her away from the bed. Four or five servants were in the room by now. I gave the housekeeper to a couple of them, telling them to take her out and quiet her down. She went away laughing and crying.

Ringgo was still staring at the bed.

"Where's Mrs. Ringgo?" I asked.

He didn't hear me. I tapped his good arm and repeated the question.

"She's in her room. She—she didn't have to see it to know what had happened."

"Hadn't you better look after her?"

He nodded, turned slowly, and went out.

The valet, still lemon-yellow, came in.

"I want everybody on the place, servants, farm hands, everybody downstairs in the front room," I told him. "Get them all there right away, and they're to stay there till the sheriff comes."

"Yes, sir," he said and went downstairs, the others following him.

I closed Kavalov's door and went across to the library, where I phoned the sheriff's office in the county seat. I talked to a deputy named Hilden. When I had told him my story he said the sheriff would be at the house within half an hour.

I went to my room and dressed. By the time I had finished, the valet came up to tell me that everybody was

assembled in the front room—everybody except the Ringgos and Mrs. Ringgo's maid.

I was examining Kavalov's bedroom when the sheriff arrived. He was a white-haired man with mild blue eyes and a mild voice that came out indistinctly under a white mustache. He had brought three deputies, a doctor and a coroner with him.

"Ringgo and the valet can tell you more than I can," I said when we had shaken hands all around. "I'll be back as soon as I can make it. I'm going to Sherry's. Ringgo will tell you where he fits in."

In the garage I selected a muddy Chevrolet and drove to the bungalow. Its door and windows were tight, and my knocking brought no answer.

I went back along the cobbled walk to the car, and rode down into Farewell. There I had no trouble learning that Sherry and Marcus had taken the two-ten train for Los Angeles, the afternoon before, with three trunks and half a dozen bags that the village expressman had checked for them.

After sending a telegram to the Agency's Los Angeles branch, I hunted up the man from whom Sherry had rented the bungalow.

He could tell me nothing about his tenants except that he was disappointed in their not staying even a full two weeks. Sherry had returned the keys with a brief note saying he had been called away unexpectedly.

I pocketed the note. Handwriting specimens are always convenient to have. Then I borrowed the keys to the bungalow and went back to it.

I didn't find anything of value there, except a lot of fingerprints that might possibly come in handy later. There was nothing there to tell me where my men had gone.

I returned to Kavalov's.

The sheriff had finished running the staff through the mill.

"Can't get a thing out of them," he said. "Nobody heard anything and nobody saw anything, from bedtime last night, till the valet opened the door to call him at eight o'clock this morning, and saw him dead like that. You know any more than that?"

"No. They tell you about Sherry?"

"Oh, yes. That's our meat, I guess, huh?"

"Yeah. He's supposed to have cleared out yesterday afternoon, with his man, for Los Angeles. We ought to be able to find the work in that. What does the doctor say?"

"Says he was killed between three and four this morning, with a heavyish knife—one clean slash from left to right, like a left-handed man would do it."

"Maybe one clean cut," I agreed, "but not exactly a slash. Slower than that. A slash, if it curved, ought to curve up, away from the slasher, in the middle, and down towards him at the ends—just the opposite of what this does."

"Oh, all right. Is this Sherry a southpaw?"

"I don't know." I wondered if Marcus was. "Find the knife?"

"Nary hide nor hair of it. And what's more, we didn't find anything else, inside or out. Funny a fellow as scared as Kavalov was, from all accounts, didn't keep himself locked up tighter. His windows were open. Anybody could of got in them with a ladder. His door wasn't locked."

"There could be half a dozen reasons for that. He—"

One of the deputies, a big-shouldered blond man, came to the door and said:

"We found the knife."

The sheriff and I followed the deputy out of the house, around to the side on which Kavalov's room was situated. The knife's blade was buried in the ground, among some shrubs that bordered a path leading down to the farm hands' quarters.

The knife's wooden handle—painted red—slanted a little toward the house. A little blood was smeared on the blade, but the soft earth had cleaned off most. There was no blood on the painted handle, and nothing like a fingerprint.

There were no footprints in the soft ground near the knife. Apparently it had been tossed into the shrubbery.

"I guess that's all there is here for us," the sheriff said. "There's nothing much to show that anybody here had anything to do with it, or didn't. Now we'll look after this here Captain Sherry."

I went down to the village with him. At the post office we learned that Sherry had left a forwarding address: General Delivery, St. Louis, Mo. The postmaster said Sherry had received no mail during his stay in Farewell.

We went to the telegraph office, and were told that Sherry had neither received nor sent any telegrams. I sent one to the Agency's St. Louis branch.

The rest of our poking around in the village brought us nothing—except we learned that most of the idlers in Farewell had seen Sherry and Marcus board the southbound two-ten train.

Before we returned to the Kavalov house a telegram came from the Los Angeles branch for me:

> Sherry's trunks and bags in baggage room here not yet called for are keeping them under surveillance.

When we got back to the house I met Ringgo in the hall, and asked him:

"Is Sherry left-handed?"

He thought, and then shook his head.

"I can't remember," he said. "He might be. I'll ask Miriam. Perhaps she'll know—women remember things like that."

When he came down stairs again he was nodding:

"He's very nearly ambidextrous, but uses his left hand more than his right. Why?"

"The doctor thinks it was done with a left hand. How is Mrs. Ringgo now?"

"I think the worst of the shock is over, thanks."

7

Sherry's baggage remained uncalled for in the Los Angeles passenger station all day Saturday. Late that afternoon the sheriff made public the news that Sherry and the Negro were wanted for murder, and that night the sheriff and I took a train south.

Sunday morning with a couple of men from the Los Angeles police department, we opened the baggage. We didn't find anything except legitimate clothing and personal belongings that told us nothing.

That trip paid no dividends.

I returned to San Francisco and had bales of circulars printed and distributed.

Two weeks went by, two weeks in which the circulars brought us nothing but the usual lot of false alarms.

Then the Spokane police picked up Sherry and Marcus in a Stevens Street rooming house.

Some unknown person had phoned the police that one Fred Williams living there had a mysterious Negro visitor nearly every day, and that their actions were very suspicious. The Spokane police had copies of our circular. They hardly needed the H. S. monograms on Fred Williams's cuff links and handkerchiefs to assure them that he was our man.

After a couple of hours of being grilled, Sherry admitted his identity, but denied having murdered Kavalov.

Two of the sheriff's men went north and brought the prisoners down to the county seat.

Sherry had shaved off his mustache. There was nothing in his face or voice to show that he was the least bit worried.

"I knew there was nothing more to wait for after my dream," he drawled, "so I went away. Then, when I heard the dream had come true, I knew you johnnies would be hot after me—as if one can help his dreams—and I—ah—sought seclusion."

He solemnly repeated his orange-tree-voice story to the sheriff and district attorney. The newspapers liked it.

He refused to map his route for us, to tell us how he had spent his time.

"No, no," he said. "Sorry, but I shouldn't do it. It may be I shall have to do it again sometime, and it wouldn't do to reveal my methods."

He wouldn't tell us where he had spent the night of the murder. We were fairly certain that he had left the train before it reached Los Angeles, though the train crew had been able to tell us nothing.

"Sorry," he drawled. "But if you chaps don't know where I was, how do you know that I was where the murder was?"

We had even less luck with Marcus. His formula was:

"Not understand the English very good. Ask the *capitaine*. I don't know."

The district attorney spent a lot of time walking his office floor, biting his fingernails, and telling us fiercely that the case was going to fall apart if we couldn't prove that either Sherry or Marcus was within reach of the Kavalov house at, or shortly before or after, the time of the murder.

The sheriff was the only one of us who hadn't a sneaky feeling that Sherry's sleeves were loaded with assorted aces. The sheriff saw him already hanged.

Sherry got a lawyer, a slick-looking pale man with hornrim glasses and a thin twitching-mouth. His name was Schaeffer. He went around smiling to himself and at us.

When the district attorney had only thumb nails left and was starting to work on them, I borrowed a car from Ringgo and started following the railroad south, trying to learn where Sherry had left the train. We had mugged the pair, of course, so I carried their photographs with me.

I displayed those damned photographs at every railroad stop between Farewell and Los Angeles, at every village within twenty miles of the tracks on either side, and at most of the houses in between. And it got me nothing.

There was no evidence that Sherry and Marcus hadn't gone through to Los Angeles.

Their train would have put them there at ten-thirty that night. There was no train out of Los Angeles that would have carried them back to Farewell in time to kill Kavalov. There were two possibilities: an airplane could have carried them back in plenty of time; and an automobile might have been able to do it, though that didn't look reasonable.

I tried the airplane angle first, and couldn't find a flyer

who had had a passenger that night. With the help of the Los Angeles police and some operatives from the Continental's Los Angeles branch, I had everybody who owned a plane—public or private—interviewed. All the answers were no.

We tried the less promising automobile angle. The larger taxicab and hire-car companies said, "No." Four privately owned cars had been reported stolen between ten and twelve o'clock that night. Two of them had been found in the city the next morning: they couldn't have made the trip to Farewell and back. One of the others had been picked up in San Diego the next day. That let that one out. The other was still loose, a Packard sedan. We got a printer working on post card descriptions of it.

To reach all the small-fry taxi and hire-car owners was quite a job, and then there were the private car owners who might have hired out for one night. We went into the newspapers to cover these fields.

We didn't get any automobile information, but this new line of inquiry—trying to find traces of our men here a few hours before the murder—brought results of another kind.

At San Pedro (Los Angeles's seaport, twenty-five miles away) a Negro had been arrested at one o'clock on the morning of the murder. The Negro spoke English poorly, but had papers to prove that he was Pierre Tisano, a French sailor. He had been arrested on a drunk and disorderly charge.

The San Pedro police said that the photograph and description of the man we knew as Marcus fitted the drunken sailor exactly.

That wasn't all the San Pedro police said.

Tisano had been arrested at one o'clock. At a little after two o'clock, a white man who gave his name as

Henry Somerton had appeared and had tried to bail the Negro out. The desk sergeant had told Somerton that nothing could be done till morning, and that, anyway, it would be better to let Tisano sleep off his jag before removing him. Somerton had readily agreed to that, had remained talking to the desk sergeant for more than half an hour, and had left at about three. At ten o'clock that morning he had reappeared to pay the black man's fine. They had gone away together.

The San Pedro police said that Sherry's photograph—without the mustache—and description were Henry Somerton's.

Henry Somerton's signature on the register of the hotel to which he had gone between his two visits to the police matched the handwriting in Sherry's note to the bungalow's owner.

It was pretty clear that Sherry and Marcus had been in San Pedro—a nine-hour train ride from Farewell—at the time that Kavalov was murdered.

Pretty clear isn't quite clear enough in a murder job: I carried the San Pedro desk sergeant north with me for a look at the two men.

"Them's them, all righty," he said.

8

The district attorney ate up the rest of his thumb nails.

The sheriff had the bewildered look of a child who had held a balloon in his hand, had heard a pop, and couldn't understand where the balloon had gone.

I pretended I was perfectly satisfied.

"Now we're back where we started," the district attorney wailed disagreeably, as if it was everybody's fault but his, "and with all those weeks wasted."

The sheriff didn't look at the district attorney, and didn't say anything.

I said:

"Oh, I wouldn't say that. We've made some progress."

"What?"

"We know that Sherry and the servant have alibis."

The district attorney seemed to think I was trying to kid him. I didn't pay any attention to the faces he made at me, and asked:

"What are you going to do with them?"

"What can I do with them but turn them loose? This shoots the case to hell."

"It doesn't cost the county much to feed them," I suggested. "Why not hang on to them as long as you can, while we think it over? Something new may turn up, and you can always drop the case if nothing does. You don't think they're innocent, do you?"

He gave me a look that was heavy and sour with pity for my stupidity.

"They're guilty as hell, but what good's that to me if I can't get a conviction? And what's the good of saying I'll hold them? Damn it, man, you know as well as I do that all they've got to do now is ask for their release and any judge will hand it to them."

"Yeah," I agreed. "I'll bet you the best hat in San Francisco that they don't ask for it."

"What do you mean?"

"They want to stand trial," I said, "or they'd have sprung that alibi before we dug it up. I've an idea that they tipped off the Spokane police themselves. And I'll bet you that hat that you get no *habeas corpus* motions out of Schaeffer."

The district attorney peered suspiciously into my eyes.

"Do you know something that you're holding back?" he demanded.

"No, but you'll see I'm right."

I was right. Schaeffer went around smiling to himself and making no attempt to get his clients out of the county prison.

Three days later something new turned up.

A man named Archibald Weeks, who had a small chicken farm some ten miles south of the Kavalov place, came to see the district attorney. Weeks said he had seen Sherry on his—Weeks's—place early on the morning of the murder.

Weeks had been leaving for Iowa that morning to visit his parents. He had got up early to see that everything was in order before driving twenty miles to catch an early morning train.

At somewhere between half-past five and six o'clock he had gone to the shed where he kept his car, to see if it held enough gasoline for the trip.

A man ran out of the shed, vaulted the fence, and dashed away down the road. Weeks chased him for a short distance, but the other was too speedy for him. The man was too well-dressed for a hobo: Weeks supposed he had been trying to steal the car.

Since Weeks's trip east was a necessary one, and during his absence his wife would have only their two sons —one seventeen, one fifteen—there with her, he had thought it wisest not to frighten her by saying anything about the man he had surprised in the shed.

He had returned from Iowa the day before his appearance in the district attorney's office, and after hearing the details of the Kavalov murder, and seeing Sherry's picture in the papers, had recognized him as the man he had chased.

We showed him Sherry in person. He said Sherry was the man. Sherry said nothing.

With Weeks's evidence to refute the San Pedro police's, the district attorney let the case against Sherry come to trial. Marcus was held as a material witness, but there was nothing to weaken his San Pedro alibi, so he was not tried.

Weeks told his story straight and simply on the witness stand, and then, under cross-examination, blew up with a loud bang. He went to pieces completely.

He wasn't, he admitted in answer to Schaeffer's questions, quite as sure that Sherry was the man as he had been before. The man had certainly, the little he had seen of him, looked something like Sherry, but perhaps he had been a little hasty in saying positively that it was Sherry. He wasn't, now that he had had time to think it over, really sure that he had actually got a good look at the man's face in the dim morning light. Finally, all that Weeks would swear to was that he had seen a man who had seemed to look a little bit like Sherry.

It was funny as hell.

The district attorney, having no nails left, nibbled his fingerbones.

The jury said, "Not guilty."

Sherry was freed, forever in the clear as far as the Kavalov murder was concerned, no matter what might come to light later.

Marcus was released.

The district attorney wouldn't say good-by to me when I left for San Francisco.

9

Four days after Sherry's acquittal, Mrs. Ringgo was shown into my office.

She was in black. Her pretty, unintelligent, Oriental face was not placid.

"Please, you won't tell Dolph I have come here?" were the first words she spoke.

"Of course not, if you say not," I promised.

She sat down and looked big-eyed at me.

"He's so reckless," she said.

I nodded sympathetically, wondering what she was up to.

"And I'm afraid," she added, twisting her gloves. Her chin trembled. Her lips formed words jerkily: "They've come back to the bungalow."

"Yeah?" I sat up straight. I knew who *they* were.

"They can't," she cried, "have come back for any reason except that they mean to murder Dolph as they did Father. And he won't listen to me. He's so sure of himself. He laughs and calls me a foolish child, and tells me he can take care of himself. But he can't. Not, at least, with a broken arm. And they'll kill him as they killed Father. I know it. I know it."

"Sherry hates your husband as much as he hated your father?"

"Yes. That's it. He does. Dolph was working for Father, but Dolph's part in the—the business that led up to Hugh's trouble was more—more active than father's. Will you—will you keep them from killing Dolph? Will you?"

"Surely."

"And you mustn't let Dolph know," she insisted, "and if he does find out you're watching them, you mustn't tell him I got you to. He'd be angry with me. I asked him to send for you, but he—" She broke off, looking embarrassed: I supposed her husband had mentioned my lack of success in keeping Kavalov alive. "But he wouldn't."

"How long have they been back?"

"Since the day before yesterday."

"I'll be down tomorrow," I promised. "If you'll take my advice you'll tell your husband that you've employed me, but I won't tell him if you don't."

"And you won't let him harm Dolph?"

I promised to do my best, took some money away from her, gave her a receipt, and bowed her out.

Shortly after dark that evening I reached Farewell.

10

The bungalow's windows were lighted when I passed it on my way uphill. I was tempted to get out of my coupé and do some snooping, but was afraid that I couldn't out-Indian Marcus on his own grounds.

When I turned into the dirt road leading to the vacant house I had spotted on my first trip to Farewell, I switched off the coupé's lights and crept along by the light of a very white moon overhead.

Close to the vacant house I got the coupé off the path.

Then I went up on the rickety porch, located the bungalow, and began to adjust my field glasses to it.

I had them partly adjusted when the bungalow's front door opened, letting out a slice of yellow light and two people.

One of the people was a woman.

Another least turn of the set-screw and her face came clear in my eyes—Mrs. Ringgo.

She raised her coat collar around her face and hurried away down the cobbled walk. Sherry stood on the veranda looking after her.

When she reached the road she began running uphill, towards her house.

Sherry went indoors and shut the door.

Two hours and a half later a man turned into the cobbled walk from the road. He walked swiftly to the bungalow, with a cautious sort of swiftness, and he looked from side to side as he walked.

I suppose he knocked on the door.

The door opened, throwing a yellow glow on his face, Dolph Ringgo's face.

He went indoors. The door shut.

I put away the field glasses, left the porch, and set out for the bungalow. I wasn't sure that I could find another good spot for the coupé, so I left it where it was and walked.

I was afraid to take a chance on the cobbled walk.

Twenty feet above it, I left the road and moved as silently as I could over sod and among trees, bushes and flowers. I knew the sort of folks I was playing with: I carried my gun in my hand.

All of the bungalow's windows on my side showed lights, but all the windows were closed and their blinds drawn. I didn't like the way the light that came through the blinds helped the moon illuminate the surrounding ground. That had been swell when I was up on the ridge getting cock-eyed squinting through glasses. It was sour now that I was trying to get close enough to do some profitable listening.

I stopped in the closest dark spot I could find—fifteen feet from the building—to think the situation over.

Crouching there, I heard something.

It wasn't in the right place. It wasn't what I wanted to hear. It was the sound of somebody coming down the walk towards the house.

I wasn't sure that I couldn't be seen from the path. I turned my head to make sure. And by turning my head I gave myself away.

Mrs. Ringgo jumped, stopped dead still in the path, and then cried:

"Is Dolph in there? Is he? Is he?"

I was trying to tell her that he was by nodding, but she made so much noise with her *Is he's* that I had to say "Yeah" out loud to make her hear.

I don't know whether the noise we made hurried things up indoors or not, but guns had started going off inside the bungalow.

You don't stop to count shots in circumstances like those, and anyway these were too blurred together for accurate scorekeeping, but my impression was that at least fifty of them had been fired by the time I was bruising my shoulder on the front door.

Luckily, it was a California door. It went in the second time I hit it.

Inside was a reception hall opening through a wide arched doorway into a living-room. The air was hazy and the stink of burnt powder was sharp.

Sherry was on the polished floor by the arch, wriggling sidewise on one elbow and one knee, trying to reach a Luger that lay on an amber rug some four feet away.

At the other end of the room, Ringgo was upright on his knees, steadily working the trigger of a black revolver in his good hand. The pistol was empty. It went snap, snap, snap, snap foolishly, but he kept on working the trigger. His broken arm was still in the splints, but had fallen out of the sling and was hanging down. His face was puffy and florid with blood. His eyes were wide and dull. The white bone handle of a knife stuck out of his back, just over one hip, its blade all the way in. He was clicking the empty pistol at Marcus.

The black boy was on his feet, feet far apart under bent knees. His left hand was spread wide over his chest, and the black fingers were shiny with blood. In his right hand he held a white bone-handled knife—its blade a foot long—held it, knife-fighter fashion, as you'd hold a sword. He was moving toward Ringgo, not directly, but from side to side, obliquely, closing in with shuffling steps, crouching, his hand turning the knife restlessly, but holding the point always towards Ringgo.

He didn't see us. He didn't hear us. All of his world just then was the man on his knees, the man in whose back a knife—brother of the one in the black hand—was wedged.

Ringgo didn't see us. I don't suppose he even saw Marcus. He knelt there and persistently worked the trigger of his empty gun.

I jumped over Sherry and swung the barrel of my gun at the base of Marcus's skull. It hit. Marcus dropped.

Ringgo stopped working the gun and looked surprised at me.

"That's the idea; you've got to put bullets in them or they're no good," I told him, pulled the knife out of Marcus's hand and went back to pick up the Luger that Sherry had stopped trying to get.

Sherry was lying on his back now. His eyes were closed.

He looked dead, and he had enough bullet holes in him to make death a good guess.

Hoping he wasn't dead, I knelt beside him—going around him so I could kneel facing Ringgo—and lifted his head up a little from the floor.

"Sherry," I said sharply. "Sherry."

He didn't move. His eyelids didn't even twitch.

I raised the fingers of the hand that was holding up his head, making his head move just a trifle.

"Did Ringgo kill Kavalov?" I asked the dead or dying man.

Even if I hadn't known Ringgo was looking at me I could have felt his eyes on me.

"Did he, Sherry?" I barked into the still face.

The dead or dying man didn't move.

I cautiously moved my fingers again so that his dead or dying head nodded, twice.

Then I made his head jerk back, and let it gently down on the floor again.

"Well," I said, standing up and facing Ringgo, "I've got you at last."

11

I've never been able to decide whether I would actually have gone on the witness stand and sworn that Sherry was alive when he nodded, and nodded voluntarily, if it had been necessary for me to do so to convict Ringgo.

I don't like perjury, but I knew Ringgo was guilty, and there I had him.

Fortunately, I didn't have to decide.

Ringgo believed Sherry had nodded, and then, when Marcus gave the show away, there was nothing much for Ringgo to do but try his luck with a plea of guilty.

We didn't have much trouble getting the story out of Marcus. Ringgo had killed his beloved *capitaine*. The boy was easily persuaded that the law would give him his best revenge.

After Marcus had talked, Ringgo was willing to talk.

He stayed in the hospital until the day before his trial opened. The knife Marcus had planted in his back had permanently paralyzed one of his legs, though aside from that he recovered from the stabbing.

Marcus had three of Ringgo's bullets in him. The doctors fished two of them out, but were afraid to touch the third. It didn't seem to worry him. By the time he was shipped north to begin an indeterminate sentence in San Quentin for his part in the Kavalov murder he was apparently as sound as ever.

Ringgo was never completely convinced that I had suspected him before the last minute when I had come charging into the bungalow.

"Of course I had, right along," I defended my skill as a sleuth. That was while he was still in the hospital. "I didn't believe Sherry was cracked. He was one hard, sane-looking scoundrel. And I didn't believe he was the sort of man who'd be worried much over any disgrace that came his way. I was willing enough to believe that he was out for Kavalov's scalp, but only if there was some profit in it. That's why I went to sleep and let the old man's throat get cut. I figured Sherry was scaring him up—nothing more—to get him in shape for a big-money shakedown. Well, when I found out I had been wrong there I began to look around.

"So far as I knew, your wife was Kavalov's heir. From what I had seen, I imagined your wife was enough in love with you to be completely in your hands. All right, you, as the husband of his heir, seemed the one to profit most directly by Kavalov's death. You were the one who'd have control of his fortune when he died. Sherry could only profit by the murder if he was working with you."

"But didn't his breaking my arm puzzle you?"

"Sure. I could understand a phony injury, but that seemed carrying it a little too far. But you made a mistake there that helped me. You were too careful to imitate a left-hand cut on Kavalov's throat; did it by standing by his head, facing his body when you cut him, instead of by his body, facing his head, and the curve of the slash gave you away. Throwing the knife out the window wasn't so good, either. How'd he happen to break your arm? An accident?"

"You can call it that. We had that supposed fight arranged to fit in with the rest of the play, and I thought it would be fun to really sock him. So I did. And he was tougher than I thought, tough enough to even up by snapping my arm. I suppose that's why he killed Mickey too. That wasn't on the schedule. On the level, did you suspect us of being in cahoots?"

I nodded.

"Sherry had worked the game up for you, had done everything possible to draw suspicion on himself, and then, the day before the murder, had run off to build himself an alibi. There couldn't be any other answer to it: he had to be working with you. There it was, but I couldn't prove it. I couldn't prove it till you were trapped by the thing that made the whole game possible—your wife's love for you set her to hire me to protect you. Isn't that one of the things they call ironies of life?"

Ringgo smiled ruefully and said:

"They should call it that. You know what Sherry was trying on me, don't you?"

"I can guess. That's why he insisted on standing trial."

"Exactly. The scheme was for him to dig out and keep going, with his alibi ready in case he was picked up, but staying uncaught as long as possible. The more time they wasted hunting him, the less likely they were to look elsewhere, and the colder the trail would be when they found he wasn't their man. He tricked me there. He had himself picked up, and his lawyer hired that Weeks fellow to egg the district attorney into not dropping the case. Sherry wanted to be tried and acquitted, so he'd be in the clear. Then he had me by the neck. He was legally cleared forever. I wasn't. He had me. He was supposed to get a hundred thousand dollars for his part. Kavalov had left Miriam something more than three million dollars. Sherry demanded one-half of it. Otherwise, he said, he'd go to the district attorney and make a complete confession. They couldn't do anything to him. He'd been acquitted. They'd hang me. That was sweet."

"You'd have been wise at that to have given it to him," I said.

"Maybe. Anyway I suppose I would have given it to him if Miriam hadn't upset things. There'd have been nothing else to do. But after she came back from hiring you she went to see Sherry, thinking she could talk him into going away. And he lets something drop that made her suspect I had a hand in her father's death, though she doesn't even now actually believe that I cut his throat.

"She said you were coming down the next day. There was nothing for me to do but go down to Sherry's for a showdown that night, and have the whole thing settled before you came poking around. Well, that's what I did, though I didn't tell Miriam I was going. The showdown wasn't going along very well, too much tension, and when Sherry heard you outside he thought I had brought friends, and—fireworks."

"What ever got you into a game like that in the first place?" I asked. "You were sitting pretty enough as Kavalov's son-in-law, weren't you?"

"Yes, but it was tiresome being cooped up in that hole with him. He was young enough to live a long time. And he wasn't always easy to get along with. I'd no guarantee that he wouldn't get up on his ear and kick me out, or change his will, or anything of the sort.

"Then I ran across Sherry in San Francisco, and we got to talking it over, and this plan came out of it. Sherry had brains. On the deal back in Cairo that you know about, both he and I made plenty that Kavalov didn't know about. Well, I was a chump. But don't think I'm sorry that I killed Kavalov. I'm sorry I got caught. I'd done his dirty work since he picked me up as a kid of twenty, and all I'd got out of it was damned little except the hopes that since I'd married his daughter I'd probably get his money when he died—if he didn't do something else with it."

They hanged him.

DASHIELL HAMMETT was born in St. Mary's County, Maryland, in 1894. He left school at fourteen and held many jobs thereafter—messenger boy, newsboy, clerk, timekeeper, yardman, machine operator, and stevedore. He finally became an operative for Pinkerton's Detective Agency. After serving in World War I, he turned to writing, and in the late 1920's, became the unquestioned master of detective-story fiction in America. He was a sergeant in World War II. He died in 1961. Among his books are *The Big Knockover, The Dain Curse, The Glass Key, The Maltese Falcon, Red Harvest,* and *The Thin Man.*

STEVEN MARCUS is a professor of English and Comparative Literature at Columbia University. Among his numerous writings are *Engels, Manchester & The Working Class* (1974), *The Other Victorians* (1966) and *From Pickwick to Dombey* (1965). He has also edited *The World of Modern Fiction* (1966), and with Lionel Trilling, Ernest Jones's *Life and Work of Sigmund Freud.* He is Associate Editor of *Partisan Review.*

DAPHNE du MAURIER was born in 6th Century... London. He... and had many jobs. Then he married Power... He... Daphne... and married... He finally became to operative by Pinkerton's Detective Agency. After serving in World War I, he turned to writing, and in his later years, became the undisputed master of detective fiction in America. He was engaged in World War II. He died in 1961. Among the books are The Big Sleep, Dahl, Farewell, My Lovely, The Long Goodbye, and The High Window.

Shawn Harris is a professor of English and English Literature and Language. Among the numerous fiction are Diamond Stars, The Flying Class (1975), The Cuba Vietnam (1996) and Arrow Vietnam to Berlin (1965). He is also editor in chief of Modern Literature (1962), and Bill Liberal editor. He edited a Little Guy Peace of Sigmund Freud, the essential Library of Darwin Work.